EVERY DAY
OF MY LIFE

LYNN
KURLAND

ONE

Scotland
Fall, 2009

THE SWORD HUNG IN THE air, motionless, the blade glinting faintly in the morning gloom, with yet more steel peeking out from under the well-loved leather wrapped around the hilt, and all of it covered in a relentless mist that blanketed everything in sight.

Oliver Phillips lay sprawled on his back, staring up at that massive sword, and wondered if he might manage a final thought or two before the blade descended and sent him off to take up a place in his family's slightly ostentatious mausoleum. He had very definite opinions on not only his current location but the people who had in one way or another led him to that same place. The first was simpler, so he started there.

Scotland was a bloody awful place for a holiday.

Now, for the second, the list was relatively short, but simply bursting with men who were ripe for a bit of retribu—

He swore, then rolled quickly out of the way of that perilously sharp Claymore that suddenly descended toward his chest. He managed a second roll to his feet, snatching up his own sword on the way. His current sparring partner, the truly exhausting Ian MacLeod, seemingly couldn't be bothered to offer even a morsel of praise for that feat, something he surely could have considering he'd been the one to kick the damned thing so far out of the way that Oliver hadn't been able to reach it.

Oliver didn't hope for anything supportive from the two men watching silently from thirty paces away. James MacLeod was standing there with his arms folded over his chest, studying the carnage in progress with a thoughtful frown. Jamie's younger brother Patrick was yawning and looking as if he might soon need a nap.

Oliver knew, having had his share of encounters with the lord of the local castle, that he would have a thorough assessment of his efforts after the work was done. His experiences with that lord's brother were far fewer, but he knew that no matter how nonchalant Patrick MacLeod looked at present, he was the one to watch.

Then again, perhaps that was Ian instead who almost slit his throat before he managed to heave his sword up in time to spare himself the same.

"Best pay attention, lad," Ian suggested.

Very sensible advice, that. Oliver took a firmer grip on his sword, ignored the absolute improbability of holding the same, and forced himself to focus on the task at hand.

The morning wore on in a way that could only be equaled by the most tedious of stakeouts that dragged on for hours only to leave him scrambling at the last minute to catch the prize. Slowly, then all at once, to poorly paraphrase Hemingway, which was exactly how his own morning of torment ended as he watched his sword leave his hands. He stood there, drenched in sweat and covered in mud, and aching in places he hadn't known existed, and watched his sword spin lazily in the now-afternoon gloom.

Patrick simply held up his hand and caught Oliver's sword before the hilt clunked his brother on the head, then stabbed it into the ground in front of him.

Jamie stroked his chin thoughtfully, no doubt contemplating that lengthy list of ways Oliver needed to improve his swordplay.

Oliver would have listened to an all-day lecture on his failings if he could have had half an hour to first sit, then hopefully not drown himself in the enormous pitcher of water he fully intended to pour down his throat.

He looked at his current swordmaster and wasn't above enjoying a moment of relief that Ian had resheathed his sword and handed it off to his cousin. Patrick MacLeod with two swords wasn't any more terrifying than he was with no swords at all, so Oliver felt fairly safe ignoring him in favor of the man in front of him who looked as if his wretched tasks for the day weren't complete.

"Well?" he asked warily.

"Are you asking me if we're finished or what I think?"

Oliver couldn't bring himself to do either, so he simply stood there and waited.

"I personally think we've made a proper day of it," Ian conceded, "but I do have my instructions."

"I can hardly wait to hear them," Oliver said before he could stop himself.

"Well, let's see what they are," Ian said, patting himself for a moment or two and frowning. He smiled suddenly, then pulled a slip of paper from the pocket of his tracksuit bottoms. He squinted at it, rotated it ninety degrees a couple of times, then nodded. "Here they are: *Kill him if you can and show no mercy in the deed. Mercy makes him sad.*"

Oliver was utterly unsurprised. "Is that all?"

Ian shook his head. "Several warnings about how becoming sad might leave you comforting yourself by sucking on your thumb, huddling in a corner singing off-key nursery rhymes, or, more direly, bawling like a gel whilst sucking your thumb and attempting to sing those off-key nursery rhymes."

Oliver took a careful breath. "I'm going to kill them all."

Ian nodded wisely. "They warn that you might say that, at which point I've been advised—how did they put it? Ah, here it is. *When he begins to threaten bodily harm to those who love him so dearly, he's at his most dangerous. At this point, do not, under any circumstances, offer cuddles.*"

"One by one," Oliver said, because he thought it only fair to state his intentions. "Slowly. Painfully. Permanently."

Ian laughed. "I understand, believe me. I once took a glorious holiday in a Fergusson dungeon thanks to my cousin running his fat mouth, a holiday I didn't particularly enjoy. As for you, all I can offer is directions to Jamie's kitchens. You can't plot a proper revenge if you're hungry."

Oliver knew the way to the kitchen given that he'd been there before on his way to other places, but at the moment he suspected it might be best not to think about those other places.

He made Ian a bow, fetched the scabbard for his own sword, then walked over to where the laird of the local clan MacLeod was holding out his sword. Hilt first, which he appreciated. He took it and resheathed it, then waited for the verdict on his day's work.

"Not a bad showing," Jamie conceded.

Oliver made him a low bow. "Thank you, my lord." He took a deep breath and looked at Patrick MacLeod, fully prepared for anything from a brutal assessment to a knife in his gut.

Patrick only lifted his eyebrows briefly and said nothing.

And that was likely the best he was going to have from that quarter. He made Patrick an equally polite bow, then excused himself and did his damndest to walk in a straight line around to the front of the keep before the invitation to find a meal was rescinded in favor of more torture in the lists.

He stopped on the hall's front stoop and put his hand on the massive wooden door for a moment to catch his breath. He loathed admitting to any sort of weakness, but in his defense he'd had a long day. That day had begun in the middle of the night when he'd woken to find himself being roughly trussed up like a misbehaving Christmas goose. His subsequent journey, first by private plane, then by an equally private helicopter, had ended with his being heartlessly deposited onto the doorstep of a certain Highland laird. The note secured with gaffer tape to one of his bonds where he hadn't been able to chew it off had informed James MacLeod that he was there to have a holiday.

He suspected much darker things were afoot.

Then again, the retribution he would exact for those darker things was going to be *exceptionally* unpleasant, so balance would eventually be restored. With that happy thought to keep him from blurting out any off-key nursery rhymes—which was a filthy lie; he had perfect pitch—he knocked, then gingerly opened the door and peeked in to see if anyone friendly might be home.

Elizabeth MacLeod was coming out of the kitchen and waved him inside. He accepted the invitation, then shut the door behind himself, suppressing the urge to throw not only a bar over it but stack a few pieces of heavy furniture in front of it as well. He shuffled over to the lady of the hall where he made her a bow.

She laughed. "Oliver, you don't have to do that."

"I'm hoping to flatter you out of something to eat," he said honestly.

"I'm already putting dinner together, so no flattery needed. I'm just waiting for you to finish with the boys."

"I sincerely hope that I have," he said with feeling. "And I owe you for breakfast this morning. It was the only thing that saved me."

"You answer my endless research questions about modern spy stuff, so it's a fair trade."

"Is that useful?" he asked.

"It is when Patrick's answer to any of my questions on how to deal with bad guys is a blank look and a sword-poking motion."

Oliver suspected Patrick MacLeod's skills were exponentially more extensive than that, but again, he hadn't had the pleasure of a personal encounter, something he fully intended to keep on with for as long as possible.

"I'll go clean up, then," Oliver said, "and I'll try not to drip overly on your floors."

"I've seen worse," Elizabeth said with a shrug.

Oliver imagined she had, so he made her another bow, then tried not to squelch his way too aggressively across her floor and up the stairs to the guest room he'd been given. He'd been offered the same accommodations precisely seven times in the past, something he also decided was best not to think about at the moment. It would get in the way of less unsettling thoughts of vengeance perpetrated on those who absolutely should have known better.

He walked inside, locked the bedroom door behind himself, then propped his sword up against a chair bearing the duffle bag that had so thoughtfully been packed for him. He looked into the corner of the room and scowled at the collection of zip ties and steel-banded cables that were piled atop enormous chains that could have comfortably moored a small cruise ship. He likely should have been flattered that his kidnappers had considered him dangerous enough to merit all three, but that might have stirred up feelings of mercy which would have indeed made him sad, so he forbore.

There was no silencing duct tape joining the rubbish there, but that indicated how well those hapless lads knew him. He had considered commenting on what fates awaited them as they'd been about their foul business of transporting him to places he hadn't wanted to go, but he'd decided that silence had been a more terrifying option.

He imagined Patrick MacLeod would have agreed with that, at least.

He stripped off his medieval gear and ignored the fact that he was trying to keep a saffron shirt and what amounted to a plaid-patterned blanket in a tidy pile atop his muddy boots. It was a bit more difficult to ignore the bright pink ankle monitor that had been applied to his own poor self whilst he'd been wearing the aforementioned cables and chains, but he limited himself to a brief hope it wouldn't electrocute him whilst he was having a wash.

Half an hour later, he followed his nose into the kitchen. The lady of the hall was there, dividing her time between keeping watch over a stew that smelled very promising and keeping her children focused on their homework. The youngest of the spawn, a wisp of a thing named Patricia, jumped up from her stool and raced across the room.

"Oliver!"

He caught her as she flung herself at him and couldn't help but feel a bit flattered by her enthusiasm. She hugged him tightly, then pulled away.

"Which do I pick?" she asked. "Treat or a card?"

"Patricia, he doesn't always have to bring you something," Elizabeth said mildly.

"But if he doesn't bring me a treat, I get to pick a card."

"Us, too!" a pair of lads said in unison.

Oliver looked at the collection of MacLeod spawn and sorted them into ages and potential for mischief-making out of habit. He supposed Patricia was well into her seventh year and her next older brother, Robert, a trio of years older than she. The eldest, Ian by name and early teens by age, was leaning back against the range, warming his backside and smiling in understanding. Oliver had seen that one indulging in a little swordplay with his father, though, and suspected he might be worth keeping an eye on as well.

"I'm afraid I neglected to pack either," he said, pulling himself back to the matter at hand. He'd made a point of bringing a hostess gift for the lady of the house on each of his visits, but cards containing Useful Skills to Know had been a spur-of-the-moment idea for the brood that first weekend. "I could make up a handful now, if you like."

"Actually, we have something for you," Patricia said, pulling him over to the table. She held out an envelope toward him. "I found it on the front steps, but no one had knocked which told me it was a secret."

Oliver could only imagine.

"Are you going to open it?" Robert asked.

Oliver could bring to mind half a dozen unpleasant things he would rather have been doing besides opening what he was certain would be a continuation of the indignities he'd already suffered so far that day, but Patricia had pulled him down onto the stool next to her and patted his shoulder.

"If it's a quest, I'll help you."

It was hard to argue with a seven-year-old prepared to hoist a sword with him, so he nodded his thanks, then opened the envelope that indeed had his name scrawled on it and pulled out the single sheet of paper.

> *Dearest Oliver, welcome to your holiday! Because we love you so very much—hugs and kisses!—we've planned the whole fortnight for you. A tailor-made routine of self-care awaits you, perfectly designed to refresh and restore. Attached to each carefully curated task is a set of points which, as they are earned, entitle you to other new and exciting indulgences!*

He was going to end them all. One by one, slowly, cheerfully, and painfully. He set that thought aside as something to be enjoyed later, then continued on.

> *What delights can I expect? Clever you for asking, but let's not spoil any surprises! Today, content yourself with meditating for a quarter hour, supervised. If you accomplish that, you'll receive further instructions in the morning along with a book in which to record their accomplishment.*

> *Do the tasks properly. Don't cheat on the maths. A prize for being good in school—perhaps a car that runs—will be yours when you've finished.*

> XOXO

He took a deep breath. In fact, he took several. It didn't help one bloody bit.

"What does it say?" Patricia asked.

"It's a list of things to do," Oliver said pleasantly. He said it pleasantly because he'd been asked by a child and growling might have frightened her.

"Fun things or chores?"

"Fun things," Oliver managed.

"Will you have anything for doing them," Ian asked, "or are they just exercises in strengthening character and stamina?"

Oliver exchanged a glance with Elizabeth that needed no words to accompany it. If both those lads—and likely Patricia as well—hadn't heard that same phrase from their father a dozen times a day, every day, from the moment they'd managed to make sense of the words being spewed at them, he would have been very surprised.

"I believe there might be a prize involved," Oliver conceded.

"Which kind?" Robert asked, getting up and walking around the table to peer over his arm. "Wait ... a car of your choice?" Robert looked at him, his young mind seemingly reeling at the very thought. "What sort, do you suppose? A Jaguar? An Aston Martin? Nay, a *Bugatti?*"

Very likely a used Fiat with a chipped Ferrari medallion glued to the arse-end of it, but perhaps that didn't need to be said.

"I don't think they've narrowed it down yet," Oliver offered.

"And what's that part at the end in those strange-looking letters?" Patricia asked.

Oliver squinted—he couldn't deny that he might need more sleep on occasion—and took a moment to untangle the words cut from various supermarket circulars. Unoriginal, but a bit alarming all the same.

"It says," he said, "that the process must begin again if at any point there is failure to adhere to the programme as outlined."

The two younger spawn nodded wisely. Oliver looked at Young Ian and had an eye roll and a smile in return, something with which he heartily agreed.

"I could make you a list of cars, if that would help," Robert volunteered.

"Make them very dear."

Patricia jumped up. "I'll choose the color!"

"I'll look for very expensive after-market accessories," Ian said, pushing away from the range. "Mum, we'll need your computer."

Elizabeth started to speak, but he put his arm around her shoulders and smiled.

"I'll supervise the young ones," he promised, "and be careful myself."

Oliver watched Elizabeth's eldest gather up his younger siblings and usher them out of the kitchen, then looked at the lady of the hall.

"Apparently I've been sent on an extended holiday."

"Hard to take them," she conceded.

"Do you?"

"Three kids and deadlines," she said dryly, "so, no, not often."

He hardly dared ask, but couldn't keep himself from it. "Does your husband?"

She seemed to be considering what to say.

"That was too personal," he added quickly.

She shook her head. "It isn't that at all."

"Then the Cameron/MacLeod feud ..."

She laughed. "Well, you did pledge your fealty to the dastardly laird up the hill."

Oliver refused to shiver at the memory. He had indeed done so, which had eventually led—in an admittedly roundabout way—to finding himself in medieval Scotland with

Jamie, just for a mug of ale and a sword fight he absolutely hadn't been prepared for.

"Then again, you are a Phillips," Elizabeth continued, "which means you're related back in the mists of time not only Sunny, but Madelyn as well who happens to be married to my brother-in-law. That makes you family, so I'll give you the family answers. Jamie is driven, as you know, in the same way Lord Robert is and for the same reasons."

"My lady, your husband is an entirely new level of driven."

She laughed uneasily. "I'll admit he is, but even he puts his feet up occasionally. And he does sleep."

"I sleep," Oliver muttered.

"In a bed?"

He blew his hair out of his eyes, smiled in spite of himself at her laugh, then pushed himself to his feet to offer help with getting supper on the table.

The afternoon had well and truly waned when he found himself standing in the middle of the great hall without quite knowing how he'd gotten there. He was certain he'd eaten and made polite conversation with Jamie and his family, but he had little memory of it. He rubbed his hands over his face, then looked around himself to see what he'd missed.

The lord of the hall was sitting in front of his fire, no doubt thinking deep thoughts about possible flaws in the fabric of time. Oliver realized Jamie was waving him over, so he took the invitation whilst it was still good, then accepted a heavy pewter mug of what he was certain would be a most excellent ale.

"I understand my wee Patricia gave you your letter earlier."

Oliver nodded. "She did, my lord."

Jamie smiled slightly. "And of course you didn't growl at her."

"I was far too busy marveling with your daughter and her brothers at the delights that await me."

Jamie looked to be struggling not to laugh. "And the retribution you'll enact upon those who devised the same?"

Oliver conceded the point with a nod.

"I think that might be why once they delivered you to my doorstep, your errand lads scampered off with all due haste."

"I would imagine so," Oliver agreed, "though it won't serve them. I believe I advised them before they fled that they shouldn't rest easily for too long."

Jamie did laugh then. "Och, Ollie lad, I don't think they will. Why do you think they're having women hand things to you?"

"It won't save them," Oliver assured him. "But as I prefer my revenge to be very well chilled, they'll have a few more days of breathing easily before they meet their timely and painful ends."

Jamie nodded and made himself more comfortable. "I would expect nothing less. Until that happy time arrives, let's enjoy our drink in silence and count it as meditation." He shot Oliver a look. "I've been charged with setting you off on the right path, if you're curious. Happy thoughts, though, my lad, not ones of mayhem."

Oliver raised his mug in as much of an assent as he could muster.

"I'll make a note that you've completed the task once we've finished."

"Good of you, my laird."

"Magnanimous," Jamie agreed, "but a bit self-serving. Don't want to lose a fine traveling companion."

Oliver supposed that was the second compliment he could consider his that day. He didn't care what others thought of him as a rule, but he also wasn't one to discount the good opinion of those whose opinion mattered to him.

And with that happy thought to keep him company, he stared into the fire and forced himself to simply watch it instead of imagining it wrapping itself around a pair of lads who deserved it, namely Peter Wright and Ewan Cameron, they of the maniacal cackling and ribald jokes at his expense as he'd been too fettered to hit them and too stubborn to point out how miserably they would die when he'd managed to free himself.

His boss, Derrick Cameron, and his über-boss, Robert Cameron, he would unfortunately need to allow to breathe a bit longer. They had wives and children to take care of. He wasn't above torturing them a bit, though, which he would get to as soon as he'd completed the promised record-book of misery and could use it to give them at least a score of vicious papercuts each. He was fairly certain lemon juice would then be the thing to pour into those wounds to cleanse them so they might heal properly.

Jamie drained his cup and looked over. "Pleasant thoughts?"

"Citrusy, actually."

Jamie grinned. "Interesting choice. I hope they run and hide well."

"It won't matter."

Jamie conceded the point with a nod. "You do have a gift for tracking things."

"Antiques live in fear," Oliver agreed modestly.

Jamie laughed a little. "Antiques and several of your comrades, no doubt. But what would you say to putting those skills with both antiques and nosing about to the test with a little adventure to break up your holiday?"

Oliver considered. "I think I might need to first earn the key to free myself from my ankle monitor."

"Can't you cut the bloody thing off yourself?"

"I could, but doing so will send me to the back of the queue."

"Diabolical."

"Unoriginal," Oliver corrected grimly, "and yet so unsurprising."

"And you're going to agree to this?"

Oliver shrugged. "I've been promised a car at the end of this if I'm good."

"Which I suspect you could easily buy yourself."

"I could," Oliver conceded, "but they didn't specify what sort. Your son Robert suggested a Bugatti."

Jamie did smile then. "If that's the case, I can see why you'd want someone else to pay for it. And if you don't mind me saying so, my lad, you look to have had a long day. I won't mention it if you go have a proper night's rest for a change. You never know what tomorrow will bring, so you might be grateful for the extra sleep."

Oliver suspected Jamie might know more about what lay in store for him than he would be comfortable with, so he rose, made the lord of the hall a low bow, then walked across the great hall and started up the stairs. He hesitated to ruin all that healthful meditation he'd just engaged in, but he was having thoughts that perhaps deserved some attention.

The truth was, he could have cut off that damned pink ankle bracelet, gotten himself home, then planned the demise of a handful of men who deserved it. Unfortunately, he also had to admit that there was a part of him—a very small part, of course—that very briefly and casually had to admit that if the world were ending and he had to be honest as his last act before a meteor fell on his head—

15

He tripped over the top circular step and almost went sprawling face-first into the hallway, but caught himself just in time. Obviously that was a sign that admitting anything at the moment—particularly anything having to do with whether or not he might or might not have needed a holiday to begin with—was the very last thing he would be doing.

He paused with one foot on the landing and one foot on the step below and considered. He could have sworn there was something there, but there was nothing.

Odd.

He took a deep breath, shook aside specters that were obviously leaping directly from the part of his brain that needed a great deal more sleep, then heaved himself up the final step and continued on down the hallway.

He would wait for that meteor and instead concentrate on keeping his ire burning brightly. During the daytime, of course. He would use the nights well by sleeping more than a handful of hours at a stretch.

It would at least help him avoid yawning through his retribution.

TWO

Scotland
1583

MAIREAD MACLEOD THREW HER HANDS out against the sides of the passageway, her foot hanging half off the top step of the steep circular stairs that led down to the great hall, and struggled to keep her balance.

She looked over her shoulder, fully expecting to find the lad she'd just encountered, but no one was there. There was no one in front of her, either, which led her to wondering if she might be losing her wits. She was normally quite steady on her feet, but that perhaps came from the necessity of living in a hall full of men with swords and tankards and foul tempers that needed to be skillfully avoided. She looked about herself one last time, then shook her head at her own foolishness. There was nothing there to stumble over save her own imagination.

'Twas possible she thought too much about too many things.

And what she was thinking about at present was how to get herself out of her brother's keep without being marked so she could finally be about the business she'd intended to see to that morning. She brushed her hand over the pouch she'd sewed to the underside of her apron just to make certain it contained what it should, then made her way down the stairs to the hall.

"Auntie Mair, save me!"

Mairead found her arms full of her niece who unleashed a torrent of more words than any bairn of five summers should have been full of, mostly complaints about her brothers—both the older ones and the three younglings trailing after her like ducklings—and supper and the length of the day that had included more chores to do than she'd been pleased with. Mairead pulled Fiona behind her and faced off with her nephews who were hard on the gel's heels.

"Have you nothing better to do with your energies than torment your sister?" she demanded. "Go improve your minds or sharpen your swords—nay, 'tis time for supper already. Go help with the tables."

"I'll see to them, Auntie," the eldest of the brood said. He shot her a quick smile. "I did attempt it before, but there are just so many of them. Siblings, not tables."

Mairead reached out and ruffled the hair of her brother's firstborn. Young Ambrose was a quick lad and perhaps a bit too accustomed to keeping his half-dozen siblings in line. It would likely serve him well in the future, though, so she handed Fiona over to his care, then considered the state of the keep and her chances of escaping the same.

Her father was sitting in his accustomed place by the fire in his great chair, silent and watchful. He could manage little more than that, unfortunately, but Ranald MacLeod was laird still for as long as he drew breath even if it were in name only. She noted the men about him who kept watch, though in truth they weren't needed. There wasn't a soul in the keep who wouldn't have leapt to his defense should it have come to that.

Well, perhaps not everyone, but definitely the man sitting near him on a bench pushed up against the wall, his head leaned back against the stone, his snores coming as regularly as the tides. Snores were, though, far preferable to the fantastical things her uncle Lachlan was wont to natter on about. Her father was usually his best audience, but it wasn't as if her sire could have heaved himself to his feet and run off to a quiet bit of meadow for some peace.

The rest of the men were still outside, lingering a bit longer in the fresh air before they were forced to come indoors. She understood that, no doubt better than she should have. She had no call to train with the sword or hunt game, but she had her small flock of sheep to look after which kept her free of the hall for as long as the weather allowed it. That time outside afforded her not only peace for thinking but also freedom from the incessant demands of her brother who had wed himself a girl who couldn't manage herself, never mind a keep the size of theirs.

"Mair," a voice said sharply.

She realized her brother was standing in front of her. By the tone of his voice, she suspected he might have been there for a bit. She nodded to herself over the look of irritation on his face. She wasn't entirely certain why she was generally the focus of his ire whilst his wife and her own younger sisters escaped. Knowing the reason likely wouldn't change anything, so perhaps there was no point in trying to divine it—

"*Mairead.*"

She schooled her features into an expression she hoped was pleasant enough and fixed her attentions on her elder brother. "Aye?" she asked politely.

"Supper," Tasgall said shortly, "for us, then take some to Deirdre before you feed yourself. She's ill upstairs, which you already know." He started to say something else, then frowned and turned away.

Mairead didn't trouble herself with speculating on what that might have been. Tasgall was the laird in everything but name, so he'd become accustomed to everyone jumping to his commands. She humored him out of respect for her father and because she loved his children, but it went no further than that. She watched him greet her trio of their younger sisters with consideration, but she half suspected he was no fonder of them than he was of her. They were ridiculously lovely, though, so perhaps he strove to keep them pacified until he could use them as pieces on his board.

She blew out her breath, rubbed her eyes with the heels of her hands, then turned and marched herself off to help with supper.

It seemed an endless number of hours later that she managed to carefully set a stool down by the hearth in the kitchens and perch atop it without scraping it against the stone. She looked around herself, but all were comfortably senseless. She'd already promised Cook she would keep the fire going for a pair of hours, so she expected privacy for at least that long—privacy and a bit of light for examining what she did her damndest never to bring inside her father's keep. That treasure would still be hidden in a spot far from the hall if there hadn't been such a terrible storm the day before and she hadn't had to run home so quickly down the meadow. She knew she wasn't entirely safe inside, but perhaps it was late enough that the kitchen lads and lassies would sleep through her dangerous activity.

She shifted a bit closer to the fire and carefully removed her most precious possession from the pouch she'd made on the underside of her apron. She only had a trio of things she called her own: a ring of her mother's that she had hidden behind a loose stone in her brother's bedchamber where he would never think to look and the shawl she had woven for herself out of a pattern that had pleased her.

And the manuscript she held in her hands.

She'd managed to keep it hidden for the past year, but that was likely because she had a decent hand with a needle and thread and she'd taken great care to make certain no one looking at her would notice anything she might or might not have added to her apron. She pulled her shawl over her shoulder to shield her book from even sleepy eyes, then turned a bit more toward the fire so she could examine what she held in her hands.

That she could read at all was something of a miracle. Fitting, then, that she had a clergyman to thank for it, one who had simply appeared at the keep one stormy evening, begging for shelter. Strangers were a rare enough sight, but her father had always done his duty of offering hospitality to whomever had survived the weather long enough to ask for it. The bedraggled friar who'd collapsed on their doorstep a trio of years ago had been poorly clad and, once he'd warmed himself sufficiently, not terribly eager to carry on to find other souls to rescue. He'd offered his services to the laird and been granted leave to remain.

Knowing her father's lack of patience for long conversations, she'd kept the man busy with other things. Having him instruct Ambrose not only in his letters and sums, but in French and the King's English had seemed wise. Making a production of assuring her father she was willing to make the sacrifice to supervise her nephew as he sat through those lessons had seemed the very least she could do.

She'd never let on to anyone that she'd learned to read and tally numbers right along with her nephew. Whilst her clan wasn't particularly suspicious by nature, she'd never wanted to give anyone a reason to believe she might possess the supernatural talent of actually making sense of all those scratches on parchment. Besides, she was a score-and-five and too old to be anything but a maiden aunt to her brother's children. She'd been certain she would be useful to them by making certain messengers bearing the written word were actually reading those words faithfully.

She took a breath to steady herself, but that was the normal progression of things when it came to the astonishing manuscript she seemingly had care of. Once her hands were steady, she permitted herself yet another in an endless series of studying the thing to make certain she hadn't missed anything vital.

She ran her fingers over it, regretting the fact that at some point in the book's journey to her possession half of it had obviously been lost. The covering was torn and the rear half of the book missing. She knew the first because she could see where it had been damaged, and she'd suspected the latter because she'd realized at a certain point in her lengthy study that the sheaves of parchment bore numbers. She'd made a careful search of the area where she'd found the manuscript, half-buried as it had been in a bed of fallen leaves, to see if she might have missed any sheaves, but there had been nothing else there to help her.

That, and she hadn't been particularly eager to remain near the spot where she'd found it. The little house half an hour's walk up the meadow where the MacLeod's healer had lived for as long as Mairead could remember now stood empty. The previous woman who had lived there had disappeared a pair of years earlier and there wasn't another soul in the keep with the courage to take up that place, times being what they were. She had no use for silly rumors of witches and their ilk started by foolish souls with too much time on their hands, but that didn't mean she had any desire to take up residence in that house.

Nay, 'twas enough that the forest had gifted her the book she dared call her own. She tilted the manuscript toward the fire and admired the painting on the outer cover. It was very fine, obviously something done in a particularly modern and elegant place—London, or perhaps even Paris. The book bore a title that she supposed had at least something to do with the faithful retelling of a history recorded on those very fine sheaves of parchment.

The Duke and the Kitchen Maid.

Obviously the man depicted there was the Duke himself. His blond hair was cut above his shoulders, his clothing clearly expensive, and his black boots that came almost to his knees shiny and well-made. There was a hint of what she had to assume were the kitchen lassie's skirts there as well, though she couldn't say for certain.

What she did know was that the Duke called a place named Birmingham home. He was fantastically wealthy, a bit aloof and reserved to those whose acquaintance he had not yet made, and he had been quietly living his privileged life full of many exciting escapades when he'd run into a serving gel—literally. She'd spilled the contents of a chamberpot onto his trousers, yet instead of striking her, he'd saved her from a thrashing by the master of servants and sent her on her way with a grave nod.

The scribe had taken great pains to point out that the kitchen gel had also indulged in her share of thrilling adventures. Not only was she fond of dressing in trews, she could shoot a pistol, best even sober men in games of chance, and toss back a shocking amount of port without it affecting either her aim or her ability to endure scorching looks from the Duke.

Mairead wasn't entirely certain what *scorching looks* were, but she suspected they might be a prelude to something truly shocking, such as kissing. She had never experienced either, but the thought left her feeling as if she'd spent too long by the fire and a trip to the back garden for a breath of fresh air was called for.

All in all, she could scarce believe that such a lass existed, though perhaps 'twas more difficult to envision a man such as the Duke who had put himself in harm's way to save that lass a sharp blow. Then again, her father had never struck her and she'd always managed to step out of her uncle's way if the flat of his hand had been accidentally aimed in her direction. Knowing his fondness for ale, she suspected that her uncle was simply throwing his hand out to keep his feet, not intentionally meaning to strike any of his kin.

Her brother was a different tale entirely, but she'd learned early on to avoid him when he'd either had more than his share of strong drink or too much responsibility.

She wondered about the gel described in her book, though, more particularly where she'd come from and how she'd come to have work in the Duke's hall. No doubt she was from London, for surely clothing so fine wasn't to be found in Edinburgh.

The final thing that puzzled her was the tongue the manuscript used. The words weren't in her language, nor in French, nor in the King's English that she had taken such pains to learn right along with Ambrose, though sounding them out carefully—inside her head where she wouldn't be marked—had suggested that they might be some sort of English.

The letters used in the Duke's diary had been difficult to make out at first, but she'd done what she could there as well. She'd given it quite a bit of thought over the past year and decided that perhaps it was simply a very sophisticated variant of the king's tongue spoken only by those high-born souls living in the south. Whether or not she was pronouncing them properly was beyond her ken.

What she was certain of was that the tale was nothing less than a faithful history of the Duke of Birmingham, a city she was certain was a very famous and notable place south of Hadrian's Wall.

"Bloody fool, get yerself out of my way!"

Mairead shoved her book—for that was what the clergyman had termed wee collections of the printed word—quickly under her apron and safely into its pouch, then stood and made her uncle a spot near the fire. She helped him sit on the sturdiest chair she could find, then resumed her place on her stool as if she'd had nothing better to do.

"Don't suppose you'd fetch me ale," Lachlan said wearily.

"I wouldn't want to wake anyone," she whispered. "The stew might suffer tomorrow because of it."

He nodded, which she found to be something of a relief. He continued to speak, though, which was less of that same sort of thing.

"You'd best be careful out minding the sheep and goats," he said, nodding knowingly.

"I always am," she said soothingly.

"You're not nearly as handsome as your sisters, of course, but the forest won't see that."

"I'll remember that—"

"Best do more than just remember it," he said crossly. "The faeries there, gel! Either they're making off with a MacLeod—even an unhandsome one—or they're leaving behind magical gifts. You'll avoid anything you find, if you're wise."

Mairead smoothed her hand over her apron before she could stop herself. Magical gifts were one thing; a book left behind by a nobleman taking his life in his hands to travel into the Highlands and drop it a quarter league from her home was quite another. Surely.

"I won't go into the forest, uncle," she assured him.

"See that ye don't, gel," he said, yawning. "See that ye don't."

She couldn't consider her promise a lie because her uncle hadn't specified which forest to avoid and she never went into the one behind her home to the west. She had very vivid memories of her father's wounds after he'd been attacked by a boar there. The animal's head had been stuffed and hung over the mantel until he'd finally roused himself enough to demand that it be taken down.

The forest to the north and east, the part that surrounded the healer's house, the part that led toward Cameron lands, though, that was different. Healers had lived there occasionally without undue peril. She had found her book there, so obviously even men managed to come and go without injury.

Her uncle moved his chair closer to the hearth, put his feet as close to the fire as was reasonable, then leaned his head against the stone of the wall behind him. "Faeries and bogles," he said, smacking his lips sleepily. "Don't forget the tale of Laird Jamie and his bride. They walked into the forest ... one evening at twilight ..."

Mairead watched him as he surrendered to sleep, something she envied as she never managed to have enough of it. That might have been because she generally avoided sleeping upstairs with her sisters and settled instead for a scrap of floor in the kitchens.

A bit like the lass the Duke had described in his history.

Or, rather, the half of his history that she had. She couldn't help but wonder about the man and what had happened to him after his activities in the pages she'd read. Had he returned to Birmingham and taken up his duties in his fine house? More importantly, what had become of the kitchen maid? The girl had been mocked for being unhandsome and uneducated, which likely had presented its share of difficulties.

Mairead looked into the fire and considered the difficulties of her own life. She was herself very plain, something she'd been told her entire life and had confirmed for herself by several looks in still lochs and the occasional polished bit of steel. She was not unlearned, though, and her father—when he'd been able to voice an opinion still—had quietly complimented her with quick smiles on her damnable curiosity—his words, not hers. She imagined he was very aware that her three younger sisters would always catch the eyes of whatever men came to see what sort of bride Ranald MacLeod might have on the fire, so to speak, where she would be relegated to fetching ale and serving soup.

That was just as well. She had no use for the men who pushed her out of the way so they might have a better view of her sisters. Even her brother was embarrassed by her, which suited her well enough there. His children found her to their liking, which was lovely. Also, when she finished with her serving of food and ale to family and guests, she always had a spot waiting for her by the fire in the kitchen where she could be safe and warm.

But what she truly wanted ... she looked into the fire and supposed it wouldn't be an untoward thing to actually admit what she truly wanted for a change. She took a deep breath and allowed herself to admit the truth: She wanted to find the Duke of Birmingham and give him back his book.

And once she had his gratitude and attention, she would ask him very directly what he had done with his kitchen maid. Had he left her behind at some other hall?

Had he done the unthinkable and made her his wife?

"Mistress Mairead?" a voice whispered.

She pulled herself away from her contemplation of the fire and smiled at the young lad standing there hesitantly. "Aye, John?"

"I've come to watch the fire, if you please."

"Thank you, lad," she said. She pushed herself to her feet, turned the stool over to him to use for the remainder of the watch, then found herself a spot near the hearth and sat down with her back against the stone.

She leaned her head against the wall, closed her eyes, and waited out the night.

She left the keep at dawn, mingling easily with the lads whose business it was to tend the animals and relieve the night-time guards. She promised one of the fostering lads who didn't seem quite awake yet a second portion of supper if he kept an eye on her sheep for a bit, then made her way quickly along the edge of the meadow and to the forest surrounding the healer's croft.

No one lived in the little house, of course, because the last witch had disappeared, though Mairead had always suspected the woman had run off with the priest who'd come from Ireland to save them all. Perhaps she'd grown tired of being called things she wasn't, which was one of the reasons Mairead refused to accord that wee hut any supernatural properties. 'Twas a house and one where a sensible woman might have peace and quiet and dry her herbs by the fire if she so chose.

Mairead supposed if she'd been able to, she would have taken up that place in her father's clan. She had enough learning to understand the various types of herbs the good Lord had provided for them to use in healing brews and poultices. The souls that made up her clan were sturdy and healthy, so perhaps there wouldn't have been too much use for her skills, which would have left her with enough silence to actually entertain the odd thought or two.

She stopped on the path that led to the house and looked around as if she were merely interested in what might be growing along the path. Finding herself alone, she pulled the knife from the back of her belt, removed a large square of bark from its usual place in the fifth tree from the doorway of the croft, then carefully removed her book from its hiding place under her apron. She had wrapped it in a spare piece of plaid as well earlier that morning, just to make certain it remained protected.

She put it in the hollowed-out spot she'd discovered long before she'd found her book—no doubt someone else had decided a tree could spare a bit of itself for such an activity—then replaced the piece of bark.

She put her hand over that place and wished that she could, for once, have someone step in front of her and protect her. Just once.

Which was a foolish desire and had nothing to do with her life. She had her brother to avoid, her father to watch over, and more callous and unpleasant remarks to endure from suitors who arrived and found her simply too plain to be endured for the rest of their lives.

She wondered briefly about Laird Jamie and his lady wife ... but surely that couldn't be anything but folklore. Tales of magical things found in the forest were best saved for children. If their clan's bard occasionally ventured off into that sort of thing whilst about the critical task of keeping the clan's history fresh in his mind, well, life wasn't always bloodshed and darkness.

She wondered what sorts of stories might have been related by the scribe who had written down the Duke of Birmingham's tale.

She took a deep breath, then took another look around herself to make certain there were no faeries peeking out from behind trees to see if she might suit a piece of their mischief, then turned and walked away before she lingered overlong. No sense in tempting fate—or any number of her kin—to be more curious about her doings than necessary.

She walked out from under the last of the trees and came to an ungainly halt.

There was a man walking toward her. He wasn't wearing light-colored breeches and a dark coat; his trews were a bluish color that she would have found at the loch that lay farther east from her home and his coat was black. She honestly had no idea if he wore boots or not.

What she did know was that the morning sun peeking over the mountains behind her had fallen on his hair that was still the color of golden summer grasses. She could scarce believe her eyes, so she rubbed them, then looked again.

He was gone.

She whirled around but only found herself with a face full of morning sunlight.

Well, it was obviously something ... she took a deep breath. She didn't believe in faeries or sprites, though she wasn't above the odd charm put in her pocket or the willingness to concede that there were a few mysterious happenings in the distant aforetimes of her clan.

She shook her head, then turned away from the sun and continued on her way. She had spent far too much time looking at the painting on the front of her book and it had inflamed her frenzied imagination—her uncle's words, not hers, though he was scarce one to be criticizing anyone else for that sort of thing. She hadn't just seen a fair-haired man walk past her; she had seen a shaft of sunlight and drawn a finely fashioned lad out of her imagination.

She rubbed her arms and walked quickly back to the hall to get on with her endless list of sensible, unmagical tasks.

Life was far safer that way.

THREE

O LIVER WAS BEGINNING TO SUSPECT the place between too much sleep and not nearly enough might be the only spot where a man didn't need to consign what he thought he might be seeing out of the corner of his eye to either a hallucination or an overly rested imagination.

Day Two of the Horrible Highland Holiday was off to a brilliant start.

He squinted against the rays of post-dawn sunlight that filtered through the trees, catching motes of whatever it was trees deposited in the air—it was for damned certain that those same flickers of light weren't revealing a woman dressed in a rustic Highland gown, wearing a shawl, and no doubt looking for a hair band to catch up absurdly long waves of hair. He would have hazarded a guess at the color, but he was obviously hallucinating so perhaps the color could be up to him.

He considered, then shook his head. He had been too long out of the company of women, which left him obviously needing to hallucinate one. Maybe he needed to date more. Unfortunately, he seemed to be limited to an excruciating and ever-lengthening series of terrible first dates. He wasn't certain why he seemed to frighten off all sensible dating partners so quickly, though that might have been his inability to make inane small talk, which left him discussing things that interested him.

Perhaps 12th-century art, Renaissance swordmaking, and the inner workings of not only Regency pistols but how quickly a man might down half a bottle of port yet still accept the invitation to pick the lock to his equally Regency-era mistress's bedchamber weren't interesting to anyone else.

All the other things he could have discussed—several things that flirted quite heavily with the line between good taste and illegality—were likely best left alone, along with attempting to unravel what he might or might not have just seen out of the corner of his eye.

He liked to be thorough, though, so he took another look around himself to see if there were any lost Scottish maidens to rescue. He found none, so he turned himself back to the matter at hand which was to get himself to what the MacLeods referred to fondly as *the witch's house up the way*. He'd also heard it referred to as Moraig's house, a woman he knew had been the last clan witch to live there. He hadn't quite managed to investigate the illustrious Miss MacLeod past her name for the simple reason that, the surrounding environs being what they were, he wasn't entirely certain he wouldn't run afoul of her birthdate finding itself firmly entrenched in some century that would make him uncomfortable. He shivered in spite of himself, then carried on to the cottage twenty feet away.

That cottage had been offered to him as a spa-like retreat from the cares and worries of the world, though the pithy warning he'd had from Jamie that morning on his way out the door had been limited to *mind the threshold*.

He stopped on the edge of that threshold, looked up to make certain nothing was going to drop on his head and kill him, then looked at the lock there. Completely inadequate given that a small running start and a firm shoulder against the door would easily accomplish entry, something he imagined Jamie also knew. He pulled a pair of well-loved tools from their usual resting place on the underside of his watch, made quick work of the deadbolt in front of him, then let himself inside. He flicked on the lights and caught his breath a little at the sight that greeted him.

He felt as if he'd stepped back in time half a century.

He looked over his shoulder to make sure that wasn't the case, but the outside looked as he'd just left it. He'd heard the story, of course, about how Robert and Sunshine Cameron had tried to cross that threshold together and wound up in two entirely different places. He had no reason to disbelieve it—and several reasons to accept it as the absolute truth—but that had nothing to do with him.

He set his bag down on the floor near the kitchen, propped his sword up against the small counter that separated that same kitchen from the rest of what seemed to serve as a reception room. He made note of the sleeping nook that absolutely wasn't going to allow him to do anything but curl up in a ball and hope for the best. Maybe he would throw a blanket on the floor in front of the fireplace and call it good.

He heard the crunch of tires against gravel outside and was half tempted to go hide in the loo. A coward he was not, though, so he took a firm grip on his company manners and went to stand in the doorway. Sunshine Cameron was being given a hand out of the car by one of Patrick MacLeod's lads, Bobby, who fortunately for his ability to continue to breathe hadn't been a part of the recent madness. Oliver nodded at him, had an answering nod that obviously contained a fair amount of manly sympathy, then made his laird's wife a low bow as she approached.

"Lady Sunshine," he said politely.

She inclined her head regally. "Master Phillips."

"Perhaps you would care to take your ease by the fire I haven't built yet, my lady?"

She laughed a little. "That would be lovely, but you know me and doorways. Well, particularly this doorway."

"I understand," he said. He paused. "Not sure I believe it entirely, but I understand."

"After what you've been doing on bank holidays with Jamie recently?"

Oliver shuddered for effect. "Please don't remind me."

"Deny it while you can," Sunny advised with a smile. "And in the spirit of that, why don't we just chat out here? But let me run back to the car first and grab what I brought you—and I need the exercise, so stay right here."

He nodded, though it went against his grain not to exercise his gentlemanly prerogative and fetch. He only lasted until she was halfway back to the cottage before he walked out and took a large black shopping bag from her. The sunlight falling down through the trees was pleasant and she didn't seem to want to sit, so perhaps it was best to stay as far away from the threshold as possible.

He set the bag down, certain it would hold delights he could certainly save for later, then accepted a black book which sported a pair of serene-looking cats sitting back on their haunches and dangling from what were obviously intended to be bookmarks. The cats matched the ones plastered all over his ankle monitor so at least he would be fashionable whilst wallowing in misery. He considered, then looked at Sunny.

"Do I dare?"

"I think you should. Would you like me to periodically remind you not to kill them as we read along together?"

"That would be extremely helpful."

She laughed softly. "I'm sure it will be, so go ahead and dive in."

He steeled himself for the worst, then looked at the title emblazoned on the cover.

Self-Care for Eejits

He exchanged a glance with the wife of the laird he'd pledged his fealty to, the woman who also happened to be the one who anonymously covered him with a blanket or a coat whenever she found him catching a few winks on some flat spot in the Cameron empire's London offices. He'd known, of course, though he hadn't said anything because he tried never to say anything. Life was safer that way.

Sunny was, though, a very lovely woman who deserved every happiness possible, as well as a place to sit presently given her delicate condition.

"Are you sure I can't get you a chair?"

She was watching him with an affectionate, older-sister sort of smile. "I'm too excited about all the things you have to look forward to for any relaxing. What's inside your book?"

He opened the tidy little triple-ring notebook and winced. "There are sections."

"How exciting."

He could think of other words that would have been more apt, but he kept those to himself. He braced himself for absurdities galore and flipped through the tabs. They included but were not limited to: outdoor activities, yoga classes, restorative meditations, nurturing his inner child, and bettering his mind. He took a moment to study the final tab labeled *Little Luxuries*, then turned the page and noted that the first item on the list was a mani-pedi to be enjoyed whilst sipping a spirulina smoothie.

He looked at Sunny in alarm. "A what?"

"Manicure and pedicure," she clarified. "And a healthful drink."

"Absolutely not."

"You might get a paraffin bath to dip your toes into," she said. "I'd reconsider that. And you already know the benefits of green things."

He did, though he liked to follow up any suppertime forays into health foods with a generous glass of something very boozey, but he was a man of simple tastes. And perhaps he was being too hasty about the manly pedicure. He could, if it came to it, roll up the extra wax into tiny balls and blow them through a straw at his mates. They might at least sting if the right amount of force were applied.

He filed that away as a possibility, then turned to the very back of the book. There was a, *Don't blame me, I just wrote what they told me to, luv ya!–Sam* penned discreetly on the very last page surrounded by a selection of charming hearts drawn to fill up the rest of the area, no doubt to leave no room for any more torturous activities.

The women would be spared, to be sure, and he might even unbend enough to mourn with them at the terrible straits their men would find themselves in, but he was a forgiving sort.

"At least they're leaving you to the honor system," Sunny noted.

He pulled up the leg of his tracksuit trousers and pointed at the shocking pink ankle monitor that clashed painfully with his green trainers. Sunny looked at him in surprise.

"Is it bugged?"

"I haven't investigated that yet," he admitted, "but I'm certain it's at least sending a detailed record of my movements."

"What do you have to do to get it off?"

"Tick a few items off their list."

She smiled. "They love you, you know."

"A horrifying thought," he said promptly. "I don't suppose your husband is coming along later with the key for this?"

Sunny laughed. "Not a chance. He's in an undisclosed location, sharpening his blades. I was sent because they were certain you wouldn't do me in."

"Terrified of me, are they?"

"If you want the uncomfortable truth, they were worried."

"About me?" Oliver asked with a snort.

"Oliver, you demolished a nursery full of plants."

"It was six inches of a decrepit fuchsia hedge," he protested. "Besides, I was well repaid by a very tough bloke with a heavy metal pole."

"I heard it was a granny—"

"She was spry—"

"And every day of ninety," Sunny continued. "I also heard her weapon of choice was a rolled-up newspaper."

"It still hurt," Oliver muttered.

She looked at him seriously. "They said you fell asleep at the wheel."

He let his breath out slowly. "I did, but I was parked." He paused. "Mostly."

"They also said the hedge was of great historical significance."

"Only because it was in front of some granny's house, and again, she repaid me by beating me about the head with a heavy copy of the Sun on Sunday."

"Terrible."

"I also only bent half a foot of the hedge, which was hardly visible unless you were to look closely." He hesitated, then supposed there was no reason not to be completely honest.

"There might have been a handful of blossoms that suffered bruising as well."

She smiled. "They're still worried about you."

He sighed deeply. "I don't make mistakes."

"I know," she said quietly. "They know, too."

"I don't want to give up what I do," he said unwillingly.

"Well, I certainly wouldn't want you to, and the lads don't either. They're teasing you a little with all this, but I really do think it's with the best of intentions."

"That still won't save them."

She smiled. "I imagine they would be disappointed if it did." She nodded at the shopping bag next to him. "Those are things you can wear to yoga class in the village. Nothing in leopard print, which should come as a relief, though you can thank Emily for that."

"I am relieved." He hesitated. "Are you certain I can't at least fetch you a glass of water?"

She shook her head. "Now that my dastardly duty is done, I'm headed back to Maddy's to pick up Breac. We'll come along for your mani-pedi if you like, but I think we'll have to go to Inverness for it."

"I wouldn't bolt if I went on my own."

"It might just be that we enjoy your company," she said. "You are, after all, a Phillips and we don't have a little brother to watch over."

And with that little morsel dropped on his poor heart, she gave him a quick hug, smiled, and walked away.

Oliver exchanged a slight nod with Bobby after Sunny had been carefully tucked back into the car, then picked up the shopping bag and made his way back into the house. He wasn't going to credit that doorway with any sort of magical properties and he absolutely refused to pay any attention to the fact that there was obviously something inside the house that was ferociously setting off his allergies. He dragged his sleeve across his eyes, indulged in a few foul words to bring balance back to his world, and wondered if there was a section in that damned book that would require him to distract himself from too many uncomfortable emotions by eating a hearty breakfast every day.

He shut the door behind himself, locked it out of habit, then indulged in a more thorough investigation of Moraig's magical little cottage. The great room and sleeping nook he'd already looked over, so he opened the lone door to be found inside and discovered an absurdly luxurious loo with a walk-in closet attached. He realized there were things there with his name on them: modern clothes, thankfully, mostly in black and in what he could only assume were styles for the well-dressed lad off on a discreet holiday. Also Emily's doing, no doubt.

He walked back out into the great room and decided there was no time like the present to see if they were planning on starving him to simplify his dietary tasks.

The modest fridge was stocked with green things he would have wagered a week of yoga classes had been provided by Sunny, along with heartier fare he suspected perhaps Jamie had insisted he be allowed to eat.

He had hardly managed to liberate a handful of cold chips from someone's leftovers cunningly hidden behind a cluster of carrots and shove them into his mouth before there came a banging on his front door. Well, Moraig MacLeod's front door. At the moment, he wondered why Jamie hadn't turned the place into a holiday let, but perhaps that was something he could suggest later. He opened the door, fully expecting to find Bobby having returned to drop off leopard-print yoga gear after all.

Instead, he found Patrick MacLeod, medieval clansman, dressed to impress.

Oliver considered the man's gear—saffron shirt, plaid belted tidily around his waist, dirks down the sides of his boots and sword strapped to his back—and decided a distraction might be his only hope.

"Breakfast?" Oliver offered.

"Already had it," Patrick said. "'Tis the most important meal of the day."

Oliver agreed, though he couldn't deny his eating schedule was sometimes as erratic as his sleeping one.

"I thought a hunt might suit," Patrick said with a yawn, as if he could scarce muster up the enthusiasm for the idea.

"Brilliant," Oliver said. If it got him out of the house, he was all for it. "Is this on my list?"

"Nay, 'tis an extra-curricular activity out of the goodness of my heart."

Hard to argue with that. "Do I get any points for surviving the exercise?"

Patrick only smiled briefly—and a little evilly, it had to be said, so perhaps the current offering wasn't anything to be put in that damned book he wished he could pitch. Unfortunately, he suspected one of those kitty bookmarks might actually be a bell which was no doubt designed to alert any watchers in the woods if he accidentally hurled it as far away from himself as possible.

Possibly.

He turned back to the disaster at hand. "What are we hunting?"

"Whom."

Even better. "*Whom* are we hunting?"

"I," Patrick said pleasantly.

"You?"

He nodded. "*I* am hunting."

Oliver felt the first frission of unease slide down his spine. "And whom, if I'm allowed to ask, are you hunting?"

Patrick smiled. "You."

Oliver swallowed past the hunk of fried potato that had inconveniently lodged itself in his throat, something that took more effort than he enjoyed. "And what," he managed, "will you do if you find me?"

Patrick shrugged. "Let's just say if I find you, no one else ever will."

"You're having me on—"

"I'll give you to the count of one hundred."

Oliver could count that far in a handful of languages thanks to very boring thugs over the years who had left him with plenty of time to listen to courses on tape. He could ask for the loo in thirty countries plus find fish and chips almost anywhere, but all he had time for at present was to swear in his favorite language which was his own and wonder if Patrick MacLeod had a sense of humor.

He suspected not.

And he was still wearing that damned tracking anklet that he hadn't dared remove. He couldn't credit Patrick with stooping so low as to use that in his morning's sport, but it also chaffed abominably which might leave him fleeing at a less-than-optimal velocity. All in all, being hunted was not what he wanted to see on the schedule for the morning.

He rubbed his hands together in his best imitation of someone who'd looked over a deal and found it just not quite the thing. "So sorry, old bean," he said, listening to the last two words come out of his mouth and wondering if he'd just lost the rest of his sleep-deprived mind, "but I haven't a thing to wear."

Patrick pursed his lips. "An extra twenty, then," he conceded. "Go find something suitable."

"You can't be serious," Oliver managed.

"Do I look like I'm not serious?"

He looked capable of all sorts of mayhem, but who was to say? Those damned medieval clansmen were just so bloody unpredictable. A bloke never knew if they were joking or if they genuinely intended to use their swords for more deadly business.

"And then you'll give me to a hundred?" Oliver asked, just to make certain he understood the rules of what he sincerely hoped was a game.

"Unless I grow bored." Patrick shrugged. "I don't have much of an attention span, if you want the truth."

There were several things Oliver wanted, but the truth about Patrick MacLeod's attention span was not one of them. He didn't bother wasting time shutting the door. He jumped back into the cottage, pulling off clothes and flinging on vintage gear at the same time—

"Sword, lad," Patrick called.

Oliver hadn't intended to engage in any lollygagging, actually, and a sword would only slow him down. There was wisdom in the old *When in Rome* trope, but he was in Scotland and he would have a medieval clansman on his tail. Speed was of the essence.

Besides, he wasn't planning on pitching through any time gates, which precluded the need for steel. Well, except the knives down his boots, but that was one of those slightly illegal things he'd been more than flirting with for years. He took a very brief moment to curse himself for not having worked out a utility belt to go under his kilt for use in precarious vintage situations, but in his defense he'd been designing one on the evening he'd been so callously wrapped up and delivered to Scotland.

He wished he'd had time for a decent breakfast instead of someone's takeaway leftovers, but obviously that wasn't on the schedule for the day, either.

He stepped out into the fresh air and left the closing of the door to his new friend. With any luck, Patrick would forget to lock it and someone would steal not only all his clothes but that damned book he was certain was only going to add to the unpleasantness he could sense coming his way—and tracking him from behind—for the rest of the morning.

"Oh," Patrick said, frowning thoughtfully, "I've been going by tens. You'd best run away very quickly."

Oliver tossed a sufficiently vile curse in the direction of his current tormentor, then bolted, still cursing Patrick for being far more awful than he'd anticipated. He wasn't unaccustomed to outrunning all sorts of people—he'd been doing it since boarding school, as it happened—but skipping off into the wild in rustic boots and a skirt whilst not having done any prior reconnaissance of the area was a bit trying.

Also, the truth of the current situation was he just wasn't entirely sure about that younger MacLeod brother. Patrick was delightful to his wife and spawn, but any man who'd been through one of his training courses tended to grow a bit pale and refuse to comment on the particulars when asked.

Holiday? Not, apparently, in the current lifetime.

He wasn't incapable of turning himself into a ghost on the fly, however, so he ruthlessly slammed any further useless thoughts behind the usual door in his mind he reserved for that kind of thing, took stock of his surroundings whilst he was sprinting past them, and made a plan. Obviously being out in the open was going to be best avoided. Doubling back and hiding in Patrick's kitchen where he might manage a decent breakfast was likely out of the question for the moment as well. Obviously he would need to simply make the best use possible of his usual methods of disappearing.

The morning wore on.

Unfortunately, Patrick didn't wear out, which likely contributed to the eternal nature of the hours. Oliver finally stopped in the shadows of the forest slightly to the north of Moraig's to catch his breath and decided that the best he could do was hope that Patrick's middle-aged—plus a few hundred years—knees would give out. His own knees that were sliding toward thirty-two trips around the sun would obviously have the advantage.

He heard a twig snap behind him, shot Patrick a smile over his shoulder, then bolted.

He didn't feel any blades going into his back, didn't find himself tackled to the ground and smothered, and he most certainly didn't hear the plaintive calls of a medieval Scotsman begging him in lilting tones to slow down so he could be vanquished.

He did, however, run directly through a time gate.

The fact that he could feel himself blundering through the centuries was appalling enough. That he continued to run until he'd run into a situation he wasn't sure was going to go all that well was just ...

Well, he wondered how he might manage to count it as self-care because it was for damned certain no one else would be coming to rescue him.

Then again, the woman standing there surrounded by a clutch of Highlanders he didn't recognize, trying to pull herself away from one of them, perhaps didn't have anyone to rescue *her*, and that he couldn't allow.

He took a quick reading of his position, wondering how any time traveling might affect his precise longitudinal location, made himself a mental note to make an addition to Jamie's master map, then continued on into a situation he definitely hadn't asked for but perhaps might be able to put to rights. At least he was wearing sleeves that covered his watch and a plaid in colors Jamie had claimed were authentic covering the rest of him. He could have been in jeans and a Led Zeppelin sweatshirt.

On the less-helpful side of things, he wasn't their kin and he was also minus his sword, which might be the last time he would leave home without it.

He downshifted mentally into baffled nobleman and prepared to do whatever it took to keep himself alive.

FOUR

MAIREAD JERKED HER ARM AWAY from her cousin, wishing she had the courage to use either a sharp knife or a sharper tongue on the fool. Unfortunately, she knew at least what the latter would earn her and that was only more abuse from her uncle's youngest son. He was ten-and-eight, surely old enough to know better.

"Kenneth, enough," one of the other lads there said, stepping in front of her. "Pick on a man, why don't you, instead of a gel?"

Kenneth bounced on the balls of his feet and glared at the Cameron clansman who dared voice such an invitation. "Who, you?"

Mairead would have pointed out to her cousin that Giles, eldest son of the Cameron himself, was not going to be an enjoyable sparring partner, but with any luck Kenneth would find that out for himself. Giles had not only the cheek to venture over the border that lay between Cameron soil and theirs often enough, but the swordplay to match his courage.

Then again, the reason Giles and his younger brother routinely came south was to catch a glimpse of any of the fairer daughters of Ranald MacLeod, so perhaps when romantic notions seeped into a lad's wee head, he did things he shouldn't have.

Whatever wits they might have lost to the cause of romance aside, those Cameron lads at least had decent manners, something she couldn't say for her own family. Kenneth shoved Giles aside and grabbed her arm again, fair wrenching it from its moorings. She jerked it away for the third time and wondered, for more than just the third time, if perhaps she should have snuck into her father's lists instead of shadowing his priests as they were about their scratching on parchment. It would have provided her with skills she most certainly didn't possess.

"Leave me be, Kenneth," she exclaimed. "Find someone else to vex with your vile self."

He swore at her, but that was nothing new. She was halfway to giving him a sharp shove when she enjoyed the same from him. She landed on her backside, which would have been less unpleasant if she hadn't landed on a rock. She winced, then crawled uncomfortably to her feet, fully prepared to give back as good as she'd had and the consequences be damned only to realize that the men around her had drawn their swords.

She was halfway to turning and bolting off back down the meadow when it occurred to her that they hadn't turned on her. She considered that for a moment and wondered if perhaps they would brawl with each other, leaving her free to stroll back down the meadow to the keep without any trouble. She rubbed her abused backside and looked at the lads to mark how the battle was proceeding so she might have that to mull over and enjoy as she limped back home.

They were all turned toward the east, toward the forest where she knew for a fact most of them never ventured. And why not? One never knew what magical thing it might spew out ...

Apparently today that thing was a man.

She watched as the newcomer came to an easy, graceful halt, though he was breathing heavily, as if he'd run a long way. He held up his hands carefully, no doubt to show he had no weapon in them.

"Friend, not foe," he said clearly.

Mairead would have patted her surroundings for a chair or a stool, but she was outside and she'd already sat down quite heavily on the ground. She forced herself to keep her feet whilst she gaped at the man standing not twenty paces from her.

He was wearing a proper shirt as well as a plaid wrapped around him and a belt holding it there. She could see the hilts of dirks peeking up from the sides of his boots, though those boots looked to be much finer than any either her cousins or the Cameron lads owned. His Gaelic, all three words she'd heard from him, had a bit of an accent, but 'twas intelligible enough.

And that was exactly where her common sense ended and her turn as a witless kitchen maid began.

Her cousins weren't altogether ugly. Giles, being a Cameron as he was, had a markedly handsome visage. All the lads standing nearby were strong and well-built, but that was also nothing out of the ordinary. When they weren't practicing with their swords, they were hunting or keeping themselves busy with some other noble labor. They were braw enough to turn the head of any lass with two good eyes.

But that man there, standing some twenty paces away from her, dressed in simple, unremarkable gear, outshone them all.

He was taller than any of the rest of the lads, which she appreciated, being rather tall herself. His shoulders were broad, the rest of him pleasingly fashioned, and his mien one of soberness and the careful noting of what was going on around him. She was, as she had reminded herself very recently, not unaccustomed to looking at handsome men. It had been a very poor preparation, however, for looking at *that* handsome man.

She could hardly do justice to his firm jaw, pale eyes, and a nose that was fine and almost straight. She imagined he'd likely broken it at some point, but since she'd been surrounded by that sort of thing the whole of her life, she didn't think anything of it. The rest of his face was a pleasing collection of the usual business which she would have lingered over but she couldn't stop looking at his hair which was longish, though not nearly as long as her relatives kept theirs.

And it was still the color of golden summer grasses in the meadow when the day was fine and the sun shining.

Kenneth gestured at him with his sword. "Who are ye?"

Mairead pulled herself back to the matter at hand which might very well include putting herself in harm's way to save that man standing there with his hands still in plain sight.

"I'm called Oliver," he said carefully. "I mean you no harm."

"Where's your gear?" Kenneth demanded. "And your horse?"

The golden-haired man winced. "It was taken from me."

"You were robbed?" Giles asked, resting his sword against his shoulder. "By whom? McKinnons?"

"I didn't stop to ask."

Kenneth made a sound of disbelief. "And you came here with no guard? No friends?"

"He's just been robbed," Mairead said pointedly. "Perhaps he needs something to eat and drink before he has the strength to tell—"

Kenneth whirled on her. She supposed it was nothing but the fact that she'd been avoiding him for so long that allowed her to move out of his way. It helped that Giles's brother had stepped in front of her and given her cousin the shove she hadn't dared to. She left them to sorting themselves and found herself joined by Giles who was shaking his head in disgust. He resheathed his sword, then nodded toward the stranger.

"Let's see if he needs aid."

Mairead thought that a very useful suggestion, so she avoided her cousin and Giles's brother who were still scrapping like hounds and stopped with Giles a few paces away from the man who had seemingly come straight out of the forest.

'Twas a most providential happening, to be sure.

Giles held out his hand. "Giles Cameron," he said easily. "And your name again?"

The other man shook his hand without hesitation. "Oliver."

"And your clan?"

"That is a long tale."

Kenneth tried to shove Giles out of the way and earned a fist under his chin as a result. Mairead thought that one of the better events of the morning, so she let her cousin lie where he'd fallen and turned back to the man named Oliver.

"We've ready ears for a good tale," Giles said pleasantly.

"It might be difficult to believe."

Mairead had to bite her tongue not to agree that such was indeed the case, but she was nothing if not disciplined. That and she was so astonished by what she was seeing that she could only stand there, mute and overwhelmed, and contemplate the truth of what was staring her in the face.

She was looking at the Duke of Birmingham.

She wondered, now that she was closer and had a fuller view of his face that was so perfectly noble and handsome, how his portrait painter had dared even attempt his likeness. She had very little time to amuse herself by rendering things on parchment, but even had she been skilled in that art she would have hesitated to depict that man there.

She watched his mouth move and realized that aside from the perfection of it and his very fine jawline, he was speaking her tongue. That was unexpected, to be sure, but she knew him to be very well-educated and intelligent. He might have been wearing Highland dress, but obviously 'twas as he'd said. If he'd been robbed of his sword somewhere along his road, he'd likely also bid a fond farewell to the rest of his dukely *accoutrements*. To be sure, she saw no fine contraption behind him, nor any guardsmen, and definitely no kitchen maid.

"You wear the plaid."

Mairead wrenched her thoughts away from problems that weren't hers and concentrated on what was before her. Giles had resheathed his sword before, which augured well for the peace and tranquility of the afternoon, but he was wickedly proficient with his knives, which might bode less well for that sort of thing. He'd also reached out and casually pulled her not so much fully behind him, but a pair of steps behind where he stood. She could still see their guest and his lack of servants, though, which she thought a decent piece of good fortune for herself.

"It was given to me by a MacLeod I met very far away," Oliver said carefully. "He's related to the current laird, surely."

Giles nodded thoughtfully. "No doubt. And why did he gift it to you?"

"Kindness," Oliver said. "In return, I agreed to tasks that included bringing greetings from the south."

"Where in the south?"

"I've been recently in Edinburgh, though London before that."

Mairead forced herself not to nod in agreement. At least that was something that sounded reasonable. It also explained why his Gaelic was decent but not perfect, though she likely would have listened to him babble in Latin all day and not complained.

"Are you English?" Giles asked in surprise.

Mairead managed to suppress her snort only because she did occasionally have a bit of self-control. Of course he was English.

"An accident of birth," Oliver said with a deprecating smile, "thanks to my sire. My mother is French."

Mairead thought she was far too old to be finding herself somewhat weak in the knees over a man's smile, but perhaps she should have had something a bit more substantial for breakfast. Her wits were suffering, to be sure.

"Then let's try that instead," Giles said in his own excellent French.

Mairead listened to them wander off together into that tongue and was grateful she'd made such a thorough study of it with various priests over the years as well as using Giles for practice. The Camerons were decent hosts, so perhaps he'd had the benefit of clergy as well. His Latin was better than hers, but she could read far better than he could, so perhaps the scales were balanced well enough there.

She was half tempted to point out that she could also read Lord Oliver's native tongue, but that would have given away more than she cared to. That, and she wasn't sure she was pronouncing things properly. Then again, whilst his Gaelic was serviceable enough, and his French quite obviously second nature to him, the latter was pronounced with a bit of an accent she couldn't place.

Birmingham, obviously.

She hardly had time to think that through properly before Kenneth had regained his feet and found not only his tongue and his sword. She moved well out of his way, half tempted to go hide behind the Duke, but found immediately that there was no need.

"Stop it, ye wee fools!" a voice thundered.

Mairead wasn't sure if she should have been relieved or concerned that her uncle had arrived, but she imagined her opinion wouldn't be asked on the matter. She took the opportunity to put a bit of distance between herself and Kenneth's sword, though not so far that she couldn't hear what was being said.

"And who would ye be?" Lachlan demanded.

"He's called Oliver," Giles said mildly. "An Englishman by birth, but his mother is French and he fostered with the king's household in Edinburgh."

Mairead would have added a few details from his history, but she thought that might be impertinent. Besides, she was fairly busy wondering how it was that out of all the souls she could have encountered—

She stopped herself before she went any further with that. Of course she would have encountered him. She had his book in the pocket of her apron. Well, not at the moment because it was safely tucked away in her tree, but given that he was currently in the area, she understood how he could have lost it nearby. Perhaps he had passed through their lands a year ago and no one had been the wiser.

There was a mystery there, to be sure.

"Weel, come on, lad," Lachlan said, gesturing expansively toward the keep. "Come inside out of the weather and leave these rambunctious pups to their scrapping. You'll need something to eat and a place for the night."

Mairead felt Giles take her arm and found, oddly enough, that it was somewhat reassuring. At the very least, it left her feeling as if she were still in her own skin, not lost in some magical realm where people simply stepped out of her uncle's most treasured fables.

"So, tell me of yourself, man," Lachlan said, clapping a hand companionably on Lord Oliver's shoulder.

Mairead found Giles pulling her along directly behind her uncle. He shot her a quick look.

"We'd best be here to translate," he said with wink. "I'm not sure Lord Oliver's equal to your uncle's chattering."

Mairead couldn't have agreed more. She was also rather more grateful than she likely should have been to find Giles's brother Dougan on her right, leaving Kenneth marching along behind them, grumbling loudly. The fact that she needed Cameron guardsmen in the company of her own kin was ridiculous, but there it was. She set that thought aside as something not to think about any longer and focused her attention on the conversation going on in front of her.

"So you've been in London, have you?" Lachlan said in surprise. "Quite a distance, that, or so I've heard."

"The journey here was very difficult," Oliver agreed.

"And why were you there, lad?"

Oliver smiled very faintly. "Just flattering important souls, as one does."

Mairead imagined that was indeed the case and she could only imagine the importance of the souls he flattered.

"I was fairly recently in Edinburgh—"

"Not in the gaol, eh?" Lachlan said, waggling his eyebrows and laughing a little.

"Fortunately not," Oliver agreed with a nod, "though I visited the castle and frequented many fine tradesmen on my way to Holyrood—"

"You didn't," Dougan said breathlessly, leaning up to look at him. "Did you see the king's magical beasts?"

"Later," Lachlan said, elbowing Dougan away. "Hobnobbing with King James, were you?"

"As close as one manages to get," Oliver agreed. He glanced over his shoulder at Dougan. "I'll tell you later of the fierce beasties I saw, if you like."

Mairead supposed Lord Oliver would understand that he'd just earned the undying loyalty of Giles's brother. If not, she imagined he would realize the same very quickly, indeed.

"I took up my travels in a hasty fashion," Oliver said easily, "then had my belongings purloined."

"McKinnons?"

"It was very dark."

"Terrible," Lachlan said.

Mairead thought it worse than that, but 'twas no wonder he had no sword or carriage or matched set of white horses to pull that carriage. It said much about his resourcefulness, she supposed, to carry on without the trappings of his rank.

"And now that you've reached our beautiful land?"

Oliver stopped, then made Lachlan a small bow. "I will gladly carry back to those I know a fine report about the condition of a proud and noble people."

"Well," Lachlan said, puffing up a little, "not too long a report, eh? Don't want to be overrun by a flood of Englishmen."

"Nay," Oliver said seriously, "you wouldn't want that."

Lachlan clapped him on the shoulder. "Let's have a meal. Come inside the hall and we'll find you a proper seat by the fire."

Mairead realized the Duke had paused by the front door. He looked at her, then gestured for her to go inside first. She knew she shouldn't have been surprised. After all, the man had perfect manners when it came to kitchen maids.

She ignored Kenneth's snorts and walked inside, passing so close to Lord Oliver that she could have reached out and touched his arm if she'd cared to. She looked up at him on her way by and had the most ridiculous thought occur to her.

Had she seen him earlier that morning on her way back from secreting her book in its tree?

She put her head down and hurried into the hall. She hadn't slept enough, that was it. If she'd passed by a man that handsome, she surely would have remembered it.

Then again, perhaps he'd taken shelter in the healer's wee croft after having been chased by McKinnons. None of their ilk would dare set foot on MacLeod soil, though she had to admit the Camerons had more trouble with them than her family did. Lord Oliver was fortunate to have survived being hunted, if that were the case.

She stopped a few paces in and looked behind her. Her uncle still had Lord Oliver's ear, though he was soon swarmed by the rest of her clan. He was polite and grave and, she had to admit, fearless. She wasn't sure she would have walked into a strange hall without at least having a guard, but perhaps he had more confidence in his knives than she did in hers.

Her uncle shepherded him inside the hall and introduced him to her father. He obviously noticed her father's lack of response, but he did him the courtesy of a low bow and a freely proffered compliment on the sturdiness of the hall. He was equally polite to the endless number of people who wanted to make his acquaintance.

She noticed, though, that he marked where everyone was. Perhaps she wouldn't have realized what he was doing if she didn't do the same thing herself every time she came inside. And why not? Her brother and several of her cousins were unpredictable. Her sisters, on the other hand, were not, and she was half surprised they didn't immediately begin brawling with each other to determine which of them would sit next to their guest at table.

She rolled her eyes and turned to make her way to the kitchens. There were simply some things a woman shouldn't have to watch.

An hour later, she was waiting on the edge of the hall, watching as the tables were set up for supper. Lord Oliver was still standing by the fire, looking as if he might have preferred to blend into the wall. If the reports held true, he wasn't opposed to conversation, but preferred it to be short and to the point. That he was enduring it said much about his good manners.

She found herself pushed out of the way and realized that it had only been her brother's bairns to do the like. Ambrose threw her a smile over his shoulder, then ran after his siblings, though he arrived too late to save Lord Oliver from their attentions. She shook her head. The bairns were behaving as if they'd never seen a man before. Fiona actually threw herself into his arms and he picked her up with all the gentleness of a man who valued children.

He smiled.

Women—and a few men—swooned.

Mairead was tempted to tell them all to make another grab for their senses, but that was obviously a lost cause. That also might have been because she was close to swooning herself. The man had perfect teeth, not missing a one, and that quick, charming little smile he'd given to the bairns?

"Mistress Mairead, will you not serve the young gentleman?"

She looked over her shoulder to find one of the swooning kitchen maids there. She supposed it might be the only way the man would have anything land in his bowl, so perhaps she would do well to take on the task herself. She nodded, then waited until the company had taken places around the tables before she made her way over to where Lord Oliver sat to the right of her uncle, with Tasgall on his right.

She would have been fine, she supposed, if he hadn't looked up at her when she was attempting to ladle something into his bowl.

She imagined he would later think it a stroke of good fortune that she hadn't upended the entire pail of soup she'd been carrying onto his leg. For herself, she felt very fortunate that her uncle had jumped to his feet and taken her bucket out of her hands before her brother had leapt out of his chair, swearing, and turned to strike her. She turned away to save what she could of her visage and steeled herself for Tasgall's usual response to any mistake she made.

The sound of a slap echoed in the great hall, but she felt nothing.

She turned around and realized that Lord Oliver had stood, put himself directly behind her, and taken the blow himself.

She ducked out of the way and pushed herself back against the wall, fully prepared to watch bloodshed happen before the rest of the clan had managed to get their suppers pushed away from themselves and their swords into their hands.

Instead, Lord Oliver only put his hand on Tasgall's shoulder in a friendly fashion.

"You slipped on the floor," he said calmly. "I did as well. Let's sit back down comfortably and enjoy our meal, shall we?"

He shrugged aside her brother's blustering as if all the excuses were naught to fret over, then sat back down with him. She didn't argue with her uncle when he put her bucket back in her hands, then pulled his chair back from the table so she could serve Lord Oliver from his other side. She did manage to get food into his bowl that time, though she supposed someone else would need to feed the rest of the men at the high table.

Lord Oliver looked up at her gravely. "Thank you."

"Forgive me—"

"Nothing to forgive."

She nodded, then managed to hand her burdens off to one of the serving lads so she could retreat to the kitchens and calm her racing heart. She had no idea why she was trembling so badly, though she knew it had nothing to do with her brother.

She lingered at the edge of the hall for the rest of supper, wondering about Lord Oliver.

After supper, she found herself too busy with the usual tasks of putting the house to bed to consider what she might ask him did she have him cornered without anyone from her family gaping at him as if they'd never seen such a fine specimen of manhood in their lives.

She understood that last thing, actually.

In time, the hall settled down for the night. Lord Oliver had been offered a spot close to the fire, which spoke well of his comportment that evening. Her kin wouldn't have trusted him otherwise. There were a pair of cousins standing post by the front door, but that was nothing unusual, either.

She watched him sit down on a stool near her father, then listen politely to her uncle who sat down next to him and began filling his ears with the saints only knew what. Her uncle was obviously quite pleased with that, though

Lord Oliver offered his own words now and again. Nobly, of course, and discreetly, but why would she have expected anything else?

She had one last look at him before she went to find her own spot in the kitchen. Perhaps there would be time in the morning to ask him her questions when he wasn't surrounded by her kin and could answer freely. She could speak French well enough—and his English with enough courage—so perhaps between the two of them, they would manage a bit of speech.

She drew her shawl around her, sat down in the corner of the kitchen nearest the fire, and closed her eyes. She was left with more questions than answers, to be sure, but she knew one thing.

The book she'd been reading was exactly what she'd thought it was, namely a bard's faithful recounting of his lord's travels through the world. And she had just met the Duke himself.

And if that were the case, he was the one person who could tell her how his tale with the kitchen maid had finished.

She could scarce wait to find out.

FIVE

O LIVER WALKED THROUGH THE WOODS near Moraig's house and hoped that if his unerring sense of direction were ever going to fail him, it wouldn't be presently. That didn't begin to address the fact that along with going in the right direction, he needed to get himself back to the right spot on the cosmic timeline because he didn't particularly want to find himself living out his life in 16th-century Scotland.

Day Three and his holiday was threatening to go completely sideways.

He squinted at the compass on his watch, though the truth was that the terrain hadn't changed all that much over the past four hundred years. He was probably fairly safe continuing to head to the gate he knew lay on the border between MacLeod and Cameron lands.

Knew was a very hopeful sort of word, but he was a hopeful sort of lad when he wasn't cynically assessing his surroundings for random thugs. He paused under the eaves of the forest and looked out over the landscape in front of him to retake his position and make certain he was still alone. It was barely dawn and he hadn't lingered over breakfast. He'd paid his respects to Laird Ranald, nodded seriously over warnings about odd happenings in the forests near the keep from Ranald's brother Lachlan, then promised the laird's son

Tasgall that since he'd brought greetings from those in royal power in Edinburgh, he would be returning there to carry MacLeod felicitations as well.

He was fairly certain he had a five quid note stuffed into his boot which was as close to royalty as he—or any of his dinner companions from the night before—was ever going to get, so perhaps that would excuse him for his creative bit of fiction.

He'd made a production of heading east that morning, only doubling back through the forest surrounding Moraig's house when he was certain he'd lost the scouts following him. Perhaps he could have been less fastidious about that given that he had no desire to tempt fate again with another visit without a sword, a plan, and perhaps a good reason to be where he shouldn't have been, but as he'd noted before, he liked to be thorough. That, and James MacLeod liked to keep things in the past tidy, a principle he agreed with when it came to slightly sketchy doings.

He rubbed his hands over his face and shook his head sharply. He wasn't unaccustomed to all-nighters for various reasons, but he had to admit that engaging in one whilst lingering in a medieval keep inhabited by late 16th-century Highlanders was definitely not the norm. Coming to from an unwilling half hour of slumber to find himself still in the great hall with his English self unpierced by half a dozen Claymores and his plaid almost dry from where he'd had soup spilled on him the night before had been an additional relief.

At least he'd only seen the inside of the keep and not the inside of Jamie's dungeon, which was a stroke of good fortune. He would relay that happy news to Jamie when next they met over a mug of ale and some meditation.

He rubbed his arms briskly, but that didn't help him warm up any at all. The next time he traveled through time, he would be better kitted out. He was much more comfortable in a pair of jeans with sensible trainers on his feet than draped in a plaid with boots on his feet and his arse covered but bare to the wind. Perhaps there was good reason his ancestors had opted for the southern side of Hadrian's Wall. Puritanical about their knicker choices, no doubt.

Or perhaps it had been the weather. He would have to research it, but he was fairly certain he'd just spent the night in the middle of a Little Ice Age. Four hundred Scottish words for snow? He understood why. The damned country likely had just as many words for rain.

He took one more look to make certain he was still on his own, then carried on out to the spot where he knew the gate lay, admiring the scenery just a bit as he went. Admittedly, there was plenty of spectacular scenery to be gawked at in Scotland—fabulous stretches of glorious beaches, majestic mountains, and the occasional restaurant where they knew how to cook up cattle that hadn't been raided earlier in the week—but that didn't mitigate the horrors of midges, soggy feet, and yet more midges.

The next time he went on holiday, it would be to some sunny Caribbean island where he was just certain there couldn't possibly be any gates through t—

"MacLeod!"

Oliver jumped away from the shout, then whirled around to face a rather unfriendly looking clansman who didn't seem at all reluctant to use Oliver's collarbone as a resting place for the point of his perilously sharp blade.

"You shouldn't," the clansman began politely, "ever lose your sword."

Damn it, did none of these bastards ever sleep? Oliver would have glared at Patrick MacLeod, but he didn't know him well enough to anticipate how that might go for him. He set aside the relief he felt at being—or so he hoped—back in his own time and prepared to keep himself alive in a different century.

Holiday? The word didn't begin to apply.

"I didn't have one to begin with," he said briskly.

"Not my problem."

"I didn't sleep well last night."

Patrick snorted. "And I should care about that, why?"

"Because killing your quarry before you've stalked it to your satisfaction would be stupid—"

He missed losing his head only because he had decent reflexes. That was the only thing that he could say about the encounter that was positive, however, because he had no sword, Patrick's sword was very sharp and obviously well-used, and he—still—hadn't had enough sleep. He managed to keep himself from becoming a resting place for what he was certain was medieval steel, but he suspected that was nothing more than dumb luck. That made him angry—mostly at himself—and anger inspired him to reach for and use his hands and feet in ways he generally only resorted to when his need was very dire.

A pity Patrick MacLeod seemed to know the same techniques, which left him wondering just where in the hell the man had learned such an impressive array of martial arts.

He eventually found himself in the usual place he wound up whilst on his Scottish pleasure trip, namely flat on his back, looking up into a misty sky and not having to wonder why the Scots had so many bloody names for what that sky produced. He glanced to his left to find his companion resting comfortably a few feet away with his hands clasped over his belly, looking perfectly at ease. Oliver sat up, dragged his hands through his hair, then shifted to face his current torturer.

"My apologies," he said without hesitation.

Patrick looked at him. "For what?"

"Resorting to other things than steel."

"You didn't hurt me."

"Clearly not."

Patrick sat up without so much as a huff of exertion. "You might want to work on not losing your sword, lad."

"Again, I didn't have one to begin with."

"You would have lost it just the same."

Oliver took a deep breath. "You startled me."

"That's generally the idea," Patrick noted. "Something you likely also know is that you cannot do that sort of unapproved fighting business in the past. Well, perhaps you might post-1800s if you limited yourself to proper fisticuffs, but anything earlier and they'll think you're a demon."

Oliver suspected that might very well be the case.

"That, and you might find it failing to serve you whilst you're facing a man pointing a six-foot broadsword at you."

"What a thought," Oliver said, attempting a light tone.

Patrick leaned back on his hands and crossed his feet at his ankles. "I pushed you."

"Why?"

"I wanted to see what you were made of."

"And did you?"

"Only scratched the surface, I imagine, though time will tell the rest."

"I'm not a thug," Oliver said lightly.

"Never said you were, not that it matters what I think. Didn't Robert Cameron have you investigated before he hired you?"

Oliver didn't particularly care to remember that meeting with his potential employer when Cameron had gone over a private investigator's findings with Oliver sitting in front of him, but there were also things about his past he didn't particularly care to remember. He would credit Cameron with skipping over his family situation at least, which he had appreciated. He looked at Patrick and nodded.

"If you think he wasn't satisfied with that piece of nosiness, then you obviously don't understand why he continues to allow you near anything he loves."

"I'm loyal," Oliver managed. "And discreet."

"And you have a tolerable right hook." Patrick touched the side of his mouth with the back of his hand. "My wife won't appreciate this."

Oliver would have smiled if he'd been able to breathe a bit better. "I'll look for somewhere to hide."

"I might hide with you," Patrick said with a snort. "I was, if you can believe it, warned to be gentle with you."

"By whom?" Oliver asked in surprise.

"Madelyn, of course. Over a leisurely and delicious breakfast this morning, my beloved wife said, and I quote: 'Sunny and I are related to Oliver somewhere back in time, so we've decided to claim him as a little brother. Don't hurt him.'"

Oliver did smile then. "She might be offended you didn't listen to her."

"She might well be." He stretched, then winced. "I think you may have given me a single bruise, damn ye."

"My apologies."

"Don't make me work so hard next time," Patrick grumbled.

"Of course, my lord."

He studied Oliver for a moment or two. "Want to talk about where you were last night?"

Oliver shivered in spite of himself. "I'm not sure where to begin."

"The date?"

"Late 16th century," Oliver said. "Or thereabouts."

"Jamie will want all the particulars, of course, but I'm only interested in how you kept yourself alive. What did you tell them?"

"That I'd been robbed and abandoned by my friends," Oliver said darkly, "but that I brought greetings from those in power in Edinburgh."

Patrick laughed a little. "Clever, but have you ever *been* to Edinburgh?"

Oliver looked at him unflinchingly. "Boarding school, but didn't you already know that?"

He shrugged. "Ferreting out those sorts of details is my brother-in-law Alex's purview, not mine. All I know is Cameron trusts you and my brother has the same level of confidence in you or he never would have taken you on any of his insane gallops through time."

"I appreciate that."

Patrick slid him a look. "I'm still taking your measure before I claim you as kin."

"I understand, my lord."

Patrick rolled his eyes. "A younger brother. What the hell am I going to do with one of *those?*"

"*Not slit the poor lad's throat* might be something to consider."

Patrick laughed and heaved himself to his feet. He held down his hand and hauled Oliver to his. "So it might be, laddie, but where's the sport in that?"

"I might need a bit more experience with steel, my lord, before I can provide you with that sort of entertainment."

"I thought in addition to being scrutinized by Cameron, you'd been occasionally training with him—or do I have that awrong?"

Oliver hesitated to use the word *training*. Facing Robert Cameron over swords for any reason at all was something he was still trying to wrap his pitiful wits around. The truth was, that was a side of his employer he'd never been privy to during the first five years he'd worked for him as something more than security and something less than family. At the time, his place in that exclusive group hadn't bothered him in the slightest. He'd been happy for a way to make pots of money and put to good use all the fighting skills he'd paid a very steep price for.

And then Sunshine Phillips had walked into Cameron's life and turned it upside down.

Well, she'd upended the entire apple cart, actually, but that was something to think about at a different time. He supposed they were indeed related back in the mists of time, something she had first pointed out to him quite gingerly, as if she hadn't been quite sure if he would be pleased or not. He was beginning to think he might need to work on his company manners if he ever hoped to date, never mind anything more serious.

And somehow during that time when Sunny and Cameron had been sorting their lives and winding up marching down the aisle to wedded bliss, he'd begun to notice things about his employer's habits that he'd previously assumed were simply opinions accumulated by a man who had perhaps watched a few too many historical documentaries about Scotland and its glorious history. After all, that certainly could have explained Robert Cameron's uncanny feel for old things, or his ruthless defense of those he considered in his care, or his unassailable honor in his business dealings.

Then again, those things also could have been quite easily acquired in a previous century.

And then he'd found himself kneeling in Cameron Hall and placing his hands in Cameron's to pledge him fealty in a particularly medieval sort of ceremony, something that left him thinking about all sorts of impossible things over the subsequent few months.

He might have consigned it all to utter fiction if he hadn't been part of an elite little crew that had busted an innocent if not completely annoying man out of the Tower of London in 1602. The Tower, that was. And the man. Both loitering in 1602 as if they belonged there and thought nothing of the same.

He'd spent the ensuing year continuing on with the usual business of tracking down antiques and convincing people they really wanted to give them up so he could sell them to others who wanted to pay eye-watering sums to possess them. And somehow, because he'd become a full-fledged member of the clan Cameron, he'd had even deeper lines drawn in his code of honor, deeper than the places where his own had been drawn before. He didn't force anyone to do anything they didn't want to and he was scrupulously honest.

But the time-traveling bit ...

He pulled himself back to the present, profoundly grateful to be *in* the present, and looked at the man who hadn't killed him quite yet. Patrick was studying him silently and in a way that left Oliver wondering if even the loo might fail to provide enough of a hiding place. He endured the study, though, because he had definitely experienced worse.

"We've crossed swords a time or two," he conceded finally, dragging himself back to the present conversation. "Cameron and I."

"It shows," Patrick said. "But now, you and I will work."

"Thank you, my lord," he said, wondering if that might be the only time he said that. "In a fortnight or two?"

"Tomorrow."

Of course. "First thing?"

Patrick shook his head. "Mid-afternoon."

"But won't you be needing a nap—erm ... ah ..."

The look Patrick sent him left him wondering if *he* might do well to have an early nap so he might manage to keep himself alive for more than five minutes.

"Mid-afternoon," Patrick repeated, "after you've had a long morning of pampering yourself. Wouldn't want you to be anything but perfectly rested."

Oliver suspected that would absolutely not be the case, which he couldn't argue with. The more exhausted he was when under the stress of trying to keep Patrick from killing him, the better. He made the man a bow and escaped falling on his face only because his yet-to-be-christened elder brother caught him by the shoulder and heaved him back upright.

"Bobby's doing you the favor of fetching something from the village," Patrick said.

"How did he know—never mind." Oliver scowled in spite of himself. "I've got to get rid of this damned tracker."

"You might want to," Patrick agreed. "And until then, if you need anything, you know where I am."

"Not as often as I'd like."

Patrick did laugh then. "If it flatters you any, I didn't have to recite obscure Latin declensions to keep myself awake whilst tracking you yesterday."

"I am flattered."

"You should be," Patrick agreed. "Did you meditate last night?"

"If methodically studying the position of every man inside the MacLeod keep so I might avoid their swords and remain alive long enough to bolt out their front door counts, then absolutely."

"Close enough," Patrick noted. "Where's your copy of my brother's map?"

"Tacked helpfully to my fridge at home."

"Then you'd best hie yourself down the meadow and get another one."

Oliver thought that might be a very good idea indeed.

"I'll meet you here at three tomorrow. Don't be late."

Oliver nodded, then watched Patrick pick up his sword and walk off with a spring in his step he couldn't help but envy. Oliver watched him go for a moment or two, then remembered a most pressing item.

"Does this count as meditation for today?" he called.

Patrick's succinct two-word answer in the negative was unfortunately very clear.

He smiled to himself, then gathered up his own pair of knives and trudged through the forest to what actually seemed like a spa-like retreat. At least he had a decent shower and a bed to look forward to, no matter how inadequate the latter might have been.

Bobby was waiting for him near the doorway, take-away bag in hand. Oliver took a deep breath, then sighed happily.

"Smells delicious."

Bobby held it out. "Enjoy." He turned away, then turned back. "Spend a night out in the wild, did you?"

Oliver nodded. "Got lost."

Bobby snorted, then walked away, making no further comment.

Oliver found the door unlocked, which was slightly unsettling, but none of his gear had been taken, which was deeply disappointing. His clothes were flung everywhere, however, and one of his trainers had landed in the kitchen sink, but since he'd been the one doing the flinging, he wasn't surprised. He made a thorough search of the premises and found everything else still in its place. Perhaps Patrick had assumed he'd been through enough that day without having the contents of his extended stay holiday let ransacked.

He considered what to do first, eat or shower, though he was half tempted to eat whilst *in* the shower to save time. He decided he hadn't become quite that desperate yet, so he ate half his supper, then went to wash off the Renaissance grime he'd acquired.

An hour later, he was sitting in front of the fire, meditating on things he was certain the lads couldn't have possibly predicted. He'd taken one of the longest showers of his life, had a marvelous second half of his supper, and washed the remains of soup out of his medieval gear whilst being grateful that the fashions in the north hadn't changed all that much over the centuries.

And that led him in a less-than-roundabout way to contemplating his trip back across those centuries and considering what he'd found there.

He hadn't asked the exact date, but if James had been king of Scotland, it had to have been late 1500s. He suspected he might have to check Jamie's history for the particulars, but having a pair of Cameron clansmen breaking bread with MacLeod clansmen who hadn't slain him on sight had certainly been something he hadn't expected.

The daughters of Ranald MacLeod had been, he had to admit, stunning. He had dated his share of very beautiful girls, true, and not because of anything he'd done. Being associated with Robert Cameron had left him encountering all sorts of people as he orbited around that family. Perhaps he wasn't entirely ugly, because it was for damned sure those modern women hadn't been dazzled by his conversation. His parents had, at least, provided him with straight teeth and funds for whatever sport he'd fancied at the time which had left him fit and acceptably kitted out.

Those girls back in the past, though, whilst astonishingly pretty had left him enormously uneasy. He hardly knew what to say to a modern bird. Trying to make inane small talk with a vintage Scottish lass had been beyond him.

And then there had been that girl who had spilled soup on him. He had spent more of his time watching her than was polite, but that was likely because he was almost positive he'd seen an echo of her the morning before—and if *that* wasn't something to jot down in his book under *Paranormal Happenings I Should Have Extra Credit For*, he didn't know what was. Perhaps he would add his own section and demand something very dear for it.

He propped his elbow onto the arm of a ridiculously comfortable overstuffed chair, rested his chin on his fist, and allowed himself to contemplate things he suspected he shouldn't.

He couldn't help but wonder a bit about that woman who'd ladled his supper right onto his leg. He'd fully expected the laird's son to make her pay for it, which had left him easily absorbing that piece of hot-tempered backhanding. It had taken a surprising amount of self-control not to flatten the man, never mind the woman's place in the house. Perhaps back in the day there wasn't much distinction between servant and member of the family, not that he would have hesitated to step forward and defend her either way.

The one question he couldn't answer was who she was and why the hell she seemed so ridiculously familiar. He would have said it was because he was fairly certain he'd seen someone just like her out of the corner of his eye, but he was also profoundly sleep deprived and very much out of his element. For all he knew, the spirulina powder he'd inadvertently sniffed the morning before whilst about his fridge investigations had left him hallucinating.

But perhaps more importantly, why was a woman that twelve of a dozen men would have looked past without hesitation have to be the one he hadn't been able to stop watching himself? He could think of all the reasons why she wouldn't been have found beautiful by modern standards, especially compared to the laird's daughters, but he could think of a dozen reasons why she was far more lovely than that trio. All those things began and ended with the smile she'd given those cheeky little yobs he suspected were the laird's grandchildren who'd mobbed her for sweets after supper.

He also suspected it might take him a while to forget the sight of it.

He realized he'd been dancing around what bothered him about the whole venture and that hadn't been winding up in 16th-century Scotland on a whim. Something had felt ... uncomfortable. Like a thunderstorm brewing that simply wouldn't break. It was none of his affair, of course, but he couldn't help but feel a little bothered by it just the same.

How James MacLeod managed to never get involved in any of the historical happenings he witnessed was a terrible mystery he didn't want to solve.

He closed his eyes, trying to forget the sight of a woman he would never see again, then shook his head sharply and pushed himself to his feet. He'd had a ridiculously long trio of days and what he needed was a decent night's sleep for a change. With any luck, he might manage to make the previous twenty-four hours fit into his to-do list. Perhaps it could count not only meditation but a change of diet and some sleep.

He checked locks one more time, commended that long-haired serving girl to her proper place in time with a wish for her happiness, then put himself to bed and hoped his insomnia would consider a holiday for itself as well.

SIX

WHEN A GEL WAS OFF to engage in subterfuge, 'twas best to get an early start.

Mairead walked quickly up the meadow, keeping to the eaves of the forest, and hoped none of her cousins would decide that following her would be good sport. She'd left her flock in the care of a younger cousin, made excuses to everyone else about needing to find the last of the year's plants for dyeing, then marched off with a purpose.

If she found herself roaming a bit further afield than usual or using her well-honed tracking skills to determine where a certain guest had wandered off to, who was to know? She had a knife down the back of her belt and her favorite shawl wrapped around her to not only keep her warm but allow her to blend into the landscape. She would be perfectly safe.

Safe, but perhaps a little more curious than was good for her. Then again, what else could she do? 'Twas nothing more than a commitment to proper hospitality that demanded she make certain their guest hadn't inadvertently left anything behind: a belt buckle, a riding crop, or perhaps an extra ball from his pistol that she hadn't seen but was certain he'd had until he had been, as he'd said, robbed blind and abandoned by his friends.

And if he'd happened to leave behind any folios detailing more of his adventures, good manners behooved her to pick them up and keep them safe in case he returned for them.

She supposed it would have been easier to simply ask him about his adventures, but he'd left yesterday before sunrise whilst she'd been trapped in the kitchens, seeing to things that should have been seen to by Tasgall's wife. She might have considered a bit of a ramble later in the morning, but the scouts who had followed him had returned and reluctantly admitted that they had lost sight of him sooner than they'd cared to.

To her mind, that either meant he was a ghost, which she doubted, or he was highly skilled in keeping himself unobserved, which left her wondering how it was he'd been robbed.

Her uncle would have suggested that faeries were involved, she was sure, perhaps even those bold ones who had once upon a time made off with the Laird James and his lady wife. She, however, wasn't susceptible to that sort of foolish thinking. There was a reasonable explanation for everything and the first part of that included determining where Lord Oliver might have gone.

She stopped on a somewhat contested stretch of ground that marked the end of her clan's holdings and the beginnings of those belonging to the Camerons and studied the landscape. Lord Oliver couldn't have simply appeared from nowhere, surely. She looked around herself for clues, then reluctantly looked down at the ground under feet.

'Twas an odd patch of earth, that smallish ring of plants there in the meadow. She had always used it as a way to mark the border given that it was either in bloom with flowers in the spring or still bearing leaves in the fall with the leavings of its stems always visible against the grasses that surrounded it no matter the time of year.

Her animals never stepped inside it, though she'd led them through that meadow countless times. The lads didn't either, though she couldn't credit either her cousins or those Cameron lads with any more sense than her sheep, so perhaps she was the only one who noticed.

She considered, then decided there was no point in not testing its magical properties for herself and putting the entire ridiculous piece of speculation to rest. She put her shoulders back, then deliberately stepped into the circle, then out of it again.

She looked over her shoulder and found the witch's forest lingering there to her right. Her own meadow lay directly behind her and Cameron lands still lay comfortably to the north in the valley that gave way eventually to a rather lovely stretch of meadow that led directly to Cameron Hall.

There were, however, no sprites dancing in the fall grasses, no fairies peeking out at her from behind trees in the forest, and nothing of an otherworldly and fantastical nature galloping across the meadow to sweep her up into a tale fit for a drunken bard's worst offering. Nothing had changed save perhaps her good sense which had obviously deserted her.

She looked up and was relieved to find not only that the sun was in its accustomed place in the sky, it had apparently decided to push aside a few clouds and pour down a good deal of unexpected warmth. That was an auspicious sign, to be sure, though she couldn't decide precisely why. She drew her shawl more tightly around her just the same, turned to the east, and carried on with what she had come to do.

She shivered as she walked under the eaves of the forest. The sun filtered down through the trees here and there, but it was hardly enough to keep her warm.

If she might have been slightly unnerved by the memory of seeing a man with fair hair out of the corner of her eye, then consigning the sight to her admittedly ungovernable imagination—the one that tended to stroll hand-in-hand with her insatiable curiosity—was perhaps understandable. She put that aside as something to tell her uncle when he exhausted his own stories of ridiculous happenings and carried on under the trees.

She paused several times to study the ground. There was something ... She rolled her eyes and forced herself to simply walk on. Her imagination was truly demanding to be taken out and exercised, but she suspected she might do well to keep a tight rein on it. There was nothing unusual about the forest. The trees were simply trees, and the forest floor was disturbed either from the rain that had descended like the flood the day before or from the feet of those lads who had attempted to follow their guest. She had to admit she hadn't been completely unhappy the day before to remain in the hall where at least she'd been dry.

She wasn't one given to flights of imagination, but she was beginning to feel as though she'd wandered into a dream. The trees were the same, and yet somehow ... not. Perhaps she hadn't paid enough heed during all the times she'd wandered through that forest, keeping a weather eye out for wild animals and unruly cousins.

She blew out of her eyes a few stray hairs she'd caught on branches she hadn't paid any heed to, then continued on her way. The first thing she would do once she returned to the hall was set herself on a stringent course of pretending to listen to her uncle whilst never hearing another word about magical creatures in the forest. She was fairly certain there had been more than one woman inhabiting the witch's croft she could see in the distance who might have agreed with her.

She continued toward it, somewhat relieved to find it in its usual condition. She stopped a few paces away from it, then frowned. Perhaps that wasn't as true as she would have preferred it to be. There was something about the rock that seemed more weathered, if that were possible—

The door to the croft opened suddenly and she jumped in spite of herself. She would have ducked behind the tree closest to her, but she found that her feet were rooted to the ground.

She looked down quickly to make certain there weren't tiny faeries holding her there, but she saw nothing but the usual foliage that covered the forest floor. Perhaps 'twas just her surprise that left her unable to move. That and she didn't want to startle the creature exiting the house.

It was a man, obviously, though he was dressed in black from head to toe. Well, not his boots, which were a rich, dark brown, but he wore strange-looking trews that were black and an even stranger shirt—also black—that only came to his hips.

She looked heavenward to avoid seeing things she absolutely didn't want to, then decided that necessity dictated she venture another look.

The man wore a sword strapped to his back, that she could tell from the hilt that was visible to one side of his head. He held a book in his hands, which she didn't know how to interpret at all. The sunlight that had somehow found its way through the trees fell on his blond hair, turning it to spun gold, a heavenly sight which was at odds with the rest of his admittedly wonderfully fashioned self which she had the most unpleasant feeling had come from a different direction entirely.

He had also obviously caught sight of her poor self because he'd frozen in place, looking as if the slightest movement on her part might leave him bolting.

She couldn't stop herself from wondering if she'd wandered somewhere untoward and quite possibly perilous. She
wanted to believe that she was looking at the man written
about so capably in the pages of her book, but his garb indicated he might have sprung from a far different realm. It
pained her to suspect she had misjudged him so thoroughly,
but she hardly knew what else to think.

She considered her possible alternatives—run and hide or
stride forth and conquer—and decided upon the latter. If she
were going to be carried off to Hell, she would not go quietly.

She took her courage in hand and strode forward boldly,
stopping a few paces away from him. "Are you a demon?" she
demanded.

He looked at her blankly. "A what?"

She pointed her finger at him, just so he wouldn't think
that he would escape her scrutiny so easily. "A demon," she
repeated firmly.

He opened and closed his mouth several times without
speaking. That could have been because he was choosing a
charm to lay over her—if demons did such a thing, which she
sincerely hoped wasn't the case. He looked a little baffled
though, so perhaps she would manage to escape before he
cast any sort of unholy bit of business over her like a net.

"Do I look like a demon?" he asked carefully.

She declined to answer, instead folding her arms over her
chest and affecting her father's favorite expression of skepticism. At least that might give her time to decide just what
sort of man she was looking at.

He was holding a book, true, which was a mark in his
favor given that she was almost certain demons couldn't read.
She'd seen several paintings of them leaning over monks
diligently scribbling—the monks, not the demons—which
had left her suspecting that only the lads manning the quills

could read their own scratches. Indeed, from what she'd seen in those manuscripts, demons simply poked friars with their pointed tails, no doubt swearing quite lustily as they were about their terrible labors.

"You don't have a tail, do you?" she asked sharply.

He looked behind himself, then back at her and shook his head.

"And you *are* reading," she conceded, "which does you credit. I'm not sure if you've vexed any friars recently, but that might be something we can discuss in a moment. Your clothing, however, leaves a great deal to be desired not only in modesty but the inspiring of confidence that you aren't going to carry me off to Hell." She paused and looked at him sternly. "You aren't going to carry me off to Hell, are you?"

At the moment, he looked as if he might be asking her to carry him off somewhere so he might sit down. He was also holding up his hand in the same way she tended to when Ambrose and his wee siblings were bouncing around her skirts like a litter of pups, as if he strove to stop the madness long enough to make sense of it.

"Would you speak a bit more slowly?" he asked. "My Gaelic is poor."

She thought he spoke it very well, especially since she knew it wasn't his first language. If he was who she thought he was, of course.

"I think it is good enough," she said as casually as possible in his English.

He dropped his book, then gaped at her. She stepped forward and bent over to pick it up at the same time he did which left her running her forehead directly into the hilt of his sword. She straightened, holding her hand to her face and finding herself grateful she hadn't put her eye out.

"I'm so sorry," he said in Gaelic. "Here, come sit and I'll fetch you some water."

She had help sitting down upon a large stump that she was fairly certain had been a sapling the day before. It was such a ridiculous thought to entertain, she suspected she might do well to simply not think at all for a moment or two. She closed her eyes and put her hand against her forehead, though the pain wasn't terrible. It cleared her head a bit from her chaotically swirling thoughts, most having to do with what the Duke of Birmingham was doing half an hour's walk from her home, wearing clothing she wasn't entirely certain she also hadn't seen in some rendering of a hellish creature tormenting yet another poor monk.

She heard the door open and close and managed to squint at him as he squatted down in front of her. She took the cup, considered it, then looked at him. "Poisoned?"

He frowned. "Poisoned?"

"Poison," she said in his tongue. In his history, the Duke had been particularly vexed by enemies attempting the same in order to have his fine goods, so that word she was at least familiar with.

He shook his head slightly. "Nay, 'tisn't."

She drank and found it to be just water, as he claimed. She looked at the small wooden cup, which seemed comfortingly familiar somehow, then at him. He was only watching her carefully, as if he expected *her* to draw his sword and use it on him herself.

"You changed your clothing from your demon garb," she noted.

"I'm not a demon." He knelt next to her and sat back on his heels, looking somehow both perilous and innocent at the same time. "Why don't we begin anew?"

"Aye, with where you left your demon garb," she muttered.

He smiled. "Perhaps not that far."

"What language?" she asked loftily. "Mine or your marginally passable French?"

"My very French mother would be insulted," he said with a faint smile, "but I'll claim all the flaws there. Gaelic, then, and French when needed?"

"Or we could speak in your English," she said casually, hoping this time it might startle him into a confession.

A confession about what, she certainly didn't know. That he was a man so famous that he had a scribe following him and jotting down his more noteworthy doings? He'd obviously lost at least the first half of that recounting, so he might not want to discuss it.

He had gone very still, but perhaps that was his way of assessing the battlefield before committing to a course of action.

"I learned your tongue from a book," she said when it looked as if he might never speak again. "A book about a duke. I may not be pronouncing the words properly."

"You're doing it wonderfully."

Which he said in Gaelic, which she supposed might be the best way to continue. She waited, but he only knelt there, silent and grave. His usual method of conducting his affairs, if his diary had told the tale true.

She handed him back his cup, then started to get to her feet. He leapt up and held out his hand to help her up, which she found to be slightly uncomfortable for some reason. She wasn't accustomed to any sort of courtesies from her kin, though young Ambrose had recently taken to exercising his manners enough to see her seated before he took a stool next to her and single-mindedly worked his way through his suppers.

"So," she said casually, "you said you were returning home."

"I'm trying," he agreed.

"You might have an easier time if you had your phaeton and matched ponies," she said in as offhand a manner as possible.

He looked at her as if he'd never heard of such a thing. "My what?"

She was beginning to wonder if he'd not only been robbed, but clunked on the head hard enough to lose a few of his memories. "Your conveyance," she said, trying to dredge up a bit of patience.

"My conveyance?"

"How you came here," she clarified. "Unless you simply rode a horse."

He only nodded.

That was hardly an answer. She was beginning to suspect that there were not just a few strange and mysterious things clustered around the man in front of her and she wasn't entirely certain those things weren't several otherworldly characters from her uncle's fevered imagination.

"Were you indeed robbed," she asked sternly, "or was that a falsehood?"

He seemed to be choosing his words carefully. She was tempted to try once more to startle him into blurting out details about himself that he seemed reluctant to reveal, but there was something that stopped her. She was accustomed to instantly judging men and situations in order to avoid trouble. The man in front of her still had his hands in plain sight, he had offered her water, and he had been polite and respectful to her kin when he'd been in their hall.

He had also taken a blow for her and not made any mention of the rather hot soup she'd poured on his leg, so perhaps he had his own reasons for keeping things to himself.

"I was left here by my friends," he said carefully.

"Here in the witch's croft?" she asked in surprise.

"Aye."

"And you cannot simply return home?"

"My friends asked me to wait for them here."

"But that seems strange," she said, which she thought was a truly unholy bit of understatement.

He smiled slightly. "I agree."

"Why don't you come wait back at the hall where you at least have a hot fire?"

He inclined his head politely. "The invitation is most welcome, but I must wait here. Many horses will be mine if I do as they've asked."

"How many?"

"Twelve hundred." He paused. "Possibly fewer, but I'm hoping for that many."

She caught her breath. She wasn't sure she had over the course of her entire life seen so many animals. "And what are their terms, these lads of yours?"

"I have tasks to accomplish."

"That sounds terrible."

He smiled faintly and she wanted to sit down. 'Twas no wonder her sisters had been falling over themselves to get closer to him.

"I agree."

"Are these tasks things to increase character and stamina," she managed, "or simply foolish things with which to pass the time?"

He smiled again, as if he found something about that faintly amusing. "Simple things they no doubt thought would be amusing."

"Very well, then," she said, nodding firmly. "Let's hear a pair of them. I'll help you, then go home."

He hesitated. "I wouldn't want to be improper by accepting your aid."

She frowned. "What do you mean?"

"I am honorable," he said carefully, "but you are a woman alone."

Mairead was heartily tempted to sit back down on the stump that hadn't been a stump a pair of days ago. The only thing she could say in her favor was that the Duke wasn't sending her any scorching looks, which she thought boded well for her virtue. Then again, he likely had serving maids who were far more handsome than she would ever be, so perhaps he wasn't at all affected by her. She was indeed safe.

She watched as he went back inside. Perhaps he'd changed his mind and gone to fetch his list of tasks, though she had to wonder how his gear had found itself inside the croft to begin with. Perhaps he'd considered it a handy place to hide things before he'd continued on to the meadow, searching for aid.

He emerged once more with his sword again on his back, pulled the door shut behind him, then stopped in front of her and made her a slight bow.

"I would be honored to walk you back toward the meadow and keep watch as you return to the keep. I don't want your master to think I've been keeping you here improperly in the forest."

"My master?" she managed, then it occurred to her what he was thinking. She decided that perhaps, given his honorable conduct with all the kitchen maids he no doubt knew, there was no slur in those words. She nodded. "Very well spoken on your part."

He nodded, but he was studying her as if things were occurring to him that hadn't before.

She wasn't quite sure how she felt about that, so she nodded briskly at him, then turned and marched off through the forest toward the meadow. She didn't last ten paces before she had to look over her shoulder and make certain he was still there.

He was simply walking behind her, his hands clasped behind his back, watching her with a grave expression on his face.

By the time they'd reached the northern edge of the forest, she wasn't quite sure what to think about him.

She realized he was looking up and down the meadow in the same way she did, as if he made certain there were no souls there to cause trouble. Then again, he was who he was and that was how he conducted his affairs. She continued along the border with him until they stood on the edge of that unsettling ring in the grass. She was very surprised to hear her hounds baying in the distance, though she wondered why. Of course she would hear things of a normal and unremarkable nature.

She turned to look at her companion only to watch him make her a slight bow.

"Safely delivered."

She reconsidered her assumptions. She suspected that if she'd been a man about some sort of vexatious business, it would have been very unwise to provoke that man there. But a woman?

What a fortunate, blessed gel it was who had attracted his eye and claimed his affection.

"Thank you," she managed.

He held out his hand. "Oliver."

She put her hand in his, watched him bend over it as if she'd been a fine lady and he the duke of some fine place she'd never been, then watched him step back and nod politely.

She nodded in return, then turned and walked away because she could think of nothing else to do. The sounds of sheep and goats and hounds was louder than it had been before, but she was also walking down the meadow toward them, so that was to be expected. She forced herself to continue on until she thought a reasonable amount of time had passed, then looked over her shoulder to have a final look at a man who couldn't possibly be what she thought him.

He was gone.

She felt her hound bump her hand with his chilly nose, which startled her slightly. She took a moment for a bit of scratching him behind his ears, then sent him back off to watch over her sheep whilst she considered things she likely should have left alone.

It was possible she'd simply been walking in the forest near her home and everything Lord Oliver had said was true. He could have taken shelter in the witch's croft whilst he awaited his friends to come and rescue him.

But that didn't explain a stump she'd sat on that she was almost positive was currently a sapling five paces from the door of the healer's croft.

It wasn't possible—and she could almost not entertain the thought—that she had stepped *into* the Duke of Birmingham's tale.

Was it?

She hardly knew what to think, so she decided to put it off as something to consider later. First things first, as her father had said to her endlessly in her youth. His list had usually included food, shelter, then long winter evenings devoted to listening to their bard recite tales of glorious battles won and innumerable cattle successfully raided. Her list had always been simpler and included nothing past avoiding those who vexed her and keeping her sheep safe.

And then she'd found the Duke's faithful history and everything had changed for her. Her list that she couldn't quite bring herself to make included things that she knew were so far out of her reach as to be impossible.

A man who would love her, give her children, keep her safe, and, heaven pity her for the most foolish of gels, think she was pretty. In perhaps a very dim light, but there it was.

She pulled herself back to the present moment and continued to walk home. She was obviously going to be seeing to her usual tasks for the rest of the day, but tomorrow was another day with ample time to investigate things that perplexed her.

Because no matter how he was styling himself, the Duke of Birmingham was not a demon. No demon could possibly have been so tall, well-fashioned, and polite. Plus, the Duke had fair hair and a pair of absolutely bewitching pale blue eyes.

She paused. *Bewitching* was a problem, to be sure, but perhaps that could be addressed later when next they met. He'd denied being any sort of foul creature from the nether regions, so she would take him at his word.

The fact that stepping into what she could safely say had been some sort of strange ring of what had been flowers at some point had given her pause, but again, she was no coward.

The odd thing was, though, that when she'd stepped out of that ring, it was as if the sun had come out from behind a cloud.

The thing she couldn't simply let lie was the fact that she'd actually had a glimpse inside the healer's house as Lord Oliver had exited it, and it hadn't looked at all like the empty croft she was accustomed to. Then again, the outside didn't look much like it, either.

There were strange and mysterious things happening on MacLeod soil. Her uncle might have called them *magical*. She wasn't quite sure what to call them, but she knew one thing beyond any doubt.

She was going to find out.

SEVEN

O LIVER PAUSED JUST INSIDE MORAIG'S house and
wondered about the wisdom of going outside. After
yesterday, he was beginning to think he might do
better to make himself a little nest in the loo and hide for the
duration of his sentence.

But he was nothing if not disciplined and he had tasks
to complete. If that required him to venture out into nature,
so be it. He checked that his medieval gear was covering
everything it should and that his weapons were in their upright and locked positions, then cast caution to the wind and
opened the door.

A shopping bag was sitting on the front stoop.

That at least had come from the current century. He
picked it up and brought it inside where he could enjoy the
delights without being observed, though he couldn't imagine
who would have cared. Then again, he was wearing his medieval Highland uniform instead of a comfortable tracksuit, so
perhaps he was a little more concerned about company than
he wanted to admit.

What he was certain of was that he wouldn't be seeing
any Renaissance Highland lassies wandering around in times
not their own.

He had to wonder if she'd been the one he'd been seeing
out of the corner of his eye from the first day of his holi-

day, but he wasn't sure how that was possible. She obviously wasn't a ghost, so perhaps there was some odd quirk in the fabric of time that left them passing each other along time-travelly passageways that had very flimsy walls.

He was absolutely going to demand extra credit for all the paranormal shenanigans he was being subjected to. The next thing he knew, he would be entertaining an entire cast of Shakespeare's best ghostly offerings, all come to unsettle him at the same time.

He made a hasty grab for his good sense and walked back into the kitchen to see what had been delivered. He was utterly unsurprised to find the oft-threatened leopard-print yoga bottoms which made him shudder just to look at them. They were only marginally modest, but the note attached guaranteed him double points for donning them, so he set them aside as something to consider later.

Also in the bag was a shocking pink water bottle adorned with the usual felines—though these lads looked a bit more zen-like than the previous collection—and a key. He looked at the note the key was attached to by means of a cheerful heart sticker and braced himself for more absurdities.

> *You haven't killed anyone yet and we haven't heard any off-key yowls of terror or excessive swearing. You've earned the key, but remember we're still watching you. More delights to come.*

He could scarce wait to see what those delights might be. He also wasted no time unlocking his anklet. He was half tempted to go barefoot for the rest of the day in celebration, but one never knew where one might wind up whilst in the wilds of Scotland, so he forbore. He was fully tempted to chop that damned tracker up into tiny pieces, but it occurred to him that he might want to torture someone else with it at some point, so he popped it in a drawer for future use.

He was still without a phone or any sort of useful computing device, but he had to admit that the depravation was starting to feel a little less horrifying than it had in the beginning.

He clapped his hand to his forehead, but there was no dislodging any good sense. That he was actually contemplating the thought of an entire day of being unplugged without howling in outrage was terrifying. He was ruined, obviously, and someone would need to pay for that.

But until that happy time came, he would do his best with what he had to hand, enjoy the fact that his ankle no longer felt as if it were being slowly sawn in half, and see to ticking a few more boxes next to tasks that didn't involve wearing those obscene spotted yoga trousers.

He realized there was one last bit of misery left in the bag and decided it was best to have it all over with at once. He pulled out a tin that turned out to be full of very tiny colored pencils. The note attached instructed him to find things to sketch and be about rendering them properly on the pages to be found behind the appropriate tab in his master notebook.

He hesitated to speculate on who might be judging his skills, vowed not to draw anything obscene no matter how tempted he might have been, and decided he might as well venture out into the meadow and see what turned up. He might manage to sniff a few flowers whilst drawing them and kill two eejits with one stone.

He had a final look around the house to make certain everything was as it should have been, then opened the door and hopped energetically over the threshold before any time-traveling sprites could give him a shove into a year where he might not be so relaxed and refreshed.

He realized after the fact just how close he'd come to knocking himself out on the top of the threshold, filed that away as something to be more careful about in the future, then walked through the forest, keeping to the shadows out of habit and happily finding himself free of any hangers-on in the person of Patrick MacLeod. Perhaps the man had decided a little lie-in might be just the thing for the morning.

He reached the meadow in good time, diligently ignored the fairy ring that he knew lay fifty paces to the north of his current position, then looked around himself instead for a comfortable rock from where he might observe the local flora. If he finished quickly, he supposed it wouldn't be un-thinkable to meditate a bit on soothing things such as who he was going to kill first once his fortnight of torture was over.

He sat down, sincerely hoping there weren't any stray, soon-to-be-deceased colleagues lurking in the tall grass across the way with telephoto lenses at the ready, fully prepared to take a shot up his saffron shirt. At least he was wearing Cameron plaid boxers and not a pair of white Y-fronts with abusive language scrawled on the bum where it might be most advantageously read as he turned and mooned the blighters.

He took a deep breath and let it out slowly. He wasn't sure meditation was doing him any favors, but perhaps he needed to concentrate on more positive things.

He opened his notebook to the appropriate *Activities for Relaxation* section, found the *Draw Flowers Here* page, then looked at the little tin of tiny pencils he'd been given. How anyone expected him to do anything with those besides load them into a dart gun and shoot them into a criminal, he didn't know. He chose something useful—green, as it hap-pened—then looked around himself to see what floral delights there might be for him to attempt to reproduce—

He froze.

He wasn't alone.

He made a production of pretending he hadn't noticed anything unusual. It seemed like a perfect time to do a little yoga, so he replaced his pencil, shut the lid, and used the tin's shiny underside to make certain no one was standing directly behind him, waiting to stab him. Not a great mirror, admittedly, but sufficient for his purposes. Finding no one, he put his gear on the rock where with any luck it would get nicked, then rose and began to stretch.

He limited himself to twisting at the waist, partly because he was, as usual, in an outfit that required a princess-like commitment to keeping his knees together and partly because a little releasing of the tension in his back gave him the chance to look over his shoulder in both directions where he found ...

Nothing.

He frowned thoughtfully. He was being watched—he would have bet his favorite pair of trainers on it—so obviously he would have to go investigate. The only question that remained was did he keep his sword strapped to his back and possibly clunk himself on the back of the head thanks to a misstep, or did he leave it behind and hope his invisible friend wasn't Patrick MacLeod trying to keep himself awake?

He decided abruptly that keeping his sword with him could be considered an exercise in *Being Prepared for Scottish Adventures*—and for all he knew, Jamie could be persuaded to create a section for just that with hefty points attached—so he clapped his hand to his forehead in an exaggerated fashion, then stomped back the way he'd come, cursing himself loudly for having forgotten the very thing he'd intended to bring outside. He suspected he also might need to add a section entitled *Why Eejits Should Do Reconnaissance*, but that might become too full with all the recriminations he would be directing at himself.

Time marched on as doggedly as he did, but perhaps with a bit less grumbling.

He heard the snap of a twig behind him and quickly ran through potential suspects. Those included anyone from one of Jamie's children to Ian MacLeod taking over whilst Patrick was having his lie-in. He indulged in a quick prayer that he wouldn't turn and impale himself on a death-dealing medieval blade, held up his hands, then turned slowly around to face his fate.

A woman was standing there.

Well, to be perfectly accurate, a fearless Highland lass he recognized was standing there with the knife she'd obviously intended to use to defend herself lying at her feet. He realized he was already very still, but he felt that stillness increase exponentially. That happened, he supposed, when one encountered in the present day someone who should have been comfortably loitering four centuries, give or take a few years, in the past.

He wasn't sure who she was, especially as she hadn't given him her name. He also wasn't entirely certain about Highland clan structure past knowing in his head that when he'd pledged fealty to Robert Cameron, he'd become part of the Cameron clan. What that meant to his heart in terms of being considered family was something that generally left him feeling overly maudlin, so he didn't think about it.

"Friend not foe," he said, because that had worked well enough before. "Still."

"I don't need a knife to best ye," she said.

Oliver nodded solemnly. "I'm sure that's true." He would have attempted a smile, but the woman had called him a demon the day before, so there were obviously discussions still to be had. He dug deep for his best Gaelic and pointed to the dirk down the side of his boot. "I'm going to draw my blade and hand it to you."

"Why?"

"So you'll feel safe while I bend down and pick up your knife."

She didn't look as if she would be feeling safe any time soon. In fact, she looked as if she might be one poorly chosen word on his part away from a complete meltdown. He considered offering a soothing *calm down*, but he'd listened to more than one eejit of his acquaintance utter those fighting words to a female companion and marveled at the ensuing carnage. Caution and silence were obviously the orders of the day.

He carefully pulled the dirk free from its sheath and handed it to her haft first, then kept his eye on her as he bent and picked up her knife. He handed her that as well.

"You will not find me easily vanquished," she said, her voice shaking as badly as her hands.

"I never thought you would be." As an afterthought, he pulled the dirk from his left boot and held that out as well.

She considered that third blade, studied him for a moment or two, then stuck her own knife into what he assumed was a sheath loitering in the back of her belt. She took his second blade, then pointed them both at him, though she honestly didn't look as if she would be holding onto either for very long.

"I have questions," she said, her voice quavering badly.

He could only imagine. He took a deep breath and nodded carefully. "I'm certain you—"

"Am I in your book?"

He blinked. "My what?"

"Your book!"

He was tempted to scratch his head to see if that helped, but he had the feeling that any sudden movement might inspire her to dig answers out of his gut—with his own blades, no less. She couldn't possibly mean his book of absurdities and torments, though it wouldn't have surprised him to learn his mates had secretly designed a bit of time-traveling as part of the programme.

He had vague memories of his current companion having mentioned a book the day before—had it only been a single day ago?—about a duke, which at the time had only left him with the uneasy feeling that he should have watched more period pieces on telly.

"The book about the duke?" he ventured.

She looked as if he had just handed her—well, not the keys to an obscenely expensive sports car, but something era-appropriate. Or perhaps that was just the look a body wore when she'd taken her first decent breath of the day.

"You know it, then," she said, obviously relieved.

He had no trouble producing a baffled look. "I've forgotten, I fear. Refresh my memory, if you would."

Her relief turned a bit of a corner there, right into a cul-de-sac of skepticism. "You've forgotten your own tale?"

"Ah ..."

"And your own scribe?"

"Well—"

"Mistress Buchanan will not be pleased with you, I'll tell you that plainly."

"I only want to make sure she's written it down properly," he lied, attempting to stall. He couldn't imagine why his companion thought he had a book, though he supposed finding herself in what was indeed a different world might have led her to believe she was *in* a book.

She had begun to study him as if she expected him to do something villainous at any moment, but he'd seen that sort of thing before and had no trouble continuing to look as trustworthy as possible.

"'Tis the tale of the Duke of Birmingham," she said, watching him closely, no doubt to see if that rang any literary bells for him.

"Such a fine, strapping lad," Oliver managed, wondering if *he* had suddenly plunged face-first into the land of faeries and bogles. And books, apparently. He was torn between trying to decide where her tale might land on the literary time line and being relieved he wasn't going to be explaining any modern offerings containing either terrible weapons or superheroes in tights.

"Of course I only have the first part of it," she continued. "I fear the rest was lost somewhere, no doubt causing Mistress Constance Buchanan a great amount of vexation."

"Constance Buchanan," he repeated, nodding to keep the peace whilst rifling through his catalog of fiction to see if that name rang any bells. No tolling, unfortunately, but the beginnings of wishing he'd bypassed the Jaffa cakes and settled for something green for breakfast.

She put her hands on her hips. "Do you not know her?"

"Recent blow to the head," he said promptly, putting his hand to the back of his head and attempting to look a bit confused. "I've forgotten many things."

"She is the scribe who wrote down the duke's tale. *Your* tale, if I'm guessing aright."

He hardly knew where to begin with that, so he simply nodded and hoped that would be enough.

"There is talk of his kitchen maid," she continued, "who is in every particular his equal, especially in gaming, shooting, and tossing back port."

"She sounds exceptional," he said, hoping she wouldn't mind if he reached for more French than usual. His Gaelic was absolutely not equal to the current conversation.

"I've yet to discover the maid's name as she held it as a closely guarded secret."

"Very wise," he noted. He suspected there was romance in sickly abundance in the duke's tale which he wasn't sure was an improvement over superheroes. What he did know was that the woman standing there studying him seemed to be coming to conclusions she didn't particularly care for.

"I thought the tale was yours when I first saw you," she said, beginning to frown. "There is a painting of the man on the cover and you resemble him greatly."

"Poor lad," Oliver managed.

"Oh, nay, he's very handsome. And he would never use a sword on a woman."

"I like him already," he said promptly. He nodded toward the meadow. "Why don't we take a walk and you can tell me more about his finer qualities so I'll know where to improve."

She didn't move. "I will not be vanquished," she said bluntly. "I am very fierce in battle."

She couldn't have sounded more like a grown-up Patricia MacLeod, which would have left him smiling if he hadn't suspected any smiles would result in *his* being vanquished. He settled for the most trustworthy look he could muster, which didn't take any effort as he meant it fully.

"You are perfectly safe with me," he said. "And I would step between you and harm without a second's thought."

"Well, you have before."

He conceded that with a nod, had a brisk nod in return, then clasped his hands behind his back as they walked in the direction of the meadow. He could, however, feel her gaze boring into the side of his head. He'd endured worse so he simply let her have her look.

"You aren't the Duke of Birmingham, are you?"

He was surprised to find that he suddenly wished he were. He glanced at her and shook his head. "I'm sorry," he said simply.

"And we're not in your book."

"We're not. We are in Scotland, though."

"But things are different from how I left them this morning," she said. She shot him a look that said clearly that she suspected he might be responsible for that. "The outside of the healer's croft is different. I couldn't bring myself to look inside it."

Thank heavens for small favors. Not only were there things inside that would have sent her into an entirely different level of unsettled, he couldn't remember whether or not he'd left clothes strewn about or done the washing up after breakfast.

He suddenly had vastly increased respect for the time travelers in his circle of acquaintances. Of course he'd thought it was absolute bollocks when the notion had first floated across his brain. He'd consigned it immediately to the same place that contained his experiences with ghosts who might or might not have protested any of the antiquities he had cheerfully moved to new digs.

Ghosts could be very annoying at times.

He supposed it might be best not only to leave any antics in 1602 alone, but also his journeys with James MacLeod to places and times not their own. All seven times, each more unbelievable than the time before.

He wondered how *that* might be worked into keys to a Bugatti.

He also wondered how one went about explaining the inexplicable, especially when the one who might not particularly care for the particulars was holding—barely—two very sharp dirks. He wished he'd taken advantage of Jamie's offer to give him his full lecture series on the vagaries of time travel and its attendant social conundrums, but that was a poor excuse for his own failing to do his due diligence.

He never went into any situation where he hadn't mapped out every contingency well in advance. That he found himself at present so completely out of his depth was galling. He should have, at the very least, taken a few minutes to contemplate how a Renaissance clanswoman might feel should she find herself again in the present day instead of spending all his time enjoying the horrors he would perpetrate on his work colleagues when he tracked them with a thoroughness and efficiency that even Patrick MacLeod might have admired.

All of which left him, at the moment, with a woman standing in front of him, looking very lost, and he didn't have a damned clue where to start in fixing that for her.

"Lord Oliver?"

He pulled himself back to the tangle at hand, a little surprised at how distracted he'd become. "It's just Oliver."

He waited, but she didn't offer any of her credentials. For some reason, that didn't surprise him. There was a gel who kept her cards close to her vest. He suspected he might understand given what he'd seen of Tasgall, the *de facto* laird of the hall.

"Oliver, then," she said, then she shivered. "I do not like to admit weakness, but I fear I might be lost."

He attempted a reassuring smile. "You aren't lost," he said firmly. "You're still on MacLeod soil." He nodded in the direction of the meadow. "Why don't we go for a walk and you'll see that things aren't so different after all."

She nodded, but he could see the wheels still turning. He just wasn't entirely sure where her thoughts were going to lead her.

He forced himself to keep a weather eye out for trouble as they walked, but saw nothing more nefarious than a few birds and some stray shafts of sunlight. He realized at one point that his companion, that nameless lass with the sweet smile, was also marking their surroundings. He wondered, with a bit less detachment than the thought merited, where she'd learned that skill and why she needed it.

Though he supposed just her time period was reason enough. He was half tempted to send her back to whenever she'd come from with a can or two of safety spray, though he imagined that might have gotten her burned at the stake after the fact.

"My uncle Lachlan says there are fairies and bogles in this forest."

He glanced at her. "Do you think that's possible?"

She looked absolutely shattered. "I don't know." She stopped, stared off into the distance for a moment or two, then looked at him. "Do you think 'tis possible?"

"Well—"

She searched his face more closely than he was comfortable with. "You do," she whispered.

"Scotland is a very special place," he conceded, because he found, to his surprise, that he believed it. It was no wonder Cameron—and Derrick, for that matter—came back to it as often as possible. For the first time, he found himself envying them their connection to the land.

And then it occurred to him just what that meant. Her uncle? Was she one of Laird Ranald's daughters then?

He felt himself come back to earth in a particularly ungentle way. He wasn't looking at a simple serving girl; he was looking at a Renaissance noblewoman who was off in the wilds of the future without permission. Obviously, things had to change, and rapidly. He had years of experience in inventing reasonable-sounding excuses for being wherever he was, though he would be the first to admit that trying to convince a 16th-century clanswoman to stay in her proper time was new.

"Let's say this," he began slowly. "Have you been to Cameron Hall?"

She nodded.

"And whilst it is still in Scotland, it's different to the MacLeod hall, aye?"

She frowned. "Aye, of course."

"Then think of this place as just another place, much like a different hall. Still in Scotland, just different."

"But I left my part of the book in the bole of a tree near the witch's croft yesterday," she said carefully. "When I looked a bit ago, 'twas there no longer."

"Think of this forest as being a bit different from yours as well."

"That's daft," she said, though she looked to be considering it. "So, I'm not in a dream."

"I think we're both real enough," he said, trying to be as careful as she had been.

She looked over the meadow. "I cannot hear my flock."

"You might, if you moved a bit closer to them."

She nodded up the meadow. "Have you seen that strange patch of earth on the border of our lands?"

He had the feeling he might know the place, but he didn't want to assume anything that might interfere with getting her back home where she belonged.

"Show me?" he asked politely.

She nodded and walked with him up the meadow. She paused by that particular ring in the grass, then looked up at him.

"What is this thing, do you think?"

"I think it could be a way to get from here to a different place," he said carefully.

"What place?" she asked, her voice barely audible. "Your demon world?"

He smiled. "I thought we decided yesterday that I'm not a demon."

She scowled at him, though her heart didn't look to be in it. "I'm still coming to a decision on that, but I'll allow that your manners are too fine for it."

"Thank you."

She looked back at the ring in the grass. "Then 'tis a bit like a doorway," she mused.

He half expected Jamie to come striding up the meadow with his sword bared. He took a deep breath, then nodded.

"I think it's exactly like a doorway," he agreed.

"You know that's absolute foolishness."

He almost smiled. "I couldn't agree more."

She looked out over the meadow. "I should likely go home."

He had the most absurd urge to tell her perhaps she didn't need to quite yet. He had lunch and colored pencils and his left knee was absolutely not giving him any forewarnings of impending weather.

But he'd likely already said more than he should have and she had definitely spent more time than was wise in a century not her own. He accepted his knives back and watched her step toward that unsettling circle in the grass and actually saw the gate open for her. He'd seen the same happen at a spot near Raventhorpe a year ago, but he'd been happy to consign that to not enough sleep.

At the moment, he could safely say that if he hadn't believed in the whole ruddy business of time traveling before, he would have believed it then. He could hear a dog barking on the other side ...

"Shall I walk you home?" he asked, because he had a sword and she was a woman who might need protecting.

She looked at him and smiled faintly. "I'm on my own land."

So she was, which was likely something to keep in mind for the future. "Safe home, then," he said quietly.

She turned away and stepped into the ring, then paused. She looked over her shoulder at him.

"Mairead."

He closed his eyes briefly, then nodded and made her a low bow. He straightened, a *thank you* on the tip of his tongue.

But she was gone.

He sighed deeply, dragged his hands through his hair, and walked off to fetch his gear. He'd done the right thing, sent her back with hopefully an explanation that would make sense, and she would get back to her normal life whilst leaving him to his.

He felt surprisingly ... bereft, which was absolutely absurd and someone would pay for it—and dearly.

He kept himself company with thoughts of which of his mates he would do in first because that was better than wondering why the hell he'd been blindsided by a woman who was nothing more than a freckled girl-next-door type that a dozen undiscerning lads would have looked past.

Unfortunately, he was not an eejit, no matter what his book—not hers—called him and there was something about the way her smile took her face from plain to breathtaking that left him wishing he could ask her out on more than a first date.

He made his way back to Moraig's, let himself in the cottage without rejoicing overmuch that he'd arrived in the proper century, then made himself something to eat. He could hardly believe he was relieved that he had no device with which to do a little online sleuthing to find out a few more details about that plainly lovely woman, but perhaps that was for the best. He didn't want to find out she'd married someone likely hadn't deserved her.

He wished her well, finished up his lunch, then hoped a quick nap in a chair would restore his good sense.

If not, he would have to rely on Patrick MacLeod's very sharp sword to do it instead.

EIGHT

MAIREAD WALKED UP THE MEADOW a pair of hours after dawn, keeping to the shadows of the witch's forest to avoid attracting the attention of either cousins or sprite-like creatures peering at her through blades of grass, and considered the events of the previous day.

She'd gotten herself home after her encounter with Oliver, pled a headache to anyone who would listen, then shut herself into the small hut where she dyed her wool and kept it hanging from the eaves. She'd remained there until well after supper, only allowing herself to seek the warmth of the kitchen when she'd been certain most of the clan had already fallen into peaceful slumber.

If she'd slept, she didn't remember it. Her thoughts had been consumed by doorways and faery rings and a man who claimed not to be any sort of nobleman but had manners finer than any lord she'd ever seen. When the cock had begun to crow, she'd resigned herself to the fact that she couldn't leave unanswered the question that kept her awake for the whole of the night.

What world was it that lay on the other side of that doorway in the meadow?

She had made herself a poor breakfast from the last of the previous night's pot scrapings, bribed a different cousin to tend her animals, then slipped out of the keep whilst the household had been distracted with breaking their fasts. She wouldn't say she'd run up the meadow, but she'd definitely walked swiftly which had left her where she was at the present moment: looking down at that odd ring in the grass and wondering where it led.

She closed her eyes briefly, stepped in and out of it, then gathered her courage and looked around herself.

She could no longer see her sheep, though she'd watched her cousin gather them up and head off to their usual spot for grazing. The air was a bit warmer, though it was obviously still autumn. For all she knew, she was ablaze with a fever that had roasted her wits. The forest was full of trees just as she'd seen it not a handful of moments before and she was still in her proper form.

Perhaps 'twas time to do the unthinkable and brave the inside of the witch's croft.

She made her way along the eves of the forest until she found a path that led inward. She walked silently along that until she came to a halt twenty paces away from the healer's croft. It was still fashioned from sturdy stones, the doorway was still boasting a solid piece of wood as a defense against the night and enemies, and the path that led there was still flanked by what poor bits of land anyone had ever managed to clear for the cultivation of healthful plants.

She put her hand out on her tree, then pulled it back to herself quickly. She realized with an unpleasant bit of alarm that her tree wasn't the same, her hiding place was gone, and even the bark was so weathered that she couldn't believe the tree still lived—

She heard voices and the sound of light laughter. A woman's laughter, as it happened, as well as the sound of a man's deep voice. It wasn't a terrible noise, which was reassuring. In fact, if she'd had even two wits left to rub together, she might have considered it a good, homely sound that left her wanting to join in and become a part of what sounded like familial happiness.

The door to the croft opened and two souls crossed the threshold, light spilling out from behind them. She pushed away from her tree and staggered forward a handful of steps, not because she particularly wanted to, but because she couldn't help herself.

A woman stood there, holding onto the arm of a man. She was very beautiful, with long, curling dark hair, a lovely visage, and a blossoming belly that spoke of joys to come in a few months' time.

The man standing next to her was one she recognized. His fair hair was, as it usually was, golden in the pale light of the morning. His visage was also as it usually was, full of noble planes and angles with a beautiful mouth that gave voice to kind words and wry observations. His form was, also as usual, enough to put any of the lads of her family to shame. He wore some species of tunic that reached down to a reasonably modest level and covered things it should.

But his legs were covered in spots.

She gaped at him. "Did ye catch the pox?" she asked in astonishment.

Oliver's mouth worked industriously, no doubt as he looked for something useful to say.

And then something else occurred to her, something that left her suddenly and quite ridiculously unhappy. She gestured to the beautiful woman who had been holding onto his arm on their way through the doorway but had now released him and taken a step forward.

"Is that your lady wife?" she managed, wishing she sounded quite a bit less devastated and far more aloof.

The woman didn't even bother with a glance in Oliver's direction. She did look over her shoulder to the innards of the croft, then walked forward and held out her hand.

"I'm Sunshine, Oliver's cousin," she said in reassuringly perfect Gaelic, "though I'm more of an older sister than a cousin, actually. Who are you?"

Mairead took Sunshine's hand and wished hers weren't so chilly. "Mairead," she managed. "How are you here as well?" She looked at Oliver. "Did your mates rob her and leave her with you to tend?"

He was still wearing the sort of look she'd seen on more than one man's face when he simply didn't have the words to use in addressing the madness lying before himself. At least a closer view of his fine self—not too close, of course—revealed that he wasn't covered in pox sores, but rather oddly patterned trews.

"And what, by all that is holy," she managed. "are you wearing?"

Sunshine laughed and it was as though a merry fire had simply sprung to life there before them all. "A terrible gift from his friends, I'm afraid."

"Lady Sunshine, I do not think they are his friends," Mairead said. "They've robbed him of his goods and left him here to see to foolish tasks in order to regain their company. No number of horses are worth that."

"I would imagine Oliver agrees," Sunshine said with another cheerful smile. She began to chafe Mairead's hand, then reached for the other to attend to it as well. "How did you come here?"

"I walked," Mairead said, beginning to wonder if she shouldn't have stayed at home. "Though I'm afraid my journey here is not one you would believe. I'm not sure I believe it myself."

"You might be surprised," Sunshine said, her smile faltering slightly. "Will you tell me how it began?"

Mairead supposed there was no reason not to be honest. "I stepped inside a ring in the grass near our border with Cameron soil." She would have attempted a smile, but she was too chilled to. "No one puts foot inside it, usually."

"But you did, because you're not afraid."

"I'm afraid of several things," Mairead said honestly, "but not that."

Sunshine smiled again, her expression full of understanding and sympathy. "I understand, believe me. I imagine we would have many things in common if we had time to talk about them, but I'm afraid you might be missed if you're away too long. Shall we walk you back to the meadow and start you on your way home?"

"But I came to learn the truth," Mairead protested.

That was perhaps stating it badly. She'd spent her previous sleepless night trying to smother a curiosity that burned within her like a bonfire and refused to spend another night in like manner. She couldn't go home until she had at least had a few answers about things that perplexed her.

"Why don't we find somewhere to sit and we'll satisfy your curiosity at least about a few things," Sunshine said carefully, "though you'll need to keep what we discuss to yourself. That looks like a decently comfortable stump over there we could share."

That was a sapling earlier was what Mairead wanted to say, but she didn't. She also noted that since the woman was obviously with child, surely a seat by the fire would be more comfortable.

"'Tis chilly out," she offered. "Perhaps the inside of the croft would be warmer?"

Sunshine smiled briefly. "Mairead—may I call you by your given name?"

"Of course, my lady."

"Then call me Sunny," Sunshine said, "and we'll be comfortable with each other from now on. I think there are things inside that you might find startling until I've told you my story, so let's stay outside. If you want to go inside after that, I'll go with you."

Mairead supposed that was reasonable enough. She watched Oliver go inside the croft, then return swiftly with a pair of cushions and another chair. He made two comfortable spots from adorned chair and stump, then stepped back and made them both a small bow.

"I'll fetch water."

Mairead perched on the edge of the tree stump only after having had a lively but friendly discussion with the lady Sunshine over who deserved a softer seat, then took the opportunity to look around herself and note differences she hadn't had the courage to before. The most glaring was the forest. What trees she recognized from their positions near the croft were enormous and obviously much, much older.

Oliver came outside moments later, dressed sensibly in shirt and plaid, and bearing a wooden trencher with three wooden cups atop it. He offered her one, handed one to Sunny, then resumed his spot against the wall of the croft. Mairead suspected there was no time like the present to have difficult things over with, so she looked at Oliver's adopted sister.

"I'm ready."

"Can you bear the truth?" Sunshine asked carefully.

"Aye, unless you're a witch or a faery," Mairead said without hesitation. "Then I likely shouldn't believe you."

Sunshine smiled. "I'm neither, though I did live in this house for a while, pretending to be the clan witch to amuse the laird down the way."

"Then you're a MacLeod?" Mairead asked in surprise.

Sunshine shook her head. "I'm not, though my sister is wed to one." She nodded toward Oliver. "Oliver and I share Phillips ancestors, so my sister and I decided to claim him as our wee brother. And now you know how things are here, let me tell you a story about things that happened a couple of years ago."

"Are there faeries and bogles involved?" Mairead asked skeptically.

Sunshine laughed a little. "It might seem like that, but no, this is about a man and a woman who Fate brought together against terrible odds." She looked at Oliver briefly. "This might be more difficult than I thought it would be."

Oliver held up his hands. "Don't look at me for help. There's more romance in it than I can stomach easily."

Mairead wasn't above listening to that sort of tale if pressed, so she nodded and hoped she wouldn't make any untoward noises of disbelief.

"One evening while I was living in this house," Sunshine began, "there came a knock on the door. I opened it to find the laird of the clan Cameron standing there."

"Giles's father Alistair?" Mairead asked in surprise.

Sunshine hesitated, then shook her head carefully. "It wasn't, but I'll tell you who it was in a bit. Let's just say that a Cameron clansman came to fetch me back to Cameron Hall to try to save his brother who had been wounded in battle." She paused, then smiled sadly. "I came too late, unfortunately. Things unraveled from there, as they sometimes do, and he decided to come back here with me to this house."

"He must have loved you greatly," Mairead murmured.

"He did," Sunshine said simply, "and I him. The problem was, when we crossed the threshold there, we ..." She considered, then smiled gravely. "We found ourselves in different places."

"As if you'd walked into different keeps?"

"That's a perfect way to put it."

"Oliver suggested it."

Sunshine smiled at him, then looked at her. "That's exactly what happened. I went one place and he went another. We found each other eventually, we were married, and here we are today where he is laird of the clan Cameron." She paused. "This is where things might become a bit difficult to believe, but I promise it's the absolute truth."

Mairead was tempted to blurt out that she'd earnestly believed for a moment or two that she'd actually stumbled *into* a book and anything else might seem rather tame by comparison, but she imagined that didn't need to be said. She glanced at Oliver to find him leaning against the side of the croft, watching her. He smiled briefly, which she appreciated. She nodded, then turned back to Sunshine.

"I'm listening."

Sunshine smiled briefly. "My husband was laird of the clan Cameron in the year 1375," she said carefully. "That would make him, if the genealogy holds true, the uncle several times removed from the current laird—what did you say his name was?"

"Alistair," Mairead managed. "But, my lady, that is madness. We're in the year of our Lord's Grace 1583." She had to take a restorative breath or two. She thought waving away Oliver's attempting to hand her another cup was very wise. "How is it possible that he would be born in such a year? 'Tis two hundred years ago!"

Sunshine nodded carefully. "From the year 1583 it certainly is. But there are more years than 1583, aren't there?"

Mairead opened her mouth to argue that there certainly were not, but she found herself suddenly considering things she hadn't before. In her book, in the very beginning of it, there had been a series of numbers that she had assumed were perhaps the number of bottles of port the Duke had consumed, or chickens the kitchen maid had slain, or pistol balls either of the pair had sent winging toward a foe.

But what if the numbers 1823 weren't any of those things, but instead a date?

Some 250 years after her time?

She looked at Sunshine. "What is the year in this place?"

Oliver pushed away from the house, though his hands were still in plain sight. She scowled at him.

"I won't filch your blades, ye wee pox-marked fiend."

Sunshine laughed and it was again as if the sun had come out from behind a cloud. "You, Mairead MacLeod, are a properly fierce Highland lass. And the current year in this place is 2009."

Mairead attempted a snort, but it didn't go very well. Those were numbers that made even less sense than the lady Sunshine's delusions about 1375. Men lived and died in their proper sphere and their proper time. Anything else was something only her uncle would have believed.

"I know it's difficult to imagine," Sunshine said quietly.

"Not difficult," Mairead said. "Impossible." She considered, then hit upon a perfect way to prove her point. "Who is king presently?"

"Queen," Sunshine said gently. "We have a queen, and her name is Elizabeth."

"In Scotland?"

Sunshine hesitated. "That's a bit complicated. Scotland doesn't have a ruler any longer."

"Of course we do and his name is James," Mairead said firmly. "They have a queen down in that wasteland in the south and her name is indeed Elizabeth, so forgive me, Lady Sunshine, but that proves nothing."

Sunshine looked at Oliver, but he only held up his hands in surrender. Sunshine smiled briefly at him, then turned that same gentle smile on her. "Ours is the second one," she offered.

Mairead frowned because there was no way of confirming that and it seemed a bit too easy. She looked at Oliver. "Do you believe this?"

He nodded solemnly.

Mairead looked back at Sunshine. "Perhaps we've all been struck upon the head whilst we were sleeping and now are sharing the same fantastical dream." She cast about for something else that made more sense than people leaping over years with the same ease as they might have a pile of horse dung. "My uncle claims there are faeries and sprites in these woods that carry off the occasional unsuspecting MacLeod when it suits them. Perhaps that happened to you and your husband." She paused. "Perhaps it happened to me as well."

"Do you believe in faeries and sprites?" Sunshine asked with a faint smile.

"'Tis utter rubbish," Mairead managed. "As is a man stepping across a threshold and finding himself elsewhere."

"Or stepping in a faery ring in the grass," Sunshine said gently, "and finding himself in a different time entirely. That would be something, wouldn't it?"

Mairead had to concede it would be, but she did so silently. She looked at Oliver who was standing there, leaning against the wall of the croft, his head touching the thatching where it ended above the wall, but he was only watching her, grave and silent. She turned back to Sunshine.

"It seems ill-mannered to ask," she began slowly.

"For proof?" Sunshine smiled. "It isn't, though I don't want you to regret starting down a path that may lead you places you don't care to go."

"My lady Sunny, I'm well down the path already. Another league or two won't change things."

Sunshine laughed a little, but uneasily. "I suppose not. Let's go inside, then, and you can see if that's proof enough. There may be things there that are startling, though."

Mairead was somehow unsurprised to find Oliver stepping forward the moment Sunshine moved to push herself out of her chair. She was surprised, though, to find him offering her the same courtesy. She also decided it might be best not to comment on how Sunshine had hold of one of her hands and Oliver the other as they crossed the threshold into the healer's croft. Whatever the truth might be in its whole, there was obviously something to Sunshine's unease about that doorway.

Sunshine paused with her just inside.

"Door open or closed?" she asked gently.

Mairead wasn't one given to weakness, but she was heartily tempted to simply give up and faint.

"I don't know," she managed.

She found Oliver's hand suddenly under her elbow and his beautiful face closer to hers than was good for her wits.

"Come and sit for a minute first," he said quietly. "I'll make you a fire. You're perfectly safe here with us."

The saints pity her for a fool, she couldn't help but believe that. She walked—or was helped, actually—across the wee croft and put into a chair that was covered in the finest weaving she'd ever felt. It also seemed as though the fleece from surely a dozen of her finest sheep had been stuffed beneath that fabric to fashion a seat that surely even the King had never enjoyed beneath his royal backside.

She watched Oliver quickly bring the fire back to life and move her, chair and all, a bit closer to that warmth. She looked up at him quickly.

"Fire makes me uneasy."

He moved her back to her previous spot without delay and without comment, then squatted down in front of her. He was just so gloriously beautiful, she could hardly stop herself from reaching out her hand to put it against his cheek—something she realized she'd done before she thought better of it. She pulled her hand away, but he caught her hand and held it in both his own.

"You're very cold."

"I'm terrified I'll catch the pox from you," she managed.

Oliver shot her a quick smile, then stood up and made certain Sunshine was seated comfortably before he went to busy himself in a different part of the croft. She supposed by the sound of things that he was rummaging about to make them something to eat.

At least he was properly dressed, which was remarkably soothing. It occurred to her at that moment that Sunshine was wearing long-legged trews and a generously sized shirt, both in a cheerful color of blue she had never managed to achieve in all her years of dying wool and cloth.

Mairead sniffed before she could keep herself from it. Whatever it was Oliver had in his stew pot smelled better than anything her father's cook had ever prepared. She stared at the things loitering there in that part of the croft that seemed as though they belonged in the kitchens. Bowls on shelves, cups, crockery that might hold very useful bits of herbs and dried roots. There were also things, shiny things, that made her uneasy, so she turned away and looked back at the lady Sunshine.

"The croft was empty yesterday when I looked inside it," she said hoarsely.

Sunshine only nodded. "I imagine it was."

"And all these things inside," Mairead managed. "They have all been added in your year?"

"Perhaps a bit of the furniture," Sunshine conceded. "The walls and the hearth have been here for centuries, I would imagine."

"I've never been inside," Mairead admitted, "but it looks the same from the outside. Perhaps something added to the back. And the rock of the walls is more worn."

"Very likely. Oh, Oliver, what did you make?"

"Soup that I didn't make myself, which you know given that you brought it for me," Oliver said dryly.

Mairead accepted a bowl of something that smelled so good, she almost swooned. She had been convinced she wouldn't manage a single spoonful, but she realized only after there was no more that she'd eaten the whole thing.

"More?" Oliver offered.

She shook her head. 'Twas Future food, that soup, and who knew what it might do to her form?

A knock startled her. She watched Oliver go and open the door, then watched as a man ducked a little and came inside.

"My husband, Cameron," Sunshine said happily.

Mairead helped her up, took their bowls to the wee kitchen and set them on what she hoped was the appropriate spot, then returned hesitantly to the hearth. The Cameron, if that's who he truly was, made her a slight bow.

"My lady tells me that you're a MacLeod lass," he said.

He spoke her tongue without any trace of an accent, which she found both comforting and alarming. She was certain she'd returned an equally polite greeting, refrained from remarking on his clothing which was definitely more modest than Oliver's pox-marked trews but not at all like the garb Giles's sire would have worn, and soon found herself outside the croft with her companions. The Cameron seemed to find something slightly amusing about the glares Oliver was sending his way, which she thought rather brave on Oliver's part given who he was glaring at.

Sunshine embraced her own poor self right after she'd given the same sort of farewelling to Oliver.

"I wish we had more time," Sunshine said with a smile. "I think we would be good friends."

Mairead could only nod. Her head was too full of things she'd heard and seen and her heart a bit pained by the thought of having people around her who might want to pass time with her for her to manage any speech.

She watched Cameron take Sunshine's hand and they both turned and walked down a path to points unknown.

Mairead looked at Oliver. "Well."

He lifted his eyebrows briefly. "Indeed."

"This doesn't feel like the Future. I feel the same."

"Time is a strange thing."

"And you?" she asked. "What do you think of this?"

"I thought it was daft," he admitted. "At first."

"And now?"

"Hard to argue with it now." He paused. "What do you think?"

"I'm trying not to."

He smiled and turned to pull the door of the croft closed. She then found herself walking with him through woods that were silent save for the whisper of wind in the trees.

"How many souls do you think have been lost to this place?" she asked.

"James, your ancestor," he said, frowning thoughtfully, "and his brother Patrick. And Sunny's husband, Robert Cameron. How many others?" He shrugged. "No idea."

"My uncle claims that faeries steal the occasional MacLeod that they fancy."

He only looked at her with raised eyebrows. "This might be a better explanation for the losses than wee creatures filching them."

She had to agree, but she did so silently. She studied the forest as they walked and had to admit that it somehow didn't look as if it belonged to her time, though she now suspected that it did indeed belong to his time.

Though she could scarce believe it at all.

It took far less time to reach the meadow than she suspected it might. She looked up and down that stretch of field, but saw no enemies. She didn't hear her sheep or her hounds or men training, either.

"I would prefer to see you back to your hall," Oliver said quietly.

She wanted to say she'd forgotten he was there, but she suspected she would never stand next to him and not be aware of him. "I'll be fine."

He reached for her hand and bent over it, then straightened and looked at her. "You are the bravest woman I know."

"Braver than Sunshine?" she asked.

"Well," he said, stroking his chin with his free hand, "she is fairly brave as well, enduring Robert Cameron as her husband."

Mairead smiled a bit in spite of herself. "I wouldn't let him hear you say as much."

"His swordplay is terrifying," Oliver admitted, "so you might be right there." His smile faded. "Safe home, Mairead."

"Thank you, Oliver."

He didn't release her hand and she couldn't bring herself to pull it away from his. She looked up at him.

"I'll find my way home easily enough."

"I imagine if you don't, no message you leave me telling me as much will last."

"Not over four hundred years of rain, ye daft lad."

He squeezed her hand, then released her and stepped back. He said nothing more and she couldn't find anything in any of the languages she knew—including her very poor Latin—equal to the moment.

"What do you say in your tongue as farewells?" she asked.

"'Ta-rah,'" he said with a faint smile, "if you're a Birmingham lad."

She pointed her finger at him. "You have things to explain."

"If we had time," he agreed. "Or you could just settle for a pleasant, 'cheers, ducks.'"

"That's vile."

He smiled. "Maybe, but that's England's problem, not ours."

Not ours. The only reason she didn't break down and weep was because she never wept. Put her chin up and soldiered on, raged against the injustices of it all, but weeping? Never. She took a step backward, because she had no choice.

"Ta-rah, then," she managed.

He smiled very faintly. "Cheers, me lovely ducks."

She blushed, because he was ridiculous, but so had become her entire life. She turned and walked into the equally absurd circle in the grass, because she could see her sheep in the distance and hear her hound barking his bloody head off. She stepped out of the circle and refused to look over her shoulder.

Well, she looked over it once, but there was nothing there but fall grasses and the view of mountains in the distance that kept them safe from dastardly McKinnons and all manner of other things.

Perhaps not the Future, apparently, but that was something to perhaps think about while she was keeping herself warm in the kitchen, not sleeping through the night.

She hoped what she'd just been through didn't show on her face, because it had certainly ruined her wits given that she was vastly tempted to take her courage in hand and skip across the centuries again very soon, though she had no idea to what end.

Perhaps to have one more glimpse of a man who had called her lovely when she so perfectly didn't deserve the same.

NINE

T HERE CAME A TIME IN every man's holiday when he had to admit that he had strayed a bit too far from the programme and needed to refocus his energies on the mission at hand.

And if that mission was to burn through a bloody self-care manual as quickly as possible so he could return with equal swiftness to his normal life where he had a computer and things to do that had nothing to do with wondering how the hell it was a woman four hundred years older than he was could possibly be so charming as to trouble his thoughts late into the night, so much the better.

Oliver snuggled down into the beautiful simplicity of that, carefully avoiding any encounters with his thumb or perfectly pitched nursery rhymes. That clarity of purpose was also why he had crawled out of bed at an unseemly hour, indulged in another endless shower just short of boiling, and was current-ly walking purposefully down the meadow, forcing himself to ignore the utter improbability of watching a vintage Highland miss step through a gate in the grass whilst fretting over the fact that he hadn't been able to see her properly home. As an afterthought, he wondered if he might be arriving too early at the modern-day incarnation of the MacLeod keep for a quick bite of breakfast and a nose through the castle's library. That he couldn't decide was telling.

He would have blamed the length of his holiday for his lack of decisiveness, but he honestly couldn't remember how many days he'd been in Scotland. Five? Six? A brief eternity? Too long, by any count, but nae worries, as Patricia MacLeod would have announced before informing him, no doubt, that she could clear her schedule at any time if he needed questing help.

Hard to argue with a seven-year-old willing to make those kinds of sacrifices for a decent adventure.

He suspected Mairead MacLeod had been that sort of lass at seven, but that would have been somewhere during the 1560s, so he suspected it might be well to pick up the pace a bit, trot swiftly down to Jamie's hall, and throw himself on the mercy of the writer in residence and beg for something distracting to read before he thought any more about any early Renaissance Highland lassies. With any luck, the book might be so enthralling that he also wouldn't have time for any more trips to that damned faery ring up the meadow, thereby avoiding potentially jumping on it as if it had been some sort of daft, cosmic trampoline until it bounced him into a time period not his own.

He pulled himself back to a walk when he reached the hall, took a few deep, even breaths, then walked up to the front door and hoped there was at least someone inside who was an early riser.

The door opened before he could knock and the laird himself stood there with a pleasant expression on his face.

"Ah, Ollie lad," he said cheerfully. "Come for a bit of exercise this morning?"

"It would be an honor," Oliver said sincerely, "but I've actually come to see if I might borrow something to read. Something fictional," he added, because he'd heard about the things that made up James MacLeod's library and he was on holiday after all. "If your wife might lend me something."

"I imagine she would," Jamie said, opening the door fully and waving Oliver inside. "She's upstairs staring off out the window which I've come to learn means she's working out plot issues, not that she's learned to nap with her eyes open."

"Have you accused her of the latter?"

"Once," Jamie said uneasily. "'Twas a mistake."

Oliver would have laughed, but he had no desire to stand between a writer and her methods, so he thanked Jamie for the offer of something hot in the kitchen later, then soon found himself standing at the open doorway of the lady of the hall's inner sanctum.

Elizabeth smiled and waved him inside. "I won't yell at you and no, you weren't interrupting."

"I've been properly warned," Oliver admitted.

Elizabeth put her finger to her lips. "It's the only way I get a decent nap. I'm assuming you're here for something to read."

"As long as it's short."

"I'll just bet. Let's talk subject first. I think you'd be bored with any of the thrillers I keep here for Jamie when he's taking a break from his more esoteric studies, but I have some time-travel romances you might enjoy."

He tried not to wince. "That's a bit too close to home, don't you think?"

She laughed a little. "I suppose so. Maybe a ghost story instead? Patricia could loan you a blanket for comfort if you get scared."

He shot her a look, but she only smiled. "Do you need an early reader for your next book?" he asked. "What's the set-up?"

"Oh, it's just a little cozy mystery series," she said, shifting uncomfortably. "I'm afraid you'd have the culprit identified by the second paragraph, though you know I'll definitely be asking you later for opinions on possible murder weapons."

"Just not pistols small enough to be conveniently tucked beneath the bench of a phaeton pulled by a set of matched ponies, I beg you."

She laughed. "It sounds like you're pining for a few Regency delights, actually, so I have just the thing for you."

He followed her across what he had to admit was a lovely library. She stopped in front of one of the floor-to-ceiling bookcases there, then pointed to the middle shelf. It was stocked with a collection of very thin books, which was a relief.

"Regency era romances full of duels, debutantes, and debauchery," she said, "but very light on the debauchery. There's always a little mystery involved, but again, that might be boring for you."

"They look short," he noted.

"They *are* short," she said dryly, "but just packed to the brim with period goodness."

Oliver could only imagine. He hunched over to look at what a quick estimate told him might be a hundred books, then almost landed on his arse in surprise. He felt his way down onto a wee step-stool, then looked up at his hostess in shock.

"The author is Constance Buchanan?"

"Have you heard of her?" Elizabeth asked in surprise.

"Just rumor," Oliver managed.

"Well, she should have been the absolute queen of Regency romance in her day, but somehow she just missed that boat."

"What a pity."

Elizabeth shot him a look that made him smile, then patted a handful of her collection. "They're actually very good, so it might be. I have the complete set—well, I *had* the complete set. I'm missing number eight-two."

"What's the title?" he asked, though he suddenly suspected he already knew.

She took out the last book and flipped through the first couple of pages. "There's a list of the whole series here ... and it's number eighty-two, *The Duke and the Kitchen Maid.*"

Of course it was. "Exciting," he said hoarsely.

"Well, it was a nail-biter for me when I was a teenager and had swiped it from my grandmother's bookcase, that's for sure."

"Were these hers, then?"

Elizabeth nodded. "She left them to me because she knew how much I loved them. They had very modest print runs, so it's hard to find copies unless you want to dig through used bookstores or musty trunks in barns." She smiled. "Are you expanding into antique books now?"

"Might be," he conceded. "At least for this one. I wouldn't want to lose any sleep over the fate of the kitchen maid."

"I'm sure that's the case," she said with a smile. She put the book she was holding back in its spot, then pulled out the one next to what he could see was an empty spot. "Take number eighty-three. The hero's a Highland laird, so you might get extra points for it."

"If there's any time traveling involved, I'm not taking it with me."

"Just phaetons and women named Fanny," she promised. "Let me feed you, then you can trot right back to Moraig's and get started. There are ninety-nine—well, ninety-eight more where that came from if you find yourself hooked."

He was fairly certain he would need a distraction during his trip to the nail salon, so he wasn't about to say no too quickly. He accepted a piece of wrapping paper in a manly shade of black, wrapped his treasure up—ostensibly to preserve the vintage quality, not for any other reason, no, not a damn one—and followed the lady of the hall from her library.

He had a quick meal with the family, assured the spawn that he was indeed holding firmly to the schedule with his sights on a jet-black Bugatti when the time came, then excused himself and made his way back to Moraig's.

He found himself, honestly without quite knowing how he'd gotten there, standing on the threshold of her croft and suddenly wondering what he was doing with his life. It was absolutely absurd, but given that such seemed to be a decent description of his entire life at present, he didn't fight the thoughts. He would certainly kick up a bit of protest at the outset, though, just to make himself feel better.

He was staring down the barrel of thirty-two in a couple of months, true, but he had a ridiculous amount of sterling piled up in a trio of Swiss bank accounts thanks to his hard work, he had a job he loved, and he had his health. He wasn't entirely ugly, he dragged himself to the gym when he wasn't simply outrunning—or running after—bad guys, and he could, when pressed, converse on several esoteric topics that should have impressed the usual rabble of birds he met over drinks instead of leaving them blinking at him owlishly before declaring a pressing need to visit the loo after which they invariably hopped up on the windowsill and legged it anywhere he wasn't.

He stood there on that threshold and didn't fight the ridiculous feeling of broodiness that swept over him, though that was only part of it. The other part, the more important part, was a woman to share his life with. The wave that swept over him at *that* thought was substantially larger and more wrenching, particularly since he couldn't seem to get a particular woman out of his thoughts even when she was obviously safely inhabiting her own time period.

Obviously he'd been unplugged for too long.

He let himself inside the cottage without a key just to make himself feel a bit more himself and set Miss Buchanan's finest on a side table for later consumption. Those pressing tasks seen to, he considered the rest of his day and found himself back where he'd started. The checklist had to be attended to as quickly as possible so he could get back to his usual life as quickly as possible before he completely lost any sense of himself.

He exchanged a perfectly acceptable grey tracksuit for Highland gear and a sword, not because he had any intention of being anywhere he wasn't supposed to be or seeing anyone who should have been safely tucked back in her proper time. He just wanted any stray tourists wandering over MacLeod soil and looking for natives to gawk at to feel as though they'd been properly rewarded for the effort of ignoring Jamie's No Trespassing signs.

He was generous like that, he had to admit.

He selected reasonable snacks from the largess in the kitchen along with a bottle of water ... and then he hesitated.

There was no reason not to take a second one, was there? One never knew when one might become extra thirsty, especially when one had made a career out of always having every contingency considered and possessed the reputation of never being surprised. That casual command of every situation required careful planning.

He grabbed a second bottle—and a third to potentially share—then thought it nothing but prudent to select another undemanding snack or two. Those things collected, he decided there was no time like the present to be off and sniffing, followed immediately by sneezing and sketching. He would make serious inroads into his self-care scheme and feel very pleased with himself by the end of the day, he was certain.

He packed everything into a worn canvas satchel he found hanging on a peg by the door, helped himself to an obviously well-loved National Trust woolen blanket to keep his tender backside off any potential patches of nettles, then checked one last time to make certain everything was turned off. Moraig's was reassuringly still in the current day, which he supposed was occasionally not the case, then took a deep breath and stepped over the threshold.

He jumped a little at the sight of a medieval clansman standing there under a tree. His relief at realizing that Patrick was in jeans and trainers was unhappily mitigated by the look his current swordmaster was wearing.

Oliver pulled the door shut behind himself, then patted his satchel. "Off to do constructive things."

Patrick eyed Oliver speculatively. "You had a visitor, I hear."

"Did Lady Sunshine tell you?"

Patrick slid him a look. "I do keep an eye on what goes on in my forest." He paused. "That and aye, Sunny told me."

Oliver wasn't surprised and there was part of him that was perhaps a bit more grateful than he'd expected to be. Whatever Patrick's flaws might have been when it came to his treatment of men in his circle, he was unfailingly kind to the women. Sunny—and Cameron, for that matter—would have been concerned that Mairead be looked after if she wandered astray and Patrick no doubt would have wanted to keep her safe as well.

"You can't let her come again."

Oliver returned Patrick's look steadily. "She's an adult."

"Very well, you *shouldn't* let her come again."

"I know."

Patrick studied him for a moment in silence, then shook his head. "You poor sod."

"Her life in the past is unpleasant."

"It will be substantially more so if someone finds out she's been traipsing through the centuries to fraternize with you."

Oliver dragged his hand through his hair. "I won't be in Scotland more than another week or so."

"And that makes it better?"

Oliver looked at him seriously. "A few days to make memories to last a lifetime isn't better?"

Patrick rolled his eyes. "You should be writing greeting cards."

"Too much time spent lingering in the sitting rooms of grannies with valuable antiques placed strategically behind cards from their progeny has left its mark." He sighed. "You won't tell Jamie, will you?"

"What, that you're dating a woman who's four hundred years older than you are?" He snorted. "What am I, your mother?"

Oliver smiled faintly. "Thank you. And I'm not dating her. We're just friends."

Patrick only shook his head and sighed. "Be careful with her."

Oliver nodded. "I understand."

"I'm not sure you could," Patrick said bluntly, "but I also know it won't be for a lack of trying." He turned away, then stopped.

Oliver suddenly didn't care for the feeling in the air. He watched as Patrick turned back to look at him.

"Jamie has been poking into the late 16th century for a pair of years, you know."

"I hesitate to ask why."

"Because crowds get swept up into things they wouldn't if cooler heads prevailed."

"Even here in the Highlands?"

"Aye, even here. I wonder what he's found in the past that troubles him."

"Something foul, no doubt."

"That foul thing might be you."

Oliver closed his eyes briefly, then nodded. "If I see her again, I'll convince her to stay where she belongs."

Patrick only waited.

"And I won't go myself," Oliver said, blowing out his breath.

"You likely shouldn't."

He nodded, then watched his current swordmaster go, no doubt making his way without thinking to his own castle where his lovely wife and children waited for him.

Lucky bastard.

Oliver shook his head at himself, then turned and made his way toward the meadow, enjoying the silence of the forest and—heaven help him—the lack of technology. The horrors of being unplugged hadn't abated, of course, but he was equally horrified to find he was beginning not to care.

After all, men had gone centuries with nothing more than the same sort of skills he'd honed over a dozen years of boarding school, namely eavesdropping, being keenly aware of one's surroundings, and extricating oneself from impossible situations with just one's wits and a few tools in pockets and down boots, hadn't they? He wasn't sure Renaissance Scotland's food could possibly be any worse than what he'd eaten at St. Margaret's, so there was also that to consider.

Which didn't mean he was going anywhere, of course, but it was an interesting intellectual exercise. In fact, he might just make a new section of his self-care notebook completely devoted to the beauties of *Being Unplugged*. Surely there would be at least a pair of lads who would understand when he bound them with one set of cords and did electrical experiments with the other. He had to acknowledge that that was more on the plugged-in side of things, but perhaps there was no need to quibble over details.

He supposed the details he should fuss over—if he were contemplating a trip to a time not his own—included what to leave behind: his watch, any sachets of indigestible condiments he might or might not generally keep in the glove compartment of his car, and his fairly comfortable Cameron plaid boxers.

He took a deep breath and carried on, forcing himself to empty his mind. If that didn't count for meditation, he didn't know what would.

He walked until he came to the invisible border that lay between MacLeod and Cameron lands, then turned to face the more-than-visible doorway that had simply opened up between the centuries.

On the other side of that threshold stood none other than Mairead MacLeod, who he was beginning to suspect had a level of curiosity that rivaled his own.

There was a little voice in the back of his head that told him he was about to make a colossal error in judgment, but he ignored it. He was being polite, nothing more.

He made her a bow. "Good morning, my lady."

She smiled. "And to you, good sir."

He clasped his hands behind his back and found, to his utter lack of surprise, that small talk eluded him. Unfortunately, his companion seemed to be just as bad at it.

"How is the weather there?" he asked, finally.

She looked at him, then laughed.

Oh, that was bad on so many levels. He needed to keep his wits about him, concentrate on getting himself free of Scotland, and convince that woman there that she should remain in her proper time. But if her smile was like sunlight after weeks of rain, her laugh was closer to having an angel standing above his head, pouring that same sunlight onto only him.

"Damp and cold," she said politely. "And on your side of the doorway?"

"Warm and sunny."

"Are you certain you're in the Highlands?"

"At the moment, my lady, I'm not quite certain of anything."

Her smile faded a bit. "I wanted to see if I'd lost my wits entirely."

He shook his head. "Still there, I'd say."

She hesitated, then nodded. "I should likely turn for home, then."

He could think of a dozen reasons why that made the most sense of anything he'd heard in days, but he couldn't bring himself to voice a single damned one of them, so he settled for an innocuous platitude.

"Probably so," he agreed.

"I shouldn't come through the gate again."

He nodded slowly. "Probably not."

"It would be ... imprudent."

He nodded again. "A bit."

She said nothing else, she simply stood there and looked at him, silent and grave.

He considered all the reasons why he should give her a friendly wave, tell her to behave herself, then turn and bolt for Moraig's. He reminded himself of Jamie's single lifting of a single eyebrow on his way out the door that morning that warned him he was playing with fire. He even groped mentally for the modicum of good sense that would surely bellow at him that if he were going to date, he should likely find someone who was born in at least an adjacent century, not four hundred years in the past. He marshalled all that good sense and prepared himself to do the right, if not the difficult, thing.

And found himself holding out his hand toward her.

She closed her eyes briefly, then looked at him and put her hand in his.

He pulled her into the future and heard the gate close behind her with a soft click. She looked over her shoulder in alarm, then back at him.

"Will it open again?" she asked breathlessly.

Hopefully not was almost out of his mouth before he stopped it. He managed a smile instead.

"If not, there are others."

And that, unfortunately, was where his glib tongue left him stranded. He looked at his 16th-century miss and wondered just what it was a modern man did to entertain a woman who most definitely shouldn't have been lingering in a time not her own. Then again, he should likely have been cursing himself for inviting her out on something that couldn't possibly be considered yet another in a long series of first dates.

But if it were going to be a single first date, he would do his best to make it memorable.

He offered her his arm. "Let's find somewhere comfortable to sit."

She looked at his arm, then at him, then hesitantly tucked her fingers just under his elbow. He wasn't entirely certain what passed for inappropriate fraternizing with the opposite sex in 16th-century Scotland, so he simply nodded toward the rock where he usually sat and hoped for the best.

He set his gear down and unsnapped the little tab holding the blanket together in its folded state. He watched Mairead take one end of it and study it as if she'd never seen anything so fine. She looked at him in astonishment.

"Did the angels fashion this?"

He smiled briefly. "I imagine just some industrious weaver here in Scotland. Let's stretch it out and see if they did the sheep proud."

She gaped at him when he started to put the blanket on the ground. "Are ye daft, ye wee fiend?" she asked in astonishment. "Next you'll tell me you plan to sit on it!"

He suspected that if he spent any time with her at all, he would never look at anything the same way again. He smiled because he couldn't help himself.

"That's the purpose of it," he said. "I imagine there are other blankets inside Moraig's that are softer for wrapping around yourself, though your shawl is more lovely than anything we would find there."

She shut her mouth, then slid him a look. "I've never heard you say so many words in one go."

He smiled. "The day is lovely, you are lovely, and you're going to help me take care of a few of these tasks my former friends left me to do. Help me spread this out and we'll have something to eat."

She did so, then simply stood there, watching him with her arms wrapped around herself. He froze, then searched quickly back through his recent babblings to see where he might have drifted off into eejit territory, but couldn't lay his finger on anything overly offensive.

"Did I say something?" he asked, deciding quickly that beginning to scratch his head so early in the day would set a bad precedent.

"What did you call me?"

He put his brain in reverse and quickly backed up to examine the road, then he realized exactly what he'd said.

Which he'd meant.

He pulled the satchel over his head and set it down, then gestured to a spot on the blanket that he thought looked comfortable enough.

"I called you lovely, which you are, and if you make me say anything else I'll end up flustered and saying stupid things. Are you hungry?"

She sat down with a bit of a thump, looked at him, then nodded.

He imagined she was and he was obviously missing some sort of nutritional infusion to his own brain, but what else could he say? Outside of very fast cars and shiny things worth buckets of sterling, he didn't like things that were so perfect as to seem fake. He had dated—one time each, of course—more than enough women who were so beautiful that they were hard to look at. Nothing against perfection, of course, but perhaps it was time to set his sights on a woman who was lovely and artless and had a smile that lit the room and a laugh that broke through the clouds like a lovely ray of sunlight.

He was painfully aware that his wishes in that area didn't matter a single damned bit, especially when a woman he thought he might like to ask out on a second date was utterly beyond his reach even if she'd been amenable to a second date.

But at the moment, he couldn't bring himself to care. He'd spent a lifetime doing what everyone expected, surviving, trying to live a half-decent life while not standing out and attracting the attention of those who were, as the saying went, gunning for him.

He had the feeling Mairead might understand that very well.

Maybe it wouldn't destroy the fabric of time or send the world spinning in the wrong direction if he simply took an hour or two and did exactly what he wanted to do for a change.

He took off his sword, drew it, then laid it down on the edge of the blanket before he executed a bit of modest sitting that even Her Maj might have nodded in approval over. He fished out a bottle of water, took the cap off, then handed it to her.

"Drink. And it's not poisoned."

She pursed her lips. "I didn't truly think you would poison me."

"You thought I had a tail and horns."

"Your future garb did nothing to allay my suspicions, though you were very handsome in it." She shot him a look. "For a demon."

He smiled and unpacked lunch.

One morning. One picnic that had been casually shoved in a bag instead of packed properly in a hamper. One woman and one man who had beyond all reason and in a truly cosmic piece of serendipity encountered each other in a way he suspected neither of them would have dreamed of.

One morning.

What could it hurt?

TEN

MAIREAD LOOKED AT THE WATER she held in her hand that wasn't contained in a cup but more of a tube that made a horrible noise if she clutched it too tightly. Not only that, the jug was as clear as water slipping slowly over a rock, clear enough that she could see the innards without effort, which left her wondering if she should have examined the innards of her head and done the sensible thing and remained safely tucked into her spot near the hearth in the kitchens.

She looked at Oliver to find him watching her as if he knew exactly what she was thinking. She cleared her throat, but that didn't accomplish anything at all.

"Future marvels?" she croaked.

He nodded carefully.

"'Tis foolish to be afraid."

"I was very afraid of all those swords your clan was carrying."

She could see his sword lying there on the other side of him, unsheathed, and looking fairly perilous, and suspected he wasn't afraid of much. "You weren't truly, were you?"

He studied the sky for a moment or two as if he considered the question seriously, then looked at her and smiled. "I have great faith in my ability to outrun people who might want me dead."

"Have many people wanted you dead?" she asked in surprise.

"I was sent away to foster when I was very young and one learns, doesn't one, to out-think those who are older and larger."

And out-run was what she would have said if she'd wanted to discuss it, which she most certainly didn't. She crinkled her water, shivered, then nodded toward what she supposed could be considered foodstuffs. "What have you there in that pile of Future torments?"

"Oatcakes, apples, other things you likely shouldn't be eating, but all safe."

"The Duke of Birmingham had a taster, you know."

"I'll be yours," he offered cheerfully. "Let's see what we have."

She watched him sort through what he'd brought, accepted whatever he deemed fit for her to consume, then looked at the final pile of what she hesitated to touch. He seemed to find nothing unusual about those flattened mounds of brown ...

"You realize those are clumps of offal, don't you?"

He paused with one halfway to his mouth and looked at her with wide eyes. "What?"

She repeated it in French, just to make certain he'd understood her. He smiled then and shook his head.

"Chocolate and orange jelly on top of a little cake." He helped himself to an entire one, chewed, then smiled. "Very tasty."

She waved him on to his delights and settled for more water, though she couldn't help but study him a bit. Now that she understood where—ah, *when*—he was from, she supposed she might be allowed a few questions about why he found himself there.

"Did your friends truly abandon you here?" she asked. "And are you one of those dastardly Englishmen from beyond the lowlands?"

He brushed his hands off, then leaned back on those hands and crossed his feet over the ankle, looking perfectly at ease. She didn't miss how he'd glanced around himself as he'd done so, as if he'd simply been arranging himself more comfortably. She understood, because she did the same thing. Easier to see trouble coming that way.

"I'll watch behind you," she said casually.

"And I'll watch everywhere else."

She smiled in spite of herself. "Who are you, in truth?"

He started to speak, then hesitated. He did that more than once, which left her torn between wondering if his identity was more terrible than he wanted to admit or he feared she would find it too difficult to understand.

"I'm afraid," he began slowly, "that my Gaelic won't possibly be equal to the silliness of my current life. We might need to resort to more French than usual."

She nodded. "Given that your friends left you here with nothing more than a sword and pox-spotted trews, I think you have that aright."

He smiled and she found herself feeling ridiculously pleased that she'd drawn it from him.

She put her hand to her forehead but found no fever there. She also found a conspicuous lack of good sense, but what was she to do? She was in the Future, sitting on a piece of weaving she would have slain anyone in her family for putting on the ground, and she'd watched a man happily ravage a pile of tiny flattened droppings without so much as a wince of disgust.

"Mairead?"

She looked at him. "I think too many thoughts."

"I have the same problem. How do we save ourselves?"

She found a new piece of ridiculousness in the unaccustomed pleasure of being included in another's happy troubles. A braw, charming man's happy troubles.

"How did you come to be in the Highlands, then?" she asked, desperate to speak of something besides what was rattling around in her empty head. "In truth?"

"My friends in London captured me and brought me here against my will, leaving me with my book being the key to freedom."

She looked at the book sitting between them, the one with the black cover and the golden letters tooled on the front, and wondered at the wealth of his friends. She glanced at him.

"Why, do you think?"

"To save me from too many thoughts, no doubt."

She almost smiled at that. "And they thought a list of tasks to accomplish would aid you with that?"

"I think they thought it would distract me from thoughts of slaying them," he said with a snort. He picked the book up and handed it to her. "Have a look, but be prepared for ridiculous things."

She glanced at him to find he was watching her with an expression on his face she couldn't quite identify, but she was no coward, so she opened his book and braced herself for something very silly indeed.

What she hadn't expected was how fine such a small collection of folios would be. The sheaves of parchment were perfectly smooth and some were of a heavier stuff she'd never imagined could exist. She continued to turn pages until she came to the end, then she looked at him.

"I'm afraid I don't recognize these words."

"I wish I didn't," he said with a smile, "and I'm not sure they'll translate very well. Let's choose something to do, though, and leave the rest." He reached over and turned back pages until he stopped at a sheaf that was unadorned. He looked at it, sighed a little, then looked at her. "I am to sniff a variety of flowers, then draw them there."

"'Tis autumn, you realize."

He winced. "I know. What do you suggest?"

"A walk." She started to crawl to her feet, but found that he'd jumped to his and was holding down his hand for her. She looked up at him in surprise, but he seemed to find nothing unusual about offering aid. She let him help her up, then made a production of fussing with her shawl as he strapped his sword to his back.

Truly, she was a woman out of her depth.

Oliver seemed to think nothing of it, though, and merely walked with her along the edge of the forest. She realized after a bit that he was spending more time watching their surroundings than he was attending to his task, but perhaps he knew of dangers she did not.

"You're supposed to be looking for things to sniff."

"I don't know where to start." He smiled. "You wouldn't choose a few things for me whilst I keep watch over us, would you?"

If it would keep her from feeling so pleased at being included in his madness, she would have picked up things from the forest floor for the whole of the day.

By the time she'd filled part of her shawl with the best the season could offer—heather, leavings from trees at the edge of the forest, and a handful of rocks and sticks Oliver was certain would be sufficient for the task set him—she found herself sitting again atop that very fine blanket with their treasures in a tidy pile between them. Oliver broke open his book, took out two sheaves of parchment, then handed her one. He closed the book and set it aside, then opened a strange little box made of what she suspected was very fine silver indeed. Inside were wee sticks of wood, all the same size, with colors leaking out from one end in shades she'd never seen before.

"A species of charcoal," he said casually.

She would have reached out to touch one, but her hands were already shaking too badly.

"Mairead."

She looked at him. "Aye?"

"I'll keep you safe," he reminded her. "And I suspect you'll be very good at this, so you'll likely keep my friends safe from my wrath. These are called pencils."

"But the colors," she managed.

"I'm guessing that it's nothing more than charcoal that's been dyed, but it could also be wax. I have no idea, really. What color do you like best?"

"Purple," she said without hesitation. She looked at him then. "'Tis the color of heather, you know."

"I know," he said with a smile. He selected one of the marvels in that silver box fit for holy relics, then held it out. "Why don't you try it? We'll see who draws a better rendering of our heather here."

She hardly dared put anything on that parchment that was so precious, but Oliver seemed to think nothing of it. She considered, then decided perhaps she could at least offer him that much aid in satisfying his mates.

She drew little clusters of heather, then frowned as she realized if she were going to do it properly, she would need other colors.

Oliver held out his precious box. "Take what you need."

She chose brown and green, then imagined there wasn't any point in not putting a bit of mountain behind her plants as well as a hint of sky. She realized only as she'd filled the page with heather and a bit of forest and the sky visible in front of her that Oliver wasn't as busy. She looked at him to find him watching her with an expression of astonishment on his very braw visage.

"I'm turning over this task to you," he said promptly. "Don't tell the lads."

She would have attempted a snort, but couldn't dredge up enough enthusiasm for it. She also realized that Oliver had been busily cutting away the wood from the colored charcoal, which she suspected had been for her benefit only. She considered, then held out her sheaf.

"I can draw other things on yours, if you like."

He took her page, then handed her his. "Please."

She considered, then drew things from memory, finding that having so many colors to use was an unexpected pleasure.

"How do you know so much about plants?"

"How else would I know what to use for dyeing yarn and cloth?"

"Fair enough," he agreed. He waited until she'd finished, then handed her another sheaf. "Could you draw some things in black, then let me color them in?"

"Will that satisfy them?"

"If not, I have a sword."

She smiled in spite of herself, then drew for him several flowers she thought he might manage. She handed him the sheaf, then watched him as he drew colors inside her renderings. He looked a great deal like a monk, bent over his page with a frown marring his perfect brow. That seemed a better choice than a demon, to be sure.

And surely no creature from Hell could possibly have had such a beautiful visage. He was braw, true, but she realized sitting perhaps a bit closer to him than her father might have found acceptable, that he had a mark or two—perhaps a case of the pox in childhood—and a scar through one of his eyebrows. His eyes, however, were a beautiful shade of pale blue, full of a quiet merriment that increased slightly when he smiled.

"You're supposed to be drawing flowers," he said, not looking up.

"I drew flowers," she said, feeling her cheeks grow uncomfortably hot. "And more for you."

"Well, if you draw me now and give me a tail and horns, I'll howl."

She smiled. "Will you?"

"It depends on how ugly you make me."

"You're braw enough," she said, which was yet another unholy bit of understatement. She cast about for something else to discuss, but found herself coming back to simply sitting with a man who left her feeling an unaccustomed sense of being safe. "Will your friends find this enough?"

"Again," he said, glancing at her, "sword."

"Don't they have them, as well?"

He considered. "A few do, actually. And to be fair, I can't deny their motives in sending me here were not entirely unkind."

"Did they think a few fortnights in Scotland would balance your humors?"

He smiled. "Exactly that."

She snorted before she could stop herself, which earned her another brief laugh—

That was cut short and she was pulled up and behind him so quickly that she almost lost her breath. He released her wrist that he had hold of, then shifted to look at her.

"Sorry," he said, taking her by the arm instead and pulling her forward to stand next to him. He gestured toward the man standing there where there had been no man before.

Or perhaps she had simply not been paying attention to her surroundings, which was far more likely.

The man was obviously a Highlander, dressed properly and wearing an enormous sword on his back. He looked enough like her kin that she would have wagered he was a MacLeod, but perhaps not.

"Patrick," the man said, making her a bow. "Younger brother of the laird James."

She felt her ears perk up at that name and spared a wish that she might have the chance to meet the man who had inspired so many legends in her clan. She also rapidly considered her possible connection to the man in front of her.

"And that would make you my uncle?" she asked.

Patrick smiled and it reminded her of her father when he'd been whole and sound, a father who had been full of fine humors and affection for her.

"The very same," he agreed. "I didn't mean to startle you." He glanced at Oliver. "Did you know I was here?"

Oliver let out his breath carefully. "My apologies, my lord, but I did not."

"I was distracting him with mindless chatter," Mairead volunteered.

"I suspect that isn't all he was distracted by," Patrick said pleasantly, "which I'll repay him for later. For now, I will remain here with you and be not only guardsman but chaperon."

"Oh," she managed, "there's nothing to guard. You see, I have three younger sisters who are so beautiful that no one ever looks at me. I'm always perfectly safe."

She realized she was again babbling, but the thought of needing a chaperon was so ridiculous that she could scarce entertain it. She watched Patrick look at Oliver.

"Are they?" he asked mildly. "Her sisters, I mean."

Oliver shrugged. "Didn't notice."

"Interesting," Patrick said, nodding. "Mind if I join you?"

Mairead found Oliver was looking at her, but she suspected they wouldn't have any say in the matter given who the man was, though she wasn't opposed to another sword within reach. She smiled and nodded. "That would be lovely."

Patrick made himself at home on a corner of their blanket, then looked with interest at their renderings. He glanced at Oliver.

"Putting her to work earning your freedom?"

"She's a far superior artist," Oliver said easily.

Mairead watched him gather up their sheaves and hand them over for inspection. Patrick sifted through them, making approving noises, then handed them back to Oliver. He considered, then looked at her.

"Has he been a gentleman?"

"From the very beginning, uncle."

Patrick smiled, then looked at Oliver. "Then I suppose you'll live another day. Have you fed her suitable things? And how was it you two met? I missed that answer."

"You missed it," Oliver said pointedly, "because you didn't ask, not that I would have answered for fear I would frighten her by admitting that you had been chasing me all through the forest, threatening to slay me, and I'd run directly through that faery ring in the grass and into her time."

Mairead realized her mouth was hanging open, but she shut it when Patrick winked at her.

"I had nothing better to do that morning," he said with a shrug. "Hunting a wee fool like this one here seemed like a decent bit of sport."

"My nephews do that to each other," she managed. "Though I don't think they intend to slay each other." She paused. "Not all the time."

Patrick laughed, Oliver shook his head, and she wondered how it was she would ever go back to a life where the souls around her were so full of bile that they rarely smiled. Ambrose did, of course, because he was a sunny lad in spite of his sober nature. Her niece and other nephews smiled as well, true, but they were young and still full of life and curiosity. Her father, in his time before her mother had died and he'd been wounded, had been a cheerful man in spite of the burden of leading the clan.

Perhaps they needed to find another minstrel who played in tune with a bit more success. It might make evenings less torturous, at least.

And that, she realized an hour later, was the last gloomy thought she'd entertained. It came as a surprise to realize she'd passed a morning in pleasure. Patrick MacLeod was a delightful man with a dry sense of jest that left her laughing more than she had in years. He seemed to take an especial delight in poking at Oliver which earned him half-hearted glares and dire threats muttered under the breath. And if most of the conversation revolved around the worst things both she and her uncle had eaten—to Oliver's satisfyingly displayed horror—well, simple pleasures were a man's daily delight as her father always said.

What she did know was that for the first time in years, she felt safe.

And happy.

Patrick rubbed his hands together suddenly. "Best get her back home, lad," he said. "Before she's missed."

Mairead couldn't argue with that, though she wished she could have given that home was not where she wanted to go. She wasn't one to shy away from difficult things, though, so she helped Oliver pack up his gear, shook her head at him one last time over the blanket he made a valiant effort to brush off, then shook hands with her uncle before he made her a slight bow and walked off toward the forest.

She walked with Oliver up the meadow to the doorway, though she couldn't find anything to say and he seemed to have the same problem. He stopped a pace or two away from the faery ring, then looked at her, silent and grave.

"Thank you for coming," he said finally.

She nodded. She knew she had to go and she knew with equal certainty that she shouldn't come back. The thought of that was terrible, perhaps because it was so unexpected. Who would have thought that a book would have gotten her into so much trouble?

"Ta-rah, Oliver," she said with as much of a smile as she could muster.

"Safe home, Mairead," he said quietly.

She had one last look at him, beautiful not-a-duke lad that he was, then turned and walked through the gate.

She heard it close behind her, so she didn't bother to turn around to see if Oliver had been closed on the other side.

Well, she only took five steps before she glanced over her shoulder, but she thought that showed a remarkable amount of restraint. She found nothing there but meadow and a storm brewing, but that was nothing out of the ordinary.

A half hour's slow walk home, however, left her facing things that were definitely not ordinary. She had no idea where the disturbance had started, but her clan was in a complete uproar. 'Twas a blessing she was accustomed to slipping along the edge of things to keep out of the sights of those with too little to occupy their time, for she gained the kitchens without trouble and put herself in a useful spot for remaining unmarked. If that allowed her to watch the doorway, so much the better.

She was somewhat surprised to find Cook standing next to her a few moments later, his brow creased as if either his stew had turned out poorly or he hadn't slept well the night before.

"Trouble afoot," he said in a low voice.

"What sort?" she murmured.

"Officious looking man from down south," he said with a frown. He glanced at her then. "Hunting witches, he is."

She felt something very unpleasant slide down her spine. "Why here?"

"Prides himself on being thorough."

No doubt. She shared a silent moment of disgust with him, then decided there was no reason not to see for herself what sort of madness was being combined. At least there was space enough at the back of the hall where she could have her look without being marked.

Cook hadn't erred with his judgment of the chaos that seemed to be multiplying with every voice adding itself to what could scarce be called a conversation. She found Ambrose and his wee siblings and sent them off to the kitchen with a look that her nephew received with a nod. They would be safe enough.

For the rest of the clan, she wasn't as confident. Her father was sitting in his usual place, staring at things only he could see. Her uncle Lachlan stood behind him with his hand on his elder brother's shoulder. She spared a brief wish for Patrick MacLeod to have been standing there as well, then turned to the rest of the madness on display.

And from that moment, things happened too quickly for her to stop them. She wanted to have a few moments to study the newcomer dressed in black clerical robes with a pair of men flanking him dressed also very importantly, but she was distracted by the fuss her cousins were causing her brother.

Tasgall had never been very good at facing more than one disaster at a time which she had always supposed might make leading the clan a difficult task for him. Her uncle generally stood at his elbow and attempted to keep the confusion to a minimum, but at the moment he was too busy attending to the clergymen. She stepped forward to see if at least an offer of something to drink might calm the tempers flaring there, then thoroughly regretted it when her brother spun around and pointed his finger at her.

"Where have you been?" he snarled.

"Off looking for herbs—"

"You should have been here!" he shouted, striding across the hall and shoving cousins out of the way as he did so. "Deirdre is ill and you should have taken her place!"

"Is she ill," Mairead shot back, "or hid—"

She realized he was going to hit her as she saw the back of his hand coming toward her face. She closed her eyes because there was no time to move and she simply couldn't watch any more fury coming her way.

She heard the blow, but felt nothing.

She opened her eyes, though perhaps that hadn't been necessary. She found herself with her face pressed against the scabbard of a sword strapped to a man's back. His hand was also keeping her pressed against that back, a hand she had no trouble recognizing.

Tasgall spluttered. "Why are you here again?"

"My lord Tasgall," Oliver said politely, inclining his head. "I heard tell of trouble in the area and thought I would offer you my sword."

"Well," Tasgall said, sounding very surprised. "I'm pleased you found it, but why would I need it when ... well, these men are honorable officials from Edinburgh. Surely you know them."

Oliver made a dismissive noise. "We travel in far different circles, my lord, but I'll be polite to them for your sake, of course."

Mairead would have thanked him, but she found her hand taken by Ambrose.

"Auntie, come away," he said quickly. "The kitchen is warm."

She nodded and let him pull her out of the great hall. She wasn't one given to weakness, but she suspected that if she'd been that sort of lass, she might have sought out somewhere to sit. As it was, she didn't argue when Ambrose found her a stool, tucked her into a corner by the cooking fire, and found a pair of lads to do things that required them to stand in front of her.

And if a different lad came to lean against the wall next to her after supper had been served and the hall put to bed for the night, all she could do was look at up at him.

"Why are you here?" she whispered.

He squatted down next to her. "I thought I should be."

She closed her eyes briefly. "Thank you."

"I told your brother I would stay for a pair of days until my friends arrive as I'm certain they'll come for me. They've likely been held up by their business with the king."

"Queen," she murmured.

"I was speaking of James."

"And I was speaking of Elizabeth," she said. She shot him a look and held up two fingers.

He shot her a warning look, but then he smiled. "I'll go sit with your father for a moment and see how things are progressing in the hall," he said quietly, rising and looking down at her. "You'll be safe enough here?"

She nodded.

He put his hand briefly on top of her head, then walked away.

She had no idea why he'd truly come, but she very grateful he had. For all she knew, he brought tidings from the Future about the past that would change things for the better.

She sincerely hoped so.

ELEVEN

O LIVER DRAGGED HIS SLEEVE ACROSS his forehead, but that didn't do anything to change his view of a vintage Highlander standing across from him holding onto, as usual, a perilously sharp Claymore, no doubt contemplating all the perilously life-ending things he might do with it.

He wanted extra credit for his current activity in the form of not only the Bugatti he was definitely going to have earned, but a decently sized house on the ocean. Perhaps one perched on some Italian bit of coastline in the south where the food would be delicious, the vistas gorgeous, and the art and culture sublime.

He was fairly certain they had antiques there along with their gelato and superb wine. Perhaps he could be prevailed upon to take up the reins of the work title he'd been awarded the day before he'd been sent off to his Holiday in Hades and exercise it in a southern clime.

I'm making you Vice President of Snoopery and Skulduggery, Derrick Cameron had said to him without so much as a hint of a smirk. *Take this ridiculous raise and go book a holiday.*

He'd thanked Derrick for the tuppence, ignored the man's banging on about the beauties of time away in nature, and escaped to go hide in Cameron's enormous office and have a nap on a rarely used sofa in the corner.

Ah, how cavalierly he'd later bid everyone a fond *adieu* before heading back to his flat to call it an early night, not having a damned clue about the perils that lay in store for him.

And that had been just the contents of that bloody self-care manual. He was positive not even Derrick and the rest of those heartless sods could possibly have foreseen his lingering in 16th-century Scotland, shielding a Renaissance miss from her brother and a cousin or two who needed to have a few good manners beaten into them, and spending his morning sparring with none other than the future laird of the clan Cameron. The 16th-century clan Cameron.

He could hardly wait to drop that little nugget onto Robert Cameron's lap when next they overindulged in scones with clotted cream to counter a late-afternoon energy slump.

At least Giles seemed to think he deserved to breathe a bit longer. That future Cameron laird rested his sword against his shoulder and nodded at Oliver's sword which was, he would have pointed out to anyone who would listen, still in his hand and not lying six meters away from him.

"Nice steel," Giles said. "A gift from your father?"

Oliver couldn't even start down that road. If his father had seen him with a Claymore in his hand, he would have immediately gotten a case of the vapors and likely begun frantically quoting Oscar Wilde in an effort to restore balance to his witty, marginally titled world.

"Ah, nay," Oliver said, scrambling for something close to the truth. "My adopted sister's husband had it made for me."

Which was true. Cameron had a blacksmith thanks to Zachary Smith's having encountered that generationally maintained smithy in various ages and thereafter singing the praises of the modern smith. Oliver had the sword—still, it needed to be said—in his hands thanks to that man having

160

made it for him and Cameron having left it propped up against the wall behind a Christmas tree at Cameron Hall a pair of years before. It wasn't the first time Lord Robert had insisted they all come to Scotland and have a proper lad's week away over the holiday, but that year had been different. Sunny had been there, for one thing, and there had been the added layers of suspicions confirmed and fealty pledged and Madame Gies outdoing herself with her menus. He hadn't uttered so much as a peep in protest when she'd gang-pressed him into helping her with her baking.

He shook away the memory before it brought back others which might leave him overly maudlin, then looked at Giles.

"In Edinburgh," he said.

"A fine city," Giles said casually. "I've been a time or two."

"A good place to be familiar with when you're head of your clan," Oliver noted.

Giles smiled briefly. "I'd rather be home, if you want the truth."

That was *definitely* a tidbit to file away for future sharing. Oliver nodded with a smile.

"Scotland is a beautiful place."

"Have you traveled much?"

"A bit," Oliver admitted. "Not as many places as I would have liked." And that was perfectly true. He'd followed along as one of Cameron's ducklings for a handful of years and the man hadn't been shy about hopping off their damp, foggy isle to tramp about the Continent whenever it suited him. But he personally hadn't quite found the right traveling partner for venturing further afield.

He wondered what a woman who had been willing to travel four hundred years into the future might think of a few very long plane rides to places where they couldn't speak the language and wouldn't easily fit into a crowd.

161

And since that was something he absolutely shouldn't have been wondering, he dragged his attention back to the matter at hand which was distracting Giles Cameron long enough to catch his own breath.

"I'm unfamiliar with clan politics currently," he said with absolute honesty. "I thought the Camerons and MacLeods weren't necessarily friendly."

"It depends on the year and how our larders look," Giles said with a shrug, "though we don't lift nearly as much cattle as my grandsire did in his day. I am ingratiating myself with the future laird here for a particular reason."

Oliver nodded, then choked. "Wait," he said, holding up his hand. "You want to marry one of his sisters?"

"Grizel," Giles said with a nod.

And so the future laird of the clan Cameron would live to moon another day. Oliver immediately committed to adding whatever romantic aid he could to the current undertaking. "Does Grizel know this?"

"That's the thing, isn't it?" Giles said slowly. "I can scarce speak to her until Mairead is wed and the chances of that happening are very small indeed. Unless ..."

Oliver would have made some noise of dismissal or disbelief or distress that someone would think him muddled enough in the head to look for a bride when he was scarce out of short trousers, never mind searching for one in a time so far out of his that he might wind up with no trousers at all, but he found that all he could do was look at his sparring partner and hope his heart hadn't been laid too bare.

Because he liked Mairead MacLeod. Very much.

"It looks like Mair is off to round up her sheep," Giles said. "I'll go help." He lifted an eyebrow. "Coming, or would you rather that I go venture where you obviously dare not?"

"I'm coming," Oliver said promptly, resheathing his sword and viciously suppressing the urge to take his elbow and nestle it oh-so-lovingly between a pair of Giles Cameron's ribs.

He was also tempted to strongly suggest to Giles that he continue to fix his affections on Mairead's younger sister whilst leaving Mairead comfortably in the friend zone, but perhaps that sage advice could be offered later.

He hung back as Giles saved himself a skewering by treating Mairead in a completely brotherly sort of way, then decided it might be useful to keep his eyes open for stray relatives who were truly itching for a proper belting. He found none of the latter, which boded well for a decent day, but did manage to find some species of purple flower that wasn't heather. He considered, then plucked and held it behind his back for use at the appropriate moment.

That moment arrived more quickly than he'd been planning on which left him a bit flat-footed, but he was accustomed to exuding an air of unsurprise. He inclined his head toward Mairead who had been standing in front of him for heaven only knew how long, then held out his bounty.

She looked at him blankly. "What's this?"

"A flower."

She frowned. "Do you want me to sniff it?"

"If you like."

She took it, sniffed it, then held it back out. "It smells good."

He took a deep breath.

"Are you preparing to sniff it as well?"

He was, he had to admit, enormously glad there wasn't a gaggle of his own family and family by association and other lads who would meet their ends immediately after he'd captured them for no doubt indulging in guffaws at his expense.

He would settle for wiping that look of amusement off Giles Cameron's face later. He looked at Mairead and shook his head.

"I wasn't."

She looked slightly alarmed. "Am I to draw it then?"

"If you like."

She looked as if what she might like was to draw her knife and use it on him. Patrick MacLeod would have approved, no doubt.

"Why do you keep saying that?"

Damn it, he was just so terrible at dating. He couldn't make decent conversation when it revolved around something as quotidian as the local chippy possibly using too much vinegar. He had absolutely no idea what to do with a Renaissance clanswoman who continued to look at him as if he'd lost his mind.

It also didn't help that Giles Cameron was standing a few feet away, still watching the spectacle with an expression that was threatening to blossom into a full-blown grin. Oliver glared at him, had something just short of a laugh in return, then turned back to his present problem. He was, after all, a bloke with innumerable hours spent dealing with other humans to his credit. He could somehow manage to not make a complete arse of himself at the moment as well.

"It's for you," he said, making her the slightest of bows. "Because I thought it might please you."

She dropped it. He had very quick hands and managed to rescue it before it hit the ground, then he straightened and almost hesitated to look and see if she were nigh onto losing her breakfast over the thought.

She'd put her hands to her cheeks. He suspected that might have been to cover her blush. He was appalled to find he was in the same straits. He held out the flower again, feeling altogether ridiculous. Then again, if anyone deserved even the slightest gesture of kindness and something lovely to look at, it was Mairead MacLeod.

Giles plucked the flower out of his hand, put it in Mairead's, then slung his arm around her shoulders and tugged.

"Let's leave your poor swain to looking for more weeds to give you whilst we seek out something to drink."

"'Tisn't a weed," Mairead protested. "It is, you fool, a lovely flower."

Oliver nodded in agreement, though he imagined no one had seen him doing so. He trailed after the Cameron heir and a woman that he—and not Giles if the man knew what was good for him—found far too charming for his own peace of mind.

So in an effort to distract himself, he took a moment to study his surroundings and take a proper measure of the state of the current clan MacLeod.

It was odd, wasn't it, how useful a lifetime spent looking at a crowd of people and coming to immediate conclusions about how close that group of souls was to popping off into something untoward could be. He could say without hesitation that boarding school had been uniformly awful, but useful.

He also had to concede that he'd been blessed with a handful of tutors who had distracted him from utter yobbishness with lessons on music and art and fine literature, but that was as far as he could go with that. And though he'd loathed the rest of it, he had also learned early on how to read a room, identify the ones most likely to foment trouble, and keep himself far away from the ensuing chaos.

It was likely best to primly decline to hold up any mirrors so he might examine his own moments of raising hell, but he was discreet like that.

He cleared his throat with equal discretion when they were fifty feet from the front door where a crowd had gathered and was apparently discussing items of interest with raised voices. Perhaps Giles had had his own brushes with spotting trouble at a distance because he smoothly put Mairead behind him and waited for Oliver to come stand next to him.

"Don't much care for that lad over there," Giles murmured.

Oliver didn't need to ask which one. The man dressed in black robes and wearing an officious sneer was quite obviously enjoying the attention he was receiving, though it would be foolhardy to hope he would be satisfied with only that.

"Have you seen his like before this far north?" Oliver asked putting his hand over his mouth as if he stifled a yawn.

"Nay, but I've heard tales."

"So have I," Oliver said grimly, though his were limited to reading about them from the comfortable vantage point of several hundred years after the fact. At least in his day, he had the ability to walk through any city on either side of Hadrian's Wall and not worry about some stupid git pointing a finger and screaming himself hoarse over any imagined witchly deed.

What he knew at the moment was that whoever and whatever that man out there was, his wearing of clerical robes was hiding a serious amount of barely restrained crazy.

He glanced over the others gathered there and singled out a pair of men for further study. Mairead's uncle Lachlan was looking very skeptical, which was encouraging, but he was also not laird in any sense of the word and had his own reputation for fanciful imaginings. There would be likely be minimal help in calming the clan coming from that direction.

Tasgall, on the other hand, was a possibility for becoming caught up in mayhem. Mairead's older brother seemed to have no trouble lashing out physically at whomever was in front of him, which seemed most of the time to be Mairead. The delicate Deirdre always seemed to be upstairs with a headache or sour stomach, which could have indicated all sorts of things. But the acting laird having the temperament to cool things down before they burst into a bonfire? Not bloody likely.

No wonder both Jamie and Patrick had been concerned about the clan during the current time period. He deeply regretted not having been more prepared for his spontaneous trip to make certain Mairead got home safely. He was damned certain his own days of being unplugged and uninformed were going to come to an abrupt end when he got back home.

He considered, then looked at Giles. "I'll keep watch out here."

Giles nodded slightly, then turned and smiled pleasantly at Mairead. "Let's go inside and find something to eat in the kitchen. I'm famished."

Oliver watched them go, smiled briefly at Mairead when she looked back at him, his flower still in her hand, then moved to take up a place against the wall of the keep. He refused to waste any thought on the absolute improbability of leaning currently where he generally found himself collapsed in a different century, wheezing after a hearty workout with the lord of the manor. Time was a very strange thing.

He made himself comfortable and settled in for a decent bit of reconnaissance.

Supper was a torturous affair even by his very low standards for trying to eat whilst wondering if he might survive the meal. He would have been thrilled to stop making comparisons to his time at St. Margaret's, that exclusive-yet-austere boarding school for the children of the ridiculously wealthy and richly titled, but he felt as if he'd resumed his identity as savvy yob of fourteen. He flattered Tasgall until he thought he might be ill, kept his gaze only where he wanted others to look, and avoided until the last moment possible any conversation with Master James, witch hunter extraordinaire.

If his disgust over the insane drivel he'd politely listened to hadn't done him in, the fact that he owed his least favorite tutor at St. Margaret's for his extensive knowledge of Scottish history—which allowed him to carefully name drop in a way that set Master James back on his heels a bit—came close to it.

All in all, a terrible evening that he would have preferred to forget as quickly as possible.

He managed to slip into the kitchens whilst everyone sorted their spots for the night and sat down on a stool next to the hearth, across from a woman he could only look at silently. He was simply beyond words. She seemed to have just as few herself, which he understood. The thought of leaving her behind with that kind of madness swirling around was almost unthinkable. The only thing he supposed would save her would be that she was as adept at making herself scarce as he was.

"Where is your book?" he murmured.

"In its usual hiding spot," she said quietly.

That was definitely a piece of good fortune. He didn't want to speculate on what would happen to either of them if Master James found them lingering over the image of the Duke of Birmingham printed by a 1970s publishing house.

"Uncle," she said, looking up suddenly.

Oliver vacated his stool without hesitation and went to fetch Mairead's uncle a cup of ale. He would have protested

Mairead offering him her seat, but he imagined the less attention he drew to her, the better off she would be. He unbuckled his sword and handed it to her, had a brief smile for his trouble, then settled himself on her stool and prepared to listen to nonsense about faeries and bogles which would be less terrifying than nonsense about witches.

"Don't like him," Lachlan said quietly.

Oliver tilted his head just slightly toward the great hall.

Lachlan nodded, then studied Oliver for a moment or two. "Know him from Edinburgh?"

"I don't associate with those types."

"Good lad," Lachlan said approvingly. He glanced toward Mairead, then sent Oliver a pointed look.

Oliver nodded, once. He understood exactly what Lord Lachlan was instructing him to do which he felt confident gave him permission to ignore James MacLeod's *Don't Arse-up the Fabric of Time* lecture. He would keep Mairead MacLeod safe until that ruddy nutter had gone off to make trouble somewhere else.

And then, if he had any sense at all, he would go back to his own time and get on with his life.

He watched Lachlan make himself more comfortable against the stone of the hearth and assumed the man wouldn't fall into the fire before he woke himself up, then turned to see how the rest of the kitchen inhabitants were faring.

Mairead had sat down against the wall with his sword on the floor next to her. He considered, then supposed no one would string him up for making himself a spot on the floor next to his sword. He surrendered his stool to a kitchen lad who turned out to be Tasgall's son Ambrose, had a quick smile as his reward, then realized his plans were about to be thrown into disarray. Fortunately for him, he had longer legs than a litter of children and managed to get himself to the spot on the floor next to Mairead before they beat him to it. He took back his sword from its temporary keeper, laid it on his right well within reach, and prepared himself for a reasonably comfortable evening in a warm place.

He found himself, somewhat surprisingly, being used as a resting place for small elbows and chilly feet. He took a quick count and came up with five children that likely belonged to Tasgall, plus Ambrose who came to sit on Mairead's other side. He looked down into a wee lassie's face and wondered if he'd misjudged where his peril might come from.

"I'm Fiona," she said, looking at him with a frown.

"I'm Oliver," he managed.

"I'm cold."

The best he could do was a bit of his plaid wrapped around her. He looked at Mairead to find that she had similarly wrapped up a pair of little lads who looked perfectly at home in her arms. He supposed that if the wee ones were comfortable, there was no reason not to make certain that the adults weren't suffering overmuch from chilly hands or feet. He didn't imagine he could do anything for Mairead's toes, but he rested his hand on the floor and very suavely inched his fingers over until he could tug on her skirt.

She looked at him in surprise, then she blushed.

He couldn't help himself. He smiled.

"Ye wee fiend," she whispered with a scowl.

"I'm being gallant by offering to warm your hand."

"Well, if that's the case," she said, shifting a small pair of legs and carefully putting her fingers onto his palm.

He took what he could get and wrapped his hand around hers, then leaned his head back against the wall.

"Tell me something about your book," he murmured in French.

"*The Duke and the Kitchen Maid?*"

170

He nodded.

"Well, she is a very saucy kitchen maid."

"I would only be surprised by anything else."

"Are you mocking me?"

"I wouldn't dare," he said honestly. "You have a very saucy-looking knife stuck into your belt."

She smiled, then sighed deeply. "I think the kitchen lass was far better at using the weapons at her disposal than I am." She paused. "We had a minstrel pass through a few years ago. He performed French songs for us, though I can't say I cared overmuch for the ridiculous amounts of romance in them."

He listened to her veer off into a different fictional direction and suspected she was coming to conclusions she might not like. Unfortunately, they were likely ones she needed to consider.

"I did remind myself, whilst I was listening to him, that there are those who write tales down for others to enjoy."

He nodded carefully. "Possibly."

"It led me to wonder if perhaps my book—the half I have, of course—might not be the duke's proper doings but instead perhaps that same sort of thing."

"I think that's possible," he agreed.

She looked at him closely. "Do you believe this scribe, this Constance Buchanan, invented her tales?"

He lifted one of his shoulders in as much of a shrug as he could manage whilst holding onto a sleeping five-year-old.

"I won't stab you," she grumbled.

He smiled. "I was worried."

"I don't think you're worried at all."

"You might be surprised," he said honestly. "But, aye, I daresay she did." He imagined he didn't need to tell her just how many other tales the illustrious Miss Buchanan had invented. "Was the story good?"

"Very," she said. "Many fierce battles and scorching looks—and that was just between the duke and his kitchen maid."

"She sounds impressive," Oliver said.

"Very courageous," Mairead agreed. "The duke was full of many noble virtues and skills in battle as well, though, along with being a deft hand at cards."

"Why did you want the rest of it? Do you like knowing how things end?"

She shook her head. "I thought if I knew how the kitchen maid's own life had finished, I could see how to escape mine."

Damn it, when would he stop being winded by every damned MacLeod he met?

"Though I dislike the thought of running."

He understood that. He wasn't one for running unless it was from thugs or to rescue someone from thugs. Well, and the occasional wee scarper from overzealous bobbies, but that was likely something he could safely leave in his yob years and have done. He preferred to take firm, measured steps away from people and situations that he no longer wanted to be a part of.

But he wasn't sure how Mairead MacLeod did that. It wasn't as though she had a modern-day list of jobs to apply for or friends in other cities. She was a woman with no escape and no prospects if she did escape.

He had no idea what it was he hoped to do for her, and he was beginning to wonder if he hadn't made an enormous mistake setting foot in that ring of plants that should have been nothing but dried weeds.

But he was where he was and perhaps it was for good reason. He laced his fingers with hers and would have winced at how hard she was holding his hand if he had been made of less stern stuff.

It wasn't possible to fall in like so quickly, was it?

He suspected it would take nothing but a slight push to have him falling face-first into something far more serious. That he should have found that thing in 1583 was beyond ridiculous.

He wondered if she might ever feel the same way about him.

"Sleep," he said hoarsely. "I'll keep watch."

"I shouldn't—"

He nodded toward his shoulder. "Use me," he said quietly. "If that isn't improper."

She shifted a sleeping child, moved closer to him, then rested her head on his shoulder.

"Thank you, Oliver."

"You're welcome, Mairead. Sleep well."

He could feel her nod. It was all he could do not to turn his head just a bit and kiss her hair, but he was, as he'd pointed out so virtuously before, a gentleman.

What he was doing in 16th-century Scotland, finding himself bewitched by a woman with beautiful eyes and an angelic smile who had been quite conveniently overlooked in favor of her truly spectacular sisters, was anyone's guess.

Fortunately for the fabric of time, he was well-practiced in simply lingering on the edges of any given situation, holding a useful cup of something in his hand and acting as if he belonged where he was. It worked like a charm with bobbies, bloviating academics, and insufferable gallery owners. Perhaps he would find a cup of mead in the morning and attempt the same sort of casual loitering in Renaissance Scotland.

Because apart from anything else, he didn't believe in luck or fate, but he absolutely trusted his gut and his gut was telling him at present that Master James who was not the king of Scotland was up to no good. Add to that mix a few superstitious souls in the current clan MacLeod along with a few more with chips on their shoulders and those storm clouds he could see on the horizon might bring in more trouble than just a nasty fall blow.

He would stay another day, just to make sure the storm blew itself out.

Not even Jamie could fault him for that.

TWELVE

MAIREAD SAT ON A FLAT stone in one of her favorite high pastures and watched two men try to kill each other.

She rested her elbows on her knees and her chin on her fists and ignored the fact that all that clanging of swords and spewing of curses was leaving her sheep no peace for grazing, but she had to admit they'd been subjected to worse. At least for herself, the view was fine and the swearing entertaining.

Giles Cameron was, as any maid with two good eyes would have immediately conceded, very handsome, terribly fierce, and exceptionally charming. She'd known him almost all her life and wished more than once that she could have called *him* her brother instead of Tasgall. He was hopelessly enamored of her next youngest sister, though, which could have made him her brother had things in her own life been different. But his hopes of wedding her sister were very slim considering that any of the lads who'd come to see if she might suit had immediately dismissed her and thrust their wooing gifts at whichever of her sisters they'd clapped eyes on first.

Not like that other man out there who had given her a flower the day before.

She looked at one of his dirks that he'd stabbed into the ground at her feet, inviting her to use it if she needed to, then at the growing little pile of other things that he'd begun. If he'd nodded knowingly at her each time he'd called a halt to the wielding of swords long enough to fetch and add to his collection, all she could do was tell him he was ridiculous and advise him to concentrate on his present business whilst she sat there and tried not to blush.

He was, after all, picking flowers for her.

She watched Oliver sparring with Giles and attempted a bit of dispassionate observation. He wasn't Giles's equal with the blade, but few were. That he was even standing against him when Giles wasn't showing him any mercy spoke well of his skill. That he could wield a sword at all given where—or *when*, rather—he'd come from was very surprising. She wondered absently what it was he did to earn his bread. If he hailed from England, what was he doing in Scotland and how long would he stay?

She didn't want to think about that last bit, actually. The reason he'd come back to her time was a mystery she hadn't wanted to solve. It was enough to have him at least within view for however long he chose to remain.

She sat up as the lads put up their swords and came to cast themselves down on the soft grasses at her feet. Giles looked at Oliver's dagger, then at the wee pile of purple things he'd begun sitting next to it.

"You haven't a clue how to woo a woman, have you?" Giles remarked.

"Are you going to help me?" Oliver asked mildly.

Mairead snorted before she could help herself and found two pairs of eyes turned her way. "Dust," she said, waving her hand in front of her face.

"I think I probably should," Giles said. "I, as you might have noticed, am particularly skilled at letting a woman know she is the object of my affections."

She found Oliver looking at her.

"Is that true?" he asked.

She shrugged. "Grizel drops things when he's in the vicinity, so perhaps."

Oliver smiled and turned back to Giles. "Then what do you suggest?"

"You might start by informing the gel you fancy that she is the one being fancied."

Oliver looked at his pile of blooms, then back at Giles. "Is that not enough?"

Giles only rolled his eyes and flopped back on the ground to look up at the sky. "Absolutely hopeless."

Mairead suspected she might find herself in that same situation if she had to listen to them any longer, so she pushed herself to her feet and went off to see about her animals. The very idea that Oliver Phillips would be interested in her for anything past refilling his ale and dropping soup on his lap was laughable. That she would find herself losing sleep over that same man was beyond absurd.

Though she couldn't help but wish it weren't.

The day passed slowly until she realized with a start that the light was beginning to fade. Her two keepers—for that is what they called themselves—had managed to keep themselves entertained whilst she labored, but that had mostly consisted of driving off a selection of her cousins with threats of bodily harm if they didn't leave her in peace. She wasn't sure that would convince Kenneth and the others to behave better in the future, but she couldn't fault Giles and Oliver for trying.

Ambrose had joined them at some point during the afternoon, trailing after her keepers with Fiona trailing after him. Her nephew had peppered them both with endless questions about Edinburgh, and Fiona had listened, all ears, as Oliver and Giles discussed the delights to be found in various locales around the city. She was half tempted to ask Oliver how much the city had changed in four hundred years, but she suspected, given how easily he and Giles discussed the same sights, that it hadn't been all that much.

She turned her sheep over to one of her younger cousins whose task it was to see them put in a pen, then stopped and looked at the keep in front of her. It had been her home for the entirety of her life, but for some reason it didn't feel very welcoming at the moment. Normally she would have blamed that on either her brother or Kenneth, but they seemed to be simply players waiting for a storm to arrive that was far beyond their ability to control.

"Mairead?"

She pulled herself back from the gloomy place she'd been wandering in her head and looked at Oliver. "Sorry, what?"

"I was wondering if perhaps you might want to take your ease in the kitchens," he said carefully.

She looked at him in surprise. "Do you fear for me?"

He smiled. "Of course not. I just want you to have ample time to enjoy all the flowers I've picked for you." He held them out. "There are, if you'll notice, quite a few."

Giles clapped his hand to his head and groaned.

Mairead glared at him, accepted Oliver's offering, then looked at him. "Devil's-bit is what the witch up the way would have called these, but I think that's a terrible name."

He winced. "I didn't know."

"They're purple."

"I did know that." He smiled. "Your favorite color."

She blushed. She also had help moving out of his way so he could slap Giles on the back of the head. He turned to her, inclined his head politely, then gestured toward the hall.

"If milady will permit us to escort her inside?"

She nodded regally, tucked her blossoms inside her shawl where only she could enjoy them, then happily walked behind two men who made a handy barrier against madness. She kept Fiona close on her right and didn't argue with Ambrose when he took up a position on her left.

She'd hardly made it inside the hall before she found herself pressed back against the wall with men and children surrounding her. The shrieking was almost intolerable, but if there was one thing her brother's wife could manage on any day of the year, it was a decent bit of shouting.

"Let go of my children," she shouted, giving Oliver a shove. "You'll not take them from me."

He regained his balance and inclined his head slightly. "I wouldn't think to, Lady Deirdre."

"Then *you*," Deirdre spat, whirling on Mairead. "You are forever wanting to take my bairns from me."

"Ach, Deirdre," Giles said, pointing behind her. "Your other wee ones are fleeing—"

Mairead found herself pulled behind Oliver with Giles making a bit more of a very handy barrier. She put her hand on Oliver's back to keep her balance, and realized that however much he presented an aura of carelessness, his body told a different tale. He was not at peace.

"Don't tell me she's a Cameron," he murmured to Giles.

"Fergusson," Mairead offered.

"At least she wasn't a McKinnon," Giles said, glancing over his shoulder. "It could have been worse."

Mairead conceded the point with a nod, then had help finding her way into the kitchens. The tenor of the chamber there was no better than the courtyard outside, but she at least had allies manning the stew pots and tending the fire. She watched Oliver and Cook exchange a handful of words, then found herself sitting in the corner with a pair of fiercer kitchen lads with very sharp knives seeing to chopping up bowls of vegetables in front of her. She looked at Oliver, had a grave smile from him before he left with Giles, then looked at her new keepers.

"Need help?" she offered.

"Nay, lady," one of them said. "You sit. We'll guard."

She found the entire idea of being watched over to be strange enough to leave her simply staring, bemused, at the flowers she held securely in one corner of her shawl.

She continued to be guarded in some form or fashion by either kitchen lads or a pair of men she'd spent the day with who seemed to take a fair amount of pleasure in mocking the other over ideas on the proper way to go about a successful wooing.

In time, Giles left the kitchens to seek out his own precarious spot in the great hall. She made herself comfortable in her usual place on the floor by the hearth, holding children that weren't hers, and wondering what her future held.

Only this time, she wasn't alone.

Oliver had already seen her uncle settled after a reasonable bit of conversation about inconsequential things, then drawn his sword, laid it on the floor, then sat down next to it. A pair of Tasgall's bairns immediately deserted her to swarm him like bees. He didn't seem to mind sharp little elbows and questing toes as the wee ones made themselves comfortable. She however was beginning to suspect that she preferred it when she had Oliver all to herself.

Poor, heart-smitten fool that she was.

"Mairead."

She looked at him and had a faint smile as her reward.

"You think too much."

"You do, too."

"I do," he agreed. "Why don't we save ourselves from ourselves and talk about something far removed from where we are. What shall we discuss?"

"Where were you weaned?" she asked, latching onto the first thing that came to mind.

"Stafford," he said easily, then he shot her a look. "It's a bit north of Birmingham."

She scowled at him, had another smile for her trouble, then shifted her youngest nephew more comfortably on her lap. "And then?"

"I was sent to—well, you could term it fostering, I suppose," he said with a shrug. "In Edinburgh."

"Which makes you a Lowlander of sorts, then," she conceded. "How long were you there in Edinburgh, then?"

"Until I was released. I never returned home."

"Were your parents gone, then?" she asked in surprise.

He smiled faintly and shook his head. "They're still alive. They just have several other children and once I was released, I was a man and there was no need to go home."

There were details enough there, she suspected, but she also sensed he might be as reluctant to discuss his family as she was to speak of hers. She was heartily sorry she'd asked, so she quickly cast about for something lighter to discuss.

"Tell me more about your friends sending you to Scotland, then," she said quietly. "We might speak in French, if you'd rather."

"That might be safer for the moment," he agreed in that tongue. He considered, then moved a bit closer to her. "We call it a holiday. That horrible thing they sent me on, that is."

"A holiday," she repeated slowly. "And what does that mean?"

"It's when you take time away from your normal labors and go amuse yourself."

She frowned. "That *is* a horrifying thought."

He smiled. "I agree."

"I suspect the only amusement anyone is having, I don't mind telling you yet again, is your lads at your expense."

"I definitely agree with that."

She would have snorted, but she feared to draw any attention to herself or wake children she could feel had drifted into their usual boneless slumber. She envied them, truly she did, that bit of sleep where they knew no harm would befall them.

"Mairead."

She liked very much the way he said her name. "Aye?"

"You're safe right now," he said quietly. "You could sleep, if you like."

"I'm fine," she said, "but I thank you—"

She jumped a little at the sound of shouting coming from the great hall, but it subsided almost immediately. She looked at Oliver.

"That happens often."

"I imagine it does," he said very quietly. "Your brother has quite a temper."

"He does," she agreed, then she cast about desperately for a distraction. "Do you think James and his bride went to—well, you know where—through the little croft in the forest?"

"I think there is a spot in the forest behind the hall," he said carefully. "I haven't had time to investigate it. What do you think?"

She wondered if she would ever become accustomed to anyone asking for her thoughts on anything. Hard on the heels of that thought came the one that she wished it could be that man there asking for her thoughts far into their future.

"My uncle advises against it," she said. "My father was wounded by a boar inside it, and you've seen what that left of him. No one goes there without very good reason."

"I'm sorry about your father."

"He was a very good man. Patrick is very much like him, if I can make that comparison, though the thought that he could have traveled from a past time to ..." She shook her head. "Difficult to believe."

He smiled briefly. "I understand, believe me. I'm not sure I would have believed it if I hadn't lived it." He studied her with a faint smile. "Were there no numbers in your book that left you wondering about impossible things?"

"There were the numbers 1823 written on one page," she conceded.

"What did you think they meant?"

"I assumed they were the tally of scorching looks the duke had sent the kitchen maid."

He laughed, then clamped his lips shut as Fiona stirred in his arms, lifted her head and glared at him, then fell back asleep with her head thumping on his shoulder. Oliver huffed out another faint laugh, then looked at her with a smile.

"You're very funny," he said.

She supposed that if she'd been a kitchen maid with an equally full tally of experiences with men and their mores, she might have taken his look for one of affection. His smile didn't fade, but he tilted his head toward his shoulder.

"Why don't you sleep for a bit on that bit of good humor," he said with another smile. "I'll watch over you."

She didn't imagine she would sleep, but she did as he bid and at least closed her eyes. She supposed it would be a very bad habit to become accustomed to, so she finally lifted her head and looked at him. He was simply sitting there, looking at nothing.

Only she realized he wasn't doing that, he was watching very carefully.

"You need to sleep," she said quietly.

"I'm fine."

She straightened and shook her head sharply to clear it. "I'll keep watch."

"My chivalry will suffer."

"Better that than your gut from Giles's sword."

"There is that," he agreed. He considered, then nodded. "For an hour, perhaps. Wake me sooner if anything changes."

She nodded her assent, though she imagined he wouldn't sleep through it if her brother went on a rampage. She did, however, shift a bit so she could watch him at least pretend to sleep, braw, chivalrous lad that he was.

In time, she decided that he had managed to fall asleep in truth. She might have been tempted to join him, but there were voices coming from the great hall that sounded as if they were discussing things that were ... unpleasant. She managed to put sleeping children down on scraps of marginally clean rushes pushed up against the wall, then rose soundlessly to her feet and walked across the kitchens to discover what she could about the goings on in the keep.

Her brother was sitting with Master James in front of the hearth on the far side of the hall. She could hear their whispers slipping along the wall like shadows, whispers of things she imagined weren't entirely sane.

She felt hands come to rest on her shoulders, but she didn't jump because she knew whose hands they were.

"They're just words," he murmured.

"I don't like them."

"I don't like *him*."

"I don't think a churched lad should be doing the things he's speaking about."

"Maybe he stole the clothes."

She would have smiled, but she was too unnerved to. She felt Oliver take her hand and pull her back toward the hearth in the kitchens. She allowed him to help her sit on the floor, then looked at him as he sat down next to her.

"Stay far away from him," he said simply.

He looked as if he might have liked to have said other things, but she knew he wouldn't. Her acquaintance with Oliver Phillips might have been brief, but she knew he tended to speak less than he thought

"Perhaps he'll go soon," she murmured.

He only closed his eyes briefly, then nodded.

⁓ ❦ ⁓

She woke to absolute chaos.

She found herself pulled to her feet and tucked back into the corner by the hearth.

"I'll be back," Oliver said, strapping his sword to his back. "Stay here with the bairns."

Well, that was very sensible advice, true, but she couldn't just sit there in the kitchens and hide when there might be something she could do to calm what her brother only seemed to inflame. That she had been doing the same thing for most of her life was likely not a useful thing to dwell on.

"Ambrose—"

"I will, Auntie."

She listened to him gather up his siblings and herd them into the place where Oliver had left her, made certain her knife was down the back of her belt, then strode across the kitchens to see if there might be something for her to do.

Half the clan was already pouring out the front door, dragging none other than Deirdre Fergusson with them. She yanked her arm away from someone's hand only to find it was Oliver who had caught her by the elbow. Gently, if that mattered to anyone but her, but firmly.

"You should—"

185

"I cannot."

He closed his eyes briefly, then nodded. "Stay behind me, then. I have the feeling this will go badly."

She had the feeling it was going to be Hell arriving on their doorstep, but she imagined that didn't need to be said. She followed him across the hall out the door with the rest of her clan. She was absolutely certain the scene there in front of her was one she would never forget.

Master James had apparently woken that morning convinced that his duty lay in ridding the clan of the witch that was bringing them such bad luck. She couldn't see that exactly as they seemed to be faring well enough at the moment. They had sufficient cattle, enough mutton for even the most hearty appetites, and warm things to wear thanks to her own industry. Her father's condition was unfortunate, true, but that had been something that could have happened to any man brave enough to walk into the forest behind the ... hall ...

She looked quickly for her uncle, but he was well away from Master James and he never would have given voice to any of his more fanciful thoughts in the presence of that madman. She was certain of it.

Her brother, however, was another tale entirely and he seemed perfectly happy to complain about the endless shrieking of his wife which might indeed indicate something amiss with her.

"Aye, aye, we'll see to her in a moment," Master James assured him. "But there are others in this gathering who must be examined. Perhaps that man who came from Edinburgh without friends or baggage—"

Mairead didn't hesitate. She walked forward and continued on until she was standing five paces away from the man who couldn't possibly have been a decent member of the church.

"'Twas a terrible misfortune," she agreed. "And yet he speaks so highly of you and your work in the city."

Master James looked at her narrowly. "And what would you know of any of it, wench?"

"Nothing, good sir," she said, bowing her head humbly. "I couldn't resist the chance to compliment you on your keen eye and compassion for those who've had misfortune befall them."

Master James pursed his lips. "Perhaps."

"Let us find a text to read together," she said, wondering if that sort of thing might distract him. "In Latin, which is too lofty for me, but for you—"

"You can read?" he asked, falling back with his hand at his throat.

"Of course not—"

It was at that moment that she began to have the smallest amount of sympathy for her brother. She had watched the souls around her from the time she'd become cognizant of them, separating them into groups of ones who were trustworthy and ones who needed to be humored so she might keep herself and those she loved safe. The latter group had been unpredictable, true, but always amenable either to food or compliments or even some sort of distraction in a direction where she was not so she could slip away, safely unnoticed.

Master James was, she could say without reservation, utterly mad.

She found herself pulled aside and expected to find Oliver there. Instead, she encountered her brother who looked just the slightest bit unsettled. Perhaps he realized too late that the flames he had been fanning the night before had gotten far beyond anything he could control.

She looked over her shoulder, away from the hall, toward what was left of a wall that had once surrounded the keep.

She watched a Highlander vault easily over it and stride forward, keeping to a larger part of the crowd, but moving with a purpose. It occurred to her with a start that the man had to be James MacLeod himself. She watched him clap a hand on Oliver's shoulder and pull him away, back toward the wall, in a direction that would eventually allow them both to trot back up the meadow and return to Oliver's proper time.

Oliver argued with Jamie for a moment, then closed his eyes and nodded.

She found his gaze locked with hers and suspected that he might have uttered a pleasing sentiment or two if he'd been able.

"Where is that fair-haired Englishman!" Master James yelled suddenly.

Mairead exchanged another look with Oliver, then turned away and made her way forward to face the man behind the current madness. She had scarce begun to wonder what she might say when she found herself shoved so hard that she went down to her knees. She jumped back to her feet partly because her father had taught her to do so that she might either fight or run without delay and partly because her brother had just taken his wife by the arm and pushed her into a spot directly in front of Master James.

"Test her," Tasgall said, his chest heaving. "I cannot listen to another moment of her screeching."

Mairead felt the weight of the decision she knew she had no choice but to make fall upon her without mercy. Deirdre was unpleasant and shrill, but she was Ambrose's mother and the bairns needed her still. Mairead knew very well what it was like to lose a mother as a child. Her mother had been a cold, distant woman, even less affectionate than Deirdre, but the loss had still grieved her.

She couldn't let that happen to Ambrose and his siblings.

She caught sight of Oliver once more, wished him every happiness in his future, then turned back to the madness before her. She couldn't help but wonder how a stake had been found so quickly, who had cut it, and how many of her cousins had been willing to see one of their own sent to it. She could scarce believe that she was surrounded by people who had lost their wits entirely, but she had to admit that Master James had been persuasive.

She stepped forward through the insanity that surrounded her, pulled Deirdre out of the way, then stopped directly in front of Master James. She took a deep breath, then pushed her gown off the very top of her shoulder.

There was a mark there, not quite in the shape of a flower, but not quite a perfect circle either. She'd had it from the moment of her birth and thought nothing of it.

Master James didn't seem to share her indifference.

And she had thought Hell had already arrived.

She'd been wrong.

THIRTEEN

O LIVER CURSED HIS WAY UP the meadow, barely
scratching the surface of all the languages in which
he knew how to find the loo.

He knew he couldn't stay. He knew Mairead couldn't
come to the future with him. The knowledge of both those
things was so awful, he couldn't find words in any of those
languages to describe the depth of the agony that knowledge
dealt him.

The only thing that made it any better at all was the
equally terrible knowledge that it was Deirdre headed toward
the pyre, not Mairead. He absolutely hated the thought of
that happening to her, but what was he going to do? For all
he knew, it would be better for Ambrose and his siblings to
have Mairead as their mother. His own governess had been
a far better mother to him than his own mother had been
during the first six years of his life until they'd dumped him
at boarding school.

Now, if there just hadn't been something about the whole
scene that had seemed ... off. He hardly knew how to describe
it and wasn't entirely sure he was in a fit state to analyze it.
Had there been a look he couldn't quite remember, or a word
he didn't quite understand, or a direction he hadn't been
looking in that he suspected he should have been?

He made it all the way to the gate in the meadow before what he'd seen finally sank in.

Mairead had been standing in front of that crowd of nutters, looking at Deirdre with compassion in her expression.

She couldn't possibly have intended to take her sister-in-law's place ...

Jamie's grip on his arm was like an iron manacle. "We must go *now*."

Oliver would have fought him—indeed, he tried briefly—but Jamie's sword was sharp and he looked perfectly ready to use it for business Oliver decided immediately he didn't want to be a part of. He also thought he might be in shock, which he suspected was substantially less terrifying than what Mairead would be facing—or had already faced. He heard shouting coming from the keep in the distance, shouting mixed with curses and perhaps even a scream or two, but before he could decide, Jamie had pushed him into the future and the gate had closed behind them both.

Oliver stumbled away, then leaned over with his hands on his thighs until he'd caught his breath. He waited another moment or two until the urge to kill the current laird of the clan MacLeod had receded, then heaved himself upright.

"I have to go back."

"You cannot."

"Cannot," Oliver said, "or should not?"

Jamie resheathed his sword over his shoulder with an unthinkingness that Oliver had to admit was highly unsettling. He could scarce bring himself to imagine how many times the man had done just that very thing, unthinkingly.

"Should not," Jamie said. "I'm sure you know how Zachary and I tried to rescue that little Puritan girl across the Pond."

"At least you attempted it," Oliver said pointedly.

"And yet we failed."

"But you *tried*."

"And *failed*," Jamie stressed. "We never should have tried because events needed to proceed as they should have, which they should here as well."

"But what if Mairead took Deirdre's place?" Oliver said desperately. "I can't let her die. I *know* her!"

"And others will die just as tragically who you do not know. You cannot save everyone."

"But I could save *her*."

Jamie studied him in silence for a moment or two. "I'm not sure I want to know how you've come to know her so well."

Oliver sensed a stab at a distraction coming his way, so he made Jamie a brisk bow. "Thank you, my laird, for the pleasant excursion. I'll be on my way now, if you don't mind."

He turned and walked away before he had to see the expression on Jamie's face. He was definitely doing Elizabeth's husband a favor by preventing the man from seeing the one on his own.

He didn't hear anyone following him, which he supposed boded well for his continuing to breathe. He permitted himself a single look over his shoulder once he reached the edge of Moraig's forest and caught sight of a lone figure walking down the meadow. There was a solemnity to the sight that Oliver simply refused to put his finger on because any emotion at all would get in the way of what he intended to do. He turned away and started to run.

He ran until he came to an ungainly halt directly in front of Patrick MacLeod's front door. He lifted his hand to knock, but the door opened before he could. He took a deep breath.

"I need a computer."

Patrick simply stepped back out of the way. Oliver nodded to him and strode into his great hall, then realized he wasn't quite sure where to go. He also found that Madelyn was standing in the middle of that same great room, watching him with concern.

"Something to eat?" she ventured.

He manufactured the smile that she deserved but he could scarce feel. "I'm fine, but thank you."

Patrick walked past him. "Follow me."

Oliver made Madelyn a slight bow, had a grave smile in return, then followed after the lord of the hall to what he assumed was the man's study. Patrick pulled out a chair, logged into his laptop, then stood back from that as well.

"Make yourself at home. I'll go get you water."

Oliver nodded absently and almost sat down before he realized he was still wearing his sword. He took it off, propped it up against Patrick's desk, then sat down with a sigh. He wasn't quite sure how long he'd been unplugged from the world, but it had been long enough that hopping onto the most convenient search engine that came to mind and typing instead of trying to draw vegetation with a mini-golf pencil left him feeling very strange.

He forged ahead, though, because he was accustomed to doing what needed to be done without fretting over the cosmic ramifications of his actions. He searched, he drank an entire glass of water before he thought to ascertain the potential for poison, then realized he wasn't going to get anywhere with the tools he had at present.

He rubbed his hands over his face, then sat back and sighed deeply. He looked at Patrick who was leaning back against a bookcase.

"Nothing online," he said flatly.

And then he realized that perhaps there was something to knowing a member of a clan who lived on his family's ancestral lands and perhaps had had enough time on his hands to do a little research on that clan. He knew Patrick had written a book on medieval warfare—he had read and been unnerved by it—but whatever else the man had in his library was a mystery.

Patrick reached behind him without looking, then held out a slim volume.

"You'll find the details here."

Oliver closed his eyes briefly because he couldn't help himself. He set aside all the things he likely had no business feeling and took the book. Opening it, though, was another thing entirely.

The only decent thing he could find to note about the little book—A *History of Highland Witch Trials*—was that it had chapters demarking the terrible contents, not tabs. He scanned the chapter headings so usefully provided on the initial pages of the book, noted the journey through history those chapters would offer him, then hoped he wasn't making a terrible mistake by skipping straight to the penultimate chapter that listed in chronological order those souls who had paid the ultimate price for what he could charitably call mass hysteria based on superstition. He wasn't at all comforted to find that men had been burned as well as women, especially when he came to a particular name.

Mairead MacLeod, 1583.

He stared at her name until he thought he could speak without howling, then looked at Patrick to find him now sitting in the chair next to the desk. Oliver appreciated the fact that silence seemed to be the man's go-to response to terrible things, though he wondered if that had always been the case.

"How did you survive it?" he asked before he managed to stop himself. "The time period, that is."

Patrick smiled without humor. "I came through the forest gate behind our hall at sixteen, so I was witness to far fewer horrors than my brother."

"I'm guessing you saw enough."

"Aye," Patrick said simply. "I did rescue my lady from a journey back in time that I will readily admit was my fault and—" He paused and took a deep breath. "She suffered and that was also my fault. I took lives to save hers and fought to save my own skin in the current century, so I've lived it, however, briefly, as a man."

"Your brother would tell me to walk away."

"He would," Patrick agreed, "and he has good reason for it. He had a close-up look at what was left of Zachary after his second try at rescuing that gel from the stake."

"Pardon my frankness, my lord, but I can't imagine he cared about either Zachary or the girl."

"Do you honestly believe that?"

"After this morning?" Oliver asked. "I think I just missed watching a woman be dragged off to be burned in a fire, so I would have to say yes."

Patrick pushed his lips out as though he feared they might say something without his permission. "Let's say this," he began carefully. "If Elizabeth or one of his children or any member of his little clan here wandered off where they shouldn't have, Jamie would never admit how far he would go to rescue them. He would instead bore you silly with endless lectures on not changing the past."

"I've heard one or two."

"There are more."

Oliver imagined that was the truth. "Yet he hops through those damned gates as if he's nipping down to the village for crisps. How does he know just showing his face in a different time doesn't change the past?"

195

"He tries to tread lightly," Patrick said. "And, to be honest, he grows bored easily. As modern and tame as he seems, he spent all of his life knowing he would lead the clan and a good deal of his life doing just that—with all its attendant excitement and not just a few dire deeds. I suspect half the books on psychology he has cluttering up his study are things he's read to try to unravel his own thinking."

"The saints preserve us."

Patrick smiled. "You've spent too much time with him, obviously."

Oliver closed the book and set it very carefully back on the desk. "I cannot let her die."

"I understand."

He looked at the book on the desk, then a thought occurred to him. "If I could rescue her at the right time, leaving them thinking she had died, then it wouldn't matter what happened in the end, would it?"

He hadn't meant it to be a question and Patrick seemingly didn't take it as one.

"That is the prevailing theory," Patrick agreed.

"Zachary brought Mary de Piaget forward because she was on the verge of death."

"Are you trying to convince me or yourself?"

"I don't need any convincing, my lord," Oliver said without hesitation.

Patrick looked to be coming to a conclusion about something. Oliver decided it was best to keep his bloody mouth shut on the off chance it would turn out to be something he didn't like.

He wasn't unused to waiting people out. He'd tended to simply walk away in his youth, which saved him endless brawls and arguments he had early on decided weren't worth his time, but that had changed as he'd matured. His ability to simply sit and watch as someone else came to conclusions about everything from writing checks to calling the bobbies was something he developed and honed endlessly after watching Robert Cameron do the same.

Patrick pulled a mobile out of his pocket and set it on the desk.

"Untraceable."

Oliver closed his eyes briefly, then picked it up. "I wouldn't expect anything else."

"I don't imagine I should bother reminding you to take your sword."

Oliver looked at him. "I won't need it."

Patrick sighed lightly and pushed himself to his feet. "I'll go find you a few other things that might be useful."

Oliver nodded his thanks, then looked at the phone in his hands. He was accustomed to finding things to help him *in situ*, but his options in Renaissance Scotland were very limited. He imagined he could make a fairly accurate guess about the number of clan members, and he could certainly speculate about who might have been susceptible to being swept up into group insanity, but that wasn't useful if they became a crowd that had completely lost its mind. He was tempted to go stand in front of them and attempt a few magic tricks of the sort he'd once dazzled Jamie's children with—

He froze. Perhaps that wasn't such a terrible thought after all.

He looked at the phone in his hands, considered a bit longer, then dialed. Derrick Cameron answered on the second ring, which he found somewhat flattering.

"I'm afraid to ask who this is."

"You should be," Oliver said curtly.

There was a hint of a brief laugh. "What's new, pussycat?"

Oliver had to unclench his jaw. "I would kill you, but your wife who is far too good for you just provided you with a daughter who might like to keep you for a few more years."

Derrick laughed more easily that time. "We're just taking the piss out of you, lad."

"I can honestly not bring to mind anything I've ever enjoyed more," Oliver said. "Oh, wait, yes I can. It will be in the future whilst I'm spending a fortnight plotting the demise of each of you. A fortnight for each, not a single fortnight for the whole mangy litter of you ruddy bastards."

Derrick whistled softly. "Sounds like someone hasn't been to his mani-pedi yet."

"No, but I've been on a little jaunt to Renaissance Scotland."

"Find anything interesting there?"

"Someone who needs to be rescued."

Derrick was silent for a single blessed moment. "What do you need?"

Oliver absolutely refused to become maudlin, but he couldn't help but admit that he was grateful for a collection of mates who offered aid without question. "I need a distraction."

"What sort?"

"The sort that will take a gaggle of puritanical nutters intent on burning a woman at the stake and keep them distracted long enough for me to grab her and do a runner. I would, for obvious reasons, prefer to leave nothing substantial behind for them to lose their bloody minds over."

Derrick didn't hesitate. "Fireworks?"

"I was thinking so."

"How soon do you need them?"

"Yesterday."

"Of course you do," Derrick said dryly. "I'm at the hall, actually, and you know what we have here in the basement. I'm guessing you don't want to walk here and pick anything up?"

Oliver couldn't bring himself to begin to breathe out the threats he wished he could dredge up to leave the man on the other end of the call rushing off to hide in a corner with his thumb and a selection of unfortunately on-key nursery rhymes.

Derrick was also blessedly silent for a moment. When he spoke, it was obvious he'd used his brain for something past inventing ridiculous tasks for a lad just trying to live his best life and help the girl he was fond of do the same.

"Who is she?"

"Daughter of the laird," Oliver said grimly. "In 1583."

"Well, I suppose you aren't looking too far above your—"

"Shut up."

"I'm trying to keep you from bawling."

"It might require more than that."

"Details?"

"I'll tell you if I can keep her from getting murdered long enough to see if she'd be interested in perhaps dating me more than once," he said. He paused. "Perhaps permanently."

Derrick dropped his phone. Oliver would have found that satisfying, but he was indeed far closer to a display of unmanly emotion than he cared to be.

"I'll go give the basement treasures a wee rummage," Derrick said briskly, "and be on the road in thirty. Where are you?"

"I'll be at Moraig's getting gear together."

Derrick was silent for a moment or two. "Want company on your trip?"

"I think I have to go alone."

"Understood. Don't go load up on carbs, lad. They slow you down."

Oliver suggested something Derrick could do with his dietary advice, had a laugh in return, then the line went dead. He looked at the phone that was surprisingly state of the art and wondered if Patrick would miss it. He supposed the only thing he could do was ask, so he collected his sword and left the study. He made his way to the great hall where he found the lord of the castle packing up a rucksack that not only would likely pass muster for time-period authenticity but was small and encouragingly sleek.

Patrick looked up at him. "Food, leather soles that can be laced to fit any foot, and sutures. I don't dare send you with anything more modern."

Oliver held up the phone and shot Patrick an enquiring look.

Patrick rolled his eyes. "I'll claim you stole it."

"They'll enjoy that."

Patrick nodded at the pack. "Charger's in there already. I imagine you can find an outlet somewhere in Moraig's that'll serve you to top up what's already in the battery. Don't take it through the gate."

Oliver nodded, then put the phone in his pocket only to realize he was still wearing his Highland uniform. He promised himself a good shudder later over how accustomed he'd become to running around in basically in his altogether covered only by a shirt and a handy bit of tartan. He took the pack Patrick handed him, put the phone inside, then made him a low bow.

"Thanks are inadequate."

Patrick nodded toward the door. "Go rescue your girlfriend. You two can thank me later by babysitting so my lady and I can have a night out."

Oliver nodded, had a quick hug and a *be careful* from Madelyn at the door, which he suspected might have more meaning coming from her than just an older-sister sort of thing, then made his way back to his luxurious retreat to look for carbs.

He showered, dressed himself in a black polo neck jumper and equally black cargo trousers, and had hardly begun to dig about in the fridge for any leftover chips before he heard the unmistakable sound of a helicopter. He straightened, shut the fridge door, then closed his eyes briefly.

He might have to babysit for Robert Cameron a time or two as well before his debt was even dented.

He decided loitering on the threshold wasn't a terrible idea, so he did so, waiting only a few moments before he saw Derrick walking swiftly through the forest in his direction carrying a black duffle bag. Oliver stood back and waved him inside.

"I claim sanctuary," Derrick said, straight-faced.

Oliver refrained from telling his boss what he could do with his claims because he'd already sworn too much that day. He did roll his eyes, though, because he imagined Derrick expected at least that much.

It took ten minutes to unpack the possibilities and lay them out a discreet distance from the hearth Oliver hadn't had the heart to start a fire in.

"Enough?" Derrick asked.

"More than, thank you." He considered, then looked at his partner in crime and other more noble business ventures. "What do you know?"

"What I read on the flight down," Derrick said bluntly. "When are you going to insert yourself?"

"Hopefully after the first incarnation of me has been dragged away by that bloody bastard down the way."

Derrick smiled. "Say that to his face."

"I damn well already did!"

"Jamie's heard worse, I'm certain. So you'll set off a distraction, do a little snatch and grab, then what? Does she know when you were born?"

Oliver nodded. "She's been here several times."

"And you like her?"

Oliver scowled at him. "Are we having this conversation now?"

"It is, without a doubt, the most fascinating conversation we've ever had."

"I'm not talking to you any more."

Derrick smiled. "As you say, of course. Pick your distraction in silence, then, and I'll help you pack it appropriately."

Oliver looked over what was there, exchanged a handful of looks with Derrick over choices to be made, then decided whatever would be left behind could perhaps become another legend that Uncle Lachlan would start by announcing that the faeries had been at it again. At minimum, a pair of mortars would be better than taking his chances with bottle rockets that might cost him fingers.

Derrick held up two fingers and lifted an eyebrow.

Oliver mouthed a friendly curse at him, then sighed. "Better safe than sorry, I imagine."

"Cut the fuses to the right lengths and run quickly enough between the two and you could send them scattering in different directions, though that might not serve you very well."

"I imagine the clan will think the world is ending whatever I manage to do," Oliver said grimly. "Perhaps that bastard going around examining innocent people for devil's marks will run off to hide in a cave for the duration of the apocalypse and die of starvation."

"I think you'd be doing the world a service," Derrick agreed.

Oliver looked at him seriously. "Don't tell Jamie."

"He'll know anyway," Derrick said wisely. "He'll blame you loudly, but don't think he won't agree silently."

"I should have been nosier about her details before now," Oliver said grimly.

"The worst thing about you, my lad, is that you have such a finely honed sense of propriety. There's privacy, of course, then there's privacy that could get you killed."

Oliver shot him a look. "Like you know the difference."

"I'm talking about you."

"*I* know the difference!"

"That's the problem."

Oliver rolled his eyes. "Go away."

"Heading out now." Derrick rose, flicked him companionably on the ear on his way by, and opened the door.

"Thank Cameron for the haste," Oliver called before Derrick managed to shut the door behind him.

"Will do," came the answer that trailed off into silence.

Oliver might have worried about that silence, but he heard the helicopter soon take off to no doubt ferry Derrick safely back to Cameron Hall. The silence that then descended wasn't merely a lack of sound. It felt heavy somehow, as if the world waited for something terrible to happen.

He shook his head at his own ridiculous thoughts, pushed himself to his feet, and went to finish his search for leftovers.

Half an hour later, he was standing at the edge of the forest, looking at the meadow that wasn't nearly as free of interlopers as he would have hoped. He made the man standing in front of him a small bow, then straightened.

"With all due respect, my laird," Oliver said quietly, "please move."

"You cannot do this."

"I believe, my lord James, that I most certainly can."

"You might be mistaken about identities."

Oliver shrugged, though he felt anything but casual about the entire affair. He also knew exactly what had happened because he'd read the bloody facts in Patrick MacLeod's library. "There's one way to know," he hedged.

"Knowing the future isn't a good thing—"

"This is the past!"

Jamie rubbed his hands together as if they ached. Oliver didn't want to even begin to speculate on the things that man there had done over the course of his life to keep alive those he loved.

"You can," he said carefully, "bend a gate to your will."

Oliver didn't want to weep with gratitude, but he was damned close to it. "How?"

"I find 'tis useful to fix my mind on either a particular event or the vision of a specific person at a specific time."

Oliver considered. "Mairead in the kitchen, perhaps."

"Too vague."

"That damned witch hunter holding court by the fire the night before he ..."

Jamie hemmed and hawed a bit. "That would work," he conceded, "though you wouldn't want to make any sort of spiritual connection with him across the centuries. You might acquire a bit of his negative energy as a result."

Oliver could scarce believe his ears. "What absolute bollocks."

Jamie actually smiled. "I have many working theories, but I never said they were *all* reasonable."

"I'll take my chances with the crazy bloke because I can remember exactly what he was saying."

"'Tis likely enough then, that."

Oliver looked at him seriously. "Thank you," he said. "I know this goes against your code."

Jamie shrugged. "I'm a romantic, as my beloved wife will tell you. And if you must know the absolute truth, I've always felt there was something lingering in that time that shouldn't have been there. I've been keeping an eye peeled for stray time travelers, but perhaps that isn't the case."

"I won't stay."

"That might be wise." He held out a scrap of paper. "Have a wee peek at that."

Oliver studied the map, memorized a pair of Xs, then handed it back. "Thank you."

"Will she come with you?"

"She covets my leopard-print yoga trousers," Oliver said lightly. "I think I would be wise to humor her in this."

Jamie smiled and started to turn away, then turned back. "No sword?"

"Won't need one."

Jamie only lifted his eyebrows briefly. "Be careful then, Oliver."

Oliver found Jamie's using his full name instead of whatever nickname apparently came first to his tongue to be a bit more unsettling than it likely should have been. He nodded, watched the laird of the hall down the way walk off into the twilight, then pulled a black knitted hat out of his pocket. He shoved what of his hair it wouldn't cover up into it, readjusted the straps of his pack, then considered his plans one final time.

He had gear for flight after Mairead had been rescued. He had food enough—jerky, not crisps, damn Derrick to hell—for them to survive in the wild for a handful of days until things cooled down at the hall and they could escape to the faery ring at the top of the meadow. The other two gates Jamie had just shown him were north of Cameron Hall, no doubt farther than he would want to travel so late in the year, so he suspected he would be wise to simply use what he'd used before and assume it would work.

He also had two professional-grade fireworks guaranteed to make an impression. The fuses were long, he had more experience than was polite in lighting the same, and he was, he could admit with all modesty, a very fast runner. He would put them where their incendiary selves wouldn't burn down the whole forest, light them, then bolt like hell for Mairead. It might be wise to avoid himself in the bargain, but he was used to being a ghost.

In the end, his knives were sharp, he had lock picking tools, and his head for maps was as flawless as Derrick Cameron's photographic memory was with everything else. Anything beyond that would just have to be invented on the fly.

He looked at the faint ring of what was left of the year's plants. He closed his eyes, focused his mind on replaying as clearly as possible the scene from the night before. It wasn't difficult. Master James was definitely committed to the task of ridding Scotland of all purveyors of witchly arts. He suspected the man likely had Mummy issues and perhaps a few girlfriends who had recoiled at whatever Mr. Collins-like delicate compliments the man had been able to spew out.

Whatever the case, it made it very easy to muster up a good bit of enthusiasm for shutting the man up at least briefly, which he supposed might be all he needed.

He took a deep breath, tried not to flinch as that scarce-visible doorway simply opened in front of him, then stepped across its threshold.

FOURTEEN

T HE WORLD RENT ITSELF IN twain with a tremendous
noise.

Mairead looked up over her head and stared in
astonishment as the sky burst into light as if the very stars of
Heaven had flung themselves down to the earth like sparks
from a mighty fire in colors she'd never before imagined—

She suddenly found herself freed from her cousins who
had been dragging her toward the pyre. She would have commented on how well they crumpled to the ground, but she
found her hand taken by someone else. She immediately
tried to pull it free, then she realized it was Oliver, dressed in
black from head to toe.

She blinked in surprise. "But I just saw you—"

"Let's go."

She wanted to stop and consider, but there was no time
for it. She could either continue on to her death or she could
turn aside onto a path she suspected would forever change the
course of her life. Surely Ambrose and his wee siblings would
survive well enough without her. They would be without her
either way—

"Mairead, *now*."

She nodded, took her skirts in her free hand, and ran
with him directly toward the pile of wood ready to be set
alight. She felt someone grab her arm and almost pull her

off her feet. She was spun around and watched a hand come toward her face, but she never felt it because Oliver's hand caught that hand first. She watched him plow his fist into her brother's mouth so hard, she was fairly sure she heard something break.

"He may be eating soup for a bit," she managed breathlessly.

"If he doesn't choke to death first," Oliver said, shaking out his hand briefly. "Can you run?"

She would have answered, but the sky had again exploded into shards of colors that had surely come from some angelic realm. She looked at Oliver, had a brief smile as her reward, then she gathered her courage and nodded.

He squeezed her hand. "Brave lass. Let's go."

She fled with him past the front door of the keep and directly into the forest behind the hall where only the bravest of her clan dared tread. She imagined bravery had nothing to do with Oliver's choice of paths, but rather causing the men she could hear shouting in the distance to think again before they followed after them certainly did.

She had no idea how long they ran. All she knew was that whatever skills she had in blending into the forest, Oliver had only to an entirely new and terrifying degree. They went west, which she imagined wasn't the direction Tasgall would have expected her to take. Then again, he would have enough pain in his face that perhaps he wouldn't be thinking clearly for a bit.

At one point, Oliver stopped, looked at her bare feet, then winced.

"Your feet are bleeding."

She imagined that was the least of her worries, but she didn't protest when he pulled leather shoes out of his rucksack and laced them to her feet.

"I can keep on," she said, wiggling her toes and scarce feeling them. "Very comfortable."

He rose, looked at her for a moment in silence, then very gently pulled her into his arms. She held onto him tightly, likely more enthusiastically than was polite, but she was freezing and terrified.

"Thank you," she managed.

He pulled back a bit and pressed his lips against her forehead. "I would have done it as many times as necessary."

She shivered. "Don't say that."

He breathed out an uneasy bit of a laugh. "I won't," he said, shivering. He tightened his arms around her briefly, then pulled away. "We should go."

"Where?"

"Still west, I think," he said slowly, "then north as long as we can keep to the trees. We need to find a better vantage point if we can. I want to know what's coming."

"Likely nothing," she said honestly. "I'm not worth it to them."

"You're worth it to me, though. Let's run for a bit longer, then we'll find a place to rest. I brought food."

"Not your offal cakes, I hope."

He smiled, more truly then. "Your uncle Patrick supplied the food, so you can blame him when you see him for whatever he sent for us."

She nodded, a jerky motion that left her feeling as if she weren't at all in control of her poor form.

"Mairead, just a bit farther."

She wished she'd had a tart remark to offer about her ability to carry on under extremely trying circumstances, but she had just been rescued from death by fire by a man dressed all in black and she could still hear the men in her clan shrieking her name behind her.

"Let's run," she said hoarsely.

He nodded and took her hand.

It was midday before she could finally go no further. She'd run when she could, then walked until she'd regained enough strength to run again, but she came to the point where she simply had no more strength left.

Oliver pulled her into his arms and held her close. She wanted to point out to him that he was trembling, but she realized he wasn't the one shaking.

"I can't feel myself," she managed.

"You're in shock," he said, rubbing his hand over her back. "It's what your body does when you've had something happen to you that's past any warrior's ability to bear."

She would have smiled, but she couldn't feel her face, either.

He pulled away and nodded. "There's an outcropping of rock up that hill that will serve well enough as a perch. Can you go that far?"

She nodded, though the movement felt strange and uncontrollable. She glanced at Oliver to find him watching her with concern in his eyes.

"I am well," she croaked.

He put his arms around her again and rested his cheek against her hair. "You are the bravest woman I know."

"I don't feel brave," she whispered. She had to take a moment and simply breathe. "Thank you for saving me."

"Again, I would—"

"Don't say it."

He laughed a little, uneasily, then pulled away. "Let's go climb up that hill and make ourselves a spot for the afternoon. We'll be safe enough, I imagine."

She followed him up the hill and was more relieved than perhaps she should have been at the chance to simply sit and rest. She watched Oliver take a brief walk in both directions, then return and sit down next to her. The rock was warm and she supposed she would have been happy to close her eyes and sleep if she hadn't been so unnerved.

That, and she could also feel a stillness coming from Oliver that spoke very clearly of his watchfulness. She didn't dare hope she was safe, so she forced herself to keep her eyes open and watch the land below them for any movement.

"What happened?" he asked finally. He glanced at her briefly. "After Jamie pulled me away, which I apologize for. I assumed you would be safe from them."

"Then how did you know?" she asked wearily.

He grimaced. "I read it in a book."

She had to smile a little then. "Of course you did."

He took her hand in both of his and continued to look over the countryside in front of them. "And?"

"They wanted to put Deirdre to death," she said with a sigh. "I couldn't allow that to happen, so I showed them my mark to draw their attention away from her."

"Your mark?"

She looked at him archly. "Am I to show it to you as well?"

"I don't think I'll ask where it is," he said faintly.

She rolled her eyes, pulled her dress far enough off her shoulder to show him the mark she'd come with into her current life.

Her previous life, if luck were with her.

"It looks like a heart," he said with a faint smile.

"Does it?" she asked, pulling the cloth back up. "They didn't seem to think so."

"That was very noble of you," he said. "To sacrifice yourself for her."

"It wasn't for her," she admitted. "My mother died when I was very young and I didn't want Ambrose and the wee ones to suffer as I did." She paused. "And you were gone, so ..."

The look he gave her almost brought tears to her eyes.

"Mairead," he said in a low voice. "In truth?"

She took a deep breath. "Well, you are braw enough, so aye. But now, I don't think they'll burn Deirdre or anyone else, not after that display you put on. What was that magic?"

He smiled. "We call them fireworks, though that's just a fancy way of talking about gunpowder. It's an English thing, if you want the truth, and the most famous practitioner in your day is a man named Guy who will in a few years try to blow up important bits of London where King James will be taking a stroll."

She looked at him in surprise. "Does he succeed?"

"He doesn't," Oliver said, "and winds up in the Tower as a result. I'll leave the rest to your imagination for now, though I'll tell you later if you like." He stared out over the countryside. "I wonder about Master James," he said slowly. "It isn't as if he can put the whole clan into the fire, is it? Perhaps he'll look for riper pickings somewhere else."

"At least he won't find them at Cameron Hall," she said, shivering in spite of the sunlight. "They were a suspicious lot in the past, but no longer."

"Both Sunny and Cameron would have something to say about that," he said. "And I forgot about food, sorry. Let me show you what I brought."

She tried to eat, truly she did, but her hands were shaking too badly to manage it very well. Oliver only caught whatever she dropped—oatcakes, dried things he claimed were fruits from the Future, and equally cured meats in strips—and held it for her until she could take hold of it again. She gathered her strength to thank him, but when she turned to do so, she found him watching her as if he feared she might have some sort of fit.

"What is it?" she asked.

"Will you mind coming back with me?"

"To the keep?" she asked, surprised. "In this time?"

He shook his head quickly. "Forward, I should say. To the Future."

She was very aware there was no future for her at her home, though she would miss Ambrose and his wee siblings. But to walk into a different time entirely … that was daunting.

"You could stay with Cameron and Sunny," he said carefully.

She looked at him in surprise, but said nothing. That offer of sanctuary and shelter would be very kind, of course, but she had thought …

"Or Patrick and Madelyn," he added. "Or even Jamie and Elizabeth, if that wouldn't be too unnerving to be in the same keep yet a different year."

She nodded, because she could do nothing else. "Lovely."

He looked profoundly uncomfortable. She imagined that was because he was attempting to find a way to tell her that he would be depositing her on someone's doorstep and fleeing as quickly as possible. Perhaps that shouldn't have surprised her. It wasn't as if she'd had a long line of suitors in her time, either, so she was accustomed to it.

"It might take a few weeks to not be startled by things," he continued gingerly.

"I have a strong stomach."

He nodded and fell silent.

"You obviously have things you need to see to," she said, supposing there was no reason not to have everything out there in front of them right off.

He blinked. "I suppose so."

"I'm certain I'll have many important things to see to as well," she said, watching him to see what, if any, impression that thought might make on him.

He only nodded slowly.

"Perhaps Lord Patrick will find a place for me in his house," she added. "As a kitchen maid."

He seemed to be chewing on his words. In fact, he chewed on them so long and so well, she wondered if he might never speak again. She was a little surprised to find that she knew him well enough to be able to say that he was a man of few words and many deeds, but he had, after all, plucked flowers for her that were purple, because he'd known that was her favorite color. She suppressed the urge to simply elbow him sharply in the gut to dislodge a bit of conversation and settled for waiting him out.

He finally simply held out his hand toward her.

She looked at it, then at him.

He only regarded her with a grave expression on his face. "Or," he said very quietly, "you might stay with me."

She would have said the smoke from the fire was terrible, but they hadn't made a fire and she was freezing.

But she put her hand in his just the same. That task accomplished, she considered her next move. She supposed there was no reason not to point out things he might have missed.

"I am very plain."

"Are you?" he mused. "I disagree."

"I would say you hadn't seen my sisters, but you have."

"I have," he agreed. "And whilst they are very pretty, I think you are far lovelier."

She would have blustered a bit to save herself the discomfort of a compliment she didn't deserve, but she was honestly too unbalanced to do so. "I think you're daft."

"And I think I see very clearly."

She reached for something else he might not have noticed. "My teeth are crooked," she admitted. "Not perfectly straight like yours."

"A couple of mine are fake," he said with a shrug. "Cricket batt to the face when I was younger, so I don't care."

She wasn't entirely sure what a cricket batt was, but the result sounded painful. "Did it break your nose as well?"

He smiled. "It did, as it happened. But your nose is perfectly straight, which makes up for mine."

"'Tis a noble nose," she offered. "But for the rest of me, I don't think you've looked properly."

He turned toward her, took her face in his hands, and looked at her seriously. "I have," he said. "Your beauty comes from your soul, Mairead MacLeod, and will be shining through your features when we're both ninety and mooning over each other like a pair of wizened apples."

She was slightly appalled to find her eyes were burning, but there was nothing to be done about that. "Will I be mooning over you then?"

His expression was very serious. "I don't know. Will you?"

"Do you care if I will?"

"Very much."

"Daft man," she said, shifting uncomfortably.

He smiled and put his arm around her shoulders, pulling her close. "Is that all you have to say?"

"Daft, braw, demanding man?"

"I think there was a compliment in there," he said with a brief laugh. "Settle yourself comfortably, Mairead, and see if you can't sleep for a bit. I think we'll try the faery ring at dusk when the sunset might help us by shining in the eyes of anyone hunting us."

She shifted so she could put her head on his shoulder which she likely should have found a bit alarming given that she'd never sat with a man's arms around her, but Oliver was sturdy and solid and warm. That, and she liked very much the way he ran his hand over her hair occasionally, as if he found it, well, beautiful.

She tried to sleep, truly she did, but it was impossible. She had the feeling that what lay before them was more difficult than he wanted to admit which left her wanting to think about anything else.

"You've seen my family," she said, latching on to the first thing that came to mind. "Will you tell me of yours?"

"Hmmm," he said, shifting a bit, "well, there's not much to tell. I have four younger siblings, three brothers and a sister, but we don't speak often."

"Are they terrible people?"

"To be honest, I didn't grow up with them, so I don't know them very well. They're very involved in flattering my father, so I hear, which takes up a great deal of time."

"Is he an important man, then?"

"Well ..."

She lifted her head and put on a glare for his benefit. "If you tell me he is a duke, I will stick you."

He smiled. "Nothing so lofty, I fear, though he is a viscount. I haven't spoken to him in years, so it has little to do with me."

She suspected there was more to the tale, but whatever it was, it seemed to make him uncomfortable. She cast about for a less tender topic to discuss.

"How do you earn your bread?" she asked "Do you have a wee croft you tend, or a labor you perform?"

She didn't want to admit that discovering what he did might answer the question of how she might find a way to feed herself. Perhaps given that his father was a lord, he might have a kitchen that needed tending.

"Mairead."

She smiled before she could stop herself. There was something about the way he said her name that was far more lovely than she deserved.

"I'm thinking," she admitted.

"I recognize the activity," he said, lifting his eyebrows briefly, "and I can imagine what those thoughts are. I'll see that we don't starve."

"What are your normal labors, then?" she managed, grasping for a distraction from those very pleasing words.

He shot her a quick smile. "Other than wishing I were the Duke of Birmingham?"

She pursed her lips. "Aye, that."

"I am, I suppose you might say, a merchant." He shrugged lightly. "A bit of a fall from a duke, isn't it?"

"I believe he was little more than a landlord, so that hardly seems any loftier," she said honestly. "What sort of merchantry is your business?"

"Rich people—and nobility now and again—tell me what sort of treasures they would like to have and I get them the same."

She pushed away from him and gaped at him. "You're not a merchant, you're a pirate!"

He laughed and it was as if Sunshine Cameron's merry fire had started up, warm and lovely, directly next to her.

"My boss would be thoroughly flattered by that," he said, looking as if he found the thought particularly delightful.

"Boss?"

"The head pirate, who is also a cousin to Robert Cameron, Sunshine's husband. Lord Robert is the one who started this whole business. He has, as you might imagine, a good feel for old things."

"I daresay," she agreed, then she realized what he'd said. "Old things? Why does that matter?"

"Because some people in the Future are very fond of old things and willing to pay a great deal of money to possess them." He shot her a look. "And if that doesn't make me sound like a mercenary, I don't know what does."

"We should have stuffed our pockets then," she said frankly, "though I don't know with what."

He smiled. "We'll find things enough in my day, I suspect." He reached out and tucked a lock of hair behind her ear, then met her eyes. "Will you be all right?"

"You've asked me that before."

"I want you to be sure," he said. "I haven't given you much choice about this so far."

"You saved me from death," she said. "Life is a gift."

He smiled faintly. "Even when it might include old age with a wizened apple like me?"

She would have smiled in return, but she didn't think she dared. "Is that what you want?"

He nodded, his smile fading. "It is, but you have to decide what you want."

She couldn't bring herself to think he might be speaking of marriage, but she couldn't imagine he would have been suggesting anything else. That thought was so foolish that she had to stop herself from getting up and running away. It helped that Oliver shot her a look and took her hand, as if he could tell what she was thinking.

"Will your mates like me?" she managed. "You know, if I were to meet them." She paused. "At some point in the Future."

"They will love you. Please don't forget about me in their mad rush to surround you and wax rhapsodic about your beauty."

She pursed her lips and made a noise of dismissal, but he was only watching her with what she might have been willing to concede was affection if she'd been as daft as he was. He pulled her close again and wrapped his arms around her.

"Let's rest for a bit longer, then I think we should decide on a path back to the faery ring."

"Will they be waiting, do you think?"

He sighed deeply. "I'm hoping it's the first place they will have gone. Since they will find nothing there, hopefully they will have already returned to the keep. For all we know, Master James has spent the day accusing other people."

"I hope not," she said quietly.

"I do, too," he agreed, just as quietly. "I think your uncle Lachlan has more control over things than your brother gives him credit for, so perhaps he'll manage to stop the madness."

She couldn't deny that was true. Her uncle babbled on and on about magical things, but she had begun to suspect over the past pair of years that it was something of a ruse to draw attention away from the shrewd glances she occasionally caught him turning on her brother.

"He won't hurt Ambrose or the bairns, will he?" she whispered. "Master James?"

Oliver shook his head. "Not even your brother would allow that to happen, I don't think."

She nodded and closed her eyes, breathing carefully until she thought she could voice the terrible thought that was rattling around in her empty head.

"Might we read about what happened?"

She felt his lips against her forehead. "Of course. And keep in mind, Mairead, that if Master James went on to harm others, harming you first wouldn't have stopped it."

She nodded and hoped that was true.

The sun was setting when she found herself standing with Oliver just under the eaves of the witch's forest, well within bolting distance of the faery ring.

A pity there were so many men standing there, apparently keeping watch.

"We'll use the cottage door," Oliver murmured.

She didn't argue. She turned and slipped into the forest with him, grateful beyond measure that she'd spent her life escaping various things. The forest was still firmly situated in her day, which made things easier for her at least. She pulled on Oliver's hand when it was useful, and kept pace with him at his side when he seemed to see a clear path forward.

She saw the croft through the trees, but she didn't allow herself any of the relief she so desperately wanted to feel. She knew the threshold had worked for Sunshine and Robert Cameron ... after a fashion. She absolutely didn't want to find herself in a far different time from Oliver, not after he'd managed to save her from the fire.

She ran with him past her tree and would have insisted that they stop so she could retrieve her book—and wishing quite desperately that she'd hidden it instead in the loose stone at the back of the witch's croft—but perhaps it would be a token for someone else to study. For all she knew, it might give another Highland lass hope that she could change her own life.

Oliver threw open the croft door. The inside was completely dark, but she had expected that.

He kept hold of her hand and leapt across the threshold.

The sound of his head striking the stone above the doorway was uncomfortably loud as was the sight of him pitching forward. She felt something slam into her back and wondered if they had healers there in that Future she could see opening up before her.

She thought she might need one.

FIFTEEN

O LIVER WOKE.

The first thing that occurred to him was that he'd obviously been unconscious. That was alarming, but that was what happened to a man when he was 6'2" and not precisely made to nip in and out of vintage Scottish crofts. He wondered how it was that Cameron who was even taller than he was had managed to get himself inside Moraig's so neatly, but then again, the man had been sporting a dagger in his back and suffering from half his skull being crushed—

He sat up with a start, clutched his head, then heaved himself to his feet and staggered to the open doorway. He flicked on the lights, grateful than there were lights to turn on, then spun around to look for Mairead.

She was standing next to the hearth.

He wasn't sure what sort of sound came from him, but he hoped he never had to make the same again. He propelled himself across the cottage at something not quite a dead run and threw his arms around ...

Nothing.

He staggered back and looked at her in shock that soon turned to something very close to horror.

"No," he said, his voice hoarse in his own ears. "Please, no—"

She smiled gently. "It's all right," she said, in perfect modern English. "It's all right, Oliver, my love."

He continued to stumble backward until he felt his head make contact with that bloody doorway yet again. The pain was almost enough to do him in. Or perhaps that was the shattering of his heart. He wasn't sure and he didn't want to know. What he did know was that the first thing to do was fix what he'd botched so thoroughly—

"Oliver."

He was halfway out the door before it registered that Mairead was calling to him. He pushed himself away from impulsiveness that he had trained out of himself, then slowly turned and looked at the woman across the chamber from him.

"Build a fire, my love," she said gently, "and let us have speech together."

At least she still had her Gaelic accent. He was tempted to ask her to speak it, but couldn't bear the thought of missing anything. He was the first to admit he was absolutely not at his best, though that was perhaps the understatement of the century. Centuries. He hardly knew how to quantify it, though trying helped him bring his rampaging emotions under control.

He shut the door, locked it out of habit, then forced himself to put one foot in front of another until he'd taken himself all the way to the hearth. He didn't allow himself to look at the woman he could absolutely see out of the corner of his eye, the one wearing the same rustic dress he'd last seen her in, the one who was standing just beyond where he could have reached out and touched her.

Centuries beyond that, apparently.

He built a fire because it was something to do with his hands. He excused himself to nip in and out of the loo, wondering if things would change if he shaved and showered, then decided nothing so stupid and simple was going to change the fact that he had tried to save a woman's life by bringing her out of her time and to his.

And he'd failed.

He dragged his hands through his grimy hair, then walked back out into Moraig MacLeod's little great room.

Mairead was sitting on a hard wooden chair near the fire. He walked over and sank to his knees in front of her.

"I can fix this," he said quietly.

She reached out and put her hand against his cheek. He didn't feel it, which was one of the more difficult things he'd had happen to him over a lifetime of difficult things—

He looked at her in surprise.

Because suddenly, he remembered.

He jumped to his feet and backed away, looking at her in ... again, *horror* wasn't the right word, neither was dismay because neither had anything to do with what he was feeling. Shock, yes. Profound surprise, yes to that as well.

He almost went down to his knees again for a far different reason.

"Oliver," she said quietly.

He realized he was looking at her, yet not seeing her. He shook his head sharply, then dropped to his knees again right where he was because he wasn't entirely certain he wouldn't fall there anyway with the force of the realizations that were crashing over him like storm-propelled waves against the shore.

"You were there," he whispered.

She smiled. "What do you mean, my love?"

"For me," he said thickly. "My whole life, you've been there."

225

She looked as if she might have been weeping, though she was still smiling. He didn't want to ask, though he was ridiculously and no doubt inappropriately curious as to why he could see her.

Though he had in the past, as well.

Almost.

Memories layered themselves on top of each other, one by one, as relentless as those same waves of the sea. First was the memory of the first night his parents had dropped him off at boarding school when he'd been six. He'd had a special dispensation, of course, because his father was who he was and his mother had been eager to get him out of the house and away from her other more tractable children.

"It's more complicated than that," Mairead said softly.

He looked at her in surprise. "Can you read my mind?"

She smiled. "I can see the thoughts crossing your face, but I've been looking at that face for years, so perhaps I know you better than anyone else. Your mother is a difficult woman."

"And my father an utter arse."

"Well," she said, conceding the point with a nod, "aye. Your father is, however, a lord, which has perhaps left him a bit more arrogant than he might have been otherwise."

"He's only a viscount," Oliver said, trying not to weep. "Hardly worth saving him a decent table at supper."

His father's title had been enough, though, to win him that early entrance to boarding school which had led to some unpleasant hazing from the older lads. If he had made especial note of those same lads whilst considering doing business with them—it was odd how those deals had always fallen through at the most inopportune moment—it was likely best to leave those memories behind that door in his mind where he locked his less palatable thoughts.

"A title you don't want," Mairead added.

226

He shook his head. He would have said more, but he was suddenly awash in more memories that he hadn't thought about in years, memories he wondered if he hadn't *had* before, yet somehow he now knew he'd possessed them the whole of his life. He looked at Mairead and wondered if the agony showed on his face.

"You were there," he said hoarsely. "That first night at St. Margaret's."

She smiled faintly. "Was I?"

He would have glared at her, but he couldn't bring himself to. "You sang me to sleep." He paused, then shivered. "I can still hear the melody."

She smiled in truth that time. "You have a good ear."

"It makes pub crawls a misery."

"Fortunate are you, then, that I can string along a proper tune. And aye, I was there when they dropped you off at St. Margaret's and told you they'd be back for you in a few hours." She smiled gravely. "I also sat with you all night after the first time you ran afoul of the headmaster's birch switch."

Oliver wanted to stop her there, mostly because he preferred not to think about that first incident. He'd been but a lad of eight summers with more of a mouth on him than was appropriate and a finely honed sense of fairness that tended to inspire more words than he should have said. That first time had led to regular visits to the headmaster's office.

There were times he wondered how he'd managed to wind up as any decent sort of man.

Perhaps the answer was there in front of him.

Then he remembered, suddenly and with a clarity that left him completely unbalanced, what had happened to him on his eleventh birthday.

"Tell me."

He looked at her. "I'll weep."

"I will weep with you."

He pushed himself to his feet and decided that perhaps he could be forgiven if he spent a few minutes doing everything in his power to avoid thinking about that day. He walked over to the kitchen, poured himself a substantial glass from a bottle of whisky he was actually surprised to find lurking behind a curtain under the sink, then tossed it back without flinching. It cleared his head, but it did absolutely nothing for the state of his heart. He set the glass in the sink, then leaned on the worn wooden counter and looked out the window.

He couldn't see anything, of course, because it was pitch black outside. He imagined that was exacerbated by the fact that Moraig's was surrounded by trees, but the sight of the dark chilled him just the same.

He should have seen how many men there had been there all those centuries ago. He should have known ahead of time that Mairead's kin wouldn't give up their prey that easily. Hadn't Patrick warned him? Hadn't *Jamie* warned him? He supposed he could take the coldest of comforts in the knowledge that Mairead would have lost her life even if he hadn't intervened.

But he couldn't bear being the cause of her death.

He pushed away from the sink and walked back across the little cottage to pull up a stool and sit down in front of the fire. He looked at the woman sitting there, looking as corporeal and real as anyone else would have, and wished he'd done things better.

"I'm so sorry," he said quietly.

She shook her head and smiled, a gentle, beatific smile that held no bitterness at all. "No need, my love. It was a gift to be there for you during your youth."

He rifled back through his memories and was stunned to realize that at the worst of times when he'd thought he'd been all alone, he hadn't been.

That woman there had been with him.

"On my eleventh birthday," he said, grasping frantically for the thread of what they'd started to discuss and hoping the mere act of giving voice to his memories would keep him from weeping over them. "On my eleventh birthday," he repeated carefully, "I had snuck out the back of school, expecting to see my governess's sign that the way to her house was clear and I wouldn't be marked as missing."

"You went there often."

"She stocked my favorite chips in her pantry," he said with an attempt at a smile, "and she was a first-rate chess player."

She had also been a fabulous conversationalist with a head stuffed full of an esoteric knowledge of history and philosophy and other things that had led him to his own study of things that had completely changed the way he viewed life and what he valued.

"She was a very accomplished woman," Mairead agreed. "As well as being cannier than everyone around her."

"Especially my headmaster," Oliver said, coming close to taking a bit of pleasure in that thought. "She somehow always managed to make it so he had no choice but to engage her over whatever bait she'd set before him, which had the benefit of distracting him long enough for me to slip past him and back inside the gates." He took a deep breath, then let it out slowly. "On that day, though, our sign wasn't there, which for some reason seemed unsettling."

"And?"

"I bolted toward the school's front gates only to find her neighbor speaking to the headmaster. My governess had died that morning and her neighbor had come to tell me. The headmaster sent me away immediately, insisting that I go back inside and attend to my studies." He paused. "But you know that. You were standing behind me when I heard the news."

She nodded. "Aye, I was."

"I think he wanted to beat me the next week for skivving off to attend her funeral."

"He did," Mairead said mildly. "I believe he brought to mind the threats your governess had casually dropped in conversation, ones about how he was being watched in ways he would never discover."

Oliver found it in him to smile faintly. "I wondered why he seemed to leave most of us alone—" He looked at her in surprise. "How do you know that?"

"How do you think I know that?"

He would have smiled, but his heart was in shreds and all he could do was ignore the tears rolling down his cheeks. "Thank you."

"It was my pleasure, believe me. We might speak of it at length later, if you like. But carry on with your tale."

He took a deep breath. "Her neighbor slipped me a note at the funeral, something my governess had asked her to give me if something happened to her."

"What did it say?" she asked gently. "I know you can still see it in your mind."

He could. It was as fresh in his memory as if he were looking at it there in front of him.

"She told me that she was actually my father's youngest sister." He had to take a deep breath. "She had given up everything to buy a leaky, terrible council house next to the school so she could give me refuge."

"She was a very good woman," Mairead agreed. "And she loved you like a son."

He nodded, because he suspected that was true.

"And what was her signal atop that rock wall, my love?"

"A green house slipper," he said quietly. "She had to spend her tuppence on several pairs as the squirrels kept carrying them off."

"Oh, Oliver."

He managed some species of smile. "She finally took to wedging them under a rock in that decrepit wall that was barely standing between the sorry hovel she could scarce afford and my luxurious school that I loathed. Yet somehow she always had a lovely supper waiting for me whenever I managed to escape to visit her." He cleared his throat roughly. "I had planned to have a great deal of money some day and buy her a cozy cottage somewhere in gratitude for her care of me."

"She knows."

He didn't want to know how Mairead knew that and he most definitely didn't want to see anyone else out of the corner of his eye. He decided the best thing he could do for his sanity was to change the subject to something far less tender.

"The headmaster never threatened to hit me again after that."

Mairead inclined her head. "I won't take credit for that entirely, but I'll admit that I can be very inspiring under the right circumstances. He is also a man whose terrible thoughts showed on his visage, so it wasn't hard to distract him from them when they were so easily read."

"He had many such thoughts to be distracted from—" He sat up and looked at her in genuine horror. "You didn't watch *my* thoughts, did you?"

She laughed a little. "I left you your privacy, of course."

"Thank heavens," he said fervently. He considered, then looked at her. "You didn't watch anything else, did you?"

"What sort of saucy maid do you take me for?"

He smiled because even though she was speaking modern English, she still sounded so much like herself that he would have forgotten their terrible situation if he didn't remember it every time he was tempted to reach out and take her hand—

He blew out his breath and shook his head sharply, but that only set his head to pounding again. He looked around desperately for something to talk about that had nothing to do with what was before him, but all he could do was think about that horrible time in boarding school and how his memories of it had somehow ...

He forced himself to think about how it had been. He had, regardless of his current memories, still been dropped off as a child and left to his own devices. It hadn't taken him but a pair of years of misery to completely mentally divorce himself from his parents. They'd made that easier by always leaving him at school during holidays and over the summer, consigning him to an existence that had lain somewhere between the grimness of a Brontë novel and a genteelly austere piece of Dickensian squalor.

He'd quickly learned and then perfected his skills in being a ghost, extorting money from spoiled gits, and not talking about any of the bloody fistfights he'd engaged it. He'd never stolen anything, he'd never offered the first punch, and he'd never, ever walked away from a fight. He had spent all his time accumulating skills, knowledge, money, and nasty connections so he could one day walk up to his parents and send them into ignominity and despair.

Or he'd planned on that until he'd met Robert Cameron and his thoughts on many things had taken a much different turn. He hadn't noticed it at first, but there had been something about being trusted to do the right thing and valued for using his skills for a nobler cause that had changed him.

He also realized suddenly that there was a sweetness layered over all of his life, a deep, soul-soothing sense of having someone good love him just because he drew breath. His governess who had turned out to be his aunt Maud had certainly filled that role in his childhood.

Only now, he realized that the other constant in his life, the other stable, loving, unfailing sense of someone loving him for himself had been that woman there.

The one he could scarce see for the tears standing in his eyes.

"Thank you," he whispered.

"It was an honor," she said just as quietly.

He took a deep breath. "I'm not sure how to make this better."

Which, as it happened, was a lie. He knew exactly how he was going to make it better. He just imagined he was going to do so, as usual, less in true pirate fashion and more in superspy mode. He heaved himself to his feet.

"Oliver."

He didn't want to look at her. He wanted to be simply walking out the front door to do what was needful without fuss, without comment, without emotion getting in the way of the job to be done.

"Oliver."

He closed his eyes briefly, then looked at her. Words were simply beyond him.

She patted the chair across from her. "Rest now. Tomorrow will see to itself."

He sat only because he was half afraid he might fall if he didn't have ten minutes to simply breathe in and out and let the pain in his head ease up a bit. He looked at the woman facing him and sighed deeply.

"I can fix this."

"But at what cost?" she asked softly.

"I'll be in and out of the past, bringing you with me, in less than half an hour."

She shook her head. "You know I'm not speaking of that. I was given the chance to watch over you for the whole of your life. If you stop my death, you won't have that from me during your life."

"I'll trade that," he said without hesitation. "Not that I'm not grateful." He looked at her and hoped she could see that in his face. "I am."

"You'll need me then," she said firmly.

"I need you now more."

"But all those days," she protested. "There were so many—"

"Which I will trade without hesitation," he said firmly. He cleared his throat roughly. "I will trade all the days that came before for the days that lie ahead."

"But—"

"You are worth it," he said. "You, Mairead MacLeod, are worth it to me."

She sighed and shook her head. "Stubborn man," she said quietly. "Stubborn, braw, magnificent man."

"I think that's a compliment."

"What if you—" She stopped, then smiled. "I forget who you are."

"I won't fail."

She nodded. "I suspect you won't."

He pushed himself to his feet and tried not to have his heart lurch as she rose with him. She looked at him with what he wanted to believe was a dreadful hope in her eyes.

"I won't stop you."

"Will you regret it when I succeed?"

She pursed her lips. "I'm not going to tell you that now, ye wee fiend."

He smiled, though his heart still felt as if it were being ripped out of his chest by claws. "I'll look forward to many flowery sentiments later."

She nodded. "You'll have them."

He considered. "You don't remember anything about right now, do you?"

"How would I?" she asked with a puzzled look. "'Tis still in our future."

"Of course," he said. He considered, then looked at her. "I'll go now."

"But 'tis full dark outside."

"The gate won't care." He paused. "I might be gone for a bit, so don't worry. I'll try to get back earlier in the day—earlier today, if that isn't impossible to believe—then rescue you after I've clunked my damned head on the threshold."

She didn't look any less worried. "Please be careful."

"I will be."

He suspected that if she'd been a different sort of woman and he'd been a different sort of man, she would have begged him not to go and he would have ... well, he would have gone just the same. He very much suspected that if the roles had been reversed, Mairead would have been making one last visit to the loo to rebraid her hair before she'd bid him farewell and marched off to see to the business at hand.

He was fairly sure he might just love her.

"I'll wait for you," she said quietly.

"I'll be quick."

She only nodded, which he supposed said everything without saying anything. He would go and rescue her because the thought of living any of the days that remained in his life without her to hold as a living, breathing woman was simply intolerable.

She'd had four hundred years to get used to the idea.

He had no intention of doing the same thing.

SIXTEEN

MAIREAD SAT IN MORAIG MACLEOD'S house and contemplated a pair of things.

The first was that she was, perhaps a bit self-ishly, happy that time had caught up to events to the point where she'd actually been able to reveal herself completely to Oliver instead of just remaining discreetly outside his view.

The second was that she loved Oliver Phillips so desperately it hurt.

She would have sighed if she'd been able to, but since she couldn't, she settled for yet another in an endless series of contemplations on the mysteries of life and death and all things in between.

She had decided, once she'd resigned herself to the fact that she was indeed no longer alive, that she would simply watch the events of the world unfold in front of her without interfering. She'd managed that for the most part, though she imagined Master James, wherever he was lingering in some slag-lined pit of Hell, was still enjoying the memories of how she and her sisters of the fire had made the remains of his mortal life equally hellish.

She took a mental breath and pushed that thought aside as not helpful.

What she could say was that she'd promised herself she would stay out of Oliver's life and leave him to finding his own way. Or she had until she'd watched his parents drop him off at a school and leave him there without a backward glance.

She was, after all, very fond of children.

Outside of a few ghostly melodies sung in the quiet of the night, she supposed she'd held to her vow well enough. She'd left him to his years of yobbery and refrained from clucking her tongue at him even once. She'd absolutely left him to fending for himself in situations where she likely could have altered his path. That had been a bit more difficult than she'd anticipated, but she'd done so simply because she'd been certain that his choices then had made the man he was at present.

That braw, stubborn, magnificent man who was off in the wilds of Renaissance Scotland, trying to save her life.

Perhaps he would manage it. Several of the women he'd squired about might appreciate that, at least, given that they wouldn't have found themselves troubled at any point in an outing by any sort of restless spirit. Of course she hadn't frightened *all* of them off. Not entirely. Not with anything more than a friendly *boo* or two to liven up any given evening.

She thought she might not want to admit to any of that.

A knock on the door startled her so badly that she jumped until she realized that it hadn't been the knock of a mortal hand. She looked over her shoulder to find none other than Ambrose MacLeod, laird of her clan during those rather tumultuous and glorious 1600s, poking his head through the door.

She smiled. "Come in, nephew."

He walked through the door and snorted, no doubt for her benefit. "Auntie, I continue to tell you that I've at least thirty mortal years more than you in my current state."

"You could have chosen a more youthful appearance," she reminded him.

He sat down and plucked a mug out of thin air. "Ah, but I look so distinguished at the age of my passing. A bit like that Scottish lad who wielded all those fancy gadgets in the spy movies."

She had to admit he had a point there and she couldn't help but agree. "He was a very handsome man no matter his age, as you are in yours. What brings you to Moraig's humble hearth tonight?"

"To give you company."

She took a deep breath, then looked at him. "He's off."

"So I saw as I watched him go through the gate in the meadow."

She looked at her nephew who had indeed turned out to be an incomparable leader of their clan during his time and attempted a smile. "He is a good man."

"I think he loves you, Mairead."

"I think I feel the same way about him."

Ambrose smiled. "You know this sort of thing is my current business, don't you?"

She pursed her lips. "Matchmaking? And with your brother-in-law Fulbert and that blasted Hugh McKinnon? I'm honestly amazed Hugh is still speaking to you."

"We've made our peace," Ambrose said with a shrug. "But since this is my goodly work at the moment, I'll tell you plainly that I would like to see young Oliver succeed—for both your sakes."

She wanted to toss off a light-hearted remark about maidens in distress and those brave enough to rescue them, but she couldn't.

"What will he do without me for all those years?" she asked quietly. "And I him?"

Ambrose considered. "I'm no expert in this."

"Save for your years of unbridled matchmaking."

"I'm a romantic at heart," Ambrose admitted with a smile. "As for your very reasonable concern, even though things will change, perhaps you'll still carry in your souls an echo of those memories."

"But how?" she asked, pained. "Our paths will have changed."

He shrugged very carefully. "All I can do is speculate, but I'll give you my thoughts if you'd like them."

She wasn't sure they would be any worse than the ones she was entertaining, so she waved him on to his musings.

"We think of time as a string that stretches from beginning to end," he said, "but what if it's more like the trail of, for example, young Allan, running hither and yon to elude his exhausted parents."

"Giles and Grizel would have been less exhausted if they'd been able to stop mooning over each other," Mairead said with a snort.

"Which left Allan with several younger siblings," Ambrose agreed, "which increased the weariness and chasing for all involved. But my thinking is that time might be like his path, if you could see his path trailing behind him as he ran it, crossing and recrossing, sometimes repeating the same steps at a different moment. And surely as a mortal woman you walked over the same spots on different days, perhaps even different years. Did not the memory of your previous steps in those places ever come to you?"

"Of course," she said with a frown, "but those are memories of things you've done in the past."

"True, but what if the first time you walked to a particular spot, you recalled the memory of yourself doing the same thing, say perhaps a year later."

"That," she managed, "is daft."

"Is it?"

"That would be remembering the future," she said frankly, "and that is completely mad."

"It might be," he agreed, "but consider this: I went to Edinburgh as a youth with Uncle Lachlan and visited the exact tavern where Fiona snuck off to some ten years later. I was also there in that same tavern at *that* time, watching her spill ale down Fulbert de Piaget's front." He shrugged again, looking slightly uneasy. "Those two memories are odd to me somehow, as if I might have remembered the later one during the first one if I'd attempted it properly. Or thought it possible at all," he added.

"Ambrose, you were too busy chasing after Hugh McKinnon and wondering where to stick your dirk in him to think thoughts nearly so profound."

Ambrose laughed a little. "You have that aright, but the point still stands. You might lose your memories of being a spirit, or you might have them simply disappear until you retrace those same steps as a mortal and they come back to you." He shrugged. "Perhaps they lie somewhere between your past as a spirit and a future you will have as a mortal if Oliver succeeds, somewhere that has everything to do with both." He smiled pleasantly. "I call these *Tankard Thoughts*. What do you think?"

"I don't think you've consumed nearly enough ale," she said with a snort, then she had to smile in spite of that. "I don't think they make any sense, but I'll take comfort in them just the same."

Ambrose's smile faded. "Is he worth it to you, Mairead?"

She would have taken a deep breath if she'd been able to. Since she wasn't, she simply looked at her nephew and nodded. "Without question."

He tossed his mug into oblivion, slapped his hands on his knees, and rose. "Well, now that we've solved that, I'll be on my way."

"'Solved that,'" she echoed. "What in the world are you talking about?"

"I was just curious where your heart was."

"You already knew," she said darkly.

"And so I did." He put his hand on her head and started toward the door. "A good e'en to you, Mairead."

"You won't wait for Oliver?"

He paused and looked over his shoulder. "I've business in the south with a pair of lads who are definitely my most challenging cases yet. You and your man will sort yourselves without my aid, though I'll happily attend your wedding if I'm invited."

She rose and followed him to the door. "You know you would be, along with Fiona and her irascible husband. Can Fulbert avoid fighting with Hugh McKinnon long enough for a wedding blessing, should that miraculous day ever occur?"

"I'll see that they both behave." He smiled again, but a graver one. "Don't give up hope, Auntie. One step farther than you think you can walk might hold what you're longing for."

"More thoughts from the bottom of your cup?" she asked grimly.

"Wisdom from, if you can fathom it, John Drummond."

She shuddered. "I'm unsurprised and terrified at the same moment."

"Along with most of the northern territories of the Colonies and quite a few of his descendants," Ambrose said pleasantly, "but a shade does what he can with the tools he has to hand. The advice still stands."

"Did you offer me advice?"

He smiled, that sunny smile she'd enjoyed from him for the whole of *his* life, then walked through the door, whistling a cheerful tune. Mairead rolled her eyes, then walked back across the great room and resumed her seat by the fire. It was beginning to die out, but she didn't add anything from her own imagination to it. Her discomfort was too great for that.

She imagined that if Oliver succeeded, she would know, though how she would know was a mystery. He would lose his memories of her as a ghost, but she would lose four hundred years of being a ghost and watching the world turn before her. She had seen things she never could have otherwise, come to know kin of her own who had also taken their turns as players in the drama of life, and spent endless years wandering over her homeland.

She quite fancied the shore, if she were to be honest.

But she would trade all of it in a single heartbeat for a lifetime with Oliver Phillips.

She rested her head against the back of her chair and closed her eyes to wait.

He came inside an hour later, drenched, silent, and grim.

She stood up and moved away from the hearth. "Build a fire, my love," she said quietly.

He nodded, then knelt down by the hearth and restarted his fire. He fed it for quite a while in silence, which she understood. He was, she knew after having known him for so long in a manner she'd never expected, a man of many words when it suited him, but comfortable with silence when it didn't.

She watched him heave himself up onto a stool facing her, look at her, then go very still.

"Are you thinking of me in short pants?"

She laughed before she could stop herself. "I try not to, actually, though you were absolutely precious."

"Please, Mairead," he said with a shudder. "Concentrate on me as a man, if you would."

She made motions of putting something in a box and shutting the lid firmly, then smiled. "Done."

He smiled, then his smile faded. "Forgive me."

"For what?"

He took a deep breath. "I've obviously failed."

She shrugged lightly, though she hoped he didn't suspect her of belittling his effort. "I have no memory of it, if you'll have the truth. Will you tell me of it?"

He rubbed his hands over his face. "There isn't anything to tell. I arrived as we were fleeing into these woods, scarce managed to keep my current self from plowing into you and my former self as I did so, then I hid myself in a normal fashion and waited for events to unfold." He paused. "I didn't realize how many men there were."

"I'm surprised I was so interesting to them," she said lightly.

He lifted his eyebrows briefly. "I'm not, but that doesn't change the fact that I failed."

"Nay, my love, you retreated to rethink your plan," she corrected. "There is no shame in that."

"But you still went—"

"I know."

He bowed his head for several minutes in silence, then looked at her. "Can you forget it?" he asked, looking thoroughly devastated.

"Oliver, I did long ago. It was brief."

"I'm not sure I can bear to hear the details," he said very quietly.

"I wouldn't give them to you even if you asked," she said. "Not those, at least." She thought about that for a moment or two, then looked at him. "Is there anything else I could tell you about the night that might satisfy your curiosity, at least?"

He looked at her in surprise. "Do you remember anything about that evening?"

"I don't remember how many there were, or who was there save Tasgall and Kenneth, shrieking themselves hoarse as they dragged me away half senseless."

"Did you hear anything else? Anything unusual?"

"Besides the sound of you clunking your head against the threshold?"

He winced. "Please don't remind me. I'm still suffering from that particular headache."

She smiled. "I'll leave that then." She stretched her memory back to that particular evening that was so fresh for the man sitting across from her, then shook her head. "I was so shocked by watching you fall that I didn't think to listen. They also pulled me away from the doorway so quickly that I didn't see you lying inside the croft."

"Perhaps I wasn't."

She nodded. "I suspect that's true."

"I didn't mean to leave you behind," he said very quietly.

"It wasn't your fault." She dredged up a smile. "What else can I tell you?"

He leaned forward with his elbows on his knees and looked at her seriously. "I don't want to be indelicate, but did you ... you know."

"Pay attention to who had stabbed me?" she asked

He winced. "Yes."

"To be honest, Oliver, I don't remember much of what happened after I lost you. There was a great deal of pain, but

I think most of it came from knowing I wouldn't have you." She paused. "Though the dying was—"

"Mairead, don't," he said quietly. "You don't have to talk about it."

"I'd rather not." She smiled. "I did shout a handful of those words you mutter under your breath at them as they lit the wood."

His eyes were suddenly very red. "You, Mairead MacLeod, are terribly fierce."

"Well," she said with a faint smile of her own, "perhaps not that, but I didn't beg."

"Of course you didn't."

"Master James went on to a very bad end on a pyre himself, if you're curious."

He smiled, a crooked thing that was utterly charming. "Did you watch?"

"Of course," she said pleasantly. "Accompanied by a fairly robust collection of women—and a few men—he had put to the test of witchcraft."

"Did the gaggle of you shout any of those salty words at him as he met his well-deserved end?"

She shook her head. "We simply watched him silently because silence, as you well know, is a much more terrifying option when you have the choice."

He rubbed his hands over his face, then looked at her and smiled. "I do, as it happens, which leads me to wondering if that thought started out as someone else's."

"Nay, it was yours," she said confidently, "though I won't say I hadn't thought it myself before we met."

He nodded, then put on what she could tell was a deliberately cheerful smile. What she wanted to do was tell him to take himself off to bed, but she imagined he wasn't going to fit in that wee nook anyway. Perhaps she could eventually convince him to stretch out in front of the fire and rest his poor head.

"I had a visitor whilst you were gone," she said, looking for something to speak about that wasn't so terrible.

He looked at her in surprise. "Jamie?"

"Nay, Ambrose."

"Ambrose is a ghost?"

She smiled. "Of course. Don't you believe in ghosts?"

"Of course no—" He looked at her and shut his mouth. "Forgive me. I'm not thinking clearly."

She laughed a little, mostly because she'd had four hundred years to accustom herself to her situation. It was odd, though, wondering what her afterlife would have been like if not for Oliver Phillips and his insatiable curiosity four hundred years earlier.

And his chivalry, it had to be said.

She pulled herself back to the present moment. "He is," she said. "He's collected a little group of lads who go around with him, wreaking havoc and making matches."

"Making matches," he said, looking at her in disbelief. "As in, matches between humans?"

"The very same," she agreed. "Apparently, their success rate is very good."

"I hate to ask how they go about it."

"I would say they frighten their victims into marriage, but I'm sure there's more to it than that. I believe there is a bit of helpful nudging of various circumstances now and again."

"Ambrose MacLeod," he repeated. "Your nephew."

"He always did have a romantic streak," she said. "Who would have suspected that it would find such flowering in his afterlife? I daresay he and his companions should run some sort of service for those seeking happiness in love, but I'm not sure who would be brave enough to sign up."

He shut his mouth. "I can't believe we're having this conversation."

She laughed more easily that time. "I share the sentiment, truly. I would actually be surprised if you hadn't met at least one of his victims, though I don't think he had aught to do with your coming to Scotland."

"No, that was all the lads," Oliver agreed, then he frowned. "At least I think it was all the lads." He rubbed his hands over his face, then smiled. "I'm not sure I have the energy to think about it at the moment."

"I would prepare a meal for you, but I fear that is beyond—"

"I'll do it," he said, pushing himself to his feet. He made her a slight bow and almost landed on top of her as a result.

"I could try," she offered.

He shook his head, though rather gingerly. "I'll manage." He paused. "Wait for me?"

She looked up at him. "If you want me to."

"I can't even dance around the subject," he said seriously. "Please stay with me."

"I wouldn't think to do otherwise, actually."

He nodded, then turned away to walk into the croft's wee kitchen. He looked impossibly tired, which she understood. She hadn't wanted to grieve him any, but the truth was she could still bring to mind the events that he had recently relived. How Oliver was still on his feet when he was still carrying the weariness from their flight, she didn't know.

She realized he had turned to look at her and she smiled in spite of her sorry thoughts.

"Still here," she said, with her own attempt at cheerfulness.

He smiled gravely, then turned back to foraging in the refrigerator. She watched him pick out then put back half a dozen things before he found a baguette, broke it in half, and ate it, obviously without enjoyment. She suspected she might understand that more than she wanted to admit.

He finally came back over to stand with his back to the fire.

"What shall we do with our evening?" he asked with a weary smile.

"I'm powerfully fond of those murder mysteries on the BBC," she said promptly. "Very entertaining."

"We don't have a TV," he said.

She could have sworn she heard him add *thankfully* under his breath, but she might have been imagining that.

"A book, then?" she suggested. "I know that Mistress Moraig has several interesting titles on herbs and flowers—"

"I actually might have something better," he said, going to the kitchen to rummage about in a stack of things there. He walked back over and sat down in one of the plump chairs there. He turned on the little lamp on the table between his and a different chair covered in a lovely MacLeod plaid fabric, then reached over and patted that empty seat. "I'll read to you."

She would have blushed at the courtesy if she'd had a mortal frame, and she colored just the same as she sat down and rearranged her skirts. She looked at Oliver to find him watching her with a grave smile, though his smile faded quickly. She held up her hand.

"Please," she said quickly, wondering if she sounded as desperate as she felt. "Let us take the evening and pretend that nothing has changed."

He took a deep breath and nodded. "We'll just assume that you are your lovely self and I'm a gentleman who's decided to keep his hands off you for the moment."

"Such chivalry," she said lightly.

He inclined his head regally. "At your service, my lady." He held up the book. "What do you think?"

She read the title, then smiled. "So Mistress Buchanan has moved on to Highland lairds, is that it?"

"There is ample material here for her to use," he agreed.

She smiled at him, had a smile in return, then watched his smile fade just a bit.

"I'm very fond of you."

"And I'm very fond of you," she said. "The man you are and the boy you were."

"Thank you for leaving out the middle years."

She laughed a little in spite of herself. "Ach, weel, you were a terror."

"I've matured."

"You're perfect."

He blew out his breath and laughed uncomfortably. "That would be you, but so we don't spend our evening arguing over the truth of that, let me dive in here and see what delights await us."

She nodded and pretended that she was actually able to make herself comfortable in what she knew from past experience was a terribly comfortable chair. She would pass the evening listening to Oliver read, then see if she couldn't convince him to make himself a pallet on the floor and at least rest for a few hours. They could pretend that they had actually made it through Moraig's doorway together and they were merely taking a brief moment of quiet to rest from their journey.

The morrow would bring what it would.

She only hoped they would be able to bear those happenings when they arrived.

SEVENTEEN

O LIVER LEANED ON THE SINK in the croft's thoroughly spa-like loo and stared at himself in the mirror. Did it show on a man's face when he'd found and then lost through his own stupidity the one person he thought he might actually love?

He didn't like self-reflection. There were too many pot-holes in his past for that sort of thing to be comfortable and it was for damned sure his current straits were nothing to examine with pleasure. He suspected that if he'd been forced to meditate by some lad foolish enough to insist on the same, he would have cheerfully dealt out a great deal of gross bodily harm.

It was very tempting to wonder how much of that he could commit four hundred years in the past and not have it haunt him—

He blew his hair out of his eyes and set to the rest of his morning ablutions with an unthinkingness that somehow didn't surprise him. His eyes were full of what he'd witnessed the night before in a different century and his head equally stuffed with his own shouts of self-condemnation. It was more of an effort than he cared for to take all those very legitimate things and mentally shove them off-stage. What served him best at present was a clear-eyed, brutal assessment of what had gone wrong the evening before, not recriminations.

He'd arrived at the right time, something of a miracle in and of itself, and managed to avoid being seen by either Mairead or his own oblivious self. He'd positioned himself advantageously for a rescue, watched his original incarnation clunk his stupid head against Moraig's threshold, then watched a knife come down toward Mairead's back. It had been instinctive to take one of the stones he'd picked up on his way to the croft and fling it as hard as he could at the perpetrator.

It hadn't made much difference in the end, though Mairead had suffered a serious blow to her head instead of a hole in her back before she'd been carried off. He'd known instantly that there were too many men there for a quick grab and go, especially since he hadn't brought a sword.

He'd spared a moment of loathing for the practical side of himself that had led him to the profoundly unpleasant conclusion that it wasn't going to work. He'd slunk back the way he'd come, caught the sudden flash of a blade out of the corner of his eye, and managed a very graceful swan dive into the gate. Rolling through the centuries had been an experience he could have easily foregone, but it was over and done with.

He wondered, though, who that lad with the sword had been and how he'd known to look for someone hiking toward Cameron lands and not down to the MacLeod keep.

He pulled a t-shirt down over his head, followed by a black sweatshirt that thankfully didn't proclaim his affection for anything but remaining discreetly unnoticed, then paused to allow a very small, subversive thought to take root in his breast. It wasn't as though he didn't have those kinds of thoughts on a regular basis, but he was trying his best to be a respectable businessman in his professional life and a good guest on someone else's soil in Scotland.

But his thought at the moment was that perhaps he'd been just too polite. He'd been playing by everyone else's rules, keeping to the programme, not cheating on the maths. The truth was, he was quite a bit better at life when he was going at it as a slightly sketchy ghost.

He dragged his hands through his damp hair, looked at himself one final time in the mirror to make certain he was covered in all the right places, then faced the door and prepared to go out and pretend that everything was normal and the woman he was enormously fond of was simply skipping around in a hands-off sort of orbit for the moment. A bit of Regency cosplay, which would have suited her duke and his kitchen maid perfectly.

Only when he left the loo, he found that Mairead was wearing a Highland lass's dress with her long, glorious hair tumbling over her shoulders, looking so peaceful and good and lovely that he lost his breath. It was honestly all he could do not to stride over to her, pull her to her feet, and steal a kiss.

Perhaps more than one, if her saucy dagger remained safely stowed in the back of her belt.

But because he couldn't, he walked over to her and dropped to his knees again, right there on that uneven flagstone.

"I'm going to try again," he said without hesitation.

"Oliver—"

"Mairead—"

"You might call me Mair if you like," she said, looking remarkably shy for a ghost. "I would like it from you, I daresay."

"Mair, then," he said, realizing that his hands were balled into fists where they rested, one on the arm of her chair and the other on his thigh. Perhaps it was good she was a ghost at the moment. Perhaps by the time he managed to get her to the future as a corporeal woman, he would have gotten his rampaging emotions under control and might manage to kiss her hand a time or two before he blurted out that he was fairly certain he couldn't live without her and would she mind sharing not only his Bugatti but his bed for the rest of his life?

Put simply.

"I know what you're thinking."

"Do you?" he asked, alarmed.

"Well," she conceded, "perhaps not precisely. There is a bit of an art to it, after all. And just so you know, I've tried to leave you your privacy over the years."

"Thank you," he said weakly.

She shrugged casually. "I didn't want to pry and find that you didn't care for me as much as I wished you to."

He hardly knew where to start with that. The idea that perhaps she'd been an unseen presence in his life up until the present moment even though he'd known her—in the most chaste of ways, something he thought he should add a little extra emphasis to mentally on the off chance she was actually reading his thoughts—

"Then you don't have feelings for me?"

He blinked, then pulled himself back to the present moment with an effort. "Well, of course I do."

"You don't look like it," she said pointedly.

He rubbed his hands over his face. "I'm trying to be polite."

"Please stop."

He laughed a little, though he supposed it sounded every bit as unhinged as it felt. "Mairead MacLeod, you are without a doubt the best part of my life." He ignored the burning that had started up behind his eyes and looked at her. "I'll tell you how I feel later."

"Will there be scorching looks involved?" she asked politely.

"For you and you alone."

"Thank you," she said primly, then she seemed to be trying to decide what, if anything, needed to be added to that. "I think you should know," she said finally, "that I did my best not to intrude."

"Into what?" was out of his mouth before he realized what he was asking and how desperately he didn't want to hear her answer.

"Into your doings with other gels," she said grimly. "Though I'll admit that I did note the lassies you took to supper."

"Please tell me you limited yourself to suppers."

She glared at him. "You were hardly a monk during your university years, Master Phillips. Or afterward, if we're going to be perfectly frank."

He bowed his head and laughed because it was either that or run and hide in the loo, and he didn't run. He looked at her. "If you tell me now that you're responsible for my endless series of first dates, I'll ... well, I'm not sure what I'll do."

She shifted uncomfortably. "I'll admit nothing."

He studied her thoughtfully for a moment or two. "And here I always thought those hens never wanted to see me again because they didn't appreciate my attentions."

"'Tis possible there might be another reason," she conceded.

"Mairead," he said, dredging up as much shock as he could to put into his tone. "For shame."

"Me?" she exclaimed. "You libertine!"

He winced. "Can we stop talking about this yet?"

She scowled at him.

He pulled up a stool and managed to get his arse atop it without undue effort. He clasped his hands between his knees to keep them captive, then looked at her. He felt his smile fade in direct proportion to the silence that descended. It wasn't an unpleasant bit of quiet, as it happened, just one full of a desperate hope that likely caused every gate within a five-mile radius to shudder a bit at his determination.

"I will try again," he said quietly.

"I wish I could help you," she whispered.

He looked at his hands for a moment or two, then met her eyes. "Am I venturing where I shouldn't?"

"Don't be daft," she said briskly. "Unless you—"

"I want to."

"I want you to."

He couldn't help but a smile a bit. He started to make a list of all the things about her that he was very fond of, but he was interrupted before he even began by the chirping of his phone. Well, Patrick MacLeod's poached phone. Mairead waved him on to his business, so he wasted no time popping up and going to the kitchen to liberate Patrick's phone from where he'd hidden it under his book of torments, certain it would be the last place anyone with the brilliant idea to come steal it from him would ever look. He pulled up the message and read with hardly a flinch.

Oliver, it's Zach. I'm at Patrick's.

Oliver considered. That was an interesting wrinkle he hadn't dared put into his starched plans. He had questions Zachary Smith certainly would have answers to and if Zachary were at Patrick's, he could give those answers without James MacLeod standing there scowling over the same. He sent back his most pressing concern.

Privacy?

Bring your sword.

Oliver swore, stuck the phone in his pocket, then looked at his lady. "Care for a little walk to see your uncle?"

She rose and smoothed down her skirts. "Will they—"

"Absolutely," he said without hesitation. "They will want to see you because first, you're family, and second, you're charming. You may be offered a few opinions about why, when I manage to get you here in a different guise, you might want to make certain you haven't limited yourself to your current dating possibilities, but I suggest you ignore that bit."

She smiled. "I'll keep that in mind."

He certainly hoped she would. He grabbed his sword, opened the door and looked out to make certain there were no stray Renaissance thugs in the vicinity, then stepped over the threshold and waited for Mairead to follow him. He pulled the door shut behind them and walked with her to Patrick and Madelyn's castle.

He had scarce knocked before the door was opened and they'd been welcomed inside. He watched Mairead be welcomed without hesitation into that loving family circle and found himself questioning not Patrick's consideration for his guests, but rather the condition of his flues. Damned smoky interiors were going to be the death of his poor eyes.

"Shall we?"

He jumped a little when he realized he wasn't standing there alone, though he was grateful Zachary Smith had only asked the question quietly instead of bellowing it in his ear. He shot Mairead a smile, had a happy one in return, then followed Zachary out to Patrick's garden.

"You didn't bring a sword," he managed.

"I was giving you an excuse to rush right over," Zachary said innocently. "Besides, I figured you would just want to chat, not have a beating."

Oliver snorted, though he'd seen Zachary with a sword in his hands and been happy to have a good reason to be loitering in a different part of the man's castle. Still, there was no sense in leaving that challenge unanswered.

"I've been training with Robert Cameron," he stated, patting his sword that he'd propped up against the wall.

"And I trained with Robin de Piaget."

Oliver considered. "I hear he's good."

"He would be extremely offended by the watered-down nature of that compliment," Zachary said with a smile. "My father-in-law was, I think I can safely say, the best swordsman of his generation and quite possibly several other generations as well. Now, what do you need? Actually, what do you already know?"

"About your 1600s adventure?" Oliver asked. "The basics, but what I'd like are details about what happened when you tried to go back and rescue that girl."

Zachary made himself more comfortable atop the drystone wall. "Well, the first thing of note is that I arrived twenty-four hours *after* Jamie and I had originally walked into their little village initially."

"And you couldn't have controlled your landing more tightly than that?" Oliver asked, surprised.

"It wasn't for a lack of trying, believe me."

"Sorry," Oliver said, waving him on to the retelling of the disaster. "I'm still working on that part, so tell me all so I'm properly terrified."

"You should be," Zachary said frankly. "It was a nightmare trying to keep myself out of sight from my first me, which I didn't manage to entirely do—well, let me rephrase that. I stayed out of my own line of sight, but someone else saw me."

"Jamie?"

Zachary shook his head. "No, and I didn't stop to find out who it was. That was definitely a mistake because that person almost got us—my first incarnation and Jamie—burned at the stake right after that poor girl who in the end still met her fate."

"Brutal," Oliver managed.

"Extremely," Zachary agreed. "Jamie and I—the first me—managed to get ourselves home, but it took the second me almost two weeks to get the gate to open back up. I'm not exaggerating when I say New England winters are not anything to mess around with."

"But surely Jamie didn't leave your other self to rot there—or did he just not know what you'd done?"

"He knew," Zachary said, "and he did try, more than once. There was—and still is—something temperamental about that particular gate. I'm not sure if it was because there were two of me making trips through it at different times and the gate lost count of the return tickets, or there was something else going on." He shrugged. "It didn't work for Jamie that second time, either, so there's that."

"Couldn't you have used a different gate?"

"Well, that's the thing, isn't it? Not only did that gate take us to the 1640s, it took us across the Pond to New England." He smiled without humor. "Hopping across centuries and large bodies of water in a single bound. Hard to top that."

Oliver decided it was best to allow the utter improbability of that to continue on past them without comment.

Zachary looked at him and there was pity in his eyes. "Sometimes things happen for a reason."

"And if I could find a reason that a particular event would have been better not happening?"

"I think you could spend every moment of the rest of your life making a list of those kinds of things," Zachary said with a sigh, then he smiled. "But given that I suspect you've already made that decision for at least one thing, let me tell you why I really wanted to talk to you. Do you know Thomas McKinnon?"

"Never heard of him."

"You should look into him."

"You should save me the time."

Zachary shot him a dark look, then sighed. "Without invading their privacy too much," he said, sounding as if he were trying very hard not to do exactly that, "I'll give you a few details about Thomas and his wife Iolanthe."

"Interesting name."

"More interesting birthdate," Zachary said. "Sometime during the late 14th century, I would guess."

Oliver shook his head. "It's just a hotbed of paranormal activity up here in the wilds of Scotland, isn't it?"

"It is, which is why I sleep so well in my unassailable keep in England, though my wife's relatives do seem to show up with alarming regularity."

"Carrying swords," Oliver noted.

"More often than not," Zachary agreed. "But here's the interesting thing about Iolanthe, something I don't think she would mind me telling you. When I first met her, she'd been a ghost for over five centuries."

Oliver almost fell off the wall. He was generally a man of few, though sometimes salty, words, but he couldn't find even one of those to lay his hand on at the moment.

Zachary nodded knowingly.

"How did she die?" Oliver asked, wishing he didn't sound quite so hoarse.

"She was murdered in England, though the exact details aren't important. What is important is that Thomas met her because he'd bought the castle she was haunting."

"Yet she's here? Alive?"

"They live in Maine, but yes, she's alive."

Oliver pushed off the wall. "Let's walk."

Zachary only nodded and started across the garden with him.

"I assume he rescued her?" Oliver asked.

"He did, but that's not what I think will interest you. You see, while Thomas was off attempting a rescue and Iolanthe was still a ghost, she had anyone who would sit with her write down everything she could remember." He smiled. "Sort of as a backup, if you can call it that."

"Interesting idea," Oliver managed. He walked with Zachary for a bit, turning that over in his head for comfort, if nothing else. He finally stopped and looked at Jamie's brother-in-law. "Did she read her book?"

"I'm not sure she did at first, but in the end it didn't matter."

Oliver closed his eyes briefly, then faced his doom. "Why not?"

"Because she began to remember things from her future all on her own."

Oliver was torn between looking for a corner to use for the appropriate tear-filled activity and throwing his arms around Zachary and bawling all over *him.*

"Do you think so?" he asked.

Zachary only shrugged helplessly. "I haven't grilled her over it at Christmas, so I can't tell you specifics, but it's what I've heard. And I guess in the end maybe it wouldn't have mattered what she remembered or forgot. They're disgustingly happy together and I have to watch that up close when they're over here visiting." He shuddered. "It's really gross."

"So says the man who looks like he's been clobbered by a cricket batt every time his wife walks into the room."

Zachary laughed a little. "I'm still in a state of shock that she agreed to marry me, so that's probably true."

Oliver walked on, shaking his head at his companion's good fortune, then mulled for a bit the things he'd heard.

The first was, a successful rescue was possible. He had his own reason for believing that given that he'd managed to save Mairead at least from that initial bit of foul play in front of her home. That success was absolutely repeatable with the right plan.

The second thing that encouraged him was the idea that Mairead could have someone—possibly even him—write down her memories. Any delay in trying another trip to the past made him anxious, but the tradeoff could be worth it if she were willing.

But the third item of note ...

He looked at Zachary. "So, what you're saying," he began slowly, "is that she remembered her own future."

"The one she lived as a ghost?" Zachary asked, then he nodded. "As improbable as that sounds, yes."

"Not improbable," Oliver said. "Completely daft."

"'There are more things in heaven and earth,'" Zachary said with a smile.

"Said by an utter madman," Oliver said promptly.

"Or the only one who was sane in a cast of characters caught up in a different sort of murderous madness."

Oliver blew out his breath. "Tell me again why I agreed to talk to you?"

Zachary smiled. "You're welcome." He nodded back toward the hall. "Let's go back in through the kitchen. I know where Patrick keeps all his best snacks."

Oliver thought it wise not to pass up that opportunity, so he fetched his sword then followed Zachary around the back of the castle, forcing himself to set aside concerns and warning bells and everything else that was clamoring for his attention.

That was difficult given the sense of urgency he couldn't quite explain, one not unlike what he'd felt when he'd watched Mairead walk through the faery ring to a keep being inflamed by a madman. He would have preferred to have given her time to write down her memories, but he feared there was no time for it.

Perhaps they could simply make new ones to replace the others.

As for the business at hand, at least he wouldn't make the mistake of his first attempt, that of relying only on his ability to adapt himself to the exigency of the moment on a moment's notice. He now knew what to expect, he had a fair idea of the number of men he would face, and he had the advantage of having tried at least one method that hadn't worked.

He would go and he would do it that afternoon.

And this time, he wouldn't fail.

Three hours later, he walked through the twenty-first century forest near Moraig's house and suspected ceasing to live by everyone else's rules might not be extreme enough to do what he needed to do.

He'd made it back to the right time, avoided being seen by the men milling about the lower part of the meadow, and hidden himself in an advantageous locale where he watched two incarnations of himself—the original and his first retry— go about their business on their way to complete failure. He'd promised himself a proper assessment of the collective disaster later—perhaps with Zachary Smith, Patrick MacLeod, and a large bottle of something very strong all in the same place—then gone about trying to fix what he'd already made such a great hash of twice before.

He dismissed his unconscious self falling into Moraig's because just watching that was painful. It was even more shocking to watch his body simply disappear—presumably into the future—but he filed that away as something not to think about without that same bottle of something strong in his hand.

He'd waited until his second self had flung a rock at one of Mairead's cousins he wasn't able to name but did recognize, watched that man fall, then listened to the rest of the bloody bastards shriek that Mairead wasn't just a witch, she was a demon who could fell men around her with nothing more than her presence.

He'd known at that moment that there was no hope of rescuing her and that trying would very likely result in his own death which would most assuredly make impossible any further attempts. He had slipped back into the darkness of the forest and come back to the future, too heartsick to even dredge up a few curses with which to keep himself company.

He took a deep breath, released it slowly, then continued on his way to the twenty-first century version of Moraig's house, exhausted beyond any reasonable measure. The cottage was dark, which he knew shouldn't have chilled him as it did, but it had been that sort of evening.

He didn't care for failure.

No, that didn't come close to stating just how deeply he loathed it. In fact, he despised it so thoroughly that he'd made a career out of never being in a position where he did anything but succeed brilliantly and he did that by compensating for every contingency he'd mapped out thanks to knowing all the answers beforehand. His research methods were impeccable, his sense of direction flawless, and his competitive nature only matched by Derrick Cameron's on Wednesdays and Fridays. The lad had to have time to recover, which Oliver tended to discreetly neglect to notice.

He took a deep breath and opened the cottage door. He almost hesitated to reach inside and turn on the lights, which made him angry at himself. Better that, perhaps, than being devastated that not only had he failed to rescue Mairead, he'd watched her brother almost knock her out in his fury whilst screaming at her that she was in league with demons.

He imagined Tasgall had been talking about him, which was yet another reason to aim a little fury at himself.

At least Mairead hadn't been stabbed, which he supposed would be something to discuss with her later if she could bear it. For the moment, he would go inside, drop to his knees, and apologize for failing her.

And then ... well, he had no idea what he would do then.

He flicked on the lights to find the cottage empty.

He spun around and flung himself out the door. He ran in the only direction that made sense to his poor fogged brain which was toward the meadow. He came to an ungainly halt at the edge of the forest and simply stared into that open, moon-drenched expanse.

Mairead was standing there in that moonlight as if she'd been something from a dream. He leaned over with his hands on his thighs until he'd caught his breath, then straightened and walked until he was standing five paces from her. She turned and smiled at him, a gentle, beautiful smile that was full of nothing but affection. No condemnation, no anger, no disappointment, just love.

He stood there and watched her with the moonlight falling down on her, somehow turning her into something that wasn't quite corporeal yet wasn't quite a dream, and for the first time in years had absolutely no idea what to do. He had come to the conclusion, as he'd tried to avoid the other rescuing incarnation of himself, that he had two choices.

He either needed help.

Or he needed to give up.

"We could try living as we are," she said quietly.

He looked at the woman standing in front of him, part dream, part the embodiment of almost everything that had been beautiful in his life in a way he only understood at that moment, and could do nothing but nod.

"All right," he agreed quietly. "We'll try."

EIGHTEEN

M AIREAD SAT ON A STONE bench pushed up against the wall of her ancestral keep and marveled at the changes in her life.

Well, the changes to her post-mortal existence, if she were to be exact. It had always been full of things she had never expected: generations of family passing by her, the doings of men and monarchs parading before her eyes, the turning of the world from dawn to dusk with a constancy that had been particularly soothing.

It had also been full of a sense of waiting, perhaps more than she would have suspected it might be. In that, at least, she almost envied Oliver his not having to wait so long to see her.

Assuming, of course, that such a thing was important to him.

"He's looking pretty ferocious today."

She looked to her left to find Sunshine Cameron watching Oliver thoughtfully. "Do you think so?" she asked.

Sunshine smiled at her. "It's almost as if he's working extra hard to be prepared to have something he wants very much."

Madelyn leaned in from Sunshine's other side. "And that wouldn't be more time with my husband over swords," she said with a smile that was the echo of Sunshine's. "In case you were wondering."

Mairead couldn't help but admit that she was, so she nodded. She looked at the woman sitting on her right and only had a smile in return.

"He's not swearing," Elizabeth offered. "In my experience with Oliver Phillips, that means he's very serious about whatever he's doing. Jamie isn't showing him any mercy, in case you were wondering about that as well."

Mairead nodded over that as well, though she imagined that if she'd had a mortal form, her mouth would have been dry as dust from fear. It was a well-known fact that MacLeod men were terrifying in battle and Jamie was no exception to that. He was showing Oliver no mercy, though Oliver didn't seem to expect any. Perhaps the rub of Oliver's having gone back to try to save her irritated them both equally.

Oliver called peace shortly thereafter, which she suspected he did unwillingly and only because he looked as wrung out as she'd ever seen him. Both Jamie and Patrick spoke with him quietly for a moment or two, no doubt giving him areas for improvement, then all three shook hands like gentlemen and left the field.

Mairead watched Patrick gather up his lady and her sister and escort them back to the hall. Jamie made her a slight bow, then smiled at his wife.

"Where are the bairns?"

"Hopefully not tearing the hall to shreds with the little ones," Elizabeth said cheerfully.

"Young Ian will keep them in check, as he should."

Elizabeth stood up and kissed him briefly. "He has you as his example, my laird, of course."

Mairead watched Jamie harrumph a bit in pleasure and suspected he did it merely for his wife's benefit. He smiled at her briefly before he clapped a hand on Oliver's shoulder, exchanged a look with him she didn't try to decipher, and walked off with his lady around the side of the keep to no doubt use the front door. Mairead rose and smiled a little at the low bow Oliver made her.

"My lady," he said, straightening.

"My—"

"Please," he said with feeling, then he smiled. "You know there's nothing left at the tail-end of my father's stylings for me that requires genuflecting."

"Shall I settle for something sentimental, then?" she asked, trying to match his light tone.

He stroked his chin in a manner that reminded her so much of Jamie, she almost laughed. He considered, then looked at her.

"Beloved?" he suggested.

"Aren't you cheeky," she said with a smile.

He simply waited, smiling faintly.

"Very well, *beloved*," she said pleasantly, "let us away and see if there might be something in your book we could accomplish together this afternoon and win you your freedom."

He nodded, though she could see that he was thinking thoughts that would have been termed subversive if looked at in the right light. Then again, she knew what to look for and had years of experience with how Oliver Phillips took on things that either vexed him or intrigued him.

There was a part of her that couldn't help but wonder how it would be to forget all the things she knew about him and meet him again. She suspected that even with her brief relationship with him in the past as a beginning, she would have continued to fall in love with him just as easily.

"You're thinking."

She pulled herself back to the present moment. "A bad habit that you share."

"So I do," he agreed. He rested his sheathed sword against his shoulder and nodded up the meadow. "Moraig's, then?"

She nodded and forced herself to walk with him as if she'd actually been able to feel the earth beneath her feet and the wind in her hair and hear the measured breathing of the man next to her. If she'd dared, she might have even imagined his hand around hers, keeping her close to him as if she'd been something precious that required protecting.

He was quiet, though, and she suspected that his silence spoke of deep thoughts indeed, thoughts that wouldn't be limited to what he might find lurking in the refrigerator behind the green things Patrick's lad Bobby had brought him that morning.

So she clasped her hands behind her back, put her face forward, and decided she would do best to simply wait him out.

She began to wonder, as she sat an hour later in Moraig MacLeod's house—a place *she* had sat with Moraig MacLeod on several occasions to chat about the lovely things to be found in gardens and meadows—if the idea that she might be able to have an existence where she was a ghost and the man she loved was a beautiful, stubborn, magnificent man might just not be possible.

She looked up as the man himself came out of the luxurious garderobe. After all her years of hobnobbing with mortals, she was accustomed to their manner of garbing themselves. She had to admit, however, that whilst she might not have had a mortal frame any longer, her poor spirit's heart beat just a bit faster at the sight of Oliver Phillips in jeans and a black t-shirt.

He was fussing with his fancy silver watch, which gave her time to get her rampaging emotions under control.

Or, perhaps not.

He looked at her and lifted an eyebrow. "Are you, my lady Mairead, lusting after me?"

"If I had the strength, I would throw something heavy at you," she said, trying to manufacture a scowl for his benefit.

'Twas impossible. The man was charming and quiet and stubborn and had a very lovely pair of pale blue eyes. She watched him make her a small bow, then excuse himself to make something to eat. She supposed she should have gotten up to at least keep him company whilst he was at his labors, but she couldn't bring herself to move. It was enough to pretend that, had she been a mortal woman, perhaps he would have been her man and they might have been doing nothing more noteworthy than enjoying a holiday together in Moraig's croft.

She couldn't bring herself to entertain the knowledge that there would come a point in his life when he would want a corporeal woman to warm his bed and give him bairns.

She looked up to find him leaning back against the range, studying her thoughtfully.

"What?" she asked crossly.

"I'm thinking about second dates."

She would have blushed if she'd had a proper physical form for it. Then she realized what he was saying.

"Your second dates with other women?" she asked in surprise.

He pushed away from the range and walked across the great room to hunker down in front of her. "Actually, I was thinking about second dates with you."

"Were you?" she managed.

He nodded. "Will you date me now?"

She could scarce believe she could blush in her current state, but apparently 'twas possible. She looked at him, then nodded.

"Or something maybe a bit more permanent?" he asked quietly.

"Your eggs are burning."

He swore, then jumped up and strode over to rescue them. She watched him quickly prepare the rest of his meal, then come to sit next to her. He ate, but he was a man and likely rarely found himself put off his food.

He finished, put his dishes in the sink, then returned to sit next to her. He looked at her and simply waited.

"What?" she asked finally.

"I asked you about something more permanent than dating," he said gravely.

"Is that a proposal?" she asked.

"You knew me when I was ten," he said dryly. "I would likely be taking a very great chance even asking you out, never mind anything more serious."

"I've lov—erm, I mean *been very fond* of you for your entire life," she said seriously. "Ask me again another time."

"I'll remind you of this conversation."

"I won't believe you."

"I'll find a way to convince you."

"That won't be difficult."

He smiled briefly, then rose and went to wash up his supper things. She watched him as he did so and suspected he was dragging out the entire business because he was entertaining thoughts he knew she wouldn't care for. She had no trouble divining what those thoughts might be.

He walked over to her, then dropped to his knees in front of her.

"Let me change this," he said quietly.

271

"Oliver—"

"I beg you."

"How do I agree?" she asked frankly. "How do I leave you alone all those years in your youth?"

"I'll survive."

"I'll forget all the English I've learned," she said, trying to dredge up something that sounded reasonable.

"You can relearn it." He sat back on his heels. "And if you forget all the things you've learned about me over the course of my life, then after I've safely rescued you, you decide that you fancy someone else, I'll survive that too."

"Will you?" she asked in surprise.

He scowled at her. "Of course not," he grumbled. "I'll slink off to a corner and howl off-key pub ditties until you beg me to stop, then I'll begin again with asking you on a first date."

"Well," she said slowly, "I do know you from my mortal past and I'm fairly certain you almost kissed me on our rocky perch on Cameron soil."

"I was afraid you'd clout me in the nose if I tried."

She smiled. "You weren't."

"It's all about timing, love," he said pleasantly, then his smile faded a bit. "I'd like to kiss you for the first time on the edge of the sea, if you want the truth. To make it memorable."

"You'd best not admit that to your mates," she said, feeling a little breathless. "They'll never stop teasing you for being such a romantic."

"I'll bear it," he said, "especially if you won't bloody my nose for attempting it."

She shook her head, but found herself suddenly unequal to any more words. He was in earnest, she knew, and she wasn't sure she could stop him even if she wanted to.

Accepting that she wanted him to try one last time was more terrible than she'd suspected it might be.

He shot her a look full of what she suspected might have been a suggestion that she not think so much, then he smiled and pushed himself to his feet. He fed the fire again, then sat down on the soft chair that lay at an angle to hers.

"Time is an odd thing," he said.

"How so, my love?"

He smiled briefly at her, then he shrugged. "I was thinking about Jamie and his endless lectures on the perils of changing the past. I didn't listen and look where it's left us."

"I don't regret the time I had to watch over you."

"I don't either, actually," he said, looking at her seriously, "though those memories are rather newly arrived."

"'Tis odd, that," she mused. "That your memories now hold me, but before you came to Scotland surely you didn't know who I was."

"Yet I knew you somehow. The first night I was at Jamie's, I almost tripped over you at the top of his stairs."

She looked at him in shock. "'Twas the same for me. And I saw you in the forest."

"And I you," he agreed. "Who's to say we wouldn't have echoes of these memories just the same? Then again, you might not want to give up memories of the past four hundred years."

"I've written them down."

"You have?" He sat forward and looked at her in surprise. "How?"

"I *can* write," she said archly. She smoothed her hair back from her face. "Do you think Mistress Constance Buchanan is the only woman with volumes to her name?"

He laughed a little. "Did you write *romances?*"

"Historical fiction," she corrected. "And they were to be, if I may say so, very light on the historical part."

"Where is your book?" he asked, sounding a little breathless. "Or do you have more than one?"

"I haven't gotten to them yet," she admitted, "though I have plans for several. I had even chosen a lad to write them down for me."

He sat back and looked at her with bright eyes. "I have to know the details. Tell me who, where, and what he did the first time you arrived in his study for a wee get-to-know-you chat."

She pursed her lips at him. "He was a Victorian Englishman who'd come to Scotland to document its glories for a yet-to-be-secured audience in London. He had come to stay with the McKinnons, which I suppose was his right given that he hailed from that line. And the first time I approached him in William McKinnon's study as he was sipping on whisky he'd brought with him, he leapt to his feet and dropped his finely cut glass against the stone of the floor." She paused. "I did feel terrible about that."

Oliver was resting his chin on his fist and watching her with an affectionate smile. "I can only imagine. And then?"

"I told him I was his maiden aunt to try to encourage him to stop screaming." She shrugged. "I thought if he considered me a friendly spirit, he might stop taking refuge in senselessness every time I attempted to speak to him."

"Very sensible."

"I thought so," she agreed. "He eventually accustomed himself to me long enough to take down a few tales that he thought were fiction, though they were actually my memories. 'Twas more palatable for him that way."

"No doubt," he said, nodding. "What happened then?"

"He rushed off to make an appointment with a printer in Inverness, then fell into a bog and drowned."

Oliver put his hand over his eyes, then shook his head and laughed a little. "Oh, Mair," he said with a miserable smile. "I'm sorry."

She couldn't help but return the smile. "It was a bit of a tragedy, especially given that he'd already penned several in his series of essays about traveling through our beautiful land. He put his work in a strongbox that was buried alongside him, though who knows if it survived. He decamped for the south of France two hundred years ago, but I could find him." She paused. "Perhaps."

"I'll help you find him," he promised, then he hesitated. "Would that be enough? Those memories you have written down?"

She looked at him seriously. "I thought we were going to try to make a life as we are," she said quietly.

Though in truth, sitting with the women in Oliver's circle of family and friends that morning whilst pleasant had been difficult. Especially when she'd watched those same women be collected by their men or go off themselves to collect their children and all she'd been able to do was stand and watch.

But what Oliver would give up ...

"Jamie lifted his eyebrows this morning," Oliver said. "I think that was meant to give me complete autonomy where the gate in the meadow is concerned."

She pursed her lips at him, but he only smiled in return.

"He stroked his chin twice."

"Thrice," she corrected. "I counted."

"See? I'm sure that signals approval." He leaned forward with his elbows on his knees, his expression sobering. "Please let me try one more time."

"But your memories," she protested.

"I wrote them down last night."

"I thought you were working on your book from your lads."

He shook his head. "I thought it might be a handy thing to have. And I didn't tell you what I discussed with Zachary yesterday, did I?"

"You did not."

"It was an interesting conversation," he said began carefully. "Do you know anything about your aunt Iolanthe?"

Mairead shook her head. "Who was her father?"

"I didn't get that far," Oliver admitted. "We were too busy discussing the fact that when Thomas met her, she'd been a ghost for almost six hundred years."

Mairead felt the world around her suddenly go very still. That happened occasionally, when something of great import had been on the other side of a few hours or days from where she'd been lingering. She'd felt it several times in the past before happenings in the world or in her clan or, if she were to be precise, in Oliver's life.

She couldn't remember the last time she'd felt it in relation to her own poor self.

"A ghost," she managed. "How interesting."

"It is," he said carefully. "From what I understand Thomas went back before she was slain and saved her—which is interesting but not the most interesting part. Apparently she wrote down her memories whilst she was a ghost. Or, rather, others wrote them for her as she dictated them."

"As I tried to do with Sinclair McKinnon."

He nodded. "Exactly that. But even though she'd written those things down, she apparently began to remember things all on her own."

"Things from her time as a spirit?"

He nodded slowly.

"But those were her memories," Mairead said quietly, "not her man's. If you rescue me, you'll lose *your* memories of me."

"I wrote most everything I could remember down," he reminded her. "And I'm going to trust that I'll remember the rest on my own."

"But what will become of you in your youth?" She paused. "I know you survived it without me the first time and I'm not the reason you're a good man—"

"You put beauty where there had been none," he said seriously. "And for that I'm grateful." He smiled. "Perhaps you'll need to pick *me* a few flowers in the future to make up for it."

She couldn't make light of it. "Oliver ..."

"I know what it will mean." He paused and his expression was so serious that it almost brought tears to her eyes. "I'll trade that willingly for a future with you."

She reached out to put her hand on his arm, then stopped when she realized it was pointless. She clasped her hands together instead. "But after your aunt passes, you will be alone."

"It will make having you in my arms again that much sweeter."

She pursed her lips. "You haven't yet had me in your arms."

"That's absolutely not true, but it is something I would like to remedy as quickly as possible."

She smiled uneasily. "Is that so?"

"Are you blushing?"

Her smile faded. "Oliver, I am not—"

His phone rang suddenly. She would have been startled, but she was too old for that sort of thing and it wasn't the first time she'd heard it. He smiled.

"Excuse me a moment. I'm sure it's just the lads telling me where to go find more pages to add to the book of horrors you're helping me finish."

She watched him walk over to Moraig's tiny kitchen and wondered if it might be possible to fix into her soul somehow the memory of things that had been, over the past four centuries, lovely and good. Conversations with others who had taken their turn in her clan, standing on the periphery of happenings of historical significance, watching the seasons continue to turn and marveling at the beauty that was her homeland. She had particularly lovely memories of Moraig and her connection to that procession of the world's turnings.

Perhaps there was some possibility that, as Ambrose said, when she walked the same paths again, the echoes of her memories from each day of those same years in her past would be there waiting for her.

"Let me text you," Oliver said, putting his phone down in the kitchen.

She watched him as he walked over to her, that braw, determined man who had paid such a price in self-discipline to become so fully what he'd become. He knelt down in front of her and looked at her.

"The lads are waiting for us at Cameron Hall."

She attempted a smile. "More pages for your book?"

He shook his head slowly. "Strategy session."

She took a deep breath—well, she went through the motions of the same in hopes that it would calm what should have been her racing heart.

"I don't want to lose my memories," she admitted.

"I know."

"But we might make new ones."

"On every blessed day of all the days that lie before us," he agreed. "And I will remember at least this conversation for the both of us. We can work on the rest as the days go on."

She closed her eyes briefly. "I wish you could hold me."

"Remember that thought."

She smiled at him. "I don't think I'll need to."

He pushed himself to his feet, groaning a little as he did so. "I think that may be all the kneeling I can do for a bit. If I propose on my feet, that's why."

"I won't remember it."

He laughed softly and moved to bank the fire. "I'll remind you."

She watched him finish his work and put the rest of Moraig's house to bed. It was scarce noon, but she felt as if she'd been awake for years.

Which, she supposed, she had.

Oliver picked up his phone when it chirped at him, then looked at her. "Cameron's sending a helicopter."

"I think I'll just wish myself to his front door and save myself the trip with you, thank you just the same."

He shook his head, but he was smiling. "I don't think I want to know how. Will you at least walk with me to the meadow?"

"And keep you far from the gate? Aye, of course."

He smiled. "Everything will be all right, Mairead."

The saints pity her for a lovesick fool, she actually believed him.

She walked with him through the woods and found that there was indeed a helicopter swooping down from the sky like a terrifying bird of prey. She imagined such a thing wouldn't have been able to fit through that gate in the faery ring, but she couldn't help but wish it could have and she could have watched Kenneth faint from his terror over the sight.

She suspected she might have a bit of work still to do on forgiving a few souls in her past.

Oliver stopped and looked at her. "You'll meet me there," he said, pinning her to the spot with the force of his gaze alone.

How could she not? She nodded. "I will."

"If you get there before me, please wait for me."

She could only nod.

She watched him climb into the little glass ball, then continued to watch as the blades attached to its top spun madly and lifted the beast off the ground. She watched Oliver hold up his hand to her and she returned the gesture.

She closed her eyes and pretended to take a very deep breath, then let it out slowly. She had been waiting four hundred years for time to bring events back to a place where she might have what she so desperately wanted in the person of a courageous, honorable, beautiful man.

She imagined she could wait a few more whilst he did what he needed to do to have her in his arms.

NINETEEN

O LIVER WALKED AROUND THE CORNER of Cameron Hall and was more grateful than he likely should have been that his most recent trip in Cameron's natty whirlybird had been made whilst he'd been unfettered. He was also pleased to think that his zip ties and sundry were still safely tucked away in James MacLeod's hall where they would absolutely be used in the future, and not on him.

He came to a skidding halt on the gravel drive there in front of the hall and wondered when it had happened that he'd so completely fallen into something when it came to a certain woman of his acquaintance.

Something that felt a great deal like love.

Mairead was leaning back against the hall with her hands tucked behind her, watching the sky, a look of such peace on her face that it was all he could do not to trot over to her, drop to his knees right there in the rocks, and ask her to marry him.

In fact, that sounded like the best idea he'd had all day, so he wasted no time in approaching, then attempting the second. Or he would have if she hadn't held out her hand and stopped him.

"The rocks are sharp."

He stopped halfway to his knees, then straightened. "How do you know?"

"One of your mates came out to check on you and forgot his shoes."

He considered. "Peter?"

"Possibly," she said thoughtfully. "He looked at me, squeaked, then bolted back inside."

Oliver smiled. "He didn't."

She smiled in return. "He did blurt out a very polite greeting with my name attached, but there was definitely squeaking. Perhaps he was eager to return inside to their plots and schemes."

He felt his smile fade. "They're very good at this sort of thing," he said quietly.

"I've seen them," she agreed, "but I'll pretend I don't know anything and just enjoy your parley."

Considering the discussion would center around how he was going to get back to her time, avoid a trio of his own eejit selves, and manage to get her to the future before she was slain, he couldn't imagine she would enjoy it much. He took a step backward and made her a low bow.

"I won't fail this time."

"Oliver—"

"You don't need to spare my feelings," he said simply. He paused. "I was impulsive."

"And you're never impulsive."

He lifted his eyebrows briefly. "Not usually. Then again, I've never been trying to get anything I've wanted quite this much."

She waved him away. "Get on with you, lad, and be about your business."

He smiled and nodded toward the door, setting aside thoughts of proposals for a more auspicious moment. "Come with me? I'd like to introduce you to my terrible friends. You've already met my laird."

She nodded, then walked with him to the front door. He opened the door, ushered her inside, then paused for a moment to take the measure of the situation that lay in front of him.

First was the absolute splendor of Cameron Hall. The place had been, as they tended to say on the telly, sympathetically updated and expanded over the centuries until it had its share of homely comforts without having lost any of its medieval glory. He could remember with perfect clarity the first time he'd walked inside and wondered, unironically, if he'd stepped back in time hundreds of years.

Second and perhaps more importantly was the collection of Cameron's modern-day clan clustered around the hearth. There was Cameron himself, of course, and Sunshine, along with Derrick and Samantha and Peter and Ewan. Madame Gies was there, no doubt making certain everyone was comfortable and fed, along with her granddaughter Emily, she of the excellent taste in absolutely everything.

He looked at Mairead, had a nod in return, and walked across the great hall to join them.

He was very grateful that Sunshine immediately came to meet them halfway.

"Mairead," she said with a welcoming smile. "I hoped you would come with Oliver. Why don't you come with me and I'll introduce you to everyone?"

Oliver watched as his self-appointed older sister took his lady in hand—figuratively, for the moment—and led her over to that collection of souls he had to admit he was somewhat fond of. He would be fonder of the men once he'd repaid them all for their part in his holiday, though perhaps his vengeance would be tempered with a bit of gratitude that their actions had led in a fairly roundabout way to his encountering ...

He had to take a deep breath at the thought of how easily he could have missed meeting a woman he thought he just might love.

He watched that collection of souls welcome Mairead into their midst—even Peter, who only gulped, then put his shoulders back and got on with business.

He watched the ladies there gather Mairead up and bundle her off to the kitchens where he suspected they would at least try to make her feel as though she could enjoy a cup of tea. He, on the other hand, was abandoned in the spot where he'd stopped. Unfortunately, he was soon joined by a pair of his mates who seemed not in the slightest bit concerned over the fates that awaited them.

"You're still a dead man walking," he reminded Derrick.

Derrick pursed his lips. "I promoted you."

Ewan stuck his head between theirs. "He did? You did?"

Derrick flicked Ewan between the eyes without looking, which Oliver appreciated. He also supposed it might be considered a mercy to keep his boss at arm's length instead of in an inescapable headlock, so he stepped aside and allowed Ewan a bit of room.

"What's your new title?" Ewan asked.

Derrick cleared his throat. "Vice President of Skulduggery and Snoopery."

"It's the other way around," Oliver said crisply.

"As if you know anything about either," Ewan said with a snort.

Oliver reminded himself that he needed Ewan alive for at least another twenty-four hours, but that didn't preclude delivering an elbow to the lad's gut.

"Why don't I get a title?" Ewan wheezed.

"You wouldn't like my choice," Derrick said shortly.

Ewan slung his arm around Oliver's shoulders. "When you kill him and take over the company, will you give me a fancy title?"

Oliver shot his colleague a cool look. "What leaves you thinking you'll outlive him?"

"You need my vast stores of knowledge about the fairer sex and how not to make an arse of yourself when you're around them, which, considering your hopeless state, means that I should get a lofty title *and* a very generous raise."

Oliver had to concede that Ewan definitely excelled where the rest of them floundered when it came to women. The lad was perfectly willing to fling the Cameron name and his own unfortunately abundant amounts of charm around like rose petals, then scoop up all the willing—if not a bit bamboozled—maidens fair who found that sort of thing mesmerizing. Oliver wasn't entirely sure that Ewan could talk about anything besides the hoity-toity rubbish he himself loathed, but there were obviously girls who enjoyed that.

"Kill him first," Derrick advised, "and save yourself the aggravation. Let's go talk in Cameron's office. Your girlfriend can join us any time she likes."

"Girlfriend," Ewan said thoughtfully. "That means there's still hope—"

Oliver wondered if Ewan had permanent bruises from the elbows to the gut he seemed to take regularly, then decided it wasn't worth investigating. He did make his way with his collection of mates to the laird's downstairs office where he found that a detailed outline of Moraig's forest and the surrounding environs had been marked out on a large white board. There were magnets waiting in a patient line down one side, proper black ones only polluted with one pink kitty face.

"For your lady," Ewan said, rubbing his hands together. "She'll appreciate the utter cuteness of the kitten, which will lead her naturally to associate charm and adorableness with your sorry self."

Oliver looked at Derrick, had a shrug in response, then decided that perhaps he wouldn't kill Ewan right off. The man might prove to be useful. He held back and watched as Derrick, Ewan, and Peter arranged things to their liking for a proper strategy session, ignored the fact that they seemed perfectly happy and attached to their devices, and further ignored the truly unnerving thought that he didn't entirely loathe the idea of occasionally being unplugged.

He looked to his left to find the laird of the current clan Cameron standing there, watching him with thoughtfully.

"My laird," he said, making Cameron a small bow.

Cameron only smiled. "How are you, Oliver?"

"Wishing I'd been less impulsive," Oliver admitted.

"If there's anything I would never call you, lad, it would be impulsive, but love makes fools of us all sometimes. We'll help you sort this."

Oliver let out his breath slowly. "Thank you, Cameron." He looked at him seriously. "For more than this."

"Don't get all maudlin on me," Cameron said with another smile. "We'll either drink or weep later, whichever you like. I might also send you and your lady on a proper holiday somewhere sunny after you've rescued her. There's a useful thought for you."

"I won't argue," Oliver said. "And if you'll excuse me, my lord, I'm being summoned to go and play with magnets."

Cameron waved him on to the white board and he went, feeling a bit more himself with each step. He set aside the recrimination that he should have done this the first time around because there was nothing useful to be gained from flogging himself over things that were dead and gone, so to speak. Perhaps there was also something to the old saying that the third time was the charm.

He sincerely hoped so.

"How many lads?" Derrick asked. "And where were they?"

He shook aside his useless thoughts and focused on the discussion at hand. "Which time?"

Peter held out a bag of blue magnets. "Another color for a different time. Want green as well?"

"We'll need both, plus the black," Oliver said grimly. "We'll need to account for the first time and my subsequent two tries."

"Give me details about each," Peter said, setting out magnets, then reaching for a legal pad. "Call them black, blue, then green so I can keep it straight."

Oliver considered, then arranged magnets on the board within the outlines of Moraig's forest to the best of his memory. He put Mairead where she'd been, ignored the improbability of his own damned unconscious self disappearing just inside Moraig's doorway, then stood back and studied the board.

"Is that it?" Derrick asked.

"I'm thinking."

"What did you miss during the first two rescue attempts?"

Oliver found his hand halfway to his chin, which was alarming in and of itself. He stroked just the same and suspected he might understand why Jamie did it so often. He held up his index finger to request a moment, then walked around the perimeter of Cameron's office, ignoring his glorious surroundings and putting himself back in Renaissance Scotland.

He came back to himself an indeterminate amount of time later to find those lads he'd gone on innumerable adventures with in the present—along with that rather alarming trip to 1602—simply watching him patiently. Well, Ewan looked as if he might be brewing up a particularly annoying smirk, but since that was nothing new, it was a bit comforting.

"I missed someone," he said carefully. "And I changed things, if you want the entire truth. The first time, Mairead remembers having someone stab her in the back, but that changed after my first attempt."

"You stopped that, at least," Cameron offered.

Oliver couldn't bring himself to point out that it hadn't done Mairead any good, so he nodded and continued.

"Time One, I got to Moraig's and realized just how many lads there were. Seven or eight, at least, and not in their right minds." He looked at Cameron. "I couldn't fight that many."

"Not without a sword and a running start on a horse," Cameron agreed. "Trying to stay out of your own way yet rescue your lady is a complicated business. Just out of curiosity, how did the fireworks go?"

"Brilliantly," Oliver said without hesitation. "I suspect it became clan legend, though I haven't had the heart to go dig through history to find out for certain. Thank you, my lord, for such superior firepower."

Cameron nodded and waved him on. "We have more, if that would be useful, though I'm guessing a more surgical attempt would serve you better here."

"Agreed," Derrick said. "What else on the second trip? And leave aside your unconscious self on Moraig's floor."

"Which wasn't there in the past because I'd fallen through to the future," Oliver pointed out.

Derrick looked at him for a moment in silence, then shut his mouth and nodded briskly. "Fair enough, if not a little unsettling. I'm assuming you also avoided your first rescue-attempting self well enough."

Oliver shuddered a little at the memory, in spite of vowing that he wouldn't. "Beyond the absolute barking nature of that, yes, I managed to keep out of sight of my first self, but—" He had to stop and take a deep breath before he could admit the truth in all its unpleasant starkness. "I was tempted to ignore the cosmic ramifications of the first me seeing the second me and simply go snatch Mairead from her cousins, but I'll admit I hesitated. She was barely conscious from being struck in the head, I noticed the gleam of a blade where I hadn't before, and I didn't see how I could carry her and escape seven or eight—"

"Which was it?" Derrick interrupted. "That might be important."

Oliver closed his eyes and ran through the details with a dispassion that was oddly comforting. He considered, then opened his eyes and looked at Derrick.

"Seven I could identify," he said. "Plus one in the shadows who I can't."

Derrick waved him on. "We'll put that lad in red. Peter?"

"Here, boss," Peter said, tossing him another magnet.

"And when you came back through the gate?" Derrick asked.

"Someone followed me at least to the meadow," Oliver admitted. "If I hadn't been looking for his blade in my back, I wouldn't be breathing."

"Same magnet?" Peter asked. "Or do we need two?"

"Two," Derrick said. "We'll toss one if it turns out to be the same lad."

"We also need to know if that person knows about the gate," Cameron said with a frown.

"Or he might just have been following Ollie by chance," Peter offered. "Or one of his incarnations, rather."

"No matter," Derrick said. "We'll keep our eyes open and station ourselves at appropriate spots."

And with that, they were off in strategy mode. Oliver watched those four men then gather around the board and discuss the whole operation as if it had been a stage play with movements they were blocking. He caught an inquiring look from Derrick at one point, but shook his head. He'd already replayed the whole scenario in his mind scores of times and landed exactly where he was: back in the future without the one thing for which he'd gone to the past. He was happy to let them take a crack at it and potentially see something he'd missed.

"Two plans," Derrick said, stepping back and looking over the board. "We'll need a primary and fallback, just in case."

"We," Oliver echoed. "What do you mean, *we*? You can't come."

Derrick turned and faced him. "No choice. Sam ordered me to go with you."

Oliver would have gone to find Derrick's wife and first scold her for being willing to put her husband in harm's way, then hug her for being so kind to him, but all he could do was look at his best mate and shake his head. Just once.

"I'll go," Ewan volunteered.

Oliver hardly had the wherewithal to smother his surprise. That was an offer he hadn't expected.

"With all due respect," he said carefully, "this is for all intents and purposes medieval Scotland we're headed back to with swords and witch hunters and many people who will want you dead."

"Sounds like a rough night in Glasgow to me," Ewan said with a yawn. "I'll manage."

"Ewan—"

Oliver heard Cameron clear his throat and he turned to look at his freely chosen laird.

"My lord?"

"I know we all want him dead more often than not," Cameron said with a faint smile, "but he's more observant than you give him credit for being."

"And what," Derrick managed in a strangled voice, "are you saying?"

"What he's saying," Ewan said pleasantly, "is that you are a gaggle of dolts who had no idea what you were looking at all those years you worked for him. I, if I might be so bold, am not so stupid." He paused. "I'm also the one who picked up the phone when Moraig called, then drove Alistair to her house after which I drove both of them to hospital in Inverness."

Oliver staggered. He tripped over Derrick who had also staggered and found himself sitting in an untidy little heap with his boss on Cameron's office sofa. He looked at Derrick, then at Ewan.

"My ears are going," he said faintly.

"I won't offer details you both are incapable of understanding," Ewan said archly. "I'll just say that I know Ian MacLeod very well and John Bagley keeps my Claymore in the back of his studio so I don't have to carry it around like a Year Four lad totting his lunchbox."

"When?" Oliver asked blankly. "When did you find out anything?"

Ewan rolled his eyes. "I grew up here in the hall. Old Alistair was also my great-uncle, which you should know if you don't. Did you think I hadn't paid attention to happenings in the clan?"

"And you didn't want the title?" Oliver managed. He shot Cameron a look. "Before, I mean."

"I would have had to fight Derrick over it and that might have mussed my manicure."

Oliver felt his eyes narrow. "You're responsible for the mani-pedi, aren't you?"

Ewan only returned his look mildly. "When one has spent, as I have, an enormous amount of time becoming proficient with a wide variety of weapons including steel, one's hands occasionally require attention lest the fairer sex complain."

Oliver shuddered. "Shut up, I beg you."

"And nay," Ewan said, making Cameron a brief bow, "I never wanted the title. I was thrilled when Cameron hopped over all those centuries to take up his rightful place yet again." He smiled briefly. "As for the rest, anything for a brother, aye?"

Oliver nodded sharply, because that was better than looking around for a handy corner in which to bawl like a bairn. He looked at Cameron who only smiled.

"Go take a nap in front of the fire for half an hour," Cameron said, nodding toward the great hall. "You already know what needs to be done, but we'll have a proper schematic plotted out for your approval. You and Ewan can fly down and be there well before dusk."

Oliver would have protested, but he found himself hauled up from the sofa and shoved out the office door. It was shut in his face, so he supposed he had no choice but to leave his mates to their discussion of magnets and Highlanders with swords and eejits with books to complete.

He imagined the best use he could make of his time was indeed to nap even for a few minutes, so he walked across the hall, then cast himself down on that very comfortable sofa he'd used more than once in the past. He closed his eyes, then felt Mairead sit down with him.

He was almost certain he could feel her hand on his head.

"I love you," he said quietly.

"I love you as well."

He smiled a little in response, then considered his afternoon. He would listen to whatever his mates had to add to his plan, pretend he'd offered Mairead an unexceptional kiss on his way out the door to go to work, then he would do what needed to be done, simply and perfectly.

He had no other choice.

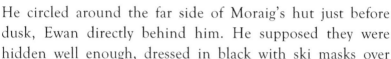

He circled around the far side of Moraig's hut just before dusk, Ewan directly behind him. He supposed they were hidden well enough, dressed in black with ski masks over their faces and minimal gear shoved in cargo trouser pockets. If nothing else, they would frighten the holy hell out of a few lads who definitely deserved it. He looked over his shoulder, had a curt nod in answer, then turned his mind to their plan.

It was beautiful in its simplicity and terrifying in the possibility of having a single wrong step send the whole scheme spiraling out of control. He did, however, have absolute faith in his ability to memorize things, and he knew from adventures in the present that Ewan was far cannier than he let on. Having Ewan with him in superspy mode was almost the same as having Derrick there.

He heard the low conversings of lads coming up the path to Moraig's and wondered how he'd been too stupid to notice that the first time. What he also hadn't interpreted properly was that it was Lachlan himself shouting at them from what he gathered was the edge of the forest. The only thing he remembered properly was that it was indeed Tasgall shrieking that he'd caught sight of the fugitives coming toward them.

Oliver wished he'd been quite a bit less polite in the past to Mairead's brother.

"Timing still good?" Ewan murmured.

"Still good," Oliver said quietly. He was very grateful that their closed-circuit communications of earbuds and mics seemed to work in whatever century they found themselves.

And if *that* knowledge wasn't enough to merit a few ticked boxes in his damned book, he didn't know what was.

"I'm going to have a proper scream after this," Ewan muttered.

Oliver smiled to himself, then continued to listen until he heard the unmistakable sound of clansmen announcing that their unwitting guests had arrived. He held up his hand, waited, then dropped his hand in the pre-appointed signal.

"Mark one," Ewan said quietly. "Three ... two ... one ..."

Oliver slipped with him around the east side of Moraig's house and flattened himself back against the side of the croft. He heard himself clunk his head against the threshold, heard the shouts that accompanied that, watched whichever clansman his second incarnation had beaned with a rock go sprawling, then looked at Ewan.

"Let's go."

Ewan nodded shortly, then stepped forward to become the diversion he absolutely needed.

TWENTY

MAIREAD WONDERED IF GUY FAWKES had decided to make a quick visit to Scotland before setting off on his foul adventure in London.

She coughed at the blue smoke that obscured even her hand in front of her face, then felt that hand be taken by another hand she suspected she would recognize anywhere. She didn't bother to question Oliver over why he'd just gone sprawling into the witch's croft whilst at the same time was pulling her through the forest at a dead run. Perhaps he was rescuing her yet again.

She didn't dare ask why.

She tripped, which wasn't surprising given the condition of the forest floor, but found herself caught by someone behind her. She looked behind her and opened her mouth to shout out a warning, but the man quickly pulled his head covering off and smiled.

"Ewan Cameron," he said pleasantly. "Oliver's second."

She would have smiled if she'd had it in her, but as it was all she could do was nod, then look at Oliver who reached for her hand again.

"We need to run," he said urgently.

"Let's fly instead."

He smiled. "We'll do that, too."

She suspected he might be referring to a Future marvel she fully intended to be alive to see for herself, so she bolted with him through the forest, his friend hard on her heels. She wasn't sure how many times she tripped, but one of those lads caught her every time, something she suspected her hands and knees would appreciate.

What she didn't appreciate was the pair of lads waiting for them just under the eaves of the forest near the Cameron's border.

"Got it," Ewan Cameron said firmly.

She hardly dared ask what he meant by that, but Oliver seemed to trust him and she trusted Oliver. They continued to run directly at those lads and then suddenly a cloud of pale red smoke billowed out, obscuring everything in sight. She watched, open-mouthed, as Ewan rendered unfit for any sort of battle both those men with several sharp movements of his hands and feet.

She continued on with Oliver and Ewan toward the proper spot, trying not to lose what breath she had left at the sight of the doorway simply standing there, ajar. She felt Oliver tighten his hand around hers.

"Ewan," he said sharply, "take my hand, damn you."

"Are you daft—"

She found herself pushed forward, which left her releasing Oliver's hand. She stumbled out of the faery ring, then turned to make certain he'd come with her only to find him standing a few feet away from her looking at Ewan who had gone sprawling behind her. Oliver stopped short when Ewan sat up and swore.

"Stop moving," Oliver said quickly. "You have a knife sticking out of your back."

Ewan crawled to his feet, then turned around. "Pull it out. I'm wearing Kevlar, dolt."

Oliver laughed a little and smoothly pulled the knife free of his mate's back. Mairead would have commented on that, but he pulled her suddenly behind him. She could see fairly well in the gloom and realized that the pair of men she found standing there were ones she recognized.

From the Future.

Oliver handed the knife to Ewan, then sighed deeply and rubbed his hands over his face. She supposed she might be allowed the same relief, so she took a deep breath and let it out, though with perhaps a bit less confidence than Oliver had used. She had another look at the gate that was still shimmering in the last of the day's light. It seemed to think its work was done because it closed with a soft *click*.

She stared at the place where it had been for a handful of moments, permitting herself time to fix the sight in her memory so she might recall the exact instant when her life had changed forever.

Well, perhaps that had been several days ago when she'd looked up from the madness of her unruly cousins and first laid her poor gaze on Oliver Phillips, but perhaps she could argue the point with herself later when she had the time.

She turned and looked at that collection of souls gathered there, the last bit of twilight surrounding them like a soft shawl. Her uncle Patrick was there along with the man who had come to fetch Oliver in the past. She suspected, given how much he resembled Patrick, that she was looking at James, his elder brother and, if she looked at it the right way, her grandfather. She smiled briefly at both of them, then looked to her left.

There standing closest to her, watching her with an expression on his face she couldn't quite identify, was Oliver Phillips, the man who had just rescued her yet again from death at the stake.

297

He closed his eyes briefly, then reached out and pulled her into his arms. If he did it with a fair bit of enthusiasm and she threw her arms around his neck and held on with just as much fervor, well, perhaps their kith and kin wouldn't make note of it overmuch.

She wanted to tell him a score of things beginning and ending with *thank you*, but all she could do was stand in his embrace and pray that if the world were to end in truth, it would end at that very moment so she might forever remain where she was. Oliver seemed no more willing to let her go, which she found very much to her liking.

"Are you shaking," she managed finally, "or am I?"

"I don't know," he said hoarsely. "I don't know anything except I'm never letting you out of my arms ever again."

"Thank you," she whispered. "For it all."

He shook his head, but said nothing. She suspected there was a great deal more to the tale than she knew, for no other reason than she'd seen Oliver fall into the witch's croft and disappear, yet there he was, dressed in other gear and bringing along one of his mates to be his support.

She shuddered to think what might have happened to her had he not been willing to make an attempt to rescue her.

A throat cleared itself suddenly from behind her.

"That's all well and good," it said in reassuringly crisp Gaelic, "but night is falling and we should be away."

Mairead pulled out of Oliver's arms and turned to look at that intimidating Highlander behind her. She felt Oliver arrange her so she was standing next to him with his arm around her shoulders, which she had to admit she appreciated. She caught the gaze of Patrick MacLeod and had a brief smile as her reward, then a nod toward whom she had to assume was the current laird James.

"My brother Jamie," he said with a shrug. "Good luck with him."

Mairead had endless amounts of experience dealing with capricious leaders, though she suspected she wouldn't need to call on any of those skills at present. Jamie had already shot her a quick smile before he turned a very lairdly look on the man standing next to her.

"Turn her loose, young Oliver."

"With respect, my laird," Oliver replied politely. "I think I'm capable of caring for her."

"Whilst I'm certain you could," Jamie conceded, "'tis growing dark and she needs to be home."

"I'm not letting her out of my sight."

"And I'm not allowing a granddaughter—" Jamie waved his hand in a vague sort of encompassing motion. "A granddaughter of mine, however many generations removed she might be, to be alone in a cottage with a man who is not her husband."

"I am perfectly—"

"Honorable," Jamie finished for him, "which I know very well, lad. 'Tis why you'll agree that she should come home and sleep in my hall until she's wed."

Mairead found her hand taken by her—well, she supposed he was her grandfather, never mind the twistings of her lineage. What she did know was that she'd just been pulled away from the man who had just risked his life to rescue her. She started to speak, then decided perhaps 'twas best to remain silent and see which way the wind blew for a bit. Oliver had rescued her, true, but he was braw and charming and perhaps he would reconsider the things he'd said whilst they'd been running away from her clan. The Future was no doubt a very large place with many beautiful women who would fight each other to have him look at them twice.

"Come along, Mairead lass," Jamie said, patting her hand, "and let's see you settled. Your lad there can visit you occasionally if you can tolerate it."

"But—" Oliver protested.

"Over the course of several months, at least," Patrick added, "before he attempts anything more serious."

Oliver took her hand back and laced his fingers with hers. "I'll do whatever is required," he said, making Jamie a small bow. "To your satisfaction, of course, my laird."

Jamie removed her hand smoothly from Oliver's. "Then, again, you'll agree that she should come to the keep."

Mairead found her hand taken again by Oliver and tucked under his elbow. "If I'm allowed to come along? Absolutely."

"Do I have a say?" Mairead asked, pulling her hands away from them both.

"You do, of course," Jamie said, reaching for her hand and tucking it under his elbow. "And as your nearest kin and laird, permit me to escort you to the family hall, just as I would do for a favored daughter. I'll make the concession that your lad might come along if it pleases you."

Mairead looked at Oliver who sighed and stepped back, as if he conceded the battle.

"Well, you needn't go that far," she said.

He looked at Jamie, then made him a low bow. "Might I hold her other hand as we deliver her to your luxurious hall, my lord?"

Mairead looked at Jamie to find him watching her with a very faint smile.

"He has decent manners, at least," he said with a wink. "Now, shall we set off and find supper? My lady will see you properly settled for the night. Your lad there is perfectly capable of caring for you, I'll admit, but propriety demands a discreet distance between the two of you until you've decided if you'll have him or not. He might hold your hand if you'll allow it."

Mairead looked at Oliver to find him watching her carefully. She supposed that if the time were ever to come to find out what the lay of the land looked like, it was the present one.

"Do you want to?"

He looked pleasingly surprised. "Of course I do."

"And you'll come for supper?"

"If you'll have me."

"I'm going to need a chair for this," Patrick muttered.

Mairead couldn't help but agree with him. He shot her a brief smile, then gathered up Ewan Cameron and invited him to go home with him for supper. She watched them walk off toward the witch's forest, then found herself being escorted down the meadow to her home. She supposed she should have been a little more concerned that the landscape might have changed, leaving her stepping into a hole and twisting her ankle, but the truth was nothing had changed all that much.

Well, aside from the obvious.

And the fact that one of her hands was tucked into the crook of Jamie's elbow and the other was being held by a man who rubbed his thumb over hers continually, as if he either sought to soothe her or remind her that he was there. She looked at him and wished for nothing more than time to sit with him and find out why he was still wearing his demon gear, but he'd lost his wee rucksack, which she hoped someone would think belonged to Master James and push him into the fire for possessing.

She considered. She might need a very long walk in the daylight to wrest her thoughts away from a very sour place and put them in more pleasant pastures.

She focused again on Oliver and found him watching her as if he feared she would dash off into the night if the wrong thing were said.

"I am well," she said. If she sounded very hoarse and a little unnerved, she suspected he understood.

"We'll talk later," he promised.

Jamie leaned in front of her and looked at him pointedly. "Not," he said distinctly, "in any sort of private chamber."

Oliver rolled his eyes. "I am a gentleman."

"And I am this lass's nearest kin."

Oliver bowed his head deferentially. "Of course, my laird. It will be as you wish."

Mairead looked at Jamie, had a pleasant smile as her reward, and suspected this might have been how her sisters felt whenever some lad came to the hall with wooing on his mind. She glanced at Oliver to see what his opinion might be only to find him watching her still with that look of ... well, *awe* was the only word she could bring to mind.

"Thank you," she managed.

"You are very, *very* welcome."

And that, she found, was the extent of the conversation she was going to have with him at the moment.

It was very odd to be walking toward her own home, yet realizing she was hundreds of years out of her time. The stables were still where they'd been, the keep itself looked as it always had, and the courtyard was happily free of men with her death on their minds.

Instead, she found strange conveyances with wheels, flowers planted in spots where none had been before, and what she could have sworn was a door that was slightly newer than the one her brother had slammed shut every time he'd come and gone through it.

The inside of the hall had definitely seen some improvements, which she heartily agreed with. There were no rushes on the floor and the entire place smelled as fresh and clean as the outdoors. There was also hanging in the air a scent that she hoped might signal some sort of decent supper. She wasn't quite sure when she'd eaten last.

Hundreds of years ago, most likely.

"Are you thinking subversive thoughts?" Oliver asked.

"Thoughts about supper, rather, and how many years it's been since I had it last."

He smiled. "I'm sure Jamie can remedy that. I'll let him introduce you to his family, but I think you'll find they're very lovely."

What she did know was that she didn't particularly care for his releasing her hand, though she supposed he would need to eventually so she might eat. She met Jamie's wife Elizabeth and had to bite her tongue not to assure her grandmother, who could scarce have been old enough to be her mother, that her fame had lived on in the past, if only in the mind of Lachlan MacLeod.

Their children were staring at her with wide eyes, but she supposed that had less to do with her face and more to do with her dress.

"Mairead has traveled a long way today," Elizabeth said in comfortingly perfect Gaelic, "so we'll save all our questions for her until tomorrow and just see that she's comfortable tonight. Who wants to sit next to her at the table? All right, Patricia you take one side and Robert the other. Ian, you and Oliver can watch over them and make certain they don't keep her from eating her dinner."

Mairead found herself taken in hand by a young girl who reminded her quite a bit of Fiona and a young lad who actually looked a great deal like Ambrose. She took comfort in that familiarity and allowed them to shepherd her across the hall to the kitchens.

She stepped inside that same chamber where she'd passed so many of her hours in the past and felt herself freeze in place. So much was the same, but how many things had changed. There were additions in the form of worktables with boxes under them and shiny things where there had been nothing but walls and kitchen lads and maids before—

Though she supposed she wasn't as surprised as she might have been if she hadn't seen similar things inside Moraig MacLeod's wee croft. She glanced at Oliver who smiled encouragingly at her, then turned back to face her doom. She had faced down the witch's house in two different centuries; she could survive supper in her ancestral home.

She had to admit she was pleased to find that Oliver had very politely bargained away something to Robert for the privilege of sitting next to her and hoped it had been worth it to him. She supposed he ate when given the chance, but every time she looked at him, he seemed to be watching her.

"Am I doing this poorly?" she whispered. "My manners—"

"Are perfect," he said. He smiled briefly. "I just have to keep looking to make sure I haven't dreamed you."

She realized Jamie's children were watching her with undisguised curiosity—and no doubt wondering why she was blushing so furiously.

"Is it a good dream?" she asked frankly.

"Mairead," he said, sounding genuinely appalled. He reached for her hand under the table and held it securely. "It is a beautiful dream. I'll tell you just how lovely when I have a chance to talk to you without your grandfather glaring daggers at me."

She glanced at the lord of the keep, then back at her rescuer. "I think he's doing that for my benefit."

"I *know* he's doing it for your benefit, which you completely deserve." He smiled, then squeezed her hand again, his smile fading. "You'll be all right?"

She took a deep breath. "I will. And you?"

Oliver shot Jamie a dark look. "I will if I manage a scrap of floor in front of the fire, actually, but I may have to do more negotiating to make that happen."

"Would you?"

He looked back at her and smiled again. "I would."

She knew his sleeping habits were as erratic as hers, so she wasn't surprised by where he was willing to lay his head—or not, for that matter. She would have thanked him for being willing to take up a scrap of floor for her, but she realized the rest of the family had finished their suppers and were simply staring at her as if they couldn't believe what they were seeing. She was very grateful when Elizabeth invited her upstairs to find clean clothing.

She was desperate to ask the lady of the hall several questions about her own adventures in Scotland, but perhaps later when she thought she had the words equal to those questions.

At the moment, the second thing she wanted most was to simply find somewhere private to sit for a moment and weep in gratitude that she was alive.

And then she would work on the first, which was finding Oliver and seeing if he wouldn't hold her until she thought she could take a decent breath again.

She suspected that might take quite a while.

It was well past nightfall when she made her way silently down the passageway and paused at the top of the steps. She remembered as vividly as if she were reliving the moment how she'd encountered someone at that same spot several days earlier. She wasn't sure how long it had been, to be honest. It felt like years.

She wondered if it might have been the echo of Oliver walking in that same spot only centuries in the Future.

The thought was thoroughly ridiculous, but she supposed she was living out things that someone else would have considered just as daft. Perhaps she wasn't the one to judge.

She could judge her current straits, though, and at least the recent pair of their hours had been passed happily enough. She'd been offered a chance to brave a bath in a tub that wasn't made of wood and provided endless amounts of hot water from a spout, a marvel she thought she might want to become very familiar with. Having a brief but heartfelt talk with Elizabeth about the challenges of arriving in a different time and adjusting to unexpected things had been comforting. Being given a chamber where she'd been able to stand in the midst of it and bawl her poor eyes out for a quarter hour had perhaps been the most useful thing of all.

Time traveling, as Jamie had remarked as he'd passed her in the passageway but a moment ago, was not for the faint of heart.

Which was all the more reason to descend to the great hall and ground herself in the current year, which was what she had replied to her laird lest he think she was off to raid his larder. If she happened to keep her eyes open for a certain lad of her acquaintance who might be amenable to sitting up all night whilst she endured whatever trembles she hadn't managed to weep out, well, who was to know?

She walked down the stairs, running her fingers along the stone of the stairwell wall and wondering just how many generations of MacLeods had done the same thing. Too many to count, perhaps.

She stepped out into the hall and saw Oliver sitting on the floor and leaning back against the wall near the hearth. He immediately pushed himself to his feet, then swayed.

"You should sit," she said, running quickly over to him and catching him by the arms. "When did you sleep last?"

"I'm not sure. Let me go find chairs and we'll do the maths."

"How closely together can we sit?"

He closed his eyes briefly, then held his arms open. She walked into his embrace as though she'd been doing it her whole life.

"Are you cold?" she asked in surprise.

"Trying not to weep, rather."

She pulled back and looked at him to find his eyes were very red. She smiled in sympathy.

"I shed my share upstairs."

"It's been a long day," he admitted.

"Are you going to tell me about it?"

He studied her for a moment or two, then reached up and smoothed the hair back from her face. "I wonder," he said carefully, "if it might be better to simply take a few days and see what you remember naturally?"

"Have I forgotten things?" she asked, feeling slightly alarmed. "Have *you* forgotten things?"

He smiled slightly. "I'll have to give it some thought. I did spend a pair of hours writing things down before I came to fetch you, though, which might help."

"Hours?" she said with a snort. "I stood over that damned Victorian scribbler for two entire … months …"

She felt her words trail off into the emptiness of the great hall, hang there for a moment or two, then fall softly to the ground. She looked at Oliver in astonishment.

"Did I?"

He only returned her look steadily, but said nothing.

"What did I tell you?" she asked. "Or, more to the point, when?"

He smiled slightly. "Why don't you come sit and be warm with me? And where's your knife?"

She pursed her lips. "I won't stab you in surprise if you say something unexpected."

"You are fierce and saucy," he said solemnly, "and I like to have all possibilities accounted for."

She pulled her sheathed knife out of the pocket of what Elizabeth had called a dressing gown. "I wasn't sure where else to keep it." She pointed at her feet for inspection. "These pleasing shoes in this rosy color of sunset are not up to the task of hiding anything at all."

He took her face in his hands, kissed the end of her nose, then smiled. "You are a wonder."

She felt herself beginning to blush. "I'll match my very fine shoes if you don't stop with that."

He smiled, took her hand, and pulled her over to the hearth.

"Who sits closer?"

"You do," she said without hesitation, putting her knife back in her pocket. "I'll be warm enough."

"Chair or the floor?"

She looked down, then gestured toward the stone of the floor next to the hearth that was cleaner than she'd ever seen it before. Oliver nodded, sat with her, then took one of her hands in both his own. He glanced at her.

"I'm just keeping your hand warm and making certain you don't catch a chill."

"In truth?" she asked in surprise.

He laughed a little. "Actually, I just wanted to hold your hand, but, again, saucy lass with a sharp knife. A bloke can't be too careful."

She scowled at him. "You're safe enough for the moment."

"And so are you, and for more than just the moment."

She considered the truth of that. She supposed it was also perhaps one of the more noteworthy events of her life to be sitting with an extremely braw man who held her hand because he was apparently daft enough to want to and there wasn't a relative in sight demanding that she hie herself off to the kitchens and prepare a meal for them.

Her life had become very strange, indeed.

"Mairead?"

She looked at him and smiled reflexively. "Aye?"

He took her hand, laced his fingers with hers, then kissed the back of her hand. "I'm just happy you're here."

"I am, too."

He sighed. "Unfortunately, you should probably go up to bed."

"Don't make me go."

"Well, *I* don't want you to go," he said, then he shot her a quick smile. "Jamie might take me outside and cut me to ribbons for keeping you downstairs, though, so keep that in mind."

"I'll protect you with my saucy blade."

He laughed a little, then tilted his head toward his shoulder. "Then I won't argue with you tonight. Lay your head and be at peace."

"You don't want me to go?" she murmured.

"Nay, lass," he said very quietly. "I don't."

Well, he had risked life and limb to come and fetch her away from her murderous kin, so she supposed he meant it.

She considered, then brought his hand close and kissed it.

She was the first to admit it was awkwardly done, but his breath caught just the same. He squeezed her hand, shifted a bit closer to her, then rested his cheek against her head.

"Sleep, Mairead," he said quietly. "You're safe."

The saints preserve her, she thought she just might be.

TWENTY-ONE

O LIVER STOOD INSIDE MORAIG'S COTTAGE and eyed the front door warily. It hadn't done him dirty so far that morning, but the day was still young.

That day had begun for him a pair of hours earlier with a quick run up the meadow from Jamie's, a shower and change of clothes, and a quick rummage in the fridge for a few carbs which someone had very thoughtfully left for him in the form of a full order of his two favorite foods. Unfortunately, all those successes had left him standing where he was: facing off with a doorway and hoping he could get back out it as easily as he'd gotten inside it.

He supposed he might as well admit that he was fretting over a doorway because he was avoiding thinking about the events of the past forty-eight hours. He was still gobsmacked it had all worked, though given the skill sets both he and Ewan possessed in that sort of skulduggery, perhaps it wasn't a surprise. What had been a surprise was finding out that in a dodgy spot, Ewan's mind worked a great deal like Derrick's. Obviously, they'd been misusing his gifts.

What he absolutely couldn't bring himself to face, though, was his past, never mind wondering why it was that he could remember Mairead's presence running like a beautiful silver thread through his entire existence yet at the same time he knew he'd never had her there in the first place.

On the other hand, he had very vivid memories of her as a ghost over the past handful of days. He could hear her speaking modern English as if she'd never spoken anything else and bring to mind the details she'd given him about his own past.

He knew, in a way he couldn't quite lay his finger on, that her being a part of his life over the course of his *entire* life had somehow now become nothing more than an echo of her presence there, but he wasn't sure that he'd so much lost his memories of her as he'd had them simply fade beyond where he could hold them any longer. Changing the future couldn't possibly change the past, but her future had changed *in* the past, which had surely changed his own past in the future.

The loss was, he had to admit, a bit devastating.

He understood on an entirely new level why Sunshine Cameron was careful with Moraig's threshold.

But if he didn't put all that emotion behind him and move on with things, he would likely spend the rest of his days simply standing in the middle of Moraig's gathering chamber, either weeping from events that floated in and out of his memory like so many ghosts, or trying to catch his breath over the fact that he actually had Mairead MacLeod in the same century as his own poor self and that she seemed slightly fond of him. And when looked at in that light, what he'd lost was so much less than what he'd gained.

He allowed himself one deep breath, then he did what he always did with things that didn't serve him. He shoved them behind the door in his mind he reserved for that sort of thing and got on with his life.

He took hold of his good sense and opened Moraig's front door. The stoop wasn't cluttered up with angry Highlanders in Renaissance dress, calling him names and threatening to drag him off to the stake, which was a good thing. There was, however, a manila envelope lying there, which might be something else entirely.

He retrieved it because his damnable curiosity was too strong to resist and opened it to find a new section to insert in his book entitled *Wooing Ideas for the Perpetually Helpless*. He was tempted, as usual, to fling it a very long way away from himself, but he found himself hesitating. The truth was, he wasn't precisely overflowing with those sorts of ideas at the moment. Though he had himself, Mairead MacLeod, and delicious takeaway in the same century, that might not be enough to win the day.

He considered that for a moment or two. Surely there was a way to help her acclimate herself to the present day whilst leaving her feeling as though she might like to have him along for the trip. He went inside to dig around in Moraig's junk drawer where he unearthed a sticky tab and made himself his own section entitled *Things that Haven't Changed Over the Years*. That useful section at least labeled, he locked up Moraig's cottage, then started off toward Jamie's. He considered the facts of the case lying before him as he walked, just to make himself feel more in charge.

First, he was a man of mature years with a rich and varied history of first dates. He could walk up to James MacLeod's front door, knock, and present himself as a very desirable dating partner without bollocking it up.

Second, he was dressed nicely in trousers and a black polo neck jumper, the latter of which would serve the dual purpose of setting off his fair hair to perfection—Emily promised that was the truth—and hiding his neck where enthusiastic swallowing might be interpreted as gulps of unease. A black jacket covering that and sensible Docs on his feet hopefully would provide a trustworthy if not slightly slick and attractive aura of, again, dating desirableness.

He was also a Man with a Plan and that plan, very sensibly to his mind, centered around making sure that a certain MacLeod clanswoman was properly introduced very slowly and carefully to the current century. Nothing too startling at first, nothing more modern than what could have been found in Jamie's kitchen with perhaps a brief foray into Elizabeth's library for Regency reading material that would also be acceptably calming and soothing. He would keep his lady corralled in the past-places that were located in the same future-places so she would see that nothing much had changed. He imagined not even four hundred years of four hundred different types of Scottish precipitation could have altered the landscape all that much.

Finally, the truth was that even though she'd been given the chance at a new life with family in the persons of Jamie and Elizabeth and Patrick and Madelyn and even Sunshine and Cameron—delightful souls who would love and care for her properly—he wanted to be at the beginning of the queue.

He found himself standing on Jamie's front stoop without remembering entirely how he'd gotten there. He hardly expected any renegade witch hunters to pop out from behind a shrubbery, but he was also accustomed to going through his life making detailed mental notes of his surroundings and planning accordingly. He would have to get hold of himself and quickly before he did something eejit-worthy.

The door opened before he could get his hand anywhere close to it which was a little alarming, but he gathered his wits about him and nodded deferentially to the laird of the hall.

"I'd like to take Mairead out on a date," he said politely.

Jamie stroked his chin. Not a rousing initial endorsement, but Oliver was prepared for some resistance from that quarter.

"And what sort of activities will you be engaging in?"

"I was thinking we would do a few things that would leave her feeling confident that many things haven't changed," Oliver said. "A walk up the meadow, a bit of flower-sniffing, perhaps a gentle ride if I could borrow a pair of horses."

Jamie stroked a bit more. "Do you know how to ride, Master Phillips?"

"I'll learn quickly."

Jamie did smile then. "Perhaps your gel can help you with that on a different day. I believe she already has plans for you today." He stepped back and held the door open. "Go have a look."

Oliver accepted the offer whilst it was still good, then came to a full stop at the sight of the absolute chaos that greeted him.

The children—well, more particularly Robert and Patricia—were bouncing around Mairead like puppies whilst Young Ian was trying to settle them down. He spared a wish that he'd asked Ambrose for some particulars on the art of keeping younger children from horning in on his time with his future, er, well, whatever she would be willing to be, but that moment had definitely passed long ago.

Patricia saw him and raced over to throw herself into his arms. He hugged her, grateful that at least one MacLeod female was glad to see him, then set her back down on her feet.

She slipped her hand into his. "Treat or a card?" she asked brightly.

He nodded toward Mairead. "I brought you a treat there."

Patricia laughed and tugged. "Come see her. She's had a wee makeover, so you might not recognize her."

Oliver suspected that might be true, which could throw a spanner into his carefully considered works. He walked with Patricia across the hall and had to take a moment to gape at the woman standing there in front of the fire, looking particularly at her ease whilst he felt particularly not at his own. He wondered if Emily had been hard at work or if Mairead had merely raided Elizabeth's closet.

She was dressed in a flowy black skirt that ended at her ankles, a tunic-like blouse adorned with flowers in a riot of colors, and a very lovely sweater covering it all that he would have bet good money was cashmere, which meant it had come from Emily given that that was her favorite fabric. He imagined he would get a bill for the whole thing which he would pay many times over for the sight of a vintage clanswoman occasionally looking at the things she was wearing—more particularly her chirpy little flower-patterned trainers—and giggling.

He suspected the day had already begun to get away from him.

Patricia abandoned him to go take Mairead by the hand. "You've met Oliver before, haven't you?"

"I have," Mairead said with a happy smile. "You look very braw in those new pieces of demon garb."

"And you," he managed, "are absolutely gorgeous."

She laughed uneasily, then looked at Patricia. "I'm not, but this wee one did help me choose these lovely things this morning."

"And I'll help you with the rest of the day," Patricia said brightly. "We'll have heaps of fun!"

Oliver suspected his lady's introduction to the current age had just been co-opted by a seven-year-old who was sprinkling her very capable Gaelic with a few modern English terms that she was doing her best to translate. She had help with that in the persons of her brothers who were obviously striving to make Mairead's transition into the future as smooth as possible. He cleared his throat.

"What about a walk in the meadow?" he offered.

"You can do that in any century," Patricia said firmly. "We want to show Mairead the beauties of *this* century."

It occurred to him then just what had bothered him from the start. He wasn't quite sure how to voice the thought without either sounding completely daft or cluing Jamie's children in to things they shouldn't have known, but he thought he should at least make the attempt.

"But it isn't as though Mairead is from, erm—"

Patricia reached out and patted him. "We know, Oliver."

He looked around for aid and found that Elizabeth had come to stand next to Young Ian.

"Not all family secrets are bad," she said with a smile.

"And I just learned our great, whacking one last night," Patricia said, her eyes wide. "But I'm to be eight in a month, so it was time." She looked at Oliver seriously. "I can be trusted with important things."

Oliver imagined she could be.

"So let's go to the village," Patricia finished. She looked up at Mairead. "There might be things that seem odd, but just hold my hand and you'll be fine."

Oliver watched the three MacLeod spawn gather up the woman he'd had every intention of spending the day dating and lead her off to the front door. Elizabeth came to stand next to him.

"I think you're in trouble."

He looked at her in alarm. "What do I do?"

"Get up earlier tomorrow?"

"Fair enough," he said, vowing to be rapping on their front door before sunrise. He made her a low bow, had a laugh in return, and hurried off to see what he could do to salvage the day.

He paused on the front stoop to assess the situation. His lady was also there, standing next to Jamie and looking with undisguised admiration at the dusty, well-used Range Rover parked there in front of her.

"Does it go very fast?" Mairead asked breathlessly.

Jamie smothered a smile with his hand. "Perhaps not this first trip, lass. We have other automobiles that might be more to your taste in a few days."

Oliver suspected he'd missed a critical part of their conversation about conveyances and exactly what sorts of ponies pulled them, but there was nothing to do about that at the moment. He accepted keys from the lord of the hall and made him a slight bow.

"I'm an excellent driver," he said. "No points on my license."

"Which young Hamish complains about endlessly," Jamie said pleasantly, "which I'm guessing means you at least keep to the posted speed when there might be children or sheep in the area."

Oliver nodded and attempted to look as trustworthy as possible. He accepted a hearty clap on the shoulder and found himself summarily abandoned to his fate. He walked down the steps with a confident air, reminded the children to buckle their safety belts, and opened the passenger side door for a woman who was still peering into the headlamps and making sounds of disbelief. She straightened and looked at him in surprise.

"Beautiful," she managed.

As was she. He wasn't entirely certain when she had gone from—if he were to be brutally honest—a fairly plain woman with a pretty smile to a luminous woman with a gorgeous smile that when she turned it on him left him feeling as if he'd stared at the sun too long. Quite a bit too long. It was all he could do to nod, then tuck her into the car and show her how to buckle herself in without then proposing that they deposit the children back inside and run off to some deserted tropical isle and never return. They could have handfasted in the doorway of a very lovely beachside dwelling he would have happily built with his own two hands. Problem solved, perfect life begun.

He pulled himself back to more reasonable thoughts with an effort. Mairead touched his hand before he shut the door and that almost sent him arse over teakettle backwards.

He was in deep trouble.

"Are you unwell?" she asked, sounding worried.

"I'm fine," Oliver said with as much confidence as he could muster.

"I could drive, you know," Young Ian said from the backseat. "In an emergency."

Oliver shot him a look, had a bland look in return that was so reminiscent of his father that Oliver almost smiled, then shut the door and walked around the boot of the car to give himself time to regroup and reassess his strategy.

Perhaps the children could be distracted by free rein in the local grocery long enough for him to ask Mairead if she might want to, first, allow him to kiss her, then second, grace him with her luminous, delightful, perfect self for the rest of their days.

It was worth a try.

He looked around himself one last time out of habit, then froze. There was something ... off ... He realized with a bit of a start that that something was nothing more nefarious than Peter Wright, leaning casually against the corner of the castle and looking slightly dangerous. He would have bet his favorite pair of green trainers on the lad having a motorbike tucked behind the keep for immediate use. Not necessarily subtle, but effective.

He nodded to his mate, then pulled Patrick MacLeod's phone out of his pocket. He suspected he might have to do a fair amount of foot-stomping to have his own back, but at the moment the one in his hands would do. He considered, then texted Derrick.

Why?

The response was immediate. **Because we luv u!**

He took a deep breath and reminded himself of all the reasons he wanted his boss alive. For Sam's sake, if nothing else.

Truth?

Jamie said to.

Oliver considered all the reasons Jamie might request such a thing and landed on only two that sounded reasonable. Either he was worried about Patricia and thought Oliver would be too distracted to properly watch her, which was less insulting than it was unsettlingly accurate, or he was worried about Mairead, which was definitely both insulting and unsettling.

He looked over to find the laird of the hall standing at his doorway. He nodded firmly, had a slower nod in return, then decided it was perhaps Jamie just being cautious. He imagined that if he'd had children going off with a man thoroughly distracted by the woman he thought he might love, he would have sent along security as well. Heaven knew Cameron did it without a second thought.

He put himself in the car, then looked at his charges in the rear seat.

"A chippy run?" he asked

The chorus of *ayes* was deafening, as was the cacophony that made up all the suggestions flying forward about things to do and Mairead's questioning about what those things meant—and all in Gaelic. Oliver revisited his idea of children and green grocers, then gave that up when it occurred to him that Mairead would likely be leading the charge down the aisles.

He thought he just might be in trouble.

The outing turned out to be less perilous than he'd feared and actually more enjoyable than he'd hoped. He'd recruited Robert into a hastily cobbled-together security detail which had seemed to delight the lad almost as much as thoughts of potentially driving the yet-to-be-awarded supercar up and down his father's drive. Young Ian only seemed to require a nod to immediately go into surveillance mode. Obviously the lad had done the current sort of thing before.

He also realized very quickly that a slow easing into the shallow end of the pool was not in the cards for Miss Mairead MacLeod. He had parked Jamie's car at the less populated end of the village, close to the countryside that lay beyond it, but she hadn't bothered with even a single glance in that direction. She and Patricia had headed directly for the town center. She had frozen in place a time or two, but on the whole it took her far less time to become accustomed to the sights and sounds of a modern Scottish village than he'd expected it might.

He, on the other hand, spent far too much of his time watching her watch everything around herself and far too little doing the same thing himself whilst looking for thugs, which he realized at one point with more than a little alarm. He shot Peter a brief text of thanks for doing what he should have been doing himself, had an equally brief **no worries mate** in return, then decided that perhaps at least for the moment, they were safe enough.

He pulled himself back from his consuming thoughts to find that Mairead was still walking in front of him with Patricia holding her hand. She was, however, reaching her other hand behind her, which he decided could only be a good thing where he and his prospects for a second date with her were concerned. He took her hand, had bright, happy smiles from both her and Patricia as his reward, and decided perhaps the day wouldn't be a complete loss after all. Undone by two MacLeod lassies. He knew he shouldn't have been surprised.

He did glance periodically at Robert and Young Ian, had solemn nods in return, and came to another conclusion which was he was very much looking forward to having teenagers at some point in the future. Quite possibly with the woman walking next to him who spent most of her time pulling him after her to examine yet more Future marvels behind glass windows.

An excellent meal at the local fish and chips shop, a lengthy troll through Mrs. McCreedy's green grocery, and an equally pleasant walk back to the car took up a decent part of the day. He had caught sight of Peter at various points in their outing, resolved to thank Jamie for the care instead of glaring at him for interfering, and managed to get the entire crew back to the keep without losing a one of them.

"Let's go watch something on telly," Patricia said as they crawled out of the car.

"I call the remote," Robert said quickly. "I don't want to watch any of that stupid romantic rubbish, Patty."

Oliver exchanged a glance with Young Ian that he supposed needed no clarifying and followed the company up the steps and into the hall.

"What sorts of programmes do you like, Mairead?" Patricia asked, keeping Mairead's hand in hers and turning to look at her.

Oliver opened his mouth to remind Jamie's youngest that Mairead hadn't exactly had access to television in the past, but apparently there was no need.

"I fancy BBC myster—" Mairead stopped speaking and looked at him, wide-eyed. "BBC mysteries?"

"Let's leave that for tomorrow," he said quickly. "We've had a busy day."

Patricia tugged on Mairead's hand. "We'll think about a show later, though Mum won't let me watch anything too scary."

Oliver could only hope Elizabeth would manage to keep control of the remote. He went along, had tea with the family, then convinced himself that leaving Mairead with her family for what was left of the evening might allow them both to get a decent night's sleep for a change.

He found himself walked to the front door by a girl who knew her way around the keep, then turned and looked at her with a smile.

"What do you want to do tomorrow?"

"Could we go to the sea?"

"Absolutely," he said with a smile. "We could call it a second date, if you like."

"Given that I frightened off all your oth—" She froze and looked at him. "Did I?"

He shivered. "To be honest, Mairead—"

"You might call me Mair," she interrupted, then she managed a smile. "If you like." She paused. "I've said that before to you, haven't I?"

He took a deep breath, then nodded. And with that, he was back to where he'd started the day. His memories of her

as a spirit in the current day were very vivid, but anything
else was starting to feel like a dream. How she was remembering any of it was something he imagined would send Jamie
directly into his library for a thorough search through his nu-
merous tomes on the vagaries of time and traveling through
it.

"Oliver?"

He pulled himself back to the present and smiled. "Aye,
Mair?"

She smiled and it smote him directly to what heart he had
left. "Thank you for the day."

"It was most definitely my pleasure."

Her smile faltered a bit. "I don't want you to go, but I
don't know how to ask you to stay."

He shook his head. "You need to sleep in a bed tonight,
not sit with me next to the fire. I'll be back first thing in the
morning."

She nodded, but didn't move. He was acutely aware of the
fact that the laird of the hall was standing with his back to his
fire, no doubt marking any possible missteps for later payback
in his lists. He looked at Mairead, considered, then thrust out
his hand.

She looked at him and slowly put her hand into his. "Are
you unwell?" she ventured.

"I'm saving myself a skewering from your grandfather."

"Ah," she said slowly. "I see. I thought—"

He considered, ignored Jamie's pointed clearing of his
throat from across the hall, then stepped forward and put his
arms around her. That she put her arms around his waist and
held him tightly was, he had to admit, one of the better moments of the day.

"I'll take you to the shore tomorrow," he whispered, "and we'll talk about anything you want. If you leave your blade in the car, I might even attempt a chaste kiss or two."

She laughed a little, then pulled away and looked at him uneasily. "I'm likely looking too far above myself."

He took her hands in his. "Mairead, I want you to choose your path, but I would be lying if I didn't tell you that I would very much like that path to include me."

"In truth?"

"In truth."

She smiled. "As you will, then, Oliver."

"Sleep well, Mairead."

She nodded and stepped back. He pulled the door shut, took a deep breath, then jumped a little at the shadow that detached itself from the side of the hall. He supposed he was fortunate he managed to stumble down the stairs without landing on his face at the bottom of them as a result, but luck was with him in that at least.

"You," Ewan Cameron said, "are pathetic."

Oliver scowled at him. "And what would you have done?"

"I would have kissed her and dared James MacLeod to stick me for it."

Oliver refrained from pointing out that Ewan had definitely not faced Jamie over blades only because he didn't want to think about all the things Ewan had been keeping from the whole bloody, clueless lot of them.

"I also made you a lengthy list of useful dating ideas for your Life Manual. Didn't you read it?"

"I was going to," Oliver muttered.

Ewan ruffled his hair, then stepped smoothly out of the range of Oliver's hand that would have delivered a friendly yet bracing slap. "I would study it closely before tomorrow morning. Let's get you home so you can do that."

He caught up with Ewan and walked back up the meadow. Day One of Mairead MacLeod's Flawless Future Adventure was successfully in the can, which was a relief. He could only hope Day Two would go as well, which might necessitate a reading of Ewan's notes. He shook his head. His life was no longer his own, it seemed. Who would have suspected that his Horrible Highland Holiday would swerve so fully into things he never would have expected?

He might have to write his mates a thank-you note almost entirely free of foul words and promises of gross bodily harm for sending him on it in the first place.

TWENTY-TWO

MAIREAD SAT IN THE FRONT of the automobile Jamie had loaned them for their journey to the shore and divided her time between watching the scenery go by at speeds she never could have imagined in her lifetime and watching Oliver, fresh-scrubbed, braw lad that he was, driving that same contraption apparently without thinking anything of it.

She smoothed her hands over her skirts and considered her own condition. She'd presented herself very early at Elizabeth's door, taking the lady of the hall up on the invitation to be turned into a proper Future miss. She'd subjected herself quite willingly to all the bathing and grooming duties Elizabeth had guaranteed would leave her looking like the gels she'd seen in the village, though they'd both agreed she didn't need to copy the very short skirts and too-tall shoes.

She'd been pleased to see that her eyes were a lovely green much like Patrick and Jamie's and that the rest of her features were not as unattractive as Kenneth's. Then again, that one had brawled endlessly where she had definitely not, so there was that. She was nervous about the crookedness of her lower teeth, especially when compared to Elizabeth's, but there was nothing to be done about that save hope Oliver wouldn't notice.

He had called for her at a respectable hour, accepted an invitation to break his fast with the family, then listened with absolutely no expression on his face as Jamie had informed her that he'd set aside a bit of gold for her to have for her very own. She'd looked at Oliver then, had a very serious smile as her reward, then hoped Jamie would mistake her rubbing her eyes to stop the burning for something spicy she'd encountered in his kitchens.

Truly the Future was a wondrous place.

Jamie had then suggested that perhaps the children might like to come along to the shore as chaperons, which she'd found both charming and a bit embarrassing. Oliver had taken it with his usual good grace and a polite bow made to her current laird, piled everyone in Jamie's marvelous conveyance, then made certain she was comfortable before he'd set them off on their journey to the sea.

A journey which had apparently reached its conclusion whilst she'd been preoccupied with fretting over things that didn't matter and missing several things that did. She looked at the beautiful greenish-blue water in front of her, then looked at Oliver. He was watching her with a grave smile.

"Like it?" he asked.

She could only nod. Words were beyond her. He smiled again, then looked at the children freeing themselves from their restraints behind them.

"Let's bring a blanket and the hamper," he suggested, "then you sprogs go play. Stay out of the water and don't get lost."

"I'm not a baby," Patricia protested.

Oliver only smiled. "Lads, look after your sister. There's a wee shop on the hill for snacks later if you get hungry. I'll buy."

That seemed to satisfy the bairns well enough. They abandoned the automobile without delay and ran toward the pale-hued shore. Mairead started to unclasp her safety belt only to have Oliver put his hand on her arm. He did it for her, then looked at her.

"Wait for me?"

She nodded, then watched him get out and walk around the car to fetch her. She accepted a hand out, then waited a bit longer whilst he fetched things out of the back of the beast. She eyed the blanket he had tucked under one arm, then frowned at him.

"You aren't going to put *that* on the ground, are you?"

"What do you think?" he asked with a smile.

She wrapped her arms around herself, not because she was cold but because she was too old to be thinking the thoughts that were rattling around in her empty head. Oliver set his burdens down, then looked at her with a wince.

"What can I do?"

She had to take a deep breath. "This will sound mad, but I find that all I want to do is be in your arms." She met his gaze. "Foolish, isn't it?"

"Well," he said slowly, "I might not be the right one to ask about that."

She almost smiled. "You wouldn't?"

He shook his head, then held open his arms and lifted an eyebrow. She did smile then and walked into his embrace. She closed her eyes and felt a sigh come from someplace inside herself that she hadn't known existed. Foolish or not, she felt as if she'd somehow come home.

She wondered if Oliver might grow bored by standing there and doing nothing but holding her, but he didn't move and she couldn't bring herself to ask him if he wanted to. The feel of his hand occasionally skimming over her hair was soothing, the steady beat of his heart beneath her ear was reassuring, and knowing she was actually safe was more comforting than she would have suspected it might be.

"I suppose we must discuss things," she said finally.

"We likely should," he agreed, his deep voice rumbling in his chest. "In a minute."

She smiled in spite of herself and remained exactly where she was, wishing she might remain there forever. It was difficult to believe that not a pair of days earlier she had been in a far different time, alone save for her brother's young children and an uncle of questionable sanity. Well, and Giles Cameron for a brother in affection if nothing else.

But now she had relatives who were kind, apparently a bit of gold to her name, and a man dressed in his favorite color who seemingly thought nothing of giving her comfort when she could scarce bring herself to ask for it.

She patted him on the back, because she knew there were things she needed to face sooner rather than later, then pulled away and looked at him with a smile.

"Do you own clothing in any other color?"

He shook his head. "Emily says black makes my hair look very pretty, so I stick with it."

"Well, she would know," Mairead agreed. "She's very fashionable herself—"

She stopped speaking abruptly as she found herself assaulted by memories she hadn't anticipated. She felt for Oliver's hands and found them there in front of her, warm and secure and attached to a man who didn't complain about how hard she was clutching him. She took a deep breath and looked up at him.

He was only watching her with pity in his eyes.

"What happened that I have these memories?" she whispered. "They aren't there all the time. Just now and again."

He nodded toward the water. "Let's go walk. Tell me if the tidings become too much and we'll do something else like look for shells or stick our feet in the water."

She nodded. "Very well."

He gathered up a basket and that blanket that reminded her a bit of the other one he'd defiled by casting onto the ground and inviting her to sit on it with him, then offered her his free hand. She held onto his hand with both her own and walked with him over a little rise and down onto what she could only assume was sand, never having seen it before. She stopped next to Oliver as he set his burdens down, then looked to make certain the children were accounted for.

"Perhaps we shouldn't leave them," she ventured.

"My mates are watching over us," Oliver said.

She looked at him in surprise. "I don't see them."

"That's how they like it." He hesitated. "You could take off your shoes, if you like. The sand is likely cold, but soft."

"I suppose the cuts are healed well enough," she agreed.

"I forgot," he said, wincing. "Let's just walk as we are today then. We'll come back a different day and go barefoot if it's warm enough."

She nodded, waved to Jamie's children, then took Oliver's hand and walked with him down to the water. He turned them so they walked along the edge of the water, then looked at her seriously.

"What do you want to know first?"

There was no reason not to head straight into battle when her other choice was to linger on the side of it as only a coward would. Supposing her sire might approve, she looked up at Oliver and marched directly into the fray.

"I keep remembering things that make no sense," she said bluntly. "These words come out of my mouth when I don't expect them to and remind me of things that I'm certain I don't know. I can't call them memories, but they seem to be just that. I'm terrified that I'm losing my wits, but I have to believe there's a reason for it all."

"There is," he said carefully. "Where would you like me to start?"

"You stopped the tale at Moraig's doorway," she said, then she stopped and looked at him. "That was her name, wasn't it?"

He nodded.

She walked on with him and promised herself to keep walking because if she didn't, they would both look as if they were losing their wits, what with all her stopping and starting.

"You fell at the threshold of Moraig's croft—" She took a deep breath. "The witch's croft. What happened then?"

"You remember our journey from your hall to Moraig's, don't you?"

"Aye. We were going to try the faery ring, but there were too many lads there."

"There were," he agreed. "We kept going to Moraig's, but we weren't alone there either. We made it to the croft itself, but I clunked my head on the threshold as we tried to run inside." He paused. "I fell into the Future, but I left you behind. Not that I wanted to, but because I had no choice."

She felt a chill run down her spine. "What happened to me?"

He stopped and looked at her. "Walk or let me hold you?"

"Both," she managed. "But walking first."

He nodded. "I'll be brief. You were carried away and—"

She looked him full in the face. "Did I go to the stake?"

He didn't reply, but there was misery written on his face.

"But," she said in surprise, "I have no memory of that."

"That's a mercy."

"Then why do I remember these other odd things?"

He tightened his hand around hers briefly, then continued to walk with her. "Let me tell you the tale as it happened in its entirety, then we'll sort what memories we both have, aye?"

She nodded, though she suspected the telling of that tale was going to be as difficult for him as listening to it was for her.

"When I regained my senses in Moraig's cottage, you were there," he said slowly, "but ... you were a ghost."

She stopped so suddenly, she suspected she'd come close to wrenching his arm from his socket. She looked at him in shock, but she could see he wasn't making a poor jest. If nothing else, 'twas obvious he believed it.

"And you saw me," she managed. "As a spirit."

He nodded.

She looked at him briefly, then walked on because it was the only thing that left her feeling as if she were still in the world and not wandering in a dream. He walked on with her, and he didn't make sport of her disbelief, which she found comforting somehow.

"A ghost," she said, sliding him a look.

He nodded again.

"And I knew you?"

He smiled, a small, wistful sort of smile. "You had, if you can fathom it, watched over me my whole life."

She did stop then, because the thought was so astonishing. "Was that useful?" she managed, because that was the only thing she could think of to say.

"Incalculable."

"Did you know this when you came to my time?" she asked.

"No," he said slowly, "but that's the thing, isn't it? You weren't a ghost until after I'd gone back to your time, then failed to rescue you on Moraig's threshold."

She shook her head, but that did nothing to either provide her with any answers or shake any good sense loose. She looked at him, but he didn't look as if he'd lost *his* good sense.

"Were you surprised I was a ghost?" she managed.

"It was," he said quietly, "quite possibly the worst moment of my life."

"Was it?" she whispered, hardly daring to believe that such a thing would matter to him.

He closed his eyes briefly, then turned and pulled her into his arms. She stood in his embrace for several minutes in silence, listening to the waves against the shore, the laughter of the children in the distance, the cry of the gulls overhead. But mostly she listened to the steady heartbeat of the man who held her as if he never wanted to let her go.

She suspected that it would take her quite a few hours in the dead of night to contemplate what he'd said, accept it as truth, then think about what that had meant to them both.

She pulled away reluctantly, did her polite best to ignore the fact that his eyes were as red as hers no doubt were, then slipped her hand into his that he offered her. She walked with him for quite a while in silence, trying to pit her poor wits against the idea that she had actually lived for scores of years after her death, albeit in a different form.

"Is that why I have these things coming into my mind that I never saw in my lifetime?" she asked suddenly.

He nodded. "I think they're memories of your time as a, well, you know."

"I might need to sit down soon."

"Do you?" he asked quickly.

"Nay," she managed. "I do better when I'm walking. But tell me why I am no longer a ghost but a woman who is capable of sitting down in surprise."

"The things you say," he said, shaking his head and smiling.

She supposed the present moment wasn't the right moment to feel a bit pleased that he found her at least amusing, but she was hearing things that were beyond ridiculous yet somehow reasonable in light of the things she found herself remembering.

Things from her future as something slightly less corporeal but undeniably still her own self.

"Tell me, if you would," she said hoarsely, then she cleared her throat and attempted a smile. "I'm braced."

He squeezed her hand, then continued on with her. "It all goes back to Moraig's doorway, unfortunately."

"The same place that separated Sunshine and the Cameron," she noted.

He nodded. "And as for what happened to us, here's the absolute truth. After I woke in Moraig's house the first time and realized that I'd failed you, I went back to a different point in time and tried again."

"As you did when they were pushing me to the stake by the hall, before the heavens exploded in fire?"

"Exactly that." He stopped and turned her hand over, then shot her a quick, uneasy sort of smile. "This is how it was explained to me. If you think of time as a straight line—" he drew the same on her palm, "and here is where you and I were separated. I went back through the gate a bit before that point."

"And it worked?" she asked, then she held up her free hand. "Obviously it did or I wouldn't be here."

"It doesn't always work," he conceded, "so we're actually very fortunate it worked for us. I went back and waited for us to come through the forest where my plan was to rescue you after I'd fallen into Moraig's house but before your cousins carried you off. Unfortunately, I failed twice for various reasons, then Ewan came with me this final time and was a pair of hands when I needed them."

"And were those other two yous wandering around at the same time?"

He nodded.

"Did I see any of these other yous?"

He shrugged helplessly. "I don't know. I don't think so." He looked at her closely. "Want to walk some more?"

She nodded, because she had to move or find herself caught up in thoughts that were so mad that not even Lachlan MacLeod could have invented them after his most robust night of cozying up to the largest ale keg in the cellar.

She looked down at her hand in Oliver's as they walked, at the imaginary straight line he'd drawn across her palm, and a thought occurred to her that was so odd, she hardly knew how to put it in words. She stopped, then turned Oliver's palm over and traced that line on his hand. If what he was saying were true and she had lived as a ghost—

She looked up at him. "How many years was I a ghost?"

"Over four hundred, if we're counting," he said carefully.

How was it, then, that she could have lived for centuries as a ghost yet still have it be in her memories whilst living an entirely different lifetime? It was as if her lives were threads, looping over each other, stacking on top of each other so they covered the same things again and again. Or perhaps 'twas more like yarn wrapping around a spindle, beginning at the same place on the wood with each round, winding each round separately but covering the same circle and in the end making up one entire whole.

It sounded completely daft, but there was no denying that she remembered things she absolutely hadn't lived through—as a mortal woman, that was.

She traced a loop over that imaginary line on Oliver's hand, going over the same pattern a time or two, feeling a little as if she were walking over her own grave, then she looked up at him.

"What if time isn't linear?"

He looked at her, open-mouthed. She realized she was looking at him the same way.

"Where did that come from?" he asked weakly. "And you realize that was a modern English word, don't you?"

She laughed a little because it was either that or howl. "I have no idea." She took a deep breath. "I'm tempted to run, but the bairns might think we've abandoned them."

He took her hand and tugged. "We'll just walk a bit more, then."

She thought that might have been one of the better ideas either of them had had so far that day. She walked with him along that glorious stretch of sand, finding it in her to pay attention for a change to the lapping of the water against the shore and the wind in her hair and the smell of the breeze. She found herself sighing several times and with each time, she felt the frustration and unease dissipate a bit more until she was simply walking with a man who was handsome and kind and had braved the wilds of her era to rescue her from a fate she had been willing to accept but had to admit was glad she'd escaped.

"Please tell me Master James met a terrible end," she said as they neared the end of the stretch of shore before them, "and that I watched it to the bitter end." She looked at him quickly. "Sorry. I'm not a fan."

He smiled. "You've been talking to Patricia."

"Robert, actually. He's a large fan of very fast automobiles."

"I'll just bet he is," Oliver agreed, then his smile faded. "Apparently you and a few others watched Master James meet his appropriate end atop a pile of wood."

She nodded, finding that to be a bit more satisfactory than it likely should have been.

"Let's turn around," he said quietly. "But we can walk up and down the beach as many times as you like."

She nodded and continued to walk with him, his hand warm and secure around hers, the smell of the sea lovelier than she would have expected it to be. She considered what she truly wanted to know until she thought she could ask it casually.

"And you weren't content to live with me as a ghost?"

His look of surprise was somehow very satisfying. "Of course not," he said, then he smiled quickly. "Well, I would have if that had been our only choice. We did try living as we were, human and spirit, but I pestered you until you agreed that I should try one more time."

"Did you pester me?" she asked seriously.

"Endlessly," he said, his expression suddenly serious. "Mairead, I wanted you here in this time as a woman, and I was willing to—"

"Wait," she said, stopping suddenly and looking at him in surprise. "But if you rescued me from the stake, I wouldn't have been there to watch over you as a spirit."

He nodded slowly. "That was what we discussed several times."

"But Oliver," she said faintly, "I can't believe I agreed to it. How could I have left you alone at St. Margaret's after your parents—"

She stopped speaking because she realized she couldn't finish. The memory wasn't a memory but something more like a wisp of mist that lay against the mountains in the morning only to simply disappear with the turning of the day. She looked at the man standing in front of her, rubbing his thumb over the back of her hand, and watching her with his pale, solemn eyes, and realized what he'd given up for her.

"You were alone."

He smiled gravely. "You were worth the trade."

She suspected they had had some variation of their current conversation before because she could feel the echo of it. She was equally sure she'd wept and not entirely sure he hadn't as well. She could only breathe carefully and look into his eyes that were full of memories and grief and something that looked quite a bit like hope.

"You, Mairead MacLeod, were worth it to me," he repeated very quietly.

She cleared her throat roughly. "Get on with ye, ye wee fiend," she said, hoping beyond hope that that would ease the ferocious burning in her eyes. She started walking again, pulling him with her.

He stopped her, turned her to him, and pulled her into his arms. She suspected it might be becoming a bad habit for her, that clinging to him as if he were all in the world that held her together, but he seemed to be clutching her to him with equal fervor.

And if she felt her tears hot against her cheeks where they fell, and if she wasn't entirely sure she didn't feel a tear or two of his fall onto her hair, well, who was to know? She realized he was breathing just as carefully as she was and she suspected it was for the same reason.

She felt him ease his embrace a bit finally, pull away just a bit, then smile and kiss her on the forehead. His eyes were very red, but she imagined hers were too.

"Let's speak of something less tender," she said, then she had to clear her throat. "Did I frighten anyone during my years as a specter? My brother? A collection of annoying Fergusson lairds?"

He laughed a little, though she could hear the roughness in his voice as well. "You didn't tell me any of that, but you did write your memories down."

"That damned Victorian fop," she grumbled. "He was here writing a series of travel notes, you know, to publish ... in ... London." She took a deep breath and looked at him. "I definitely think I might need to sit today."

"Now?"

She shook her head. "Not yet." She glanced at him. "I want to make light of this and claim 'twas something foul I ate, but I find I cannot."

"I have the feeling we might both have that experience more often than not."

She supposed there was no reason not to have things, as she was certain she'd heard someone say at some point in her existence that apparently spanned more years than she was comfortable with, out on the table. She considered their hands linked together there, then looked in his eyes.

"Are we going to be having those experiences?" she asked, then she had to take another deep breath and gather her courage to blurt out what she realized might be bothering her the most. "Together?"

He smiled very faintly. "Haven't we discussed this before?"

"My memory fails me. Either that, or we discussed it when I was under duress."

He considered. "Ewan Cameron told me that pressing one's suit prematurely can lead to flight by the object of one's affections."

She pursed her lips. "Those lads, Oliver, as I continue to warn you, are not your friends."

He smiled. "I was offered a new addition to my book yesterday which outlined useful ideas on pursuing one's desired object."

"And what were those ideas?"

He reached out and captured a pair of stray strands of hair blowing over her face and tucked them behind her ear, then smiled at her. "Well, the first was to take one's beloved on a date to the seaside. Which I'm doing."

She felt herself beginning color, but that could have been blamed on the chill in the air. "Is that going well?"

"She hasn't bloodied my nose yet, though she's been particularly reluctant to acknowledge that she might like me."

"I like you just fine," she said primly.

"And I like you more than that," he said seriously. "Unfortunately, your grandfather seems to have a schedule for these sorts of things that might override what's in my book."

"It was generous of him," she said. "What he did for me this morning, that is."

"Well, you are his granddaughter," Oliver said, "which I think leaves him simultaneously pleased and unnerved. I also think he wants you to feel that you have options in case you decide you'd rather date a man who wears more browns than black."

She shrugged lightly. "Black does make your hair look very lovely. I might like a few pieces of clothing in that same color."

He smiled and it felt as if the sun had come out from behind a cloud. "You would look marvelous in them. So, let's say you buy a few things in black and have your life in front of you. What else do you want to do?"

She took a deep breath. "Everything."

He laughed a little. "That might be the least surprising thing I've heard from you today." He glanced at her. "Want company on your adventures?"

"Are you suggesting something?"

He took a deep breath. "I'm terrible at this."

"Go read your book."

He smiled. "I will and I'll do better tomorrow. And speaking of tomorrow, what would you say to coming to Cameron Hall with me and meeting my family?"

"Sunshine and the Cameron?" she asked. Those two, at least, she had met before.

He nodded. "And the lads will want to meet you." He paused. "You did tell me—you know when—that your scribe had hidden his manuscript in a crypt."

"In the abandoned kirk up the road just inside McKinnon lands," she said, then she looked at him surprise. "When will this stop?"

"I don't know if it will," he said honestly. "Will you survive it?"

She would have answered him, but they were suddenly overrun by children needing to be fed. Oliver handed them pieces of paper that apparently served for funds in the current day, then held out his hand to her.

"Lunch?"

She nodded and walked with him back toward where he'd left their belongings. She looked at him to find he was watching her with a faint smile. It seemed like an affectionate smile, though, which she appreciated.

"Is this our third date?" he asked.

She considered. "Second, I believe. Why do you ask?"

"The new part of my book that was delivered this morning suggested that a brief, innocent kiss might be appropriate on a third date," he said solemnly. He considered. "Wasn't our first date whilst we sat atop that rock on Cameron soil?"

She conceded the point with a nod.

"Then this is number three?"

"It could be."

He leaned forward, then stopped. "Where's your knife?"

She rolled her eyes, had a brief smile in return, then closed her eyes again at the feel of his lips against hers—

"Ewww, kissing!"

The chorus was deafening. She opened her eyes and looked at Oliver. He glared at the bairns, but she could tell it was merely for their benefit as they responded with laughter and noises of disgust. Oliver looked at her.

"Let's leave them at home tomorrow."

She smiled in spite of herself, kissed him on the cheek before she thought better of it, then walked with him to set up camp on that piece of weaving too fine for the ground.

She supposed there would still be things that were difficult to believe, but somehow having that man there next to her whilst she faced them made everything seem a bit easier.

She was starting to understand why the kitchen maid she'd admired for so long smiled so often.

TWENTY-THREE

OLIVER SUSPECTED THAT IF PATRICIA MacLeod grew up to be anything like her niece—the appropriate twistings of the family tree to accommodate that, of course—Jamie was going to be in the soup.

He looked to his right to see how that same niece was reacting to being several hundred feet off the ground, but all he could see was the back of her head since she had her face pressed against the helicopter glass. She was clutching his hand rather enthusiastically, though, which he didn't protest.

Brave lass that she was.

"Och," she said, pulling on his hand and pointing. "'Tis Cameron Hall!"

Indeed, it was. He watched her watch the landscape as they flew over it and was genuinely surprised that she wasn't shrieking or fainting or having some other reaction that would have been completely understandable.

She glanced at him, then smiled. "What is it?"

"You."

"Go on with ye, ye wee fiend," she said, blushing a little.

"You're fearless," he said sincerely. He hesitated, then cast caution to the wind. "Your father would be, I imagine, very proud of you right now."

"Perhaps," she agreed with a smile, then she shook her head in wonder. "He would have found this much to his liking, I daresay."

Oliver watched her turn back to press her face against the window and could only hope that at some point in the twistings and turnings and non-linear stylings of time itself, the man would have that chance. He was simply grateful he was getting to watch Mairead MacLeod take her father's advice to heart. The modern world would never be the same.

For himself, along with the knowledge that he would never be the same with her in his life had come the realization that he needed to make serious progress toward better presenting himself as not just a desirable dating partner, but an eminently desirable mate.

The initial plan, which he'd jotted down briefly in the self-care manual that he'd taken to carrying with him, was to introduce Mairead to those residing at Cameron Hall so she might see that he had decent adopted relatives whilst simultaneously providing her with a wider circle of friends. He suspected that having relatives with a command of the language-du-previous-jour might come in useful during his attempts to woo a woman of a different vintage.

Assuming, of course, that he could pry her out of the helicopter and get her inside the hall, which he was utterly unsurprised to find was an effort to do. He promised her another trip as soon as was polite, then walked into Cameron Hall with her fifteen minutes later, his strategy at the ready.

He would have quickly sorted the souls inside into groups based on their potential for mayhem, but the truth was, they were—with the possible exception of Ewan—just perfectly wonderful. He sent looks of promise to Derrick, Peter, and Ewan as a matter of course, but he imagined they expected that.

"Oh, Mairead," Sunshine said, hurrying across the hall to embrace her and take her by the hand. "We're so happy you came today. Let me make introductions, shall I?"

Oliver was fairly gratified to have Mairead look over her shoulder at him and lift an eyebrow in question, but he waved her on to what he hoped would be a lovely morning of getting to know his adopted kin. He stood on the periphery and watched as Sunshine made those promised introductions, ones she had made just as graciously several days earlier when Mairead had been in a slightly different state of being. Mairead didn't seem to notice and Sunshine was definitely too discreet to mention it.

He watched as she was presented to Emily and was equally unsurprised at how kind Emily was to her. They immediately launched into nattering on in a delightful mixture of modern and somewhat vintage-accented French, which he found simultaneously endearing and extremely attractive.

"I think you need a whisky," Derrick breathed into his ear.

Oliver flicked him between the eyes without looking because he'd had so damned much practice doing the same to Ewan. Derrick cursed him, Ewan laughed, and Mairead looked at him with a slightly perplexed expression.

"What?"

"Oliver thinks you're beautiful," Ewan said solemnly.

"He's daft," Mairead said happily.

"About everything else?" Ewan asked. "Absolutely. Not, however, about you." He pushed past Oliver, more roughly than necessary, and stopped next to her. "I could sit next to you and wax rhapsodic about your charms if you'd like to take up a spot on the sofa here."

Oliver looked at Derrick. "Help me not kill him."

"Do you think I'd stop that?" Derrick said with a snort. "Have at him and please end him this time. You threaten and threaten, yet nothing happens."

"*You* threaten," Oliver grumbled. "I endure him because he has fairly decent ideas on obtaining those elusive second dates with gorgeous Renaissance misses."

Mairead looked up at him from where she was indeed sitting next to Ewan on the sofa. "Fourth."

He blinked. "We're on our fourth?"

"Right now, aye."

"Then what are we doing here surrounded by this annoying collection of lads?" He gave the women his best smile. "The present company comprised of you stunning ladies excluded, of course."

Madame Gies laughed happily. "Ah, Oliver, love, you have such delightful manners."

"Summon me when you need stirring help," he offered gallantly, then he reached over Ewan and pulled his lady to her feet and over to where he could hold her hand. "We'll come be your tasters, of course."

"Do you two have any plans other than taking up residence in my kitchen?" Cameron asked politely. "We'll have supper later, but I thought it best to leave everyone at loose ends for the rest of the day."

"We were thinking about a little treasure hunt," Oliver admitted.

Peter's ears perked up. Oliver saw them do it. He was also fairly sure the rest of the crew had stopped yawning.

"What sort?" Derrick asked.

Oliver looked at Mairead and smiled, figuring she would understand the unspoken invitation. She lifted her eyebrows briefly at him, then turned to face the lads.

"I have a book," she said in perfect English.

Well, perhaps English with a tinge of a Renaissance accent to it, but it left the others there delighted.

"Any details?" Derrick asked, obviously stopping just short of flexing his fingers and rushing off toward the front door.

"'Tis a manuscript penned by a man named Sinclair McKinnon," she offered in Gaelic. "He was a Londoner who'd come back to Scotland to write about his travels here. The McKinnons did him the courtesy of burying him in their kirk after his untimely demise."

"The ruin just over the property border?" Derrick asked. "I don't think they tend it any longer."

"It's definitely not listed," Ewan said. "A bit of careful exploration for loose stones and who knows what we might find?"

They both looked at Peter who smiled slightly.

Oliver suspected it was at that exact moment that he began to lose control of the day.

He watched Cameron make himself comfortable on one of the sofas there whilst the lads trotted off to his office to no doubt dig out laptops and thumb through a well-used collection of topical maps of the area. He would have offered to help, but his plan dictated that he remain by the side of his intended constantly, so he ignored his colleagues and turned his attentions to the object of his affections.

He would have perhaps carefully explained to her what the lads were off doing, but found that not only was his input unnecessary, it would go unheard. Emily had already absconded with her, leading her upstairs to see if something might be found that might make for appropriate treasure hunting gear. He looked around to see if anyone had noticed the theft but found only Ewan watching him from across the great hall.

Oliver held up his hands in surrender.

Ewan made opening and closing motions, hopefully of a book and not some sort of medieval torture device that was in Oliver's future.

Oliver shrugged helplessly.

Ewan rolled his eyes and walked back into the office, shaking his head.

He considered joining the lads, but felt the call of something from the kitchen. He made Cameron and Sunshine a small bow, waved to Sam, then wandered back into Madame Gies's domain without delay. He made pleasant conversation with her for a bit, flattering her out of a slice of chocolate cake that should have earned her a spot on some exclusive cooking competition, then excused himself to see if anyone might have returned his favorite Highland lass to the great hall. He chewed happily because the cake was indeed superb, then came to a skidding halt in the middle of the hall.

He almost dropped his slice in surprise.

"Oh, my giddy aunt," Ewan breathed.

Oliver would have spared a moment to wonder why Ewan always found himself in the most advantageous locale for an elbow to the ribs or a smart flick between the eyes, but he was too busy gaping at the apparition coming down the stairs. He reminded himself that *apparition* was a very poor choice of words, but to be honest, he found that his usually extensive vocabulary had completely deserted him.

Mairead was walking down the stairs with Emily, dressed in black. Mairead, not Emily, though Emily was dressed very nicely in black trousers and a white blouse topped off with a cream cashmere sweater. Mairead was wearing a modest pair of black cargo trousers, a black polo neck jumper, and black trainers on her feet. Her hair was slicked back and no doubt contained in an equally elegant braid.

She was, in a word, glorious.

She bounced down the final handful of steps and continued her jaunty journey over to stop in front of him and look
at him with bright eyes.

"What do you think?"

He could only stare at her, speechless.

Ewan put his hand lightly—and very briefly, because he
obviously knew what was good for him—on Mairead's shoulder. "He's overcome by your beauty."

"I'm not—"

"You are," Oliver wheezed. Though perhaps *beautiful*
wasn't the proper word. *Ridiculously sexy* was likely much closer
to the mark, but he was trying to be a gentleman and there
was still wooing to accomplish before he simply collapsed in
front of her and begged her to put him out of his misery and
marry him that very afternoon.

"Are you thinking dramatic thoughts?" Derrick murmured
from where he'd obviously come to stand next to him.

Oliver elbowed him, probably with unnecessary force, but
when a man was in the middle of dramatic thoughts about
the woman he most definitely might love, there was nothing
else to be done. He could only look at Mairead and nod,
hoping she might interpret that in a positive way. He watched
her as she was invited to gather with a few of the lads and
examine possible gear for the mission. Ewan's Gaelic was excellent, something Oliver hadn't paid all that much attention
to before, and his ability to explain the technical side of their
operation was unsurpassed. He glanced to his right to find
Derrick standing there, watching with a slight frown.

"I think," Oliver said slowly, "that we may have underesti-
mated him."

"He's still annoying."

"I never said he wasn't," Oliver conceded, "but there's
more to him than I suspected all these years."

"He didn't help *me* win my wife."

Oliver pursed his lips. "That was dumb luck on your part and a great deal of pity on hers." He paused. "I will concede that you haven't completely botched the whole affair yet."

"Make lists," Derrick advised.

Oliver looked at him narrowly. "My bloody book was your idea, wasn't it?"

Derrick tapped the middle of his forehead. "You think anyone else could have come up with such brilliance? Make a new section and entitle it, *All the Things I Love about Mairead MacLeod.* Add to it constantly. Show it to her every day." Derrick nodded knowingly. "Trust me on this."

Oliver had to admit that Samantha seemed very happy and Derrick was aggressively besotted, so perhaps the suggestion couldn't be dismissed out of hand. He caught the earbud and mic that Peter tossed him, then found that all he could do was stand and watch as his lady was swept up into the usual madness of pirates on the prowl.

"She's lovely," Sam said, smiling at him on her way past him. "We have plans to talk John Bagley into a few self-defense courses for women. I think swords might be involved."

Oliver could only stare at her, mute.

He watched her join Sunshine who was standing with the collection of souls he was rather fond of. And when the one he loved looked over and held out her hand toward him, he gave himself up for lost and walked over to see what the brief might contain.

A successful hunt and a lovely supper later, he wandered downstairs to crash on the couch which was his usual habit when at Cameron Hall, though Cameron and Sunshine had given him his own room a pair of years earlier. One of the perks of being part of the clan, no doubt.

He took his shoes off and flopped onto the sofa, sighing deeply at a day well lived and a hunt successfully concluded, though he imagined he would need to discuss the details with his beloved when she wasn't surrounded by people who seemed genuinely delighted to have added her to their midst.

And speaking of people who were delighted to know her, Jamie had been the object of a phone call from her earlier where she'd assured him that she would be well looked after—and chaperoned—so there was no cause for worry. Oliver had listened to Jamie sharpening his sword when he'd been handed the phone, then had a laugh for his trouble before Jamie had simply hung up on him.

Warning heeded, though, because he was no fool.

He also had very good ears which alerted him to the fact that someone was tiptoeing down the stairs. He lifted his head to peek over the back of the couch and saw that it was his lady, clad in new pajamas which he suspected were courtesy of Emily and her unholy relationship with couriers with shopping bags.

He was beginning to suspect she'd had a bigger hand in his torment than he'd been willing to credit her with.

He smiled up at Mairead who sat down on one end of the couch and patted her lap. He supposed that was innocent enough, so he made use of her leg as a pillow and suppressed a sigh when she began to drag her fingers through his hair.

"We've done this before," she said at one point.

He nodded.

She continued to smooth his hair back from his forehead. "And what did you say to me?"

"Something I meant then and mean now."

She smiled and waited.

He looked at her for another moment or two, then sat up, turned around and leaned forward to kiss her softly.

"I love you."

She closed her eyes briefly, then looked at him. "I love you."

He kissed her again with a bit less haste and repeated the sentiment in French.

She laughed softly and returned the favor, then smiled and put her hand against his cheek. "Very romantic."

"I know other languages." He paused. "I might only know how to ask for the loo in them, though."

"Less romantic," she noted, "but still charming."

He smiled, kissed her again whilst she still found him charming, then wrapped his arms around her and encouraged her to make herself comfortable. "Did you look at your manuscript yet?"

She shook her head. "I'm not certain I'm ready to, though I would go in Cameron's office and have a look if you wanted to."

"Mair, it's your book," he said seriously. "You read it or not, as it pleases you."

"So much freedom," she said lightly. "It might go to my head and leave me running wild."

"In any particular direction?" he asked casually.

She tilted her head back and smiled at him. "Do you have a preference?"

"Yes, Mairead," he said seriously. "Actually, I do."

She kissed his cheek, then smiled at him. "Then let us say that if I were to run off somewhere that you happened not to be, I would leave you a map."

"The lads have corrupted you."

"They have," she agreed. She looked at the fire for a bit, then at him. "Tell me about a few of your noteworthy adventures, Oliver," she said quietly, "whilst the fire is warm and we are safe."

He gathered her close, wrapped both his arms around her and pulled her back to rest against his chest. "Where shall I start?"

"With your most recent piece of business." She glanced at him. "Sunny says you ran over a wee granny's treasured piece of shrubbery, but I can't believe it."

He vowed to reward Lady Sunshine properly for tattling on him, but it had been the last straw in what had led him unwillingly to Scotland, so he would likely limit his repayment to a brief scowl.

He made certain Mairead was covered properly with a throw he found on the back of the couch, wrapped her securely in his arms, then launched into a faithful recounting of that poor fuchsia hedge and its encounter with the front of the non-descript Ford he drove for work. It hardly took getting past the pain of being reprimanded by a sturdy copy of the Sun on Sunday before Mairead was asleep.

He realized that he'd dozed off as well when he felt himself being covered by another blanket. He opened his eyes and smiled at Sunshine Cameron.

"Thank you," he whispered. "And not just for this time."

"Faker."

He smiled. "But a warm one."

"You know, you could go find a bed," she said dryly. "And two of them unless you wanted the entire clan MacLeod to chase you across Scotland with vengeance on their minds."

"I wouldn't think to do anything else," Oliver said honestly. "I'm finding, though, given our history, that I don't want to let her get too far away."

"Understandable."

"But I also don't want to move too quickly."

"Perplexing."

He hardly had to manufacture a frown. "Are you helping?"

She smiled. "Teasing you a little, actually." She studied Mairead thoughtfully for a moment or two, then looked at him. "I think she is very fond of you."

"Do you think so?" he asked.

"Didn't she say as much?"

He nodded carefully.

"Did you tell her the same thing?"

He nodded again.

"And that's it?"

"I gave her a flower four hundred years ago."

"Well," she said dryly, "I'm sure that removed all doubt."

He smiled—or tried to. "I don't want to doubt my appeal, but she does have an entirely new world of blokes to look over."

"I understand," Sunny said, "more thoroughly than I want to admit to. But some things are just meant to be and time doesn't really want to get in the way."

He took as deep a breath as he dared. "I think I can make her happy."

"Oliver, you're not watching her watch you when you're looking at something else," Sunny said seriously. "I actually think she's crazy about you. If you're crazy about her, then do something about it. Where did you and the boys go today?"

He frowned, not quite following the non sequitur. "We went to a ruined McKinnon church," he said slowly.

"And what's their motto?"

"'Tear me down before I fall there myself from neglect'— oh, you mean the McKinnon motto."

She pursed her lips. "You're only marginally funny at this time of night, you know. What's their motto?"

He closed his eyes briefly. "*Audentes Fortuna Juvat.*"

"Not our clan's, but a pretty pithy saying just the same. You don't want Ewan cutting ahead of you in the queue, do you?"

"Perish the thought," he said with as much of a gasp as he dared attempt.

She hesitated, then sat down on the coffee table in front of him. "How are you, really?"

Oliver glanced at Mairead, then looked at Sunny with a raised eyebrow.

"She's asleep," Sunny whispered. "Unless she's as good at faking as you are."

"I wouldn't be surprised," he whispered back. "And I feel a little like I'm sleepwalking, if you want the entire truth." He paused, then supposed there was no reason not to be frank. "Do you ever worry?"

"That Cam will go on a run and run into a different century?"

"It happens."

"That's experience talking there, I know." She took a deep breath, then shook her head. "We have one of Jamie's maps, of course, and Jamie updates it more regularly than Elizabeth's probably happy with, so while we don't deliberately tempt fate, we just don't worry about it. I assume Cam will come home without incident and we'll all be fine. Worrying about the alternative won't help."

He sighed. "I'm a contingency sort of lad, you know."

"But once all that's accounted for, what do you do?"

"Plan for the worst, expect the best," he muttered, then he smiled at her. "Point taken."

"What's your favorite quote?"

"Something pithy about revenge on mates who sent me on holiday, I'm certain."

"Actually, I think somewhere in your tiny little office in London you have something on the wall that says, 'What is it you plan to do with your one wild and precious life?'"

"I was suffering from too much green drink when I pinned that up there."

"*I* put that on your wall because you saw it in my kitchen in London and said you felt a deep kinship with Mary Oliver who wrote it. And if you've forgotten what you said when I hung it up for you, it was an extremely pithy, 'best fill it with good things, then, what?'" She smiled. "That's pretty good advice, don't you think?"

He took a deep breath. "You know I'm going to weep now, don't you?"

She smiled, then dug in her pocket for something that she then held out toward him. "Here's a distraction."

He pulled his hand out from under the blanket and took back his phone. "I see I have them properly intimidated if you're still delivering things to me."

"I volunteered," she said. "Had to make sure you were warm enough. It's actually charged, if that makes any difference to you."

"I'm terrified to admit that it doesn't."

She stood up, reached over and brushed his hair out of his eyes, then smiled at him. "Nighty night, brother. The hall's secure and you and your girl are safe. Sleep in peace."

He nodded in gratitude, then rested his cheek gently against Mairead's head, unable to even bring himself to swear silently to stave off a bout of ridiculously tender emotion. He indulged in several deep breaths to get hold of himself, propped his feet up on the coffee table, and decided to distract himself by thinking about a few things he hadn't had time for earlier.

The first thing that came to mind was their success in finding Mairead's manuscript along with several other authorly items of note in the old McKinnon kirk. He would happily leave to Cameron the finessing that would need to happen with the current clan chief over their find, but for his part he was merely relieved Mairead's document had survived. It had been cooling its heels in a decently fashioned stone box, which had helped, though many things survived in less ideal spots.

Not, however, in the boles of trees, which likely spelled the end of the first half of the Duke of Birmingham's infamous adventures. The location of the second half of that book was still a mystery, but he was certain it couldn't have survived for long in the wilds of 16th-century Scotland.

He wondered who had nicked it to begin with. It had to have been someone with easy access to Elizabeth's library, who could read, and who was interested in a bit of tame romance. He suspected one of Jamie's boys, but he'd been wrong before.

The final thing on his list was the identity of the lad who'd stabbed Ewan on their way through the gate. The knife could have belonged to anyone, so no joy there. He wasn't sure if having the dirk in the future was going to upset the balance of the world, but he hardly wanted to ask Jamie for his opinion on the same.

He also didn't want to make a final trip to 1583 to tie up any loose ends, though he was beginning to think he might need to. He'd never blamed Sam for wanting to keep Derrick in the future, but he could understand on an entirely new level why she wasn't keen on her husband time traveling. A brief foray to a Regency house party, perhaps, but the wilds of pre-Victorian Scotland?

A dodgy business, that.

He might have to talk to Jamie after all—perhaps beginning the conversation by conceding that the man had good reason for his rules—but maybe he could take a day or two and make a few strides in wooing the woman in his arms. Now that he had his phone back and Ewan on speed dial, his success was likely almost guaranteed.

But carefully. He might have lost control of the introduction of Mairead MacLeod to the future, but he would make up for that with a proper wooing, perhaps in the style of the Duke of B. who she seemed to think the epitome of all things heroic.

Slow. Patient. Ginger.

With watchwords like those, how could he fail? He would defy Ewan Cameron himself to come up with a better plan for the wooing and winning of Lady Mairead MacLeod, Renaissance clanswoman, and the girl he simply couldn't stop looking at.

"I love you," he murmured.

She opened her eyes and looked at him, then smiled. "I love you, too."

He smiled, tightened his arms around her briefly, then closed his eyes.

Tomorrow was another day full of possibilities.

He could hardly wait to get to them.

TWENTY-FOUR

I F OLIVER PHILLIPS DID NOT, as they said on the telly, make his move soon, she thought she might either slay him for making her wait so long or perish from that waiting and go to her grave a maid.

Mairead stood in the clan Cameron's great hall and surveyed a place that definitely smelled better than it had in her day. She'd been inside a pair of times before as a guest of Giles and Dougan and felt perfectly safe given that she hadn't been much of a temptation to anyone there. The hall had been large, but the Cameron clan had needed all that space to accommodate their rambunctious selves. Whoever had tidied up the place over the past four hundred years had certainly done a fine job.

But what made it truly spectacular were the souls who inhabited it currently. Cameron and Sunny were lovely people who had graciously welcomed her into their family circle without hesitation and shown her every courtesy. She was still struggling a bit with how to accept their kindness, which she imagined said more about herself than she wanted it to.

What was easier was to watch the way that collection of Camerons and Camerons by either marriage or affection treated Oliver.

His friends were seemingly very fond of him, teasing him ferociously about his book of ridiculous tasks, and engaging in the same sort of rough camaraderie she'd witnessed between Giles, his brother, and a few of her more tolerable cousins. Oliver's lads there, though, would have stepped up to guard his back without hesitation, of that she was certain.

The women of his family seemed to be equally fond of him, treating him as another treasured member of the clan, with Madame Gies especially lavishing extra love and attention upon his deserving head. Perhaps that could be accounted as a success for his governess who had turned out to be his ... aunt ...

She closed her eyes and let the memory wash over her. *His governess Maud who had turned out in the end to be his father's youngest sister.* She couldn't say it happened with any more or less frequency, that remembering of things she had never seen whilst in her mortal frame, but she was almost growing accustomed to them.

Time was an odd thing, indeed.

She opened her eyes and found Oliver looking at her from where he stood on the far side of the comfortable collection of Future furniture there before the fire. She smiled and shook her head. He shot her a look she had no difficulty interpreting, but he was drawn back into the conversation at hand before he could possibly have mouthed any delicate sentiments. The saints only knew it wasn't exactly the place for any scorching looks.

"Mairead?"

She jumped a little when she realized Ewan Cameron was standing next to her, wearing a more serious look than usual. He was, she would freely admit, exceptionally handsome. He looked actually a great deal like Robert Cameron himself, tall, dark-haired, with lovely, bright blue eyes.

"How can I help?" he asked frankly.

She considered. She wasn't one to speak freely of things that should have been held close, but perhaps there was no harm in asking the opinion of a man who obviously knew Oliver very well.

"I'm studying the battlefield," she admitted.

He smiled. "Is there any particular prize on that field?"

She didn't dare nod across the comfortable padded benches to where the object of the conflict was standing, rolling his eyes at the things Derrick said whilst glancing her way often, perhaps to see how she fared.

"That one there," she said, then she looked at Ewan. "If I'm not looking too far above myself."

He smiled dryly. "There isn't a person in this hall who doesn't realize he's absolutely mad for you."

"He did say as much yestereve," she admitted. "And I returned the favor."

Ewan only smiled. "What advice can I offer, then, to nudge this budding romance along?"

"Tell me what I'm to do."

"Short of locking yourself in a loo with him and hoping for the best?"

She smiled. "Aye, other than that."

Ewan clasped his hands behind his back and studied the hall for a bit, perhaps gathering his thoughts. She didn't want to gather any of her own because they seemed to center around wondering if she were daft to take Oliver at his word. Perhaps he was just slightly fond of her and didn't want to hurt her feelings—

"May I speak frankly?"

She looked at him and nodded. "I'm prepared."

He smiled. "If he's moving slowly, which even I can see he is, I don't think it's from a lack of affection for you."

"You don't?" she managed.

He shook his head. "I think that he hesitates because it's one thing to go after a treasure that's sparkly and valuable but not have your heart invested in it because it's not going to be yours anyway. It's another thing entirely go to after something you very much want to have for the rest of your life."

"Because he fears the loss of it?"

Ewan nodded.

"I should be the one worried," she said bluntly. "I am not beautiful—"

"You are," Ewan said with a smile. "And even if you don't think so, he does. That's what matters, isn't it?"

"But I'm not going anywhere," she murmured. "What I want, if I'm allowed to want it, is over there."

"I think you're allowed," Ewan said. "As for your lad over there, he's already lost you once, hasn't he? I think he just doesn't want to lose you again."

"And he thinks he will?"

Ewan shrugged. "He can be a bit of a numpty from time to time, so aye, he probably does. I think it's up to you to help this relationship along."

"By asking him to wed me?" she asked, aghast. "But that is his manly duty."

Ewan laughed a little. "I wasn't suggesting you propose. Just give him a shove in the right direction, then stand back and look beautiful. He'll figure out the rest eventually."

She considered. "I could do that."

"You could make a little sport of him as well," Ewan suggested. "He really enjoys that."

She smiled in spite of herself. "I've seen what you lads forced him to do. Not even all the horses you promised him are worth that."

"I think he could have a fairly fancy car with many horses under the bonnet if he did the maths properly."

She nodded, putting the idea of horses where she'd never imagined them going on her ever-lengthening list of things to investigate.

"He's a good man," Ewan said, suddenly looking a bit serious. "But you know that or you wouldn't love him. He's also very fortunate to have you. You'll invite me to the wedding, aye?"

She nodded.

She only hoped she would be asked to be a bride before she was too old to enjoy it.

The rest of the day passed pleasingly with good food and lively conversation. She never managed to sit next to Oliver, but she realized his mates were arranging that, no doubt to vex him. She would concede that he sent her a handful of affectionate smiles and at least one mildly warm look, which she supposed was progress.

Cameron made a generous loan of an automobile to him to use for the rest of his holiday, which Oliver seemed to appreciate. She, however, wasn't at all certain how she felt about the idea that his holiday would eventually come to an end, leaving them both perhaps wondering what the future held for either of them.

She trotted out her best manners for the farewelling, thanked Emily sincerely for what she understood to be a small trunk full of clothing for her own use, then allowed Oliver to see her securely tucked into a smaller automobile than Jamie's. It seemed very luxurious, though, and Oliver seemed to have no trouble guiding it away from the keep.

"Music?" he asked.

She looked at him in surprise. "Do you want me to sing to you?"

He shot her a look she couldn't quite interpret. "I think I might weep if you do, so perhaps later. Unless you can think of a madrigal or something akin to it."

She shrugged and did her best with what she remembered that silly Frenchman having foisted off upon them whilst he'd been about his work of looking for ready ears. Tasgall had suffered it for exactly three days before he'd sent the poor man off to look for more tolerant pastures, which Mairead discovered later he'd found in Cameron Hall.

She finished and looked at Oliver to find him rubbing his eyes.

"Are you unwell?" she asked.

He shook his head and smiled, his eyes very red. "You have a beautiful voice. I warned you I would get a little sentimental."

She shook her head. "Daft lad."

"That was a very beautiful song," he said quietly. "I think I've heard it before."

Mairead nodded to herself. He did, after all, have the benefit of several centuries of music in his past. That particular tune had always pleased her and the accompanying words were, she would allow, not entirely too syrupy sweet.

Oliver held out his hand for hers. She supposed he could drive and hold her hand at the same time, which might be, as Ewan suggested, a decent nudge in the right direction. She held his hand and decided to see if that made any difference.

Her decision was, once they'd reached her family home a pair of hours later, that whilst it had been quite lovely, it hadn't inspired any declarations of affection or proposals of marriage.

Oliver turned the car's engine off, dropped his hands into his lap, then looked at her.

"Thank you for coming with me to Cameron's."

"Of course," she said. "The helicopter was ... well, it was a marvel and nothing but." She put on a smile. "Thank you for helping me find my manuscript."

He looked at her as if he wanted to say something, but either his good sense or a lack thereof apparently stopped him.

"Wait for me?" he asked.

She suspected she might be doing that forever if something didn't change soon, but she was a woman with a plan. She wasn't entirely certain what that plan entailed past encouraging looks, but she wasn't unable to think on her feet.

She nodded, then watched him climb out of the car. She listened to him fetch her gear out of the back of the beast, then open her door. She took his hand and allowed him to help her out, then followed him up to the front door.

He knocked, which she couldn't argue with. Jamie and Elizabeth had been very kind to her, but it was still their home now and not hers. She found that the thought made her feel slightly out of sorts, which seemed particularly ridiculous.

Perhaps she needed more sleep.

Jamie welcomed them inside, quizzing Oliver about their activities as they made their way to the fire. She listened with half an ear, made polite conversation with Elizabeth and the children, promised to show Patricia all the lovely things Emily had given her, then came to a conclusion that seemed to sum up what was bothering her the most.

Dating, much like traveling through time, was not for the faint of heart.

She looked at Oliver who was sitting in a chair opposite her only to find him watching her as if he had no idea what she was thinking. She scowled at him, had a look of surprise in return, and wondered if anyone would think she'd lost her wits if she took off one of her trainers and threw it at him.

She glanced at him again, just to fix in her mind how exceptionally braw he was before she mussed his hair with one of her shoes, only to find that he'd taken to resting his elbow on the edge of his chair and his chin on his fist. He was watching her with the faintest of smiles, which she hardly knew how to interpret.

"Well, young Oliver," Jamie said suddenly, "you'd best hie yourself off to your wee cottage for the night. Mairead needs her rest."

Oliver blinked, then looked at Jamie as if he'd just woken up from a particularly lovely dream. "I'm sorry, what?"

"It might be time to end your date," Jamie said mildly.

Oliver frowned. Mairead found that to be somewhat promising because she didn't care at all for the way her grandfather was encouraging Oliver to get up and move toward the front door.

Then again, doorways were useful in certain situations.

She considered what her father might have told her, considered what Ewan had suggested, and took one final look into her heart. She wasn't surprised to find that she had nothing but love for that man standing over there scowling at her grandfather.

And perhaps in the end, all she could do was offer him a view of a particular direction and let him decide for himself if he cared to continue on that way.

She popped up out of her chair and intercepted him before Jamie could push him more than a pair of steps from his seat. She looked at her laird and smiled.

"I'll take care of him."

"You will?" Oliver asked, sounding surprised and not a little unnerved.

Jamie only clasped his hands behind his back and looked at her with a pleasant expression on his noble visage. She smiled briefly at him, then turned her attentions to Oliver. He was watching her with a look of speculation on his own handsome face, as if he weren't quite sure what she intended but he wasn't going to stop her when he discovered it.

She looked at him, then looked at the door to the hall. He looked at the door as well, then back at her, wide-eyed.

She nodded, sending him a knowing look.

He scratched his head.

Jamie sighed, then turned and resumed his seat. Mairead glanced at Elizabeth to find her smiling, which she appreciated, ignored her grandfather who was stroking his chin and shaking his head at the same time, then turned back to the man in front of her who looked thoroughly baffled. Perhaps more of a nudge was needed.

"There's a doorway there," she said pointedly.

He looked at her as if he feared for the state of her wits. "Well," he said carefully, "yes, there is."

She waited.

"Why does that—oh." He shut his mouth abruptly, then seemed to consider things he hadn't before. "A threshold," he noted carefully.

Jamie groaned.

Mairead forced herself not to scowl at him, though that took quite a bit of effort. She instead turned a smile on the man facing her. "Indeed, there is."

He studied her for a moment or two in silence, then he smiled, that dry smile that she had grown uncommonly fond of in so short a time, she half wondered if she'd dreamed that smile of his for years before she'd met him.

He held out his hand.

She looked at his hand, then at him. He was only watching her with what a duller maid might have called affection.

She smiled and put her hand in his.

"Very well," Jamie said, heaving himself to his feet. "I'll see to the handfasting, though a proper wedding would suit as well."

"I'll propose formally as well, my lord," Oliver said gravely. "But with your blessing, I would like to keep her next to me from this moment forward."

Mairead looked at Oliver in surprise, but he only sent her a glance that whilst perhaps not scorching, was full of promise.

"If she's willing," he added.

Mairead found both of them looking at her, along with Elizabeth and the children, and decided that perhaps for once, she could have what her heart desired.

"I am," she said quietly. "With all my heart, I am."

Oliver closed his eyes briefly, then smiled. She suspected he might have indulged in a fond embrace if Jamie hadn't been in his way, but she suspected that along with keeping watch over the strands of time, her grandfather felt compelled to deal out a bit of teasing as often as possible. Her uncle Lachlan would have liked him very much.

And if Jamie pulled a lovely piece of ribbon out of his pocket, she could do no more than smile at Oliver through her tears and discreetly avoid mentioning that Oliver's cheeks were just as damp as her grandfather bound her together with her love on the threshold of her family home.

An hour and a bit of supper later, she was standing outside Moraig's croft with her newly made husband and wondering if he was truly as nervous as he looked. He glanced at her.

"Are you concerned?" he asked.

"About the doorway?"

"That, too."

She shot him a dark look, had a huff of a laugh as her reward, then felt him squeeze her hand.

"We'll be fine," he said. "I'm certain of it."

She admired his confidence, but held on tightly to her wee rolling trunk with her free hand, just to fix herself in the present day should the doorway have other plans for them. Oliver opened the door, then reached inside and lit the lights. She crossed the threshold with him, then sighed a little in relief.

"The proper time," she said.

"I think I've rarely been more relieved," he said, with feeling. He took her trunk from her and set it against the front wall, then looked at her. "A fire?"

She nodded. "Please." She paused, then smiled. "It won't bother me if you're here."

He closed his eyes briefly, then nodded before he led her across the wee gathering chamber. She found herself invited to sit, which she did, and watched him build a fire in the cold hearth, ignoring the echoes of watching him having done that sort of thing before. He fed his fire for a bit, then finally sat back on his heels and looked at her.

"Might I say something serious?" he asked, his expression serious indeed.

She nodded slowly. "If you will."

He turned and walked over to her on his knees, then took her hands. "I would like to do the traditional twenty-first century marriage ceremony with you, as well."

She had to clear her throat, but that was likely from the fire. "Would you?"

He nodded. "I would."

"With a ring?" she managed. "And a trip to a honeymoon destination where we might sip champagne poolside?"

He smiled. "I'm being serious."

"And I'm trying not to weep."

He bent his head, kissed her hands, then looked at her. "Bridal magazines?"

"Emily thought I should at least have a wee peek at one."

"Well, she's definitely the one to put in charge of packing for our honeymoon trip." His smile became a bit graver. "And yes, Mairead, a ring and a priest and perhaps our families all gathered in your father and grandfather's hall."

She supposed there was no point in trying to hide the tears that spilled down her cheeks. "In truth?" she whispered.

He nodded. "But until then, I'm happy that this was for us alone. I didn't want to leave you at Jamie's again."

She supposed there was no point in hiding her blushes either. "I didn't want to remain behind."

He nodded, looking slightly uncomfortable. He looked around them for good measure, then back at her. "I suppose we just ate supper."

She nodded.

"I could read to you," he offered.

She looked at him in surprise. "Read?"

"Do you have any other ideas?"

She considered, then imagined there was no reason not to be about their marriage presently as they meant to go on. She rose to her feet and pulled him to his. She put her shoulders back and nodded briskly. "Let's be about the proper activity for a married couple. I'm braced."

"Braced?" he echoed faintly.

"I know the general particulars," she said, nodding again. "Let's have it over with."

His mouth opened and closed several times, as if he simply couldn't find anything useful to say. She frowned thoughtfully, then stroked her chin for good measure.

"Should we have asked Jamie for suggestions?"

He gaped at her. She supposed she shouldn't have teased him so terribly, but she had to admit she was beginning to understand why his lads did it so often. 'Twas especially satisfying when she saw in his eyes the moment he realized what she was doing. He looked at her shrewdly.

"I'm not sure if I should be relieved or embarrassed by what I'm about to say," he ventured, "but I have done this before so it might not be as awful as it could be."

She gasped. "You libertine!" Then she paused and looked at him with a frown. "I've said that before to you, haven't I?"

"At least once."

She took a pair of steps forward and put her hands on his chest, then smiled up at him. "I'm teasing you."

"I know."

She smiled at him. "I'm trying to put you at ease."

"I wasn't nervous," he said defensively.

"Oliver, you were speaking of another supper."

"I'm a lad," he said with a shrug. "We're simple creatures."

She laughed a little, because he was so much more than that and she loved him desperately. "But you're very charming creatures, so why don't you attend to your work?"

"Will you spend the evening blushing?" he asked.

"Will *you*?"

"Very likely."

She waited.

He looked at her and made no move.

She supposed the present moment was not the one to begin to worry in truth, but she was damned close to it. Oliver was a magnificent, braw, deliciously fashioned man, but he looked as if he might be contemplating a trip to the gallows. She lifted one eyebrow and looked at him pointedly, but that only resulted in his clearing his throat and taking a deep breath.

"We could begin by holding hands," he said carefully, as if he expected her to run screaming into the night at the first wrong word.

She blinked. "Hold hands?"

He nodded. "Very proper and polite. The Duke of Birmingham would have approved, I'm certain."

She felt herself begin to frown and couldn't stop. "Is that all?"

"I could give you a fairly interested look or two."

She glared at him and didn't bother to stop *that*.

"We could also kiss," he said thoughtfully. "One or two, perhaps, and very chaste."

"Would it ruin the evening if I reached for my knife and stabbed you?"

He looked at her solemnly. "It might."

She started to give him the proper tongue-lashing he deserved when she realized his eyes were twinkling.

"Are you teasing me?" she asked.

"I thought you might enjoy it."

"If you tell me it's something from your book, I *will* stab your mates."

He laughed a little and pulled her into his arms. "I invented it all on my own, clever lad that I am."

She permitted herself a small laugh, partly unwillingly given, because he was a braw, lovely man and she could freely admit that she loved him. She met his gaze.

"Thank you."

"For being so clever?"

She nodded. "And for rescuing me."

"It was most assuredly my pleasure."

"And," she ventured, "for loving me."

He pressed his lips against her forehead. "That is most assuredly a privilege."

She leaned up and kissed him just to, as Ewan would have advised her to do, point him in the right direction.

He smiled and returned the favor, then lifted his head and looked at her gravely. "I love you," he said quietly.

"I love you back," she said, then she smiled. "Emily told me that's a chic way to say it. What say you?"

"Very chic," he agreed. "And I'll gladly accept those words however you want to say them and in whatever language suits you." He paused. "Except Latin. Mine is nonexistent except for clan mottos."

She considered him. "Are you nervous?"

He glared at her, but it was very weak and not at all convincing. She smiled, then decided more demonstration couldn't go awrong. She put her hands on his cheeks and set to her goodly work of kissing him until he might possibly be swayed to her purpose.

He laughed a little as she allowed him to breathe. "I refuse to admit what I am," he managed. He considered her. "A little light reading from Constance Buchanan's latest?"

She looked at him evenly.

He only shrugged, but he seemed to be fighting a smile.

"You know what sort of gel I am," she reminded him.

"Stride forth and conquer?"

She nodded firmly.

"Yes," he said, looking at her with affection, "I do. I do know what sort of gel you are."

"You should know," she said, "whilst we're discussing the rest of our evening that Emily said I looked very fine in these black pieces of clothing."

"Very fine?"

She looked at him solemnly. "I believe the word she used was *hot*."

He began to smile. "Did she?"

"Do you think I look hot?"

He bent his head and kissed her softly. "Scorching."

She laughed a little. "Indeed."

He smiled at her fondly. "And before I feel well and truly scorched, why don't we speak frankly about what lies before us."

She swallowed confidently, not at all uneasily. "I am not afraid."

"Of me?" he asked, looking genuinely surprised.

"Well, of course not you," she said, feeling equally surprised. "But this ... well, you know."

He smoothed her hair back from her face and smiled again. "Let's do this. We'll make ourselves a comfortable nest on the floor not too close to the fire because there isn't any possible way I'm going to fit in Moraig's little nook over there."

She nodded. "That seems reasonable."

"We'll find pajamas."

"Emily bought me some very pleasing ones in pink," Mairead agreed. "They have these charming wee felines on them."

He bowed his head and laughed. "I can't kill her, but I might have to shout at her."

"Why? They're adorable. She said they are ones you are very fond of, so I will wear them with pleasure."

"Perfect," he said, looking as if he might like to laugh again, but didn't quite dare. "Then after we've garbed ourselves in luxurious pajamas and made a proper investigation of the freezer to see if there might be dessert, why don't we just have ourselves a wee cuddle in front of the hearth?"

"A cuddle?"

"Accompanied by a few kisses," he amended.

"Only a few?"

"Several."

She smiled. "And?"

"You're doing this on purpose."

She leaned up and kissed him softly. "I am."

He reached for her hand. "Let's go make sure the door is locked."

"And then?"

He laughed a little and tugged on her. "You'll put your knife in the fridge for safekeeping and we'll see where the rest of the evening leads."

She thought that a most acceptable plan.

TWENTY-FIVE

O LIVER LEANED BACK AGAINST A ridiculously comfortable overstuffed chair, propped his feet up on a stool where he could toast his toes against the fire, and watched his newly made wife prowling through the kitchen, investigating things that intrigued her.

He fully intended to offer himself as an item to put very next on her list, but he was content at the moment to simply watch her in her spy outfit for which he absolutely owed Emily a very large bouquet of flowers.

Mairead MacLeod was, he would freely admit, absolutely scorching in black.

And he was going to be of absolutely no use to anyone for the foreseeable future. He was half tempted to send Derrick a text informing him that the holiday had been such a success that he thought he might want to extend it for several months. The village had a decent grocery and a fabulous chippy, the camping mattress they'd made good use of the night before and tucked away in Moraig's sleeping nook had been surprisingly comfortable, and he imagined with enough flattery, Emily might occasionally bring them more clothes so they didn't have to do any wash.

He could think of much worse ways to spend the fall than holed up in a charming little cottage with the woman he simply couldn't keep his hands off. Well, except for the moment, but she likely needed a chance to breathe now and again.

He came back to himself to find that she was leaning against the sink, watching him. She was smiling faintly, though, which he thought might be a good sign. He crooked his finger at her, had a laugh as his reward, but also had his handfasted wife soon sitting on his lap with her arm around his neck.

"I love you," he said with a smile.

"I love you back," she said, kissing him sweetly. "I found something in the wee refrigerator."

"Didn't we just have breakfast?"

"We did, but 'tis important to keep up our strength."

"Well," he said with a slow smile, "I suppose that's very true."

He would have started something that might have required a bit of sustenance after the fact, but found himself facing instead a manila folder. He looked at his wife in alarm.

"What's that?"

"Something I found amongst the vegetables, though I'll tell you plain, Oliver, I don't know why you'd want to eat leaves."

He couldn't have agreed more, but he took the folder just the same. "I'm afraid to look inside."

"I'll hold you."

He started to pitch the container of doom over his shoulder, but Mairead caught it before he could.

"It might be important," she warned.

"If it's from the lads, that means they were here whilst we were not which is alarming and they're adding tasks to my book which might distract us from other things."

She considered. "Let's just have a look, then, and see how far it merits being flung out the front door."

Oliver opened the folder to find a single sheaf of paper there along with a little envelope of what turned out to be stickers in the shape of a particular feline. He handed those to his wife.

"They like you."

"I like these," she said a little breathlessly, then she smiled at him quickly. "Not as much as you, of course, but they are very wee and charming."

"If you pull off the backs, they stick on things. Please," he added, "do not stick them on me."

She laughed a little, kissed him sweetly, then nodded toward his note. "What madness are they combining now?"

He looked at the note and sighed.

Don't think this means you get out of your holiday. The book must be completed! Don't cheat any more, especially on the maths. An almost-running car awaits you ... maybe.

Mairead cleared her throat carefully. "I could purchase you an automobile," she offered. "I have gold enough for something small, I imagine."

He was torn between wanting to pull up a bank statement for her and going down on his knees again and professing undying love for a woman who apparently liked him well enough to be concerned that he have wheels. He chose a smile instead and offered another in what he hoped would be an endless succession of sweet kisses between the two of them.

"I have a car," he said a few minutes later. "Two actually." Which he did, namely a non-descript Ford for skulking around behind less savory types and a ridiculously expensive Audi that put him firmly in the category of Britain's rudest drivers, but it had suited him at the time when he'd plunked down his hard-earned sterling for it.

Her eyes widened. "Are you so wealthy, then? I—"

"Can absolutely afford to purchase yourself as many things in black as you like with my funds," he finished for her. He smiled. "I won't let us starve, Mair."

She looked at her hand that was resting on his chest for a moment or two, then met his eyes. "I like being included in your life."

He had to clear his throat not because he'd suddenly become overwhelmed by emotion but because the fire was smoky. "I am thrilled you want to be."

"What will we do after your holiday is over?" she asked hesitantly. "I suppose I could stay with Jamie and Elizabeth."

Why was halfway out of his mouth before he caught himself and put his brain in neutral. He looked at the woman in his arms and considered her upbringing, a few of her relatives who still deserved a right proper beating, and her previous expectations for her future. His usual refuge was silence so he didn't make a complete ass of himself at any given moment, but he suspected that with that woman there, that would be a poor choice.

"Did you give yourself to me yesterday?" he asked.

"Several times, if memory serves."

He laughed briefly, because he was just so damned happy. "I think you're right. Did I give myself to you?"

She lifted an eyebrow. "Aye you did," she said. "You libertine."

He kissed her firmly, then sat back. "I believe, my love, that that giving and taking has left us with no choice but to carry on with that sort of thing until immediately before we begin moldering in our graves."

"If you like," she said, looking as if the thought wasn't displeasing. "Then what shall we do after your holiday is over?"

"Go back to London for a bit, I imagine," he said slowly. "My job is there, after all. As for anything else, as long as we're together, why don't we take the days as they come?"

She nodded, smiling.

He tossed the folder over his shoulder. "Now, about that giving and taking thing—"

A banging on the front door almost sent him pitching out of his chair. He looked at his wife who was looking at him with the same expression of alarm he suspected he was wearing.

"Let's go hide in the loo," he said with feeling.

"It could be food."

He considered. "Might be."

"You need your sword."

He realized that it had been so long since he'd worried about steel that he honestly had no idea where it was. He followed her finger that she was pointing back over her shoulder to find his sword leaning up against one side of the hearth. He considered, then shrugged.

"We'll slam the door shut if it's someone sketchy."

"And if it's your mates?"

"We'll slam the door, then push something in front of it to keep it shut."

She smiled and crawled off his lap. He started toward the door, then turned and pulled her into his arms. He held her until the banging on the door began to be more than annoying, then pulled away and looked at her.

"Later."

She smiled. "I have black pajamas."

"I'll love them."

"I could place these adorable kitty stickers on them."

He imagined she didn't expect a proper response to that, so he only glanced at her, had a smile as his reward, then took her hand to pull her with him across Moraig's very small great room and over to the door. He looked at his wife briefly, had a firm nod in response, then opened the door.

He was utterly unsurprised to find three grinning eejits standing there, baskets in hand.

He started to speak, then gave up. Words were beyond him.

Mairead peeked around the door he hadn't quite opened fully. "Och, it's the lads," she said brightly.

Oliver shot those same lads a look of promise, then stepped aside so his bride could have a decent look at them and perhaps rethink her enthusiasm.

Ewan stepped forward and made her a low bow before he held out his burden. "We brought you treats and treasures, my lady."

"Pox-spotted yoga trews?" she asked breathlessly, accepting the basket and peering inside. "Look, Oliver, there is a set for me!"

"I brought food," Peter said in garbled tones. "What I thought you might fancy, miss."

"Mrs.," Oliver corrected with a scowl.

Peter shot him a look, then made Mairead a bit of a bow. "Mrs. MacLeod-Phillips, of course."

She bestowed one of her perfect smiles on him. "How kind of you, Peter. What sort?"

"Chocolate, chips, and those biscuits of Mrs. Gies's that you fancied," Peter managed, coloring furiously.

Oliver watched his handfasted wife welcome in a pair of those demons and was only slightly mollified that Derrick remained behind with him by the doorway instead of bounding into that tiny croft as if he'd actually been invited. Oliver looked at him coolly.

"You're interrupting my honeymoon," he said pointedly, "which, as you'll remember, I didn't do to yours."

Derrick clapped him on the shoulder. "Just taking the—"

"I know what you're taking out of me," Oliver muttered.

Derrick smiled. "We actually came to invite you two to lunch at Patrick's."

"Lunch?"

"A dual clan affair that will no doubt send shockwaves through Cameron and MacLeod family tree branches back centuries. Jamie's coming as well. Actually, he and Ian are right behind us, bearing gifts."

Oliver looked over Derrick's shoulder to find that was indeed the case. He made Jamie a bow, then straightened.

"My lord James," he said politely. "Come to check on your granddaughter?"

Jamie smiled briefly. "No, Ollie lad, I'm sure she's managing you well enough. Young Ian, lad, hand him your burden."

"We brought you luxuries from Tavish Fergusson's shop," Young Ian said, holding out a bag, "but Father intimidated him right proper so you can be certain the goods are untainted."

Oliver suspected, having gone with Robert Cameron a time or two to Tavish's shop to keep him properly cowed, that worrying about the quality was justified. He welcomed Jamie and Ian inside Moraig's house and sighed at the sight of his mates and his wife gathered in front of the hearth, welcoming Jamie in and making sure he was comfortably seated.

There wasn't a thinking lad amongst that group, to be sure.

He realized with a start that he had company in the person of Jamie's eldest son. He suspected by the look on the lad's face that he had something to confess, but that likely came from having a few of those sorts of moments himself during his youth.

"What is it?" he murmured.

"I lost the book."

Oliver looked at him in surprise. "What book?"

"*The* book," Young Ian said miserably. "The Constance Buchanan book." He paused and looked up at Oliver. "I'm approaching an age, you ken, when I might want to consort with the fairer sex."

Oliver put his hand on the lad's shoulder. "A very wise choice, then."

"I didn't *mean* to lose it. I'd been keeping it in a tree."

"Out in front here?"

Young Ian nodded.

"Very reasonable."

Young Ian paused, then looked at him. "Should I tell my Da, do you think?"

"I imagine he already knows."

"He knows everything."

"And what he doesn't, your mother does."

Young Ian looked out over the inside of the croft with a thoughtful frown. Oliver joined him. It had been that sort of holiday so far.

Young Ian looked up at him, his expression troubled. "Will it harm Mair, do you suppose?"

"We won't allow it to," Oliver assured him.

"I should go speak to my father."

"It might make you feel better."

Young Ian nodded briskly, put his shoulders back, and strode away, no doubt to conquer. Oliver didn't blame the lad at all if he changed his mind two steps into his journey and instead went to prop himself up next to Oliver's sword.

He sent Oliver a look of pleading that was unmistakable, so Oliver only shook his head and smiled. He wasn't going to tell the lad's tale for him, though it did answer at least the question of how the book had found itself liberated from the lady Elizabeth's bookshelf.

He supposed the next question to be answered was where both halves of it found themselves at present.

He leaned back against the door for a bit, picking up the thread of the thoughts he'd been thinking at Cameron Hall whilst he'd been about the happy labor of keeping Mairead warm and comfortable on the sofa. The manuscript Sinclair McKinnon had fashioned had been remarkably preserved, though he was still committed to the idea that it was because the little stone box had been above the flood line. Perhaps the chapel had also benefitted from a lack of patronage which had left the air inside not quite as moist as it might have been otherwise.

A book out in the open, though, was an entirely different story. He hadn't questioned Mairead as to the particulars, but he couldn't imagine the same hollowed out spot she'd used had been the same one Young Ian had discovered. The tree would have grown, for one thing. Even if the manuscript had remained in Mairead's hiding place and survived the four hundred subsequent years of tree growth and Scottish weather, it just wasn't possible that it would still be intact. He wasn't above hazarding a bit of a climb to make certain at some point, but definitely not for the next few days.

"You thought Oliver was the Duke of Birmingham?"

Oliver snapped back to himself and had the words Derrick had just choked out register. He listened to the rest of the lads have a jolly old laugh about it, treated his boss to the rude gesture he was obviously expecting, then rolled his eyes and walked over to see if he couldn't commandeer a spot next to his bride.

"The man on the cover was fair-haired," Mairead offered, "though Oliver is far more handsome. His noble qualities, though, and obvious chivalry seemed a perfect match to me."

And with that, they were off, though Oliver credited those lads there with knowing how close they were to death by his hands because the sport at his expense was mercifully brief. He imagined that had to do with Jamie rubbing his hands together as if he had something important to say.

But before he could, Young Ian stepped forward and looked at his father. "I apologize, Father," he said, making his sire a low, formal bow. "I am the one who lost the book after having pinched it from Mum's library."

Oliver suspected Jamie was trying very hard not to smile, but he did manage a very serious look at least initially.

"Stealing is wrong, son."

"I was borrowing, Father."

Oliver looked around to find the entire company conceding that with nods of agreement. He took a moment to smile at his wife who had slipped her hand into his and given him a smile of her own, then turned back to the conversation at hand.

"You see," Young Ian said, looking as if he hoped very much that his father would, "I was looking for wooing ideas."

Jamie looked as if he might have wanted to stroke his chin, but perhaps that moment hadn't quite arrived. "Do you have a lass you fancy, then, son?"

"I'm interested more in a general sense," Young Ian said frankly. "If I find a gel I like, I had planned to ask you for the particulars."

Oliver shook his head in silent admiration of the lad's technique. The clan MacLeod was in good hands with Young

Ian in line for the chieftainship. He listened to without really hearing the rest of the conversation which seemed to revolve around books lost and manuscripts found and concerns over things being in the past that shouldn't be.

"But all's well that ends well," Jamie said, rubbing his hands together. "Is there dessert?"

"Da, we haven't had lunch yet," Young Ian said, sounding slightly appalled.

"Son, if there is dessert in front of you, 'tis best to avail yourself of it whilst your mother isn't watching."

Oliver watched Young Ian absorb that advice with the appropriate solemnity. And he didn't particularly want to eavesdrop, but the cottage was so damned small that he couldn't help but overhear Young Ian coming to kneel down by his father and apologize again.

Jamie smiled and reached out to ruffle his hair. "You could have chosen much worse tomes to study."

"I'm sorry, Da."

Jamie only shook his head. "Not to worry, son. I think it did your aunt Mairead a goodly service in the past and I'm certain we'll find it here in the future at some point."

"Oliver," Ewan called, "come be a love and find us a pan we can put the lava cake into. Madame Gies made it especially for you, for some unfathomable reason."

"He does her washing up," Peter said wisely.

Oliver had to admit that was generally true, but it always allowed him the chance to drag out his French which should have been better considering it was hardwired into his genes courtesy of his mother. Plus, he wasn't too proud to admit he liked having someone in his life who felt like a grandmother. Perhaps she would be the same sort of thing for Mairead in time.

He looked over to find his lady wife currently in earnest conversation with Young Ian and left her to it. He imagined, by the look of relief on the lad's face, that she was absolving him of some unnecessary guilt. He wasn't about to interrupt that.

He took a deep breath and threw himself into the fray that was too many men in one very small kitchen. If there were a few friendly elbows thrown and a bit of happy cursing trotted out for inspection, he supposed it was nothing more than standard fare. He was fairly certain at some point in Jamie and Young Ian decided to forgo dessert and head for Patrick's, which he supposed left more for the rest of them.

The smell was, he had to admit, heavenly. He didn't imagine anyone would ever manage to lure Madame Gies away from her happy place at Cameron Hall, but if he could have found a way, he most certainly would have. It might be worth even a discreet inquiry about her willingness to perhaps provide cookery lessons. Mairead at least might appreciate his efforts.

"Oliver, where's your wife?"

He looked around Moraig's wee croft and realized she wasn't there. He tamped down a ridiculous feeling of panic and went to check the door of the loo. Finding it unlocked, he knocked. Perhaps she had simply wanted to change into those terrifying spotted yoga trews. When he heard no response, he decided that he could just poke his head inside and see if she'd hidden herself away with Constance Buchanan's Highland laird offering.

The loo was empty and so was the wee dressing room attached to it.

He strode back out into the great room and walked over to the door, then came to a teetering halt. The door was ajar, but he distinctly remembered Mairead having closed it firmly behind Jamie. They always closed the door firmly. They had damned good reason to close the door *very* firmly.

"Oliver?"

Oliver looked at Ewan and felt a repeat of the horror he'd felt that first night—

He slammed the door shut on those thoughts and wrenched the door open, intending to fling himself outside and rush off to find her. Unfortunately, he found himself held by the arms until his head cleared enough that he could stop swearing at his mates.

"She's likely just outside," he said hoarsely.

Derrick nodded. "Likely so, but let's gear up anyway." He paused. "Just in case."

Oliver supposed Derrick had good reason for that given that he'd once lost Samantha in Renaissance London and had to go after her. Derrick had also spent his share of time before he'd met Sam as Jamie's traveling companion of choice.

"I don't think ..." Oliver could scarce finish the sentence.

"I don't either," Derrick said calmly, "but let's do what we do best, shall we? For all we know, your lady has decided to lead us on a merry chase so we don't go to fat. Peter, go pull out that cake so it doesn't burn. We'll be back in fifteen to reheat it."

Oliver found an earbud and mic slapped into his hand by Ewan who had already gone into spy mode and was checking his own gear. Oliver managed to get his shoes on because he found he had no choice but to do as he always did when faced with things that were not useful to think about at the moment.

He took his fear and slammed it behind the door in his mind he reserved for that sort of thing, slipped out the front door with his mates, and paused to let Derrick set their plan of attack with his usual collection of gestures and nods. Peter and Ewan went west and he slipped around the east side of Moraig's house with his boss, keeping to the side of the house and wishing the shadows were much deeper.

He supposed, ten minutes north and much deeper into the forest, that the shadows weren't going to make any difference. He stopped beside Derrick and looked at the madness in progress twenty paces away.

"Don't let me kill him," he murmured.

"We'll see," Derrick said grimly in a low voice. "What now?"

"Surround him. I'll see if it's me they want."

Derrick signaled to Ewan and Peter, then melted into the darkness.

Oliver had a final look at the glade there in the woods, a place he'd never thought anything of during his previous explores, but now he wondered why not. It was a lovely place, actually, and would have made a fine spot for a holiday let. He would have to bring that up to Jamie the next time he saw him. But later. He had business at the moment that would not wait.

He took a deep breath, stilled his mind, and stepped out into the glade.

TWENTY-SIX

MAIREAD STOOD WITH KENNETH'S BLADE across her throat and wondered where she'd taken a wrong turn that day.

Dawn had broken very nicely with Oliver Phillips's arms around her, followed by several very lovely kisses that had led to yet more of the things they had enjoyed during the previous night, things she thought she could safely leave off the pages of her own book just as Mistress Constance Buchanan had discreetly left them off her own.

The subsequent arrival of visitors hadn't been entirely unwelcome. Oliver's mates were braw and charming and 'twas obvious they were very fond of her husband. Jamie, too, seemed pleased with Oliver's care of her and she had agreed that Young Ian could certainly do worse than to learn his company manners from the Duke of Birmingham.

She'd understood Jamie's concern over leaving that same book in 1583. The saints only knew what sort of havoc it could wreak on someone not quite as sensible as she had been. She had consoled herself at first with the thought that it simply couldn't have survived intact for very long.

That thought had been countered rather unpleasantly by reminding herself that Sinclair McKinnon's scribblings had been almost perfectly intact in that abandoned McKinnon chapel. The saving grace there was that his writings had been contained in a decently fashioned stone box whilst her book had been exposed to the elements.

She'd leaned against the wall next to Oliver's sword, enjoying the view of him being teased ferociously by his mates and bearing it manfully, and contemplated other things. Master Sinclair's pages had survived thanks to their weathering the years in a box, true, and in her day there she'd known of two hiding places that might have served the same sort of purpose. One had been the loose stone in her brother's bedchamber, something she was certain he had no idea about.

The other had been a similarly loose stone along the back wall of the witch's croft. She'd always thought the spot was altogether too small to hide any stray MacLeods—no matter what her uncle Lachlan had claimed—but the idea that it might possibly have hidden a book had been worth a look at least.

So she'd left Oliver and his mates to discussing the intricacies of something called football and slipped outside to do a little investigating on her own. She hadn't but rounded the side of Moraig's house before she'd realized that she would never reach that loose stone at the back of Moraig's house. The first reason was that someone had added to the croft, covering the wall in the process.

The other was that she'd run directly into Kenneth MacLeod loitering in a time definitely not his own, accompanied by a large knife and his own foul humors, and he had captured her without hesitation.

The only positive things she could think of about the whole damnable exercise was that he hadn't slit her throat right off and he'd been so unnerved by Moraig's house that he'd dragged her away from it. If nothing else, Oliver would continue his life without the memory of her shrieking herself hoarse before she died.

Not that she had any intention of crying out—nor dying, for that matter. She wished she hadn't left her blade in the refrigerator, but she'd made do with less before.

"I say we slay her here!"

Mairead looked at Master James who was standing five paces away from her and wished he would stand a bit farther away. She was most assuredly going to need another endless shower in Moraig's glorious bathing chamber just to remove the spittle that seemed to be flying everywhere each time he shouted something else.

That was a man who she very seriously doubted had even managed a first date.

"We have to take her back with us," Kenneth growled.

"Stop saying that," Master James spat. "We're here where she is!"

"Which is not where you want her to be," Kenneth said, "but you're too stupid to understand that."

Mairead had opinions on the wit of both of them, but imagined it would be best to keep them to herself.

"She's in demon garb!" Master James howled.

Mairead had to agree with that, at least. She was very fond of her black clothing, mostly because Oliver thought she was very hot in it. She did indeed feel very hot, but she suspected that at present that was merely from nerves.

"We have to return to the faery ring in the grass," Kenneth said, sounding as if he might be on the verge of weeping with frustration.

Mairead would have suggested that Master James push him fully toward that place so she might escape his blade and run, but Kenneth's hand in her hair suddenly was painful enough that she had to bite her lip to keep from making any sort of noise. Oliver favored silence as well, she knew.

She knew that because she had just caught sight of him moving silently through the trees. She didn't dare look for the rest of his lads, though she strongly suspected they were there as well.

"I'll go," she said suddenly. "Please, please just let me live long enough to see the hall once more!"

Master James stopped frothing at the mouth long enough to look at her in surprise. "Why?"

She manufactured a little noise of grief. "So I might go to the fire knowing that I've cleansed my clan of this evil."

"Let's go, then," Kenneth said, taking the knife away from her throat.

He obviously thought his hand buried in her hair would be enough, which she supposed she might agree with. She put her hand against her throat as if she could scarce control her grief because possibly losing a finger to his knife was better than losing her life, though she had no intention of giving up either.

It took far less time to reach the edge of the forest than she thought it might, though she had every confidence that Oliver and the lads would have followed her. She stopped still when she found not only Tasgall waiting there just outside the faery ring, but Deirdre as well.

She gasped, but that was likely because Kenneth was suddenly no longer standing behind her and his removal from her person had almost broken her neck.

"Are you all right?" Oliver asked urgently.

She clutched the back of her hair and opened her mouth to tell him that she was but he might not be in a moment, but apparently there was no need. He turned to meet her brother who had rushed forward, his sword bare in his hands and a look of madness on his face.

She found herself behind Ewan and Peter, with Derrick standing a pace or two in front of them. She peeked over Ewan's shoulder and glared at her brother.

"If you hurt him, I'll kill you!" she shouted.

Derrick shot her a smile. "Ewan, give her an earbud at least so she can hear Oliver muttering under his breath as he fights. It's very entertaining."

Mairead thought it might be anything but, but she found herself immediately outfitted in Future Spygear, as Ewan called it.

"Don't slay him," she managed into the little stick Ewan had fastened to her cheek.

"How alive should I leave him?"

"Only barely?"

She had a brief smile from her husband over his shoulder before he turned back to his business. She decided that perhaps it was best to just let him see to his affairs and prepare to heap compliments on his head after the fact. After all, her brother had made her life a misery. A bit of encouragement not to do that to anyone else in the future could only be a good thing.

Oliver rid her brother of his sword immediately by spinning around and kicking it from his hands. And then he simply stood there, which she almost shouted at him for but Ewan put his hand on her shoulder.

"He's not going to hit him first."

She looked at him in astonishment. "Why not?"

Ewan shrugged. "It's his code of honor. But if your brother is stupid enough to strike him, he'll regret it."

She turned back to the skirmish and tried to watch it dispassionately. Tasgall did indeed strike Oliver first, a feeble, glancing blow on the face that did him no credit at all. Then again, he generally hit women so perhaps he feared to truly commit to striking a man who was taller and more finely fashioned than he was.

"Are you afraid of me?" Tasgall blustered.

Oliver simply put the back of his hand to his mouth, glanced at the blood from his cut lip, then looked at him. "Don't hit any more women," he said quietly.

"Who are you to tell—"

Mairead supposed all those fights Oliver had gotten into in his youth had served him well, along with all those many hours learning various forms of martial—

She took a deep breath, let the memories come, then let them go. She forced herself to watch her love repay her brother for things he had done and inspire him not to do them any longer, though she suspected Oliver did far less damage to him than he could have.

He finally caught her brother neatly under the chin, sending his head snapping back. Tasgall's eyes rolled back in his head and he fell to the ground like a drunkard after far too much ale. Mairead watched him for a moment or two to make certain he wasn't going to be leaping to his feet and swinging at the nearest person he could find, then she pushed past Derrick to at least make certain Oliver's mouth hadn't been overly damaged.

Only instead of finding her love in front of her, she came face-to-face with her sister-in-law. She was very relieved to find that Deirdre didn't have a knife in her hand.

She did, however, have half a book.

Mairead looked at Oliver to find him watching with absolutely no expression on his face. Either he was on the verge of laughing or he feared that things might go very badly indeed. She suspected she might agree with him on both points, so she prepared herself for the worst as she turned back to face her brother's wife.

"That's an interesting treasure you have there," she said carefully.

"I had the entire thing," Deirdre spat.

"Did you?" Mairead asked, trying to be pleasant. "How clever of you to have found something so valuable."

Deirdre pointed back toward the forest with a hand that was not at all steady. "I went to the witch's croft a year ago to dare the faeries and sprites to vex me—"

"Your first mistake," Kenneth howled.

Deirdre shot him a look of loathing, then turned back to her. "The house was bolted against me, but I looked in the windows and saw it was full of demon's belongings."

Mairead didn't dare look at Oliver, though she could imagine well enough what he was thinking. Perhaps her uncle's tales of MacLeods disappearing into the witch's forest weren't so fantastical after all, for 'twas obvious Deirdre had gone through the faery ring in the meadow. She was grateful she'd had such a generous helping of good sense come to her from her father which had allowed her to investigate things without descending into madness. Her brother's wife obviously did not have that same skill.

"I found the manuscript next to the tree," Deirdre said, beginning to chafe her hands together. "But then I heard a rustling in the woods. I feared for my immortal soul so I picked up the book and fled." Deirdre looked down her nose. "Not that you would understand anything about that, being a demon yourself."

"As you say," Mairead agreed. "But if you were in a different world with odd things in the witch's croft, how did you return home?"

"I went back to the faery ring in the grass, of course. I ran through it, hoping to shake off anything that had come from the forest with me, but then it occurred to me that I might be drawing them to me with the folios. I decided to return half of them to the demons in the witch's croft to keep them at bay. I would have managed it had not *that* fool been following me."

Mairead imagined it couldn't hurt to join her sister-in-law briefly in glaring at Kenneth. She enjoyed that for a moment then turned back to the matter at hand.

"What happened then?"

"I took the half with the rendering of *that* demon on it," Deirdre said, gesturing with a shaking hand toward Oliver, "and left it by the tree where I'd found it, hoping that would be enough of an offering to appease them." She frowned. "The trees were different, true, and the witch's croft empty of all but a stool, but I suspected that was because I had angered the demons."

Mairead suspected it was perhaps more because Deirdre hadn't succeeded in getting herself back to the Future where she'd first found Constance Buchanan's book, but perhaps that didn't need to be said.

"I rushed home and hid the second part behind the loose stone in the wall in my bedchamber," Deirdre said, looking thoroughly unsettled. "I studied it for many months, but could make no sense of the scratches on the sheaves."

And so was answered the question of why Deirdre had spent so much time upstairs. Mairead couldn't fault her for wanting to learn new things, but she definitely could for making everyone's life a misery whilst she'd been about it.

"Do you still have that second half?" she asked carefully.

"Your fool of a brother found it and threw it into the fire," Deirdre said shortly. "And since that was the case, I needed another offering."

Mairead realized at that moment just how badly she'd misjudged Deirdre Fergusson and her madness. "And you think I have the first half?" she asked mildly.

"I've seen you putting it into the tree when you weren't keeping it secreted upon your person."

"I don't have it—"

"Of course you do!"

"Nay, she does not," Kenneth said, puffing up and pulling something from inside his plaid. He held up what Mairead could readily see was the first half of her book. "I have it," he said triumphantly, "and I will use it to prove she's a witch!"

"*I* want to prove she's a witch," Deirdre shouted at him.

Mairead looked at Master James who was gnawing on the edge of his sleeve. He glanced uneasily at her, then at the other two standing there.

"I just want to burn her," he offered. Perhaps he'd had a view of what Oliver had done to Tasgall and didn't fancy the like happening to himself.

Mairead looked at Oliver. He sighed and shook his head, then shot her a quick smile before he turned a frown on both Deirdre and Kenneth.

"If that is a demon's tome," he said slowly, "then why are you two fighting over it? I should think Master James would find your having touched it to be very ... unwholesome."

Master James rushed forward, shoving Deirdre out of his way. "I could not agree more, Lord Oliver. Perhaps you would care to aid me in my testing of these two?"

"I can't think of anything I would rather do less," Oliver said with a polite smile.

Mairead would have complimented him on that, but she was startled by the glint of steel in Deirdre's hand, the blade descending with terrifying swiftness—

Toward Oliver's chest.

He caught her arm readily enough and held the blade away from himself.

"Let me go," Deirdre shrieked. "I'll send her to the fire, and you'll not stop me!"

Mairead would have offered her opinion on her sister-in-law's moral choices, but she didn't have time before Deirdre tried to bite Oliver's hand that was still holding onto her. The sound was particularly unpleasant, though she realized very quickly that Deirdre had encountered Oliver's silver timepiece strapped to his arm and that those were likely a pair of teeth objecting the resistance.

Deirdre pulled back and put her hand to her mouth, her eyes wide. She backed away quickly, then tripped over her husband and went sprawling, her head coming to rest with yet another unwholesome sound against a rock.

Mairead would have commented on just desserts served right properly, but before she could, Oliver had leaped over to her and pulled her behind him. She looked around his shoulder in time to see Master James there, flapping his arms as if he were a carrion bird. Or at least he did for a moment or two. His arms fell to his sides, then he listed to one side, continuing on until he'd fallen fully onto the ground.

James MacLeod stood behind him.

"Did you slay him?" she asked in surprise.

He held up a longish tube that was very small. "Straw," he said succinctly. "Tranquilizer dart."

I know, she almost said, but she had no idea how she knew so she set that aside as something to think about later. That list was growing uncomfortably long, but perhaps she would start her own book like Oliver's and continually add things to it for study when she had the time for it.

She watched Oliver and Derrick catch Kenneth before he could flee, then truss him up with some sort of sticky rope.

Oliver did them all the favor of wrapping a bit of the same over Kenneth's mouth which contributed greatly to the peace of the afternoon.

"Thank you, my lord," Oliver said to Jamie, making him a low bow. "Your aid was vital."

Jamie shrugged with a faint smile. "I think you and your companions had things well in hand, but I thought a little aid with that vile man couldn't go amiss. I'll leave it to you to sort young Kenneth, though. He knows too much."

"I've got that," Ewan said, stepping up and making Jamie a bow. "If I might offer my services as a hypnotist?"

"A what?" Mairead asked.

Ewan pulled a gold disc out of his pocket. "This, my lady, is a magical tool I will use to send him into a trance where he will be amenable to any suggestion you might have. When he wakes, he will feel compelled to do as you've suggested but have no idea why."

Mairead was happy to have Oliver come stand next to her. "Is he daft?" she murmured.

Oliver shook his head with a smile. "Ewan is a man of many talents. I've watched him do this before—not, however, to me."

"That you know," Ewan said lightly.

Oliver glared at him, but Ewan only laughed lightly in return. He turned to her and inclined his head.

"Your wish is my command."

Mairead considered all the things she could have wished on her cousin, but discarded them one by one. He would either become a decent man or continue on to his own bad end, but she wasn't going to decide that for him. Though if she could, as Ewan might have suggested, point him in the right direction, perhaps there was no sin in that.

"What if every time he sees fire, he feels the need to make certain everyone around him is safe?" she asked. "That would keep him busy." She paused. "He could also insist on a diet made solely from offal, but that might be unkind."

"He probably wouldn't live very long," Ewan agreed. "Let's do as you suggest with the other, though, as well as inspire him to stick to all that do-gooding. Peter, what's in your backpack?"

"Beyond tape and zip ties? Only things to entertain the children after supper."

"You can do that later. Show me now."

Mairead watched Peter pull out things from his pack and stepped back in spite of herself. The sight of gossamer wings that shimmered and sparkled with an unusual purple light when Peter put them on was unsettling enough, but the mask he pulled over his face was another thing entirely. She groped for Oliver's hand.

"The wings I understand," she managed, "but what is the creature on his mask?"

"The same thing that's on your pajamas."

She considered, then looked at him. "The ones on my pajamas are very adorable. That thing is not."

Oliver smiled. "Perhaps not, but Kenneth absolutely deserves the nightmares he'll have from it. Don't watch Ewan whilst he's about this first part."

She looked away until Ewan announced that they could turn back. Kenneth was staring up at Ewan, slack-jawed and wide-eyed.

"Now, Kenneth," Ewan said in remarkably good Gaelic, "you've been naughty, haven't you?"

Kenneth started to weep, but Ewan shook his head.

"None of that," he said sharply. "Be a man. And as a man, this is what you're going to do. Every time you see any sort of fire, you will rush around and make certain everyone is safe. If you do not, this creature here—"

Mairead watched as Peter swooped over to Kenneth, causing his wings to flutter furiously. He hopped up and down several times, growling, then fluttered away, giving vent to very unnerving moans and baying.

"—will visit you and punish you," Ewan finished sternly. "Also, every time you're tempted to kiss a woman, you must first offer her three heartfelt compliments. You'll wet yourself otherwise."

"Oh, Ewan," Derrick said in disgust.

Ewan looked over his shoulder, winked, then turned back to his business. Mairead watched as her cousin blinked suddenly, as if he'd just woken up from a deep sleep. He looked at Ewan and his eyes rolled back in his head and he fell off his rock.

"Well," Oliver said, rubbing his hands together, "that's that. Let's cut him loose and shove him through the gate, but first let me find something." He walked over and retrieved the half of the book Kenneth had dropped in his terror. "Mairead, let me give this to you for safekeeping. It's been a lovely afternoon, lads, but—"

He stopped speaking. She took a step backward instinctively, then found herself pulled behind him. She peeked around him and could scarce believe what she was seeing, but there was no denying it.

Her uncle Lachlan had come through the faery ring and was currently shaking Jamie's hand.

"Well met, nephew," Jamie said, smiling pleasantly.

"It's been too long, James," Lachlan said with an answering smile. "I see we have a bit of a situation to account for here."

"Any suggestions, Lachlan?"

"A few more tales of faeries and bogles in the forest should be sufficient," Lachlan said with a thoughtful frown, "though I'm not sure that will be enough for the young ones of the clan, though. They're too adventuresome by half."

Mairead found her uncle looking at her pointedly and all she could do was smile weakly in return.

"I think we'll need to close this gate," Jamie said, stroking his chin.

"There are always others," Lachlan offered.

Jamie smiled. "Indeed, there are."

Mairead had to admit she'd become somewhat accustomed to feeling as if she weren't quite settled into her poor form, but the sight of her uncle chatting companionably with her grandfather was something else entirely. She decided that perhaps 'twas best to simply watch events unfold in front of her and not try to put them in a sort of reasonable order.

She first listened to Oliver approach her father's brother, flatter him effusively, then ask very politely if he might have her hand in marriage. She suspected the horse was already out of the barn on that, but decided to keep that to herself. There was tradition and a proper schedule about that sort of thing.

Her uncle then bestowed not only his permission but hearty felicitations on her handfasted husband, then walked over to her to pull her into a fatherly embrace. He kissed her on the forehead and smiled at her.

"He's a good lad."

She nodded. "He is."

"And you love him?"

"Desperately."

"Remind him that I have a very sharp sword and am not afraid to come find him and use it on him if he neglects his duties toward you. And perhaps we'll meet again someday and discuss faeries and bogles to our satisfaction over an order of fish and chips."

She found absolutely nothing to say that would equal the otherworldly nature of that statement, so she settled for a nod and what she was certain was a very weak smile.

She watched as he and Jamie and Oliver carried first her brother, then Master James through the gate and laid them in the meadow in the past. She then stood with Oliver as her uncle picked Deirdre up in his arms.

"Come along, Kenneth," he said sternly. "You can hie yourself through this wee spot in the grass all on your own."

Mairead watched her cousin heave himself to his feet to do just that—

Only to pull the knife from her uncle's belt and lunge at her. She wrenched out of his way, but realized immediately that stabbing her hadn't been his intention.

Cutting off her braid, though, certain had.

Oliver snatched the knife from him, stuck it back into Lachlan's belt, then turned Kenneth to face him. Mairead watched her husband repay her cousin for a bit of the grief he'd caused her, then shove him so hard through the gate that he stumbled and went sprawling. Lachlan thanked him, exchanged another pleasant farewell with Jamie, then walked through the gate.

It shut behind him with a firm click.

She reached out toward the hair lying there on the ground, a braid she'd never done anything but brush for the entirety of her life, but her hands grasped at nothing. Oliver caught one of her hands and brought it to his mouth. She appreciated the gesture, but all she could do was look at him in shock.

"My crowning glory," she said, wondering if the present moment might be the best one for bursting into tears.

She found herself gathered into strong arms and felt Oliver's hand skimming over what was left of the one glory she'd possessed.

"It will grow," he said quietly.

She was willing to concede he might be right, but that didn't ease her overmuch. At least she had simply lost her hair and not her life. Oliver pulled back, kissed her quickly, then smiled.

"I hear Cameron's helicopter coming. Let's get out of the way and see what he and Jamie have planned."

She nodded, but found she couldn't move. All she could do was look at her hair and mourn. She'd only ever had three possessions in her life that were hers: her mother's ring which was most definitely in the past, the first half of her book which she supposed she might have back once she'd picked it up from where Kenneth had dropped it, and her hair.

And now the man standing there, watching her with love in his eyes, something that was far more important than those other things. She took a deep breath, then nodded.

"I'll fetch my hair if you'll fetch Elizabeth's book."

He smiled, kissed her quickly, then did just that. She gathered up her braid, then moved with her husband out of the way of Cameron's flying beastie. She very quickly found herself where she was happiest, which was in Oliver's arms.

"Thank you for the rescue," she said, looking at him gravely.

"Where did you go?"

"Outside to see if the loose stone in the wall was still there." She paused. "I think it's in the loo now."

He laughed a little, then kissed her. "I have an idea."

"What is it?"

"Why don't you stay within arm's reach of me for a while?"

"How long?"

He considered. "Five or six decades?"

She smiled and allowed him to gather her close again. "If you want."

"I want."

"At least my hair will be long again after all that time."

He kissed the top of her head, then wrapped his arms around her. "It will be absolutely lovely either way."

She looked over his shoulder at the helicopter that was descending from the sky, carrying what looked to be a large boulder under itself. She would have enjoyed that, but she found that all she could do was stand there and pray that she had seen the last of a particular trio of family members.

The helicopter landed and Cameron himself jumped out and walked over to them. He greeted Oliver and the lads, greeted her with especial kindness, then turned to Jamie.

"I got your text." He looked at the gate, then at Jamie. "We can close it with a rock for now, but perhaps trees or something else would be useful?"

"A lovely addition to our border," Jamie said pleasantly.

"Will it be missed?"

"Only by those who shouldn't be using it," Jamie said seriously, then he smiled. "There are, as you know, others."

"I appreciate the continual updates to your map," Cameron said dryly.

Mairead leaned closer to Oliver. "Map?"

"Jamie has a map of all the time gates he's discovered."

She looked at him and found that her mind was simply aflame with the possibilities—

"No."

She looked at Oliver in surprise. "What?"

He considered. "Maybe."

She turned and put her arms around him, then leaned up and kissed him briefly.

"All right," he muttered, but he smiled at her before he hugged her tightly, then put his arm around her shoulders. "Let's go home."

"You aren't coming to Patrick's?" Derrick asked politely.

"Get lost," Oliver tossed at him.

"Well, it certainly worked out well for you."

Mairead smiled at the look her husband sent to his friend, then smiled again at the look he gave her which was of a different sort entirely.

"Best wrong turn I ever took," he said with a grave smile.

"I'm so happy you took it," she said.

"I am, too. Moraig's?"

"If we hold hands whilst crossing the threshold."

"Let's hold hands for the rest of our lives."

"Pass the sick bucket," Ewan called, "but let's go have supper first. Cameron, what can I do to see this flying contraption put to bed properly?"

Mairead put her arm around her husband's waist and walked with him back into the woods. If she made careful note of their surroundings and watched him do the same, who could blame them?

She was holding onto the man she loved and all was right with the world.

TWENTY-SEVEN

O LIVER STOOD JUST INSIDE THE door of the salon and had never been more grateful for the presence of a sturdy indoor potted plant than he was at the moment. The tree wasn't as tall as he was, unfortunately, but it did provide at least a bit of substance to hide behind.

He peered over the top of it and scanned the scene in front of him for more possible danger.

There were the owners and workers of the establishment there, of course, with their sharp tools and vats of hot wax. They were attending to several people who were important to him, though, so he assessed them brutally for their potential to execute anything but a good manicure—which they'd already perpetrated on his own poor self—and pedicure—which they'd also already inflicted on him. He would freely admit they were masters at their craft and he was half tempted to book another appointment before he went back to London, but he exercised his hard-won self-control and forbore. There were people still enjoying their spa day and he needed to keep an eye on them.

Mairead was head of the class there, obviously, dressed in her favorite black cargo trousers and polo neck jumper. He knew she mourned the loss of her hair, but he had to admit her chic little chin-length bob was absolutely the most ador-able thing he'd ever clapped eyes on. Just looking at her left him simultaneously smiling at the fact that she'd been willing to give him a second look and determinedly looking for a way to have her all to himself so he could show her yet again how thrilled he was she'd given him that second look.

The women joining her there—Elizabeth, Madelyn, Sunshine, Samantha, and Emily—were also lovely and gracious and had been so kind and welcoming to her that Oliver had already started another list in the back of his book entitled *Very Expensive Christmas Gifts for Women Who Deserve Far Better.*

Ewan was in the middle of them, of course, but he'd been the one to see the morning proceeded perfectly for all involved. Oliver supposed the only lass in danger of Ewan's charms was Emily, but she'd grown up with him and was very probably immune. He exchanged a brief look with his partner, then escaped out the front door whilst that door was unlocked.

He wasn't surprised to find Cameron right there just outside the door, leaning against a section of brick wall. He had been, after all, one of the drivers in their happy little convoy south.

"Finished with your pampering?" Cameron asked politely.

Oliver shuddered. "I want to say it was awful, but I'm horrified to find it wasn't." He paused. "You should try it."

"When hell freezes over," Cameron muttered, then he shot Oliver a look. "Who do you think put it in your book?"

"Ewan?"

Cameron laughed. "Well, that might be true, but I have subjected myself to the torture at least once to humor my lady. What's on your schedule for the rest of the morning?"

Oliver took a deep breath. "Jeweler's, then a florist."

"She deserves all of it," Cameron said with a faint smile. "I'll keep an eye on things here if you want to make a run for it. Derrick and Peter are roaming the streets keeping watch, though, so don't start weeping into your blossoms."

Oliver attempted a cool look, but he wasn't sure Cameron didn't have a point there. He made his laird a bow, then looked at Ewan who strode out of the salon like a conquering hero.

"Let's go," he said briskly. "I'll help you keep from faltering at this critical juncture."

Cameron snorted. "They're handfasted, lad. I think he's safe."

"So says the man who continues to woo his lady every day," Ewan said, nodding knowingly. "Study him, Ollie my lad, and see how it's perfectly done."

"Nay, you can't have the title," Cameron said with a snort, "but you're also not wrong. Go to, Oliver, and make me proud."

Oliver nodded, then walked away with Ewan who he assumed knew where they were going. Ewan patted him on the shoulder.

"Trust me."

Oliver was thoroughly unnerved to find that he did, but it had been that sort of holiday so far. He put his shoulders back, took a deep breath of suitably manly proportions, and marched on into the fray.

He emerged from battle an hour later with a ring in his pocket, a shopping bag containing clothing and topped with chocolate in one hand, and flowers in the other. If that didn't win him the day, he supposed there was always the fallback plan of taking his love to the local chippy, but he was hoping for better things. He spotted their crew up the street and blew out his breath in preparation for things to come.

"Steady," Ewan murmured.

Oliver shot him a glare on principle alone. "I've got this."

"And the proposal?"

"Still working out the details of that," Oliver admitted.

"Nice restaurant? Romantic walk at sunset on the beach? Drop to my knees right here on the pavement?"

"Those aren't terrible choices," Ewan conceded. "I'll help you think of something better, but whatever you do, don't just blurt out the question the moment you're within whimpering distance."

Oliver would have delivered the elbow Ewan deserved, but he was holding treasures for his beloved. There were just some things a man had to prioritize when his world had been completely rocked by a Renaissance—

"Oh, I say," a voice said sharply, "do look where you're going, what?"

Oliver felt as though he'd just fallen into a terribly proper BBC production of some high-brow Victorian house party—and he was halfway to saying as much when he looked at the couple who had emerged from the shop to his left and recognized them.

He supposed he would be thanking Ewan later for removing his burdens from his hands before he dropped everything. Further thanks would likely be necessarily tendered first to Cameron who simply stepped in front of him and then to none other than Mairead MacLeod who had smoothly stepped in front of Cameron and moved to his left, effectively blocking Oliver behind them both. He wasn't quite sure how they managed it, but he soon found himself surrounded by the family he'd acquired as an adult.

Handy, that, given that on the opposing side of some imaginary line was standing in a little cluster his family of birth.

He felt a hand resting lightly on his back. He looked to his right to find Sunshine standing there, watching him with worry plain in her eyes. Madelyn was standing on his left, also with her hand on his back. He managed some species of smile for them both, had reassuring smiles in return, then turned his attention back to the unexpected encounter unfolding in front of him.

It wasn't that he hadn't kept up with the doings of Aldous Phillips, the Viscount Felkirk. His father craved a discreet amount of the spotlight, mostly as he was seen either entering or exiting his club in London. Oliver also recognized his mother who did just the right amount of charity work to maintain the same aura of genteel compassion. His brothers were no doubt either off at Uni or doing whatever it was they did to remain in their father's good graces and within reach of his chequebook.

His youngest sister, however, was standing behind his mother, looking at him as if she'd seen a ghost.

He understood that, actually, and didn't envy her for it.

His father made very posh noises of disbelief and delight whilst his mother looked at him as if she expected him to blurt out terrible family secrets right there on the bloody pavement.

"Lord Robert of Assynt," his father said breathlessly. "How fortunate to meet you here in the middle of nowhere!"

Oliver had to concede that tact was not his father's strong suit. He only knew that from second-hand reports, but it was something to see it for himself.

"I'm sorry," Cameron said coolly, "I don't think we've been properly introduced."

Oliver would have smiled if he'd had it in him. Cameron's tone was so chilly it made him shiver. His father might have been a git of the first water, but he was no fool. Either that or he had a great deal of experience in being cut in public by those with much loftier titles than his own.

"My most abject apologies, of course," the good viscount said. "Aldous Phillips, Viscount Felkirk, at your service. My wife, Ondine."

Oliver was slightly surprised to find his sister hadn't been introduced, but then again, he likely shouldn't have expected anything else. He glanced at her to find she was looking at him less in horror than desperation. He understood that, but there wasn't a damned thing he could do about it at the moment. He could, however, get on with the speech he'd been rehearsing silently for two decades, the one where he would tell his parents exactly what he thought of them. He put his hands on Mairead's shoulders, gently set her aside, then stepped up to stand next to Cameron so he might do just that.

He looked at his über-boss briefly and found only acceptance in Cameron's expression, then a quick lifting of one eyebrow that generally augured verbal fireworks to come. Oliver had seen that look turned on annoying nobility more than once and been quite happy not to be in the man's sights.

But this was his family and he'd waited a very long time to exact at least some sort of revenge. He shot Cameron a look that he hoped said very clearly that he had dibs on taking his father down a peg, but Cameron only smiled.

"I'll draw first blood," he said in Gaelic.

Well, there was that, at least. He didn't protest when he found Cameron's arm placed around his shoulders. He imagined his father was very fortunate Cameron had left his sword at home.

"You might recognize this man," Cameron said, with a crispness to his consonants that would have put any BBC Four presenter to shame. "A member of my family and an irreplaceable part of my company's exclusive inner circle. I would find it … unfortunate if he were to be made unhappy by a chance encounter on the street."

And with that, Cameron looked at him and inclined his head slightly, the invitation unmistakable.

Oliver looked at his parents, his mother very pale and his father patting himself, no doubt for his smelling salts.

"Well, of course," Felkirk said faintly. "It's been a bit, hasn't it, son?"

Oliver started to speak, then found that, as usual, silence was a better option for him. And as he stood there, he felt a little as if his life were flashing before his eyes.

A month ago, he probably would have punched his father full in the face and sworn at his mother. Hell, two minutes ago he was fully prepared to do the same. He wasn't proud of that, but he had to be honest with himself.

But somehow when it came right down to it, things had changed.

He looked next to him and found Mairead there, watching him with nothing but love and acceptance in her eyes. She felt for his hand and he surrendered it to her just as readily as he had his heart. And when he touched her, he found himself with that same gentle sweetness washing over him that he realized had been her influence over the whole of his life, beyond any reason and surely beyond anything he'd deserved. It almost took his breath away.

It occurred to him at that moment that perhaps it wasn't so much a matter of absolving his parents from their part in the misery of his young life as it was letting go of his own bitterness over the same.

He looked at the people he loved, his family that he'd been loved into, then at the family that had at least brought him into the world but never loved him. And the bridge between the two was the woman standing next to him who still thought she had no beauty, a woman with which he would start his own loving family, a woman who had given him a gift he had finally just understood.

Perhaps he had been the means of rescuing her but she had, in turn, shown him how much better his life could be to let go of the past and move on.

He squeezed her hand, then turned back to his father and gave him his most polite client smile.

"My lord," he said, inclining his head. He looked at his mother. "My lady."

His father gestured inelegantly at Mairead. "Is that your girlfriend?"

Oliver stared at his parents for a moment or two in silence, then glanced at Cameron. "We should be on our way, my lord."

"As you will, Oliver," Cameron said with a nod. "Let's gather up our ladies and see what delights Inverness has to offer. Such a fantastic city we have here, wouldn't you agree?"

Oliver glanced at Mairead, had the briefest of smiles from her, then turned and walked away with her at his side.

"Brutal," Ewan said, taking a place on his right. "And so well deserved."

Oliver nodded, though he didn't imagine he would manage to say anything for a few minutes.

"Was that your sister?" Mairead asked quietly.

Oliver could only nod. He could feel his lady looking at him, but the last thing he wanted to do—for a change—was look at her because he knew exactly what she was thinking. He finally stopped, then looked at her reluctantly. She only leaned up and kissed him on the cheek.

"You're a good man."

"I'm not going back now," he muttered. He glanced at her. "I'll find her mobile number and text her later."

"My hero," Mairead said, putting her hand over her heart and sighing rapturously.

He smiled in spite of himself. "You, my love, have been watching far too much telly."

"They had a programme on in the salon," she said, her eyes bright. "The lad was very gallant, but not nearly as perfect as you are."

He could only imagine. He shook his head, smiled in spite of himself, and found himself surrounded by people who he was very fond of and who were apparently rather fond of him. And as he continued on down the high street, he realized that somehow, at some point where he likely hadn't been paying attention, things had changed for him. The thorn he realized he'd been carrying in his heart for all those years was gone.

He would have blamed that on his holiday, but thinking on that led him to thinking on where that holiday had led, which pointed directly at the woman who had made all the difference for him.

He smiled and squeezed her hand. "Let's go find somewhere romantic to walk for a moment or two."

"Why?"

"You'll see."

＝＝＝ ⚜ ＝＝＝

Three days later, he stood in the modern incarnation of the MacLeod keep with a ring on his finger and his formally wedded bride next to him and decided that life could simply not improve.

He'd re-termed his eejit manual to something more permanent and taken to heart Derrick's advice about making lists for his wife. They'd done a lovely bit of nesting at Moraig's, deciding to put off a return to daily life for another few days at least, and he found himself quite happily wed again to the woman who left him smiling every time he looked at her.

Their formal ceremony in Jamie's hall earlier that morning had been as lovely as he'd been able to make it, which was to say that he'd turned everything over to members of his family with far better taste than his own. He'd trusted Emily to find him an appropriate suit as well and dress the rest of the lads in something that had turned out to be an impressive array of kilts in the appropriate patterns.

Mairead had been nothing sort of gorgeous in a sleek 1950s style gown with her hair tucked behind her ears and diamonds around her neck that he would have bet several quid had been unearthed from some vintage hoard.

The subsequent toasting had been lengthy and very generous and loving toward Mairead and much stingier and more ribald when directed toward him. He had, however, finally been claimed by Patrick MacLeod as a younger brother, so there was that.

He pulled himself back to the present moment to find himself with his wife in front of the fireplace and three grinning fools standing in a cluster in front of him. Derrick was carrying a manila envelope, which Oliver suspected meant trouble.

"I'm married," he warned, "and my wife is fierce."

Mairead nodded, fiercely, then she smiled at the lads. Oliver imagined he would at some point need to suggest that she be a bit sterner with them, but the present moment was perhaps not the proper one for that sort of conversation.

"We have a prezzie for you," Ewan said, grinning madly.

Derrick rolled his eyes and Peter shoved his hands into his pockets only to realize he was in a kilt. He looked at Oliver and shrugged.

Oliver considered, then took what he wasn't entirely certain wouldn't slay him if he opened it, then set himself to the task with courage and resolve. He pulled out a certificate, read it, then looked at his mates.

"You bought me a title?"

"All hail Lord Oliver!" Ewan bellowed, then he looked at Oliver. "Like it?"

"I'm overwhelmed," Oliver said, shooting him a look of promise. He looked at the whole nasty collection of ruddy bastards. "Where, if I might ask, is my massive estate?"

"Down south by Edinburgh," Peter said, looking particularly pleased with himself. "A single but mighty square meter of the finest property we could find."

Ewan nodded knowingly. "Best go have a look right quick and make sure the peasants aren't revolting."

Derrick clapped a hand on his shoulder. "At least you can call yourself a proper lord now, eh? We thought it was the least we could do in the circs."

"Generous," Oliver managed, vowing to kill them all. He realized he'd lost the thread of that plot at some point over the past fortnight, but he was nothing if not tenacious and he was happy to be back on track.

"It cost us a bleeding £38, lad," Derrick pointed out. "Split three ways, true, but still, you'd best be taking it seriously."

Oliver sighed, but he couldn't help but feel slightly chuffed. At least if he saw his father at some gathering in London, he would have his own title to pull out and display.

"That's not all," Derrick said, nodding toward the front door. "Let's go."

Oliver laced his fingers with Mairead's. "I'm bringing my wife for protection."

Derrick rolled his eyes and walked away. Oliver looked at his bride to see what thoughts she might be having on the madness at hand, but she only smiled.

"They love you."

He shuddered, had a laugh for his trouble, then walked with her over to the door. They were invited out onto the front stoop beyond which sat two cars. One was shrouded in black silk. Oliver would have only been surprised to find that what it *wasn't* covering up was a very dinged-up Ford with mismatched hubcaps.

But the other ...

Derrick gestured expansively toward the modest little Fiat on the left. It was a pretty powder blue color, not quite the color of his eyes, and there was a Ferrari medallion glued to the front of it. He suspected there was a second one glued to the arse-end of it. He looked at his bride.

"I expected this."

"The car is new," Derrick said huffily. "And those medallions are damned pricey."

Oliver held out his hand for the keys. Derrick looked at him, snorted, then reached around him and held them out to Mairead.

"Your conveyance, my lady," he said, with a small bow. "I'm sure your husband will splash out for something a bit larger later, but this is a good start."

Oliver frowned. "Well—"

Derrick pulled a different set of keys from his pocket and tossed them at him. Oliver caught them out of habit, then watched as Peter pulled that silken sheet off the other car parked there.

He almost swooned.

Mairead squeezed his hand. "Does it go fast?"

"Extremely," he wheezed.

His wife abandoned him immediately to go run her hands over and peer into the headlamps of what Oliver could scarce bring himself to name, though he could spell the brand well enough and it began with a B and ended with an I.

He considered the beauty before him—and not just his wife—for quite some time before he trusted himself to speak. He cleared his throat roughly.

"Thank you."

"It's just a car, lad," Derrick said lightly. "No need to weep over it."

Oliver glared at him and had a brief smile as his reward.

"Anything for a brother," Derrick said simply. "And that's not about the car."

Oliver was half-tempted to turn and throw his arms around his best mate, the lad who had been there during that first interview with Cameron and listened to all of Oliver's secrets, never mind a few follow-ups after a night at the pub, and had never once offered him anything but acceptance and the hand of friendship.

Derrick rolled his eyes, pulled Oliver into a tight, quick and very manly embrace, then shoved him away and followed that up with a brisk slap to the back of his head. Oliver returned the favor with an equally quick and brisk flick between Derrick's eyes.

And balance was yet again restored.

"You didn't really spend your hard-earned sterling on this, did you?"

Derrick snorted. "Are ye daft, lad? Of course not. Cameron bought it for you, likely used. I did you the favor of your MOT fees for the year and Peter bought you some special wipes to clean your greasy, post-chippy-run finger leavings from off the steering wheel. The petrol is up to you. You can also buy your wife something bigger once she masters that wee beast over there, though I'm imagining you won't be letting her drive either in London."

"I think we'll stick to Scottish roads for a bit for her," Oliver agreed.

"And for you?" Derrick asked with a smile.

"I feel a long trip to London coming on," Oliver said, stopping himself before he purred. "Then a ferry ride to the Continent."

"Germany's going to change the laws there about tourists screaming down their motorways because of you, you know."

"I'm an excellent driver," Oliver said, cradling his keys to his chest and giving up on not purring. "I'm going to go ask my wife if she needs something from the village."

"You won't get it out of first gear."

"Probably not," he said, stopping just short of chortling with glee. He smiled at Derrick. "We'll return."

"I'll believe that when you do," Derrick said, but he was smiling as he turned and went back inside the hall.

Oliver promised himself a hearty round of thanks to all and sundry, no doubt accompanied by a gentlemanly hug or two and perhaps even a discreet tear for the appropriate ladies of his acquaintance, but he thought he might be first permitted a wee trip to the village with his wife.

"Text me if you need something from McCreedy's!" he called.

"Jaffa cakes," came the response from a youngling inside.

"And crisps!"

Mission accepted, of course. Oliver collected his bride, tucked her into his reward for being good in school, then slid under the wheel. He took a deep breath, started the beast up, then looked at his wife.

"Well?"

"How many horses?" she asked breathlessly.

"1200."

"I believe it."

He laughed and put his matched ponies in reverse, praying he would manage to get down the drive without an embarrassing popping of the clutch. At least he wasn't going to get the damned thing out of first gear, so there would be no equally embarrassing grinding of those. He glanced at his wife.

"You're still the best thing that's happened to me," he reminded her.

"This has to be a close second," she said, smiling at him sweetly.

He considered. "There might be a few other things ahead of it."

"Fashion me a list," she said cheerfully, "and I'll put it in your book."

He suspected that bloody book itself might have to go in the vicinity of the top of that particular list, though he would never admit it to the lads. He glanced at his bride.

"Where do you want to go?"

"Besides the village?"

He nodded.

"With you?"

He nodded again.

She smiled. "I've started a list."

He could hardly wait to see it. He shot her a quick smile, then concentrated on not running his new car into a tree.

TWENTY-EIGHT

MAIREAD MACLEOD PHILLIPS WALKED DOWN the steps of a very exclusive hall on the outskirts of London, holding onto the hand of an extremely braw and handsome man, and maintained a pleasant mien. They were, after all, at work and decorum needed to be maintained.

"What did you think?" Oliver murmured

She tried not to snort, but 'twas difficult. She suspected they were being monitored, though, so she put on one of her most tasteful smiles and looked at him.

"Those were fake," she said, looking at him lovingly.

"You think so?"

"If that was 16th-century bobbin lace, my love, then I am a purple-winged faery," she said pleasantly, fluttering her eyelashes at him. "Sam would have gotten up and walked out, I daresay."

"And you didn't?"

"Well," she said with another polite smile, "I had you to look at, didn't I? No reason to spoil the view by not lingering where I could watch it."

He smiled pleasantly. "And the spoons?"

"That's your purview, my lord, not mine."

"Silver plate," he said, as blandly as if they'd been discussing whether to have supper at six or seven. "Nice art, though."

"We might help them improve their taste," she offered. "They were willing to pay quite a robust sum for more items of interest."

"Should we help them?"

"I'm not sure how we could possibly refuse."

"Bettering the world wherever we go," he agreed.

She nodded with another polite smile and allowed him to help her into the back of a sleek Mercedes. She smiled politely at Rufus and kept her best side toward the window on the off chance she was being photographed. She felt for Oliver's hand once he was safely seated next to her, but continued to wear her company face until they were well off the grounds and she could relax.

"Interesting afternoon, loves?" Rufus asked.

"Lots of dosh but absolutely no taste," Oliver said with a sigh. "We'll see what can be done about the state of their collectables, but they certainly won't be selling any of them any time soon."

Mairead listened to them launch into a discussion about what sorts of new things might suit the family, then closed her eyes and allowed herself the pleasure of her own thoughts whilst she was being ferried about by someone who took great care to keep them safe.

During her original fortnight in London with Oliver, she hadn't believed such a thing was possible. The city had seemed so full of people that she'd feared she would never be comfortable.

But then she'd realized that Sunny was also there, and Samantha, and Emily, and even the granny who guarded Cameron's offices and sent messengers scurrying with just a look. She'd been grateful for that small circle of companions, especially since a great deal of Oliver's labors took place in London. They had also made many trips to several different places in England and Scotland during the fall, which had been very interesting.

And then one evening, he'd handed her what he'd called plane tickets and showed her a photograph of an island in what he called the Caribbean.

She had discovered that she was exceptionally fond of flying.

She was also hopelessly fond of the man sitting next to her, rubbing his thumb over hers and looking as if he might soon fall asleep. He opened one eye and looked at her.

"I'm awake."

She smiled and shifted a little to look at him. "I had an email from Jamie yesterday."

Oliver looked slightly uneasy. "Is he rescinding his blessing?"

"'Tis a bit late for that," she said dryly, "but nay, he likes you well enough, which you know. He actually had a few details he thought I might like to know about."

"Concerning bad actors in the past?"

She nodded.

"Well," he said, "you do like to know how things end. So, what happened?"

"Where shall I begin?"

"In the middle?"

She laughed a little. "That, I believe, is your favorite place to start anything, so I shall. I don't think you'll be surprised to learn that Ambrose took over the clan at ten-and-three."

He winced. "I'm not surprised, but I can't imagine the transition was an easy one for him. What happened?"

"After we last saw her, Deirdre returned to the hall, but not quietly. She brewed a very warm quarrel with Master James who convinced Tasgall to put her to the fire."

Oliver closed his eyes briefly, then looked at her. "I'm sorry," he said quietly. "She was crazy, but she didn't deserve that. What happened to your brother?"

"I'm afraid he didn't fare much better," she admitted. "Apparently he got into an argument with Angus Fergusson and found his life coming to an end on the man's sword."

Oliver rubbed his free hand over his face, then smiled at her. "I'm so glad you're here."

"So am I," she said with feeling.

"So what of your uncle?" Oliver smiled. "I half expect him to show up for dinner so he can tell us of his adventures himself, but maybe not."

She smiled. "I daresay neither of us would be surprised. But in his own time, he was a great comfort to Ambrose." She paused. "I'm not certain how Jamie would know that, but I'm also not going to ask how many times *he* travelled to another supper table to gather those sorts of tidings."

"I'm guessing it was more than once," Oliver offered.

"They did seem to know each other well," she agreed.

He looked at her hand in his for a moment or two, then looked at her seriously. "What of Master James?"

"He survived his encounter with Jamie, unfortunately, and put five more people to the fire before he had the misfortune of wandering north and attempting to ply his trade on the Camerons. Jamie claimed that young Alistair had no patience for superstitions, which led to Master James moving on to seek his victims elsewhere."

"If you tell me he now fell into a bog and drowned, I won't believe you."

She looked at him archly. "He fell off a cliff and dashed himself against the rocks below." She paused. "I think he had help with that, but that soul was never identified. It could have been just a sudden gust of wind."

He smiled. "It's probably best to leave it at that. What about Kenneth?"

"Jamie didn't have much to say about him past he kept to himself and was very kind to my father to the very end."

Oliver squeezed her hand gently. "How much longer did your father live?"

"Five years," she said. She knew it was in the past, centuries in the past, but she still couldn't help a twinge of sorrow over the tidings. "He passed peacefully in his sleep, surrounded by clansmen who loudly proclaimed how blessed and fortunate they'd been to have such a man as head of their clan. Songs were sung and tales told of his prowess in battle and his care of his people. Ambrose styled himself as such a man in every particular."

Oliver studied her for a moment or two. "That's pretty specific."

"I'm guessing Jamie was there to witness it."

Oliver smiled. "I would imagine so. He's very protective of his clan members."

"He is," she agreed. "And in case you were curious, Fiona turned out to be a lass determined to take charge of her fate."

"That sounds familiar."

She smiled. "Doesn't it, though? Jamie told me to do some digging into clan history if I wanted the details."

"She's just following in the footsteps of her terribly courageous aunt who didn't let anything stop her from having what she wanted."

"Except maybe long hair," she muttered. She looked over at him to find he was watching her with an affectionate smile. "What?" she asked, reaching up self-consciously to tug on her hair.

He caught her hand, kissed it, then smiled again. "I think it's adorable."

"You just think I'm adorable," she said. "And there's my third time of repeating that today for your satisfaction. Where's the box ticked in my notebook?"

He looked at her briefly, then pulled a slim volume out of his inner jacket pocket and made a production of flipping through the pages. "Let me see," he said, tapping his chin with a pen he pulled from a different pocket. He shot her a look. "We'd best be thorough here."

She rolled her eyes, but not very hard. He was, as she reminded him regularly, a wee fiend, but she loved him beyond reason. She thought she was terribly plain, but he seemed to find her beautiful and she wasn't going to argue.

"Meditation," he said, turning the sheaves. "Mastering all the languages your husband doesn't know so we don't starve in foreign countries, allowing your husband to shamelessly pamper you at all hours, reminding your husband how gorgeous you are if he's too dazzled by your gorgeous self to think straight." He looked at her. "Have I missed anything?"

"I think there is something inside about spotted yoga trews."

"As long as you're wearing them," he said with feeling. "And you're right. Yoga, continuing your self-defense classes, plotting ways to kill off Ewan Cameron and make it look like an accident." He glanced at her. "*Now* have I missed anything?"

She smiled. "Nay, nothing but what I will have once my book is complete."

He tucked the book back into his jacket and took her hand. "What would you like?"

"Besides you?"

"You already have me," he reminded her. "Every day for the rest of your life." He smiled. "What other thing would you like?"

"A holiday in Scotland?"

He burst out laughing. Mairead shared a look with Rufus that needed no words. They had discussed several times the joy they both took in Oliver's cheerful laugh, something Rufus said he'd heard far too seldom in the past.

Oliver laced his fingers with hers. "If you like," he said, his eyes twinkling. "Or we could go to Italy again and gawk at some more Renaissance art."

"That is tempting," she conceded. "It is my era, after all."

"They lost out on a fabulous model," he conceded, "but Michelangelo's loss is my gain. Let's add another trip to Florence to our list, shall we?"

She nodded happily and watched him jot that down before he pocketed the goods and reached for her hand again to hold it between his own. She'd tried to have a view of his new little notebook that was covered just in black with no foul names stamped into the front of it, but he'd claimed there were lists in there of wooing ideas. Not being one to want to spoil surprises, she'd left him to his secrets and counted herself fortunate that she was the delighted recipient of so many of them.

At the moment, though, he was obviously not a delighted recipient of his phone alerting him that a text had been received. Several, by the sound of things. He pulled his phone from his pocket, flipped it open and looked at a handful of things, then put it back in his pocket with a sigh.

"The lads?"

He sighed and handed her his phone. "Siblings."

"Your sister?"

"And a younger brother," he muttered. He shot her a quick look. "What am I going to do with one of *those*?"

She smiled. "Love them, I imagine. And at least with your sister, there is merit to her desire to be free of your parents. I think you might become her knight in shining armor."

He pursed his lips and shot her a look. "I've hung up my spurs."

She smiled. "Have you?"

He blew his hair out of his eyes, but said nothing.

She smiled and leaned her head back against the seat and simply watched him as Rufus wove his way through London traffic.

He sighed finally. "I'm thinking about it."

"She needs a rescue."

"I know."

"You're very good at that sort of thing."

"And what will I have if I trot out my chivalry?"

"Me," she said with a smile, "for the rest of your life until we're a pair of wizened old apples, grinning foolishly at each other over our porritch."

"For you, then."

"You're a good man, Oliver Phillips."

"After we get back from Scotland," he said firmly. "Maybe."

"Are you going to tell her that before we go?"

He looked at her and scowled, but that didn't last long. He smiled briefly, leaned forward and kissed her not quite as briefly, then sat back and sighed.

"You're persuasive."

"I understand what it's like to be rescued from my terrible life by the Duke of Birmingham."

He laughed briefly. "I suppose she'll have to settle for the older brother she doesn't know."

"Then it will be a happy new beginning for her," she said.

431

He smiled. "I suppose so. And I think we do have a few cousins scattered around the isle. She might prefer refuge with them until she finds her feet, though I'm not sure what sort of life skills she has."

"Sam and I will take her to John Bagley's when we're in Scotland."

"The saints preserve me," he muttered in Gaelic.

She laughed at him, kissed him sweetly for his trouble, then rested her head on his shoulder and happily watched him as he held her hand between his, stroking her thumb with his as was his habit. She'd originally thought it was to either soothe himself or remind her he was there, but she had come to suspect over the months that it was that he wanted to remind himself that she was there.

Because he loved her.

She closed her eyes and permitted herself a bit more thinking about the state of things.

It had taken time, but she'd eventually read her book of memories that her Victorian scribe had so faithfully recorded. It had taken less time than she'd feared to become used to the letters, and she'd endlessly ignored the feeling she'd had that whispered that she'd learned those letters in a different time and place. which had led quite naturally to an investigation—gingerly, of course—of Master Sinclair McKinnon's other offerings. She'd happily tucked her tale into the safe in Oliver's flat, then gone with him to negotiate the proper curation of Sinclair's best works.

She hadn't been entirely surprised by how a small card with the Cameron name printed so boldly upon it could have earned them such respect, but she had put on a dress and Oliver had looked perfectly scrummy in his black suit and tie over his crisp white shirt. If she'd been buying any of his goods, she would have immediately handed over all her money and thanked him for the pleasure of it.

Her life, quite obviously, had not turned out in any way to be what she'd thought it would. She'd spent so many years wondering how she might escape her straits when all it had taken was an insertion into her life of a certain man at the right moment in time. Not even Mistress Constance Buchanan could have imaged up anything that would have suited her more perfectly or given her such endless joy.

She was very blessed, indeed.

EPILOGUE

OLIVER PHILLIPS STOOD IN THE kitchen of his London flat, leaning back against a rather lovely range he'd had installed because his wife fancied a contained fire, and looked at the state of his life.

Actually, he looked for the woman who had come into his life and stayed to fill it with so many things he'd never expected, but since that was one of his favorite things to do, he decided to stick with it.

There was a little snug adjacent to the kitchen that contained a couch, a television, and a coffee table piled high with books on everything from medieval metal-smithing to Victorian cookery. The cozy little room also contained his favorite person who was currently wearing headphones and grooving to some 70s rock band for which he was certain he owned at least one t-shirt. She was wearing jeans, which she only did when her favorite pair of black cargo trousers were in the wash, and dusting when she wasn't simply standing there and singing with a heart-stoppingly lovely voice that was, he was happy to say, perfectly on key on every note.

She was also just as likely to don a lovely evening gown and go weep through Rachmaninoff or Chopin at the Royal Albert, or watch with delight whatever Drury Lane had on tap at any given time, which also made him ridiculously happy.

He was, as it happened, simply ridiculously happy about his surprisingly wonderful life.

He was still doing the job he loved, of course, trotting out his title of Vice President of Snoopery and Skulduggery as often as necessary to remind his mates that he wasn't a man to be trifled with—nor zip tied and hauled off to the wilds of Scotland and abandoned. Mairead had early on offered herself as a perfect candidate to be his assistant on his business assignments, complete with conservative business attire and librarian's glasses that made him absolutely crazy. He generally kept his hands to himself and merely watched in awe as she smoothly discussed the pernickety details of any given transaction with a finesse that even Cameron admired.

If all that working and finessing required a regular schedule of naps in the afternoon in the privacy of their own home, well, he liked to indulge her as often as possible so she would smile at him equally as often.

She'd also insisted on braces, which he'd provided without hesitation though he didn't think she needed them. Her smile was perfection because it was hers and he was happy to be the beneficiary of it as often as possible.

He jumped a little when he realized she'd taken out her earbuds and was simply watching him with a smile on her face. He considered, then lifted his hand, pointed his pointer finger at her, then turned his hand over and used that same finger in a way that could only be taken as a motion beckoning her to come to him.

She put down her duster, raised an eyebrow, and crooked her finger at *him*.

And so, he noted happily, was the state of their marriage. He was simultaneously bemused by and arse over teakettle in love with that woman there who had arrived in the Future only to, as she would have quoted her father saying, stride forth and conquer everything in her path, including him. He suspected if her uncle Lachlan could have seen her presently, he would have been very proud of the very confident modern woman she'd become. He knew he was.

He pushed away from the range and started around the island to acquiesce to her demand, but found himself coming to a halt at the sound of a knocking on their front door.

"Och, nay," Mairead said, reaching out and taking hold of his arm before he could react. "I've business with you."

He pulled her into his arms. "I am, as always, your humble and devoted servant. But I think we have company. There they go, knocking again as if they very much want to get inside."

"Kiss me briefly, then."

"If you insist."

"You know you want to."

He laughed and kissed her as thoroughly as he dared because, as she had so rightly divined, he most certainly did indeed want to. He lifted his head and looked at her.

"I'm having a thought."

She looked a little flushed. "So am I. Let's ignore the knock."

He smiled, because he was just so damned happy he couldn't seem to stop. "They are persistent."

She sighed. "Very well, let's go—wait, what was your thought?"

"I'm wondering if we dare answer given that it's a door and we've run afoul of them in the past."

"Let's hold hands whilst we do."

He nodded, then paused. "Let's examine your thought later."

She smiled. "If you like."

"You know I do."

She laughed a little at him, which he enjoyed more than he would ever admit, then kept hold of her hand as he walked with her across their flat, promising himself to boot out swiftly whoever had dared arrive on their front stoop at the truly indelicate hour of 7 PM.

A quick look through the spyhole revealed souls no more nefarious than Jackson and Olivia Kilchurn, whilst an opening of the door disclosed that Jackson was carrying dessert. Mairead squeezed his hand briefly, then abandoned him in favor of drawing inside one of her favorite new London friends. Jackson held up the bag.

"Mint chip and something else with seven types of chocolate."

Oliver waved him inside without hesitation, then popped Jackson's offerings into the freezer for later consumption.

He found himself once again leaning back against his AGA only this time he was listening to rapid-fire, authentic Gaelic being tossed about with enthusiasm by those three there. His headache was far less than it had been at first on those same sorts of evenings, but perhaps that was due to spending every day of his current lifetime speaking the same with his, again, favorite person.

He watched them for a bit, then found himself joined in his leaning by Jackson himself.

"Any interesting finds lately?" Jackson asked.

"A few swords," Oliver said with a shrug. "A handful of rare gems and some priceless art. The usual."

"You're jaded."

Oliver shot Jackson a look. "You're one to talk."

Jackson smiled pleasantly. "Agreed. And since I am, I'm wondering if you might be up for something different."

"I'm all ears," Oliver said. "What's on offer?"

"A bit of a hunt."

"What are we hunting?"

"Whom," Jackson corrected.

"You know," Oliver said with a grimace, "I did this dance fairly recently and *I* ended up being the one hunted." He imagined he could save for later a detailed recounting of how that hunt had left him sprinting into the past where he'd met the love of his life.

"Who was after you?"

"Patrick MacLeod."

"I haven't met him yet."

"You'd like him."

Jackson considered that. "How did it go?"

"Tiringly," Oliver said with a faint smile. "In the end, I gave him a fat lip and he left me limping home, barely breathing."

Jackson considered. "I suspect that isn't the entire truth, but I'll let it lie for now. What of my venture?"

"I'll bite," Oliver conceded. "Whom are we hunting?"

"I have a pair of wee cousins who need to be found."

"Medieval ex-pats?"

Jackson nodded.

"Do you want them to survive the experience?"

"Hard to torture them if they don't."

Oliver held out his hand and shook Jackson's firmly. "I'm in."

"Awesome," Jackson said. "So are Derrick and Zachary, who have their own reasons for corralling the little blighters to at least thank them for their efforts."

"Text me time and place."

"We're planning a strategy meeting at Wyckham next week. Bring your lady if she likes."

"She will."

"Mine will as well." Jackson rubbed his hands together. "Let's celebrate our future success with dessert."

Oliver couldn't think of a better way to do it.

Several hours later, he woke to an elbow placed very gently in his side and realized that the mystery on the telly he and his lady wife had turned on after their guests had left had reached its end. He yawned, shook his head sharply, then looked at Mairead who was nestled in his arms and looking perfectly comfortable in her spot.

"Is it over?" he managed.

"It is," she said. "Who did it?"

"The deacon with the purple trainers."

She smiled. "When did you know?"

"Four minutes in," he admitted, "which was all I could manage before I fell asleep." He put his feet back on the floor and looked at her. "And speaking of mysteries solved, I found something for you."

She smiled and reached out to touch his cheek. "Is the gift your own sweet self?"

"You could call this Episode Two in the same series."

"I like those sorts of programmes," she said approvingly. "Very convenient to have all that time between viewings to work out the details of the crimes."

He kissed her, smiled, then went to fetch what he'd found the week before in a very musty old bookshop full of all sorts of interesting things. He sat down, then handed her the treasure, wrapped as it was in discreet brown paper.

She unwrapped it, then looked at him in surprise. "'*The Duke and the Kitchen Maid*,'" she said breathlessly. "The entire thing."

"Are you going to finish it now?"

She studied the book in her hands for several moments in silence, then looked at him. "I'm very grateful for the gift and I will treasure it," she said slowly, "but I don't think I'll read it."

"Really?" he asked, though he was smiling as he said it. "And why is that, my lady?"

"Because, my lord, I'll write my own story."

He was utterly unsurprised. He leaned back against the couch and studied her thoughtfully. "What sort of tale will it be?"

She slipped her hand into his. "A tale of adventure, great battles won, and hedges vanquished."

He shot her a look, but she only smiled.

"It will be a love story," she assured him.

"Whose?"

"Ours."

"Shall we go add a chapter to it where the happy couple actually sleeps for a change?"

"They can sleep tomorrow," she said. "I think they have other things to do tonight."

Who was he to argue with that? He laughed and pulled her up with him to go indulge in a bit more of that not-sleeping business.

He woke somewhere during the middle of the night and experienced a moment of panic when he looked to his right and didn't see Mairead lying next to him. He realized, however, that her toes were wedged beneath his calf which was somewhat reassuring. He lifted the covers to find her reading by flashlight. He noted the title, then clucked his tongue.

"You're incorrigible."

"I had to know how it ended."

He made himself more comfortable in her cave and smiled at her. "Finished yet?"

"Not yet."

"What's happened so far?"

"Well," she said, glancing at him briefly, "there have been many scorching looks, a handful of equally incendiary kisses, and a single reference to what I'm too much a lady to name."

He put his arm under his head and made himself a bit more comfortable still, though he had to pull the covers off from over their heads before claustrophobia did him in.

"You know," he said slowly, "We've been married for a handful of months now and there has been quite a bit of that sort of activity—"

"Oliver," she said, shooting him a look, her face flaming.

He leaned up, kissed her sweetly, then put his head back down. "Very well, my lady. I will remain discreetly silent on the matter."

She blew her fringe out of her eyes and flipped a page, but she was still blushing. He tried to see how much more she still had to go, but she turned the book so he couldn't.

"Look at your mobile," she said, glancing at him briefly.

He reached behind him for his phone, promising himself to leave it charging in the kitchen more often, then pulled up a text from his wife. It contained a photo of what looked to be a fairly substantial hoard of Regency-era weaponry.

He let out a low whistle. "Very nice."

She kept hold of her wee romance with one hand and handed him a folder with the other.

He leaned up on his elbow. "Clues?"

She looked up at him with wide, innocent eyes. "Who knows?"

"You obviously do," he chided her. "Be a love and put me out of my misery."

"Ach, well, if you must know, Jamie feels there's something perhaps ... *off* in this particular year. Something missing. Or perhaps two missing things in the same time where they shouldn't be. You know how uneasy that makes him."

He did indeed know that. "What's in here, then?"

"Tidbits," she said absently, turning back to her book. "Really, Oliver, I have to at least finish this chapter. The Duke and his gel have encountered each other in his orangery and I think there may be, well, you know." She shot him a look. "Happenings of interest."

He waved her on to her reading, smiling to himself as he did so because he knew she knew how much he loved trolling through details for clues. He turned on his bedside lamp, made himself more comfortable for the perusal of what she'd given him, and dove in.

He flipped through a dozen pages of photographs, property descriptions, and the bios of a pair of possible miscreants. He considered, then looked at his wife to find her watching him instead of reading her book.

"When did you find all this?" he asked.

"Whilst you were having a wee nap on Cameron's sofa a fortnight ago. Emily and I asked Mrs. Paxton for help in our investigations. She was a wealth of information."

Oliver imagined she was. Emily was, of course, accustomed to all sorts of unusual happenings, and she had pledged her fealty to Cameron just as they all had.

Mrs. Paxton, however, whilst in the thick of all the goings on, had remained discreetly aloof from the madness. She held court as Cameron's personal secretary, which lent an air of distinction to the place and surely impressed those coming in to gawk at the business face of the Cameron empire.

Her encyclopedic knowledge of social protocols and what he suspected was a photographic recollection—updated frequently—of the Debrett's guide to everything peerage-related had also been very useful on many occasions. But it was her unflappability in the face of the rag-tag lot of them about their usual business of uncovering potentially unsavory but always exciting things that had been a constant in their lives and, he had to admit, felt like a bit of the glue that held them all together in proper order.

"Did Mrs. Paxton enjoy it?" he asked with a smile.

"She chortled at least twice," Mairead said solemnly.

"A record."

She smiled. "I thought you'd think so." She nodded at the papers. "Does it seem like cheating to know so many details now that they couldn't have possibly known then?"

He considered. "We could term it *thorough preparation* and call it good. It might be wise, though, to do a little onsite investigating."

"A little stroll through the grounds," she agreed. "Just to observe."

"The current estate grounds?"

She smiled pleasantly. "Now, where would be the sport in that?"

"Well," he said, drawing the word out until he thought he could finish without rubbing his hands together with glee, "we *could* just go observe wherever our skipping feet take us."

"Don't tell Jamie."

"He'll know anyway," Oliver said, with feeling.

"I'm afraid that might be true, but we're too far away for him to grumble at us."

"Unless we go home to your keep or to Cameron Hall or that wee house we're building around the bay from Derrick and Sam and then he'll absolutely know where to find us and grumble at us."

She looked at him with her beautiful, luminous face and gorgeous eyes and smiled again. "You aren't afraid."

"Why would I be?" he asked politely. "My wife carries a very saucy knife in her belt and I know a few stern words to mutter in moments of peril."

She laughed a little and turned back to her book. He watched her for a moment or two before he decided there was no time like the present to celebrate the fact that his life had turned out to be so much lovelier than he ever would have expected, full of so much more than grinding through every day on determination alone.

Living every day in bliss was so much nicer.

"Read faster," he suggested.

"I'm trying to, but you're distracting me."

"Read tomorrow?"

She laughed a little, then shut her book and set it aside. "What do you suggest?"

"I might have to consult my Life Manual—"

Or, perhaps not. He smiled as his wife put her arms around his neck, described to him in great detail just how much she loved him, and he, not being any sort of eejit at all, returned the favor.

Life was sweet.

Every single blessed day of it.

ABOUT THE AUTHOR

Lynn Kurland is the *New York Times* bestselling author of over forty novels and novellas. She can be reached through her website at www.LynnKurland.com.

Printed in Great Britain
by Amazon